About the Authors

Carol Marinelli recently filled in a form asking for her job title. Thrilled to be able to put down her answer, she put 'writer'. Then it asked what Carol did for relaxation and she put down the truth—'writing'. The third question asked for her hobbies. Well, not wanting to look obsessed, she crossed her fingers and answered 'swimming'—but, given that the chlorine in the pool does terrible things to her highlights, I'm sure you can guess the real answer!

Fiona Lowe is a RITA® and RUBY award-winning author who started writing romances when she was on holiday and ran out of books. Now writing single title contemporary romance for Carina Press and Medical Romances for Mills & Boon, she lives in a seaside town in southern Australia, where she juggles writing, reading, working and raising two gorgeous sons with the support of her own real-life hero! Readers can visit Fiona at her website: fionalowe.com

Kate Hardy has always loved books, and could read before she went to school. She discovered Mills & Boon books when she was twelve and decided this was what she wanted to do. When she isn't writing Kate enjoys reading, cinema, ballroom dancing and the gym. You can contact her

The Hot Docs on Call
COLLECTION

July 2019

August 2019

September 2019

October 2019

November 2019

December 2019

Hot Docs on Call: One Night to Forever?

CAROL MARINELLI

FIONA LOWE

KATE HARDY

MIX
Paper from
responsible sources
FSC
FSC C007454

This book is produced from independently certified FSC™ paper
to ensure responsible forest management.

For more information visit www.harpercollins.co.uk/green

MILLS & BOON

First Published in Great Britain 2019
By Mills & Boon, an imprint of HarperCollins *Publishers*
1 London Bridge Street, London, SE1 9GF

HOT DOCS ON CALL: ONE NIGHT TO FOREVER?
© 2019 Harlequin Books S.A.

Their One Night Baby © Harlequin Books S.A. 2017
Forbidden to the Playboy Surgeon © Harlequin Books S.A 2017
Mummy, Nurse…Duchess? © Harlequin Books S.A. 2017

Special thanks and acknowledgement are given to
Carol Marinelli, Fiona Lowe and Kate Hardy for their
contribution to the *Paddington Children's Hospital* series.

ISBN: 978-0-263-27672-5

THEIR ONE
NIGHT BABY

CAROL MARINELLI

CHAPTER ONE

'HELLO, BEAUTIFUL!'

Victoria's smile was friendly as she walked into the lounge ahead of Glen, to where little Penelope Craig, or Penny, as she liked to be known, lay on the sofa. Victoria had already had a conversation with Julia, Penny's mother, in the hallway.

Usually, two paramedics dressed in green overalls entering a home would be a somewhat nerve-racking sight for a six-year-old, but little Penny was more than used to it.

'Victoria!'

Even though she was unwell, little Penny sat up a touch on the sofa where she lay, and her huge grey eyes widened in delight. She was clearly pleased that it was her favourite paramedic who was here to take her to Paddington Children's Hospital, or the Castle as it was more generally known.

'She hoped that it would be you coming to take her,' Julia said.

Victoria gave a friendly smile to Julia and then went to sit on the edge of the sofa to chat to her patient. 'Yes, I was just thinking the other day that I haven't seen you in a while.'

'She's been doing really well,' Julia said.

There was a three-way conversation going on as Victoria gleaned some history from Julia and also checked Penny.

Penelope Craig had been born with a rare congenital heart condition and had spent a lot of her life as a patient at the Castle, but for a while she had been doing well. Her dark hair was tied in braids and she was wearing pyjamas. Over the top of them was a little pink tutu that she wore all the time.

Penny was going to be a ballet dancer one day.

She told that to everyone.

'Your mum said that you've not been feeling very well today?' Victoria said as she checked Penny's pulse.

'I'm nauseous and febrile.'

Whereas most children would say that they felt sick and hot, Penny had spent so much time in medical settings that she knew more than a six-year-old should.

She was indeed febrile and her little heart was beating rapidly when Victoria checked her vital signs.

'She's being admitted straight to the cardiac unit,' Julia said as Victoria checked Penny over. It wasn't an urgent transfer but, given Penny's history, a Mobile Intensive Care Unit had been sent and Victoria was thorough in her assessment.

'Though,' Julia added, 'they want her to have a chest X-ray first in A&E.'

Which might prove a problem.

Accident and Emergency departments didn't like to be used as an admissions hub, though it was a problem Victoria dealt with regularly. In fact, just three days ago she had had an argument with Dominic MacBride, a paediatric trauma surgeon, about the very same thing.

Victoria just hoped he wasn't in A&E this evening, as they tended to clash whenever she brought a patient in.

Generally though, things were better at Paddington's than at most hospitals. The staff were very friendly and there was real communication between departments.

And also, Penny was a little bit of a star!

They'd just have to see how it went.

'I like your earrings,' Penny said when Victoria had finished taking her blood pressure.

'Thank you.'

Usually Victoria wore no jewellery at work. It was impractical, given that she never knew what her day might entail. Her long dark brown hair was tied up in its usual messy bun and, of course, she wore no make-up for work. So yes, her diamond studs stood out a touch.

The earrings had been a gift from her father and Victoria wore them for special occasions. She had been at a function yesterday and had forgotten to take them out.

Penny was ready to be transferred to the hospital. For such a little child, often Glen or Victoria would carry them out, the goal being not to upset them. Once though, Victoria had referred to the stretcher as a throne and Penny, who loved anything to do with fairytales, had decided that she rather liked it.

Penny insisted on moving onto the stretcher herself and Julia took a moment to check that she had all of Penny's favourite things to bring along. They were very used to a 'quick trip' to Paddington's turning into a longer stay.

'Ready for the off?' Victoria asked, and Penny gave her regular thumbs up.

Spring was a little way off just yet, and so even though it was only early in the evening, it was dark outside.

'Are you just starting or finishing?' Julia asked as

Victoria took her seat in the back of the ambulance with them.

'Just finishing,' Victoria said.

'Have you got anything planned for tonight?'

'Not really,' Victoria answered, and turned her focus to Penny.

In fact, Victoria was going out on a date.

A second one.

And she was wondering why she'd agreed to it when the first hadn't been particularly great.

Oh, that's right, she and Glen had been chatting and he had suggested that she expected too much from a first date.

Not that she said any of this to Julia.

Victoria gave nothing away.

She was very discerning in her dealings with people. She was confident yet approachable, friendly but not too much.

The patients didn't mind; in fact, they liked her professionalism.

Socially, she did well, though tended to let others talk about themselves.

Victoria relied on no one.

She and Glen had worked together for two years and it had taken a long time for Victoria to discuss her private life even a little with him. Glen was a family man, with a big moon face that smiled rather than took offence at Victoria's sometimes brusque ways, and he loved to talk. He was happily married to Hayley and they had four hundred children.

Well, four.

But while Glen chatted away about his wife and children and the little details of his day, Victoria didn't.

Certainly she wasn't going to open up to her patient's mother about her love-life.

Or lack of it.

Julia, as she often did, told Penny a story as the ambulance made its way through the Friday rush hour traffic. They weren't using lights and sirens; there was no need to, and Penny was too used to them to want the drama.

'I think it looks like a magical castle,' Penny said as Paddington Children's Hospital came into view.

The Victorian redbrick building was turreted and Victoria found herself smiling at Penny's description.

She had thought the same when she was growing up.

Victoria could remember sitting in the back seat of her father's car as he dashed to get to whatever urgent matter was waiting for him at work.

'That's because it *is* a magical castle,' Victoria said, and Penny smiled.

'It's her second home,' Julia said.

It had been Victoria's second home too.

She knew every corridor and nook. The turret that Penny was gazing at could be accessed from a door behind the patient files in Reception, and had once been Victoria's favourite space.

She would sneak in when no one was looking and climb up the spiral stairs and there she would dance, or dream, or simply play pretend.

On occasion she still did.

Well, no longer did she play pretend, but every now and then Victoria would slip away unnoticed and look out to the view of London that she somehow felt was her own.

'Such a shame they're closing it down.' Julia sighed.

'It's not definite,' Victoria said, though not with conviction. It looked as if the plan to merge Paddington's with Riverside, a large modern hospital on the outskirts of the city, would be going ahead.

There was a quiet protest taking place outside, which had been going for a few days now, with protestors waving their placards to save the hospital.

Victoria's father now worked at Riverside. The only real conversations she had ever had with him were about work. The function she had attended yesterday had been for an award for him, and in a conversation afterwards Victoria had gleaned that it really did seem the merger was going to go ahead.

Of course, the beautiful old Paddington's building was prime real estate.

As always, it came down to money.

'I don't want it to close,' Penny said as they pulled up under the bright lights of the ambulance bay outside Accident and Emergency. 'I feel safe here.'

And Penny's words seemed to twist something inside Victoria.

That was how she had felt as a child whenever she was left here.

Yes, left.

Her father's quick check-in at work often turned into hours but, though alone, and though lonely, here Victoria had always felt safe.

'I don't want it to close,' Penny said again.

'I know that you don't.' Victoria nodded. 'But Riverside is a gorgeous hospital and the staff there are lovely too.'

'It's not the same.' Penny shook her head and there were tears in her grey eyes.

'You don't have to worry about all that now,' Victoria soothed. 'It might not happen.'

She wished she could say it probably wouldn't but it was looking more and more likely with each passing day.

And it mattered.

'Penny!' Karen, a charge nurse, recognised Penny straight away. 'You didn't come all this way just to see me, I hope!'

'No.' Penny gave a little laugh, but just as Victoria went to hand over, Karen was urgently summoned.

'It's fine—we can wait.' Victoria nodded.

They stood in the corridor and made sure that Penny was okay, while Glen chatted with her mother and Victoria started to fill out the required paperwork.

He was there.

She knew it.

And although they clashed, although she had told herself that she hoped he wouldn't be there this evening, Victoria had lied.

She wanted to see him.

Dominic MacBride had been working at Paddington's for a few months.

He was from Edinburgh and that low Scottish brogue had Victoria's toes curl in her heavy boots. Or was it his blue eyes and tousled black hair?

Or was it just him?

She couldn't quite place why she liked Dominic so much. He was crabby with the paramedics and he and Victoria tended to clash.

A lot!

And he was making his way over.

'Here we go,' Glen said under his breath, referring to the argument that Dominic and Victoria had had three days ago.

Victoria was very confident in all her dealings and her assertion seemed to rub Dominic up the wrong way.

He made his way straight over.

'Are you being seen to?' he checked.

'Yes, thanks,' Victoria said. 'Karen's taking care of us. She'll be back shortly.'

Victoria got back to filling in the patient report form but, just as she did, Julia chimed up.

'She's a direct admission but she's just going to have a quick chest X-ray before she goes to the ward.'

'I see.' Dominic nodded and then he came over to where Victoria stood. She could feel him in her space and that he was requiring her attention but she carried on writing her notes, refusing to look up.

His scent was subtle, soapy, musky and male and the faint traces cut through the more familiar hospital scent.

And still she did not look up.

'Could I have a word, please?' he asked.

And now Victoria looked up, quite a long way, in fact, because he was very tall and broad.

He was wearing dark navy scrubs and he needed a shave. He looked as if he had either rolled out of bed or should be about to roll into one and she did her best to stop her thought process there.

'Sure,' Victoria said. She was about to be churlish and add, *In a moment*, and then take said moment to finish her report, but instead she moved away from the stretcher and followed him into a small annexe.

He leant against a sink and she stood in front of him, not quite to attention but she was very ready to walk off.

'Can you not see how busy we are?' Dominic said. 'We don't have time to do the wards' work as well.'

'I don't make the rules.'

'You know them though and your patient is a direct

admission,' Dominic said. 'If she goes up to the ward she can wait in a comfortable bed.'

Victoria said nothing.

They both knew the unofficial consensus was that Penny would be pushed to the front of the X-ray list, just so she could quickly be moved up to the ward.

The annexe was very small.

Dominic was not.

He was tall and broad and his eyes demanded that she look at him; Victoria rose to the challenge and met his angry glare as he spoke.

'I've just come from explaining to a father that there's a three-hour wait for an X-ray. Your arrival has just added to that load.'

'So what would you like me to do?' Victoria asked.

She just threw it back at him because, despite the comfortable bed that Penny would have on the ward, once there she would be shuffled to the bottom of the X-ray pile. It could well be midnight before she was brought down to the Imaging Department.

'It's not just a matter of filling in an X-ray request,' Dominic said. 'She should be examined before she goes around. If anything happens to her without her being seen—'

'So,' Victoria calmly interrupted, 'what would you like me to do?'

She did not engage in small talk; she was confident and assertive and refused to row.

'There you are.' Karen came into the annexe. 'Cubicle four has opened up if you'd like to bring Penny through.'

She and Dominic stared at each other.

The choice was his.

'Fine,' he eventually said, and Karen nodded and went back to Penny.

'Next time…' Dominic warned, but Victoria just shrugged and walked off.

'Victoria!'

She halted.

There was an angry edge to his voice, but that wasn't what stopped her—she didn't think he even knew her name, so his use of it surprised her.

'Don't just shrug and walk off when I'm trying to have a conversation.'

'A pointless one,' Victoria said as she turned around. 'In fact, we had the same conversation three days ago.'

His mood had been just as bloody then and she watched as his eyes shuttered for a moment.

'As I said then, I just go where I'm told and deal with the inevitable angry consequence—I get your ire if I bring the patient here, or the ire of the ward if they arrive without the X-ray.'

She went to walk off, but this time it was Victoria who changed her mind and continued the conversation.

'Sometimes it's made easy though and the staff get that I'm just doing my job. That's generally the case at Paddington's, though I guess it just depends who's on. I have to go and move my patient and then I'm out of here. Which is just as well…'

And then she crossed the line.

For the first time she made it personal. 'Your misery is catching.'

Dominic watched as she swished out of the annexe and he let out a long breath.

They were both right.

There were limited resources and the staff all fought for the charges in their care.

She had rattled him though, not just with her little sign-off comment, but the reminder that they had had this conversation three days ago.

It was a difficult time for Dominic and he was self-aware enough to know he had been less than sunny on that day as well.

And he knew why.

Dominic had always been serious and a bit aloof but he loathed that, of late—Victoria was right—he was miserable.

Not to the patients though.

He shoved his messy personal life aside there.

And then from outside he heard laughter.

Victoria's.

He came out of the annexe and there she was making up the stretcher with her colleague.

'Victoria.'

She turned around. 'Yes.'

'Could I have a word?'

She rolled her eyes but came over. 'Are we really going to do this again?'

'No, I wanted to apologise for earlier.'

'It's fine.'

She didn't need it.

In Victoria's line of work, a small stand-off with a doctor barely merited a thought and she was trying to keep it at that.

But this was a genuine apology and he offered her a small explanation.

'Today's a tough one.'

He offered no more insight but Victoria knew she was hearing the truth.

'Then I hope it gets better,' Victoria said.

'It shan't.'

She gave him a smile and Dominic knew he had lied because it already had got a bit better.

Victoria was stunning.

She was wearing green overalls and heavy black boots and it should have been impossible to look stunning in those, yet she did. Her hair was worn on the top of her head but glossy waves tumbled over her face and her hazel eyes held his.

Yes, she was stunning.

And that was why she annoyed him.

Dominic was not looking to be stunned.

His personal life was very messy and, furthermore, Victoria was far from his type.

She was very direct and he usually liked subtle. He liked women who, well, stayed a bit in the background and didn't demand too much headspace.

And lately Victoria was starting to command a lot of his thoughts.

'I'm sorry too,' she said. 'That bit about you being a misery...well...' She couldn't resist a little play. 'I meant crabby.'

He got her little joke and smiled.

It was not the smile he gave to the patients, because they did not have to fight not to blush, as Victoria was doing. This smile felt as if it had been exclusively designed for her and he was holding her gaze as she completed her apology. 'I went a bit far.'

'That's okay.'

And suddenly things could not go far enough.

There was no way he was going to move things along.

Dominic had a hell of a lot to sort out before he should even consider that.

But...

'I'd offer to apologise properly over a drink but in my current mood I wouldn't foist myself on anyone.'

Foist.

That word made her smile.

First, for the way he said it—his accent was light but very appealing.

And second, because there would be no foisting required.

He was gorgeous, sexy, rugged and, yes, she fancied him like hell. He was older than she usually liked; but then again, Victoria liked few.

She guessed him to be late thirties and she was twenty-nine.

He made her feel like a teenager though.

Dominic made her want to blush, but she steadfastly refused to.

And they kept staring.

'It's fine,' she said again, and then the communication radio on her shoulder started cracking and there was suddenly another voice in the room.

'Victoria!' Glen called, and he must have picked up on the tension as he walked by because he paused.

Thankfully Glen seemed to miss that the tension was of the sexual kind.

'Is everything okay?' he checked.

'Everything's fine,' Dominic said, and walked off.

And everything *was* fine now that he was out away from her gaze. Dominic had been very close to asking her out and now he wanted her gone.

It was that simple.

He did not want anyone closer.

But that did not mean he did not want.

CHAPTER TWO

DOMINIC PICKED UP the patient card and went to check on
the new patient before she went down to X-ray.

He was a trauma surgeon and so he found himself
working in Accident and Emergency a lot and often
pitched in.

'Hey,' he said as he went into the cubicle where the
little girl had been placed. 'Penelope, I'm Dominic.'

'Penny,' she confidently corrected him. 'And you're
new here.'

'I've been here for nearly six months now.'

'Penny hasn't been an inpatient for ages,' Julia said.
'We've had a good run.'

'Well, that's good to hear.'

The little girl's medical notes were so extensive he
could be there till midnight if he read them, but Dominic had caught up on the vitals and Julia was very well
versed in her daughter's health.

Penelope Craig had hypoplastic left heart syndrome,
or HLHS, a rare congenital defect. She had had surgery
as a baby and all her life she had been either an inpatient or outpatient at Paddington's. She had presented a
few times with infections and that was the concern now.

Examining Penny, Dominic saw that just from the

minor exertion of sitting forward she became breathless and the slight blue tinge to her lips darkened.

And of course, as Victoria would have well known, it wasn't just a chest X-ray that was required.

Dominic took some bloods as a baseline. Penny would require a nurse escort if she went out of the department for her X-ray. But it wasn't to keep staff levels up that had Dominic call for a portable chest X-ray—he was concerned enough that she was really rather unwell.

And so he paged the on-call cardiologist and asked him to come down and see Penny here rather than waiting until she was on the ward.

It was a locum that he spoke to.

Again.

With the prospect of Paddington's closing down, a lot of the regular staff had gone elsewhere and it was proving difficult to attract new staff when no one really knew if the hospital would even be here next year.

Having spoken to the locum, Dominic went back into cubicle four to inform patient and parent of the new plan.

'Look what Penny just found,' Julia said as Penny lay there holding up an earring.

Dominic didn't need to be told whose it was; he had already noticed that Victoria had been wearing earrings this evening when usually she did not.

He noticed rather too many details about Victoria.

And even her earrings had intrigued him. They were large diamonds, and during their discussions he had been trying very hard not to picture Victoria dressed up to go out.

'It's Victoria's earring,' Penny said to Karen as she came in.

'There it is.' She smiled. 'I've just had a call from

Victoria to ask me to look out for it. You've saved me a job. Good girl, Penny. I'll put it in the safe. Oh, and, Dominic, there's a phone call for you.'

'Take a message, please.'

'It's your father,' Karen said. 'And he says that it's important.'

'Thank you.'

Deliberately Dominic left his mobile phone in his locker at the start of each shift. He did not want his private life intruding on work.

Yet it was about to.

This call was, in fact, three days overdue.

Yes, there was a reason he hadn't been sunny on that day.

The receiver had been left lying on the bench and Dominic hesitated. He let out the tense breath that he was holding on to. He had had months to prepare for this moment and had examined it from many angles, but even as he picked up the receiver, still he hadn't worked out what he would say.

'Hello.' His voice was as abrupt as it had been with Victoria.

'Dominic…' William MacBride cleared his throat before speaking on. 'I'm just calling to let you know that as of an hour ago you're an uncle.'

And still, even with the baby three days overdue, Dominic did not know what to say.

'Dominic?' William prompted.

'Are they well?'

'They're both doing fine.'

Dominic knew that he should ask what Lorna and Jamie had had and whether or not he had a niece or nephew.

He looked out to the busy Emergency Department,

and given it was a children's hospital, of course there were children everywhere. There was Penny, being wheeled over to rhesus for her portable X-ray and in the background there was the sound of babies crying.

Dominic fought daily to save these precious little lives and so, naturally, he should be relieved to hear that mother and baby were well and doing fine.

And somewhere he was.

Yet it was buried deep in a mire of anger and grief, because for a while there he had thought that the baby born today was going to be his.

Dominic tried his best not to recall that first moment of truth—when he had realised the baby that his long-term girlfriend was carrying could not possibly be his.

But then his father spoke of the brother who had caused the second painful moment of truth.

'Jamie's thrilled.'

Dominic held in a derisive snort.

What had taken place wasn't his father's fault. Dominic knew that his parents simply did not know how to handle this.

Who would?

'Will you speak to your brother?'

'I've nothing to say to him.'

A year ago it would have been unfathomable that on the day Jamie became a father Dominic would have nothing to say.

They had always been close.

Dominic had been five when a much wanted second child had been born. Jamie was spoiled and cheeky and always getting himself into trouble, but the rather more serious Dominic had always looked out for him.

Or he had tried to.

Jamie had been run over when he was ten and Dominic was fifteen.

It hadn't been the driver's fault. Jamie simply hadn't looked and had stepped out onto the street and on that occasion Dominic had been too late to haul him back.

It had felt like for ever until the ambulance arrived, and then Dominic had watched the paramedics fight to save his brother's life. Later, at the hospital, as his parents cried and paced, Dominic had gone to try and find out some more. The doors to Resuscitation had opened to let some equipment in and he had seen the medical team in action, doing all that they could to save Jamie.

He had been steered away and sent back to the waiting area but on that terrible day Dominic had decided on his future career.

Jamie had survived and Dominic had really pushed himself to make the grades and get in to study medicine.

Family had been everything to Dominic—right up until the day he had found out that his girlfriend had been cheating on him with his brother, and that the baby Dominic had thought was his had been fathered by Jamie.

Jamie and Lorna had married a couple of months ago.

Dominic had declined his invitation.

Did they really think he was going to stand there dressed in a kilt, smiling for photographers and pretending to family and friends that things were just fine?

No way could he do that.

Not yet anyway.

'We have to move on from this, Dominic,' William said.

'That's why I'm in London,' Dominic responded.

'Because I have moved on.' He went to hang up, yet there was more he had to know. 'What did they have?'

'A wee boy. They've called him—'

'You don't need to tell me,' Dominic interrupted.

'You don't want to know?'

'I already do.'

Dominic was named after his paternal grandfather, as was the Scottish tradition for a firstborn son.

The new baby, if a boy, had always been destined to be called William—whatever brother Lorna happened to be sleeping with that month.

Hell, yes, he was bitter.

'Dominic…' William pushed. He wanted resolution for his family but it would not be happening today.

'I have to get on,' Dominic said.

He didn't.

Dominic's working day was over, but he headed up to the wards, then to ICU to check on a patient.

All was in order.

Only he was in no mood to go home.

That would mean collecting his phone and seeing all the missed messages, as well as spending the night avoiding going online. Oh, he'd blocked Jamie and Lorna ages ago, and his parents weren't on there. But there were cousins and mutual friends, and all would be celebrating.

A baby had been born after all.

'You're very quiet,' Glen commented as he drove them back to the station. 'Did MacBride upset you?'

'Please!' Victoria made a scoffing face and Glen grinned.

He knew firsthand just how tough Victoria was.

And she was.

Men.

She worked alongside them.

And, in her line of work, she saw a lot of them at their worst as the pubs and clubs emptied out at night.

Victoria had seen an awful lot.

She relied on no one and hid her feelings well.

But that tough persona had been formed long before she had chosen her profession.

There had been no choice but to be independent growing up, for there had been no one who had cared to hear her fears and thoughts.

She was outwardly calm and did not get upset about things others might. Even when she realised she had lost an expensive earring, she just checked the ambulance thoroughly and then called Paddington's and asked Karen if she could look out for it.

'You're taking it very well,' Glen commented. 'Hayley would be hysterical.'

'Well, I'm not Hayley.' Victoria shrugged.

Sometimes, she could make life easier playing sweeter, careful of a man's ego.

And sometimes she did.

Like now, as she went into the female changing room to get ready for her date.

She showered and then let down her hair and brushed it so that it shone. Wrapped in a towel she put on some mascara and lip gloss and then pulled on a gorgeous black dress and high shoes.

Sometimes it was nice to dress up, given that she wore overalls for most of her day. But even as she dressed, Victoria knew tonight wasn't going to work out.

He didn't want to hear about her work.

Which wasn't really a good sign, when Victoria worked an awful lot.

As for attraction?

Well, she had rather hoped that might develop.

And that wasn't a good sign, surely.

The condom in her purse would remain unused.

God, it had been ages, Victoria thought, and there was almost an ache for contact and to be close to another, even if just for a little while.

No, her date tonight could in no way deliver the zaps that Dominic's eyes had.

And so she cancelled it.

Right there and then, Victoria pulled her phone out of her purse and told him that she'd changed her mind about going out tonight.

'Another time…?' he went to suggest, but Victoria didn't play games.

'No.'

All dressed up and nowhere to go.

Or nowhere she wanted to be.

She had broken up with someone a few months ago when he had started to make noises about them living together.

No way!

There was no way on earth that Victoria would consider sharing her space with another.

And so she had ended it.

With the same lack of drama as she ended things tonight.

Victoria pulled on her coat and headed out.

'Goodnight,' she called out to her colleagues, but as she walked off Glen called her back.

'Paddington's just called. Your earring is in the A&E safe.'

'Oh.'

'Do you want me to drop you off?' he offered, but Victoria said no. The ambulance station was just a ten-minute walk from Paddington's and, though cold, it was a clear night and she wouldn't mind the walk.

Her heels clipped on the pavement as the familiar building came into view.

Outside were a couple of protestors holding placards with various messages to save the hospital from closure.

They might just as well go home, Victoria thought sadly. From the way her father had spoken there would be a formal announcement soon.

She thought of little Penny's comment about feeling safe there, and that was exactly how Victoria felt as she stepped into the hospital.

There was a feeling that wrapped around her like a blanket, one of being taken care of. There was a sense of security when you were within these walls, Victoria thought as she walked into A&E and saw Karen.

'You're one lucky woman,' Karen said as she made her way over to her. 'Penny found your earring in the blanket. It's locked in the safe in Reception.'

'Thank you so much.' Victoria smiled.

Dominic wasn't here.

She could just tell.

And, Victoria conceded, she was disappointed. She knew that she looked good, and deep down she had hoped that maybe, just maybe, Dominic might revise his suggestion and take her for a drink.

But then what?

She didn't want a relationship. That was the simple truth, and the real reason why she always called things off.

Victoria didn't trust anyone and certainly she didn't

want to get involved with a colleague who she would have to run into day after day.

They walked into Reception and Karen took out the keys and went into the safe, then handed Victoria the slim envelope that contained the earring. As Victoria put it on, Karen started chatting with the receptionist.

'See you!' Victoria called, and went to walk off but then she halted.

She checked that Karen and the receptionist were still talking and realised she could go behind the screen unnoticed.

It was something she had always done as a child and something she still occasionally did, though she always made sure that no one saw her.

Up the steps she went.

Remembering being little, and the hours that she had had to kill.

Growing up, Paddington's had been more of a home than the house where Victoria had lived and she could not stand the thought of it being sold.

She looked out to the night. The moon was huge and she could see the dark shadows of Regent's Park in the distance. There were taxis and buses below and she could see the protestors who, despite a shower of rain, still stood waving their placards.

They didn't want to lose their hospital.

That's what it was.

Theirs.

It was a place that belonged to the people, and now it was about to be sold off and possibly razed to the ground.

Victoria was tough.

She didn't get involved with the patients; she had

made the decision when she started her training to be kind but professional.

But this place, this space, moved her.

The walls held so much history and the air itself tasted of hope. It seemed wrong, simply wrong, that it might go.

There was so much comfort here.

She thought of Penny and how un-scared she was to come to Paddington's.

Victoria had felt the same.

'I shan't be long,' her father would say.

Her mother had left when Victoria was almost one year old and her father had had little choice sometimes but to bring her into work. He would plonk her in a sitting room and one of the staff would always take time to get her a drink or sandwich.

Of course, then their break would end and she would be left alone.

Often Victoria would wander.

Sometimes she would sit in an old quadrangle and read. Other times she would play in the stairwells.

But here was the place she loved most and she had whiled away many hours in this lovely unused room.

Here Victoria would dance or sing or simply imagine.

And maybe she was doing that now, because the door creaked open and she heard his deep voice.

'Excuse me.'

CHAPTER THREE

DOMINIC HAD BEEN about to make his way home after visiting his patients on the wards but, not ready to face it yet, he had decided to spend some time in a place that was starting to become familiar.

He had never expected to see Victoria, yet here she was. Despite the heels and coat and that her hair was down, and despite that he could only see her back and that it was dark, still he recognised her.

But it seemed clear, not just from the location, but from the way her hand rested against the window, and Victoria's pensive stance, that she wanted to be alone.

'Excuse me,' Dominic said, and she turned at the sound of his voice. 'I didn't think anyone was up here.'

'It's fine.' Victoria gave him a thin smile.

'I'll leave you,' he offered, but Victoria shook her head.

'You don't have to do that.'

He walked across the wooden floor and came and joined her at the window.

He was still in scrubs and she could see that he was tired.

'I thought only I knew about this place,' Victoria said. 'It would seem not.'

'I don't think many people know about it,' he said.

'At least, I've never seen anyone up here and it looks pretty undisturbed.'

'How did you find it?'

Dominic didn't answer.

They stood in mutual silence, staring ahead, though not really taking in the view of London at night.

Unlike the thick modern glass in the main hospital, here the windows were thin and there were a couple of cracked ones. The shower had turned to rain and the air was cold but it was incredibly peaceful.

'Where did you work before here?' Victoria asked him.

'Edinburgh.'

'So you're used to wonderful views.'

He thought of the city he loved built around the castle, and of Arthur's Seat rising above the city, and he nodded and then turned his head and looked at something just as beautiful, though he could see that she was sad.

'Are you okay?' he asked, and Victoria was about to nod and say she was fine but changed her mind and gave a small shrug.

'I'm just a bit flat.'

She offered no more than that.

'Has a patient upset you?'

She frowned at the very suggestion and turned to look at him.

'Penny?' he checked, because he had found out this evening that the little girl had wormed her way into a lot of the staff's hearts here at Paddington's. But Victoria shook her head.

'I don't get upset over patients and certainly not over a routine transfer. If I did, then I'd really be in the wrong job!'

'And I doubt it was me that upset you,' he said, and she gave a little laugh.

'No, you I can handle.'

And then Victoria was glad that it was dark because she had started to blush at her own innuendo, even though she hadn't meant it in that way. And so, to swiftly move on from that, she offered more information as to her mood. 'If you must know it's this place that I'm upset about. I can't believe it might be knocked down or turned into apartments. I was practically raised here.'

'You were sick as a child?'

'No! My father worked here in A&E and he used to bring me in with him. Sometimes I'd sneak up here.' She didn't add just how often it had happened. How her childhood had been spent being half-watched by whatever nurse, domestic, secretary, receptionist or whoever was available.

And she certainly didn't mention her mother.

Victoria did all she could never to think, let alone discuss, the woman who had simply upped and walked away.

'My father now works at Riverside—Professor Christie.'

She turned and saw the raise of his eyes.

It wasn't an impressed raise.

Dominic had spoken to him on occasion and knew that Professor Christie wasn't the most pleasant of people.

'He's crabby too,' Victoria said.

And Dominic decided to make one thing very clear. 'At the risk of causing offence, I might be crabby, Victoria, but I'm not cold to the bone.'

Dominic did not cause offence. It was, in fact, rather a relief to hear it voiced as, given her father's status, people tended to praise him rather than criticise, and that had been terribly confusing to a younger Victoria.

It still confused her even now.

She had stood at the award ceremony yesterday hearing all the marvellous things being said about him. Afterwards, at the reception, more praise had been heaped.

The emperor had really had on no clothes, though there was not a person brave enough to voice it.

Until now.

'Well,' Victoria said, 'I saw him yesterday and he seems to think the merge is going to go ahead.'

Dominic nodded; he had heard the same. 'It's a shame.'

'It's more than a *shame*,' Victoria said, and for the first time he heard the sound of her voice when upset—even when they had argued she had remained calm. 'This place is more than just a facility,' Victoria insisted. 'Families feel safe when they know their children are here. It can't just close.'

'Do something about it, then.'

'Me?'

She looked down at the protestors and wondered if she should join them. But in her heart, Victoria knew it wasn't enough and that more needed to be done.

'If you care so much,' Dominic said, 'then fight for what matters to you.'

It did matter to her, Victoria thought.

Paddington's really mattered.

And it was nice to be up here and not alone with her thoughts, but rather to be sharing them with him.

'How *did* you find this room?' Victoria asked again.

He still hadn't told her, and now when he did it came as a surprise.

'I saw you sneak behind the shelves a couple of

months ago and I wondered where you'd gone. When I got a chance I went and had a look for myself.'

'You can't have seen me.' Victoria shook her head at the impossibility of his explanation. 'I always make sure that no one does. Anyway, I'd have known if you were around...' And she halted, because that was admitting that any time she was at this hospital she was aware of where he was.

'I was in the waiting room talking to a parent,' he said. 'I saw you through the glass...'

'I guess I stand out in those green overalls.'

'I don't think it's the green overalls, Victoria.'

She gave a soft laugh.

She was dressed in black now after all.

Yet he was confirming that he noticed her too.

'Did you see me come up tonight?' Victoria asked.

'No. I just wanted some space. I thought you were finished for the night.'

'I am. I was supposed to be going out,' Victoria said, explaining the reason for heels and things. 'But I cancelled.'

And now he thought he knew the real reason she was sad.

'Have you just broken up with someone?'

'I don't think you can really call it a break-up if you cancel a second date.'

No, she wasn't sad about that; Dominic could tell from her dismissive shrug. It would seem it really was just the building.

'Well,' he said. 'I'm sure he's very disappointed.'

And then he went to retract that because it came out wrong, as if he was alluding to how stunning she looked.

'What I meant was that—'

He stopped; whatever way he said it would sound like flirting, and he was avoiding all that.

'I think I've done us both a favour,' Victoria said. 'He didn't seem to understand the concept of shift work. So,' she asked, 'if it wasn't me, then what brought you up here?' She wanted to know more about those difficult days he had alluded to.

'I'm in the middle of something right now...' Dominic said. 'Well, not in the middle—I've taken myself out of the equation. I'm staying back from getting involved with anyone.'

'Good,' Victoria said, 'because I don't like to get involved with anyone at work.'

Yet here they were and the tension that had been in the annexe wrapped and slivered around them.

'Are you married?' she asked.

It was a very specific question and the answer was important to Victoria, because the cold air had turned warm.

'No.'

'Seeing someone?'

'Of course not,' Dominic said, or he would not be doing this—and his hand moved to her cheek. 'You got your earring back.'

'They were a gift from my father.'

'That's nice,' Dominic said.

'Not really, it was just a duty gift when I turned eighteen. Had he bothered to get to know me, then he'd have known that I don't like diamonds.'

'Why not?'

'I don't believe in fairytales and I don't believe in for ever.'

There was, to Victoria's mind, no such thing.

She held her breath as his fingers came to her cheek and lightly brushed the lobe as he examined the stone.

If it were anyone else she would have pushed his hand away.

Anyone else.

Yet she provoked.

'It was the other earring that I lost.'

And he turned her face and his hands went to the other.

This was foolish, both knew.

Neither wanted to get close to someone they had to work alongside but the attraction between them was intense.

Both knew the reason for their rows and terse exchanges; it was physical attraction at its most raw.

'Victoria, I'm in no position to get involved with anyone.'

They were standing looking at each other and his hands were on her cheeks and his fingers were warm on her ears. There was a thrum between them and she knew he was telling her they would go nowhere.

'That's okay.'

And that *was* okay.

'If you don't like diamonds, then what do you like?' he asked. His mouth was so close to hers and though it was cold she could feel the heat in the space between them.

'This.'

Their mouths met and she felt the warm, light pressure and it felt blissful. That musky, soapy scent of him had been imprinted and, this close, it made her dizzy. His tongue sliding in made her move closer and the fingers of one hand reached into her hair as the other hand slid around her waist.

It was almost like setting up to dance, as if the teacher had come in and said, *Place your hands here.* But not.

Because then she hadn't felt a tremble, no matter how warm the palm.

They kissed softly at first as his hand bunched in her hair; he explored with his tongue and it met with hers and he tasted all that had been missing.

Passion coiled them tight; his palm took the weight of her head and pressed her in at the same time.

The pent-up rows and the terse exchanges had been many and could not be dispersed with a single kiss.

It was a deep slow kiss and it birthed impatience in both. He held her head very steady and kissed her hard, and the scratch of his unshaven jaw and the probe of his tongue was sublime. But then, unlike with most men, she tasted resistance.

There was resistance, because Dominic knew very well where they were leading. 'I don't have anything with me,' he said.

And she wanted to feel him unleashed.

'I do.'

And when most would kiss harder, instead Dominic made her burn with his stealth. He stepped back and moved her coat down her shoulders and did not drop it to the dusty floor. Instead he placed it on the window ledge and she went for her purse that was there.

He came up behind her as she rifled through her purse, praying that the condom was still there and trying to find it. One hand wrapped around her and rested on her stomach as his other hand slid up between her inner thighs to the damp in the middle. His fingers stroked her and she closed her eyes to the bliss.

'Here.' She had never been so pleased to find a condom as he peeled her knickers down and she straightened up and stepped out of them.

Still he stood behind her and he lifted her hair and kissed her low on her neck. His hand pressed into her stomach and she could feel him hard against her bottom. Victoria was shaking a little, wanting to turn to him, yet wanting to linger in this bliss.

'Come away from the window,' he said, and took her over to a wall in the shadows and he kissed her hard against it. His hands held her hips and now Victoria felt the delicious hardness of him against her stomach. She stretched up onto tiptoe and he moved his hips down so he met her heat.

It was nice, so nice, to be so raw and open with him.

He caressed her breast through the fabric and, since he could feel no zipper on her dress, with a moan of want he just slid his hand inside and it was the most thorough and deliberate grope of her life. Meanwhile, Victoria was doing the same to him; she was trying to hold on to the condom as she freed him from his scrubs and underwear.

Finally, she held him in her palm, and her hand was soft on skin that was so very firm to her touch.

'I want this dress off...' Dominic gasped, but it was impossible because they could not move their mouths for more than a second from each other.

They wanted nakedness and hours to explore, but their bodies would only give them minutes.

He took the condom and began sheathing himself, while she was pulling up her dress, and when he was done, he lifted her thigh and placed her leg around his hip.

And they were not dancing!

She balanced on one stiletto but his grip of her was

firm and the wall behind her solid. Then her hips angled and both were just as urgent as the other as Dominic thrust and took her.

Victoria had never felt anything so powerful. He was rough and delicious and she felt matched for the first time in her life, because he held nothing back.

Everything he delivered.

Dominic's hand was behind her back and he could feel the scratch of stone on his knuckles but that was so far from his mind that it barely registered.

'There…' she said in a voice that was both demanding and urgent.

He met that demand and heightened it too.

She felt amazing. Dominic was rather more used to holding back, but Victoria invited intensity. It had been ages for Dominic, and he had wanted her for a very long time.

There was almost anger in him for how much she made him want her, so he thrust hard and fast and then harder still to the sound of her pleasurable moans, and then he lifted her.

Victoria had never had both feet off the ground like this; she had never been so consumed. His fingers were digging into her bottom as he took her hard against the wall.

Their faces were side by side and she wanted to find his mouth, but there was no time for that as she was starting to come. Never had she climaxed so deeply, and if she were not wrapped around him she would have folded in two at the pleasure.

He released to her deep shudder and together they hit high, and finally she found his mouth, tasted the cool of his tongue as she drank in his kiss. They rested their foreheads together, sharing those last beats of pleasure and breathing the same air until gently he lowered her down.

With long slow kisses he moved them away from the wall now. She pulled down her dress and then they broke contact and she moved out of the shadows.

Victoria picked up her discarded knickers but had to lean on the ledge, not just so she could put them on, but because her legs were shaky and she was still breathless.

She had never let herself go like that, she had never come so hard and she had certainly never been made love to so thoroughly.

When Dominic emerged from the shadows he, too, was dressed, though his hair was rumpled. It should have been really awkward between them, yet it was not.

'I look like I've been in a fight,' he said as he examined his hands in the moonlight. Victoria took his fingers and looked at them, and made him smile with what she said.

'You're going to have some trouble explaining those injuries, Doctor,' she teased, because it really did look, to her trained eyes, as if he had punched the walls.

Yes, it should have been really awkward but instead he came and sat beside her on the ledge.

'Victoria...' he started, but really he did not know what to say. Dominic was in no position to start anything. And what had just taken place was very far removed from his usual nature.

He felt amazing though, as if on the top of a high mountain.

And she saw him struggle with what to say, so she said it for him.

'You don't have to explain anything,' Victoria said. She was not referring to his knuckles, but still she smiled.

'You're sure?' he checked.

'Yes.'

What had happened was something she could never have imagined, something so far removed from her usual wary approach to intimacy, but he did not need to know all of that.

She felt liberated.

And feminine.

With him she felt she had found herself.

So, instead of an awkward parting they shared a kiss that was deep, long and slow, and ended by her.

'I'm going to go,' Victoria said, and stood.

And still she waited for awkwardness, even as she walked to the door.

So did he, yet awkward did not exist in this room.

'So, if you don't like diamonds,' Dominic called. 'What do you like?'

And she opened the door and laughed as he went back to the original question.

'Pearls.'

He sat in the room and looked around. The moon shone through the window and the air was still stirred and seductive from them; his knuckles were grazed and he was somewhat reeling.

Dominic had never really given pearls any thought before.

They were just something his mother or grandmother wore for weddings and such occasions.

Certainly he had never considered them sexy.

He did now.

CHAPTER FOUR

'PREGNANT?'

Victoria watched as her father took off his glasses and cleaned them. And, as he did so, she remembered the time she had got her first period and it had been almost an identical reaction—slight bemusement, mild irritation, though more at the intrusion of conversation rather than what was actually being said.

Victoria sat in her father's office at Riverside Hospital and waited. For what, she didn't know.

She had read somewhere that some terrible parents made the most wonderful grandparents. That without the responsibility of parenthood, they enjoyed the experience. And she had hoped, truly hoped, that it might be the case here. That this might breathe some life into her relationship with her father.

Apparently not, if his cool reaction was anything to go by.

And Victoria knew deep down that there had been no real relationship with her father. At least, not the sort she wanted. She hadn't seen or spoken to him since the function they had attended, despite Victoria having tried to call.

Her father was brilliant but completely self-absorbed. Completely.

'How far along are you?' he asked.

It had been six weeks since her time with Dominic, and with the requisite two weeks added, Victoria knew her dates.

'Eight weeks,' she said.

'Do you want it?' Professor Christie asked.

He thought she was here to ask for a referral for an abortion, Victoria suddenly realised.

And he'd write her one, Victoria knew.

'Yes,' she said. 'I very much want my baby.'

She stared at him but he was reading through some notes that lay on his desk.

'What about the father?' he asked, and looked up.

'I haven't told him yet. We're not together or anything. He's in Scotland.' Victoria had heard that in passing. 'On annual leave,' she added to her father.

She was forewarned as to the response she might get from Dominic, when her father spoke next.

'Well, he's in for a pleasant surprise when he gets back.'

The sarcasm was evident in his voice and it told Victoria all she needed to know about her father's thoughts on parenthood.

'Victoria, you really need to give this some consideration. Being a single parent is hard work—I should know. It interferes in every aspect of your life. You're the one who always bangs on about your career—think what it will do to that…'

She hadn't seen him since the function and then it had been for an award for *his* career. Victoria didn't bang on, as her father described it. Given he was a professor and specialised in Accident and Emergency and she was a paramedic, she had, on occasion, tried to find some common ground.

But there was none and there never had been.

There was no room in this narcissist's world for anyone other than himself.

'I can't help you financially,' he said, for Professor Christie had amassed a small collection of ex-wives.

'I've never once asked you to.'

Victoria hadn't.

She had left home as soon as she had finished school and had never asked her father for anything.

But she was about to.

She looked at her father and knew that really there was no point even being here. He did not want to be a part of her life, and the occasional public showing of his daughter was only when he was between wives.

'Victoria, I need to get on.'

'There *is* something I want…' Victoria said, and he let out the little hiss of irritation that he always did when she asked for a moment more of his time. 'I was hoping to have the baby at Paddington's.'

Victoria had decided as she'd walked through the corridors of Riverside that she didn't want her baby to be born here. There was nothing wrong with the hospital—she often brought patients here—but it felt bland to Victoria, and her father worked here too.

She felt closer to a building than her own parents. It was sad but true, and that was why she asked the favour.

'They only take complicated cases,' Professor Christie said.

'Not always,' Victoria refuted. And she didn't point out that she'd been born there and that members of staff tended to choose, where possible, to have their child there, but she would not be fobbed off.

'It's closing.'

'Not necessarily,' Victoria said. 'And if it does close

before the baby comes along, then I'll be referred else-where, but I'd really like to have my antenatal care there.'

As an adult she had never asked her father for any-thing, not one single thing. 'Can you get me in there?'

'I'll see what I can do.'

'Now,' Victoria said, because she knew this conver-sation would be forgotten the second she walked out of the door. 'I want to be seen before I tell work.'

And so, more to get rid of the inconvenience, her fa-ther made some calls and finally she was booked in to Paddington's maternity unit.

'You need an ultrasound before he sees you,' Pro-fessor Christie said, and he went through the details, telling her she had an appointment for tomorrow and that the referral form would be at Reception. Finally, he asked her to reconsider. 'I really suggest you have a long hard think about going ahead with this, Victoria.'

That hurt.

On so many levels it hurt.

Victoria knew he had never wanted her. She was certain that had her mother not left first, then he would have gone.

As she got to the door Victoria turned and could see that she was forgotten already—her father was straight back to work, though she still stood there.

Dominic was right—her father was cold to the bone.

'I can see why she left you,' Victoria said. 'My mother, I mean.'

Professor Christie looked up from his notes and he stared at his daughter for a long moment and then, just before resuming writing his notes, he, as always, had the last word.

'She left you too.'

* * *

His words shadowed and clung to her right through into the next day.

'You're quiet,' Glen observed as she was driven towards the children's hospital with Glen, for once not in an ambulance.

Glen had offered to come with her for her ultrasound appointment. Victoria had declined, though she was touched that her colleague had given her a lift. She had felt very sick on the underground but that was fading.

Glen knew that she was pregnant.

Of course he did.

He had no idea, though, who the father was.

They worked together, and when Victoria had started to turn as green as her overalls at the smallest thing, he had asked if everything was okay.

Victoria had said she was fine.

Then, a couple of days ago, he had asked outright.

'Hayley had terrible morning sickness, with Ryan,' Glen had told her.

It had been hard to deny a pregnancy when you were sitting holding a kidney dish in the back of an ambulance.

'You have to tell work,' Glen said.

'I know.' Victoria closed her eyes.

It was starting to be real.

For the last couple of weeks she had been in denial, but now she was facing up to things and telling work was something she knew she had to do.

She had this week to get through and then a weekend of nights before she went on two weeks' annual leave and she had decided that she would tell them at the end of her nights.

And now they sat in his car as Glen offered some further advice that she certainly didn't need.

'You have to tell the guy he's going to be a father.'

'Thanks, Glen,' she snapped.

'Listen to me, Victoria—'

'No.' She turned and looked at him. 'I accepted a lift, not a lecture.' And though she told Glen to stay back she knew he was right and that Dominic needed to be told.

When he came back from his leave she would tell him.

If he came back.

He might have decided that he missed home.

Victoria really didn't know him at all.

They had gone straight back to being strangers.

There was no flirting and certainly there had been no reference to what had taken place.

He was still moody and she was her usual confident self.

Really, if it hadn't been for the fact that she was pregnant, by now Victoria would be wondering if it had even taken place.

That night still felt like a dream.

Albeit her favourite one.

'Are you sure you don't want me to come with you?' Glen checked, but Victoria snorted at the suggestion of needing someone to hold her hand.

'For an ultrasound?'

'Hayley gets nervous whenever she has one...' Glen started, referring to his wife, as he always did.

'I'm not Hayley,' Victoria pointed out as she often did. 'I'll be fine on my own.'

She would be better on her own, in fact.

It was what she was used to after all.

Victoria walked through the familiar corridors of Paddington's and turned for the Imaging Department. There she handed over her referral slip to the receptionist.

'We're running a bit behind,' the receptionist explained.

'That's no problem,' Victoria said, even though she was desperate to go to the loo.

She had been told to have a lot to drink prior to the ultrasound so that they might get the best view of the baby.

Still, she had expected to have to wait and had plenty to do.

Apart from a baby, something else had been created that night.

Victoria was on the social committee and had decided to use her position there to start a campaign to save the hospital from the merger.

They met each week over at the Frog and Peach and there was a meeting being held tonight.

It was proving difficult to get things rolling though.

Most people seemed to think it was a foregone conclusion that Paddington's would close. Apart from the odd small write-up in the press, the campaign was not getting any real attention and Victoria was at a bit of a loss as to what to suggest next.

Rosie, a paediatric nurse, along with Robyn, who was Head of Surgery, were both a huge support and Victoria was hoping to catch up with them before the meeting kicked off.

Victoria sent a group text, reminding everyone of the meeting, and then she answered a few emails, but though she was passionate about doing all she could to save the hospital from closure, she could not give it her full attention right now.

She *was* nervous.

Oh, Victoria would never let on to Glen that she was, but she had butterflies fluttering in her chest. She was seated next to a heavily pregnant woman who, from the conversation taking place, was accompanied by her mother.

When Victoria was less than a year old, her mother had decided that motherhood and marriage were not for her and had walked out; Victoria hadn't seen her since.

Not once.

Growing up, she had asked about her, of course. She had craved information, but there had never been much. Her father refused to speak of his first wife and, apart from a couple of photos that Victoria kept to this day in a drawer in her bedside table, she knew very little about her, other than that she had worked at Paddington's.

As Victoria had got older, and she could more readily see her father's very difficult behaviour, Victoria had decided her mother had walked away because she was depressed. A few years ago, Victoria had decided that no mother could walk away like that and have nothing to do with her child.

And so she had to be dead!

It had been a shock and black disappointment to find out that no, her mother was alive and well.

Thriving, in fact, Victoria discovered when she found her on social media.

She lived in Italy with her second husband.

And was a proud mother of two grown-up sons.

Victoria didn't merit a mention.

She had contacted her but there had been no response.

That had been the final hurt and Victoria had decided she would never allow herself to hurt over her mother again.

Yet she was, and today, especially so.

Sitting in the ultrasound department, she was jealous of the stranger that sat beside her.

With her mother by her side.

She tried to focus on an email she was writing on her phone, rather than them. Hearing the doors swish open Victoria moved her legs to let a trolley carrying a patient past.

The child was crying and Victoria looked at him. She was just trying to guess what was wrong with him when she looked up into the eyes of Dominic walking alongside the trolley.

Usually they ignored each other, or spoke only about their patients. Eye contact was pretty much avoided, but today his met hers and she saw that he frowned.

And well he might.

She was sitting in a children's hospital ultrasound waiting room after all!

It hadn't once entered Victoria's head that it might be a problem to see him here today. It wasn't just that she'd thought he was on holiday, more the fact that Victoria was so used to Paddington's, so completely used to being here, that it simply hadn't entered her head that it might be an issue for her to see him.

Yet it had become one.

He couldn't come over—the child on the trolley was very ill—but he turned his head and gave her a questioning look as he walked past.

Victoria didn't quite know what to do.

Dominic was speaking with a nurse and they were about to be shown through to one of the imaging rooms; Victoria wondered if she should go down to Emergency after her ultrasound and speak with him then.

As he steered the trolley he turned and looked at her again but thankfully her phone buzzed and she could legitimately look away.

And, as she did, all thoughts of babies and fathers and ultrasounds rapidly faded.

Major Incident Alert
All available staff are to report to the station.

Sometimes there were mock-ups of major incidents and you were still supposed to attend, so that staff response times could be evaluated. Telephone lines and operators could not be clogged up with calls to check if this was real or not.

And something told Victoria that this was.

She looked up at the television on the wall but there were no breaking news stories yet.

Her phone bleeped again with another urgent alert and Victoria knew that the ultrasound would just have to wait.

Victoria was a terribly practical person and so the first thing she did was go to the ladies' room.

One problem solved.

As she came out, emergency chimes were starting to ring out as Paddington Children's Hospital's own major incident response was set into action.

'Victoria Christie,' she gave her name again to the receptionist. 'I'm a paramedic. I have to go.'

The receptionist nodded. She herself was already

moving into action. If it was indeed a major incident then all non-urgent cases would have to be cancelled, and the department cleared for whatever it was that might be brought in.

'I'll call and reschedule,' Victoria said, and as she went to run off Glen called and said he would meet her at the front.

This was real, Victoria knew, for someone must have rushed to relieve Dominic from his patient because he was running out of the ultrasound department too.

'Do you know what's happening?' she said as he caught up with her.

'No.'

She was very fit but so, too, was he and he passed her.

By the time she reached Accident and Emergency, Dominic was wearing a hard hat and she realised that he was being sent out.

Hard cases were being loaded into the ambulance that would bring him to the scene and Karen was bringing out the precious O-negative blood that was kept in Accident and Emergency for days such as this.

The ambulance station wasn't far from the hospital but Glen, having received the same text as Victoria, had come to collect her.

As she got into the car Glen told her the little that he knew.

'There's a fire at Westbourne Grove,' he said, pulling off as soon as the door closed while Victoria put on her seatbelt. 'It sounds bad.'

Victoria said nothing—she never showed her true feelings, even in the most testing of times—but her heart started to beat fast.

Westbourne Grove was a primary school, and today was a weekday…

'Apparently there are children trapped in the building,' Glen said grimly.

CHAPTER FIVE

EVERY MOMENT MATTERED.

Victoria was well trained to respond to major incidents, and as soon as they were out of the car they ran to get changed.

The station was busy with many vehicles already out at the fire and off-duty staff arriving to provide backup and relief.

She went to the female changing room and took off her jeans and silky rust-coloured top that she had been wearing and then pulled on her overalls and boots. In the main station area she then collected her communication radio and ran out to the Rapid Response vehicle, which Glen was just boarding.

They hit a wall of traffic as soon as they left the station.

Already ambulances, perhaps the first vehicles at the scene, were making their way back to Paddington's with sirens blaring.

It felt as if it was taking for ever to get there.

They had their lights and sirens on but the streets of London were gridlocked. Drivers were moving their vehicles and mounting the kerbs in a bid to try and let the emergency services through.

As well as ambulances there were fire engines, po-

lice cars and emergency response workers on motor-
bikes heading there too, and there was the sound of
many sirens as finally they approached the school.

They could hear the chatter over the airwaves. Children were being dragged out and there were reports of
firefighters going back in over and over again in an effort to reach the ones that were trapped. Most had been
evacuated and, as per protocol, were lined up on the
playground, far from the burning building. The numbers
had to be checked and constantly updated but panicked
parents were also starting to arrive on the scene and
the police were having trouble keeping some of them
back as they desperately wanted to see for themselves
if their own child had made it out.

'Your children don't go to Westbourne Grove?' Victoria checked.

'No,' Glen said. And then he added, 'Thank God!'

The stretch of silence between those words felt like
the loudest part of his response and, Victoria knew,
Glen was picturing just that—his children trapped in
a fire.

A couple of months ago, when they had been called
out to a particularly nasty motor vehicle accident, Glen
had started relating everything back to his own family.
He took it all so personally, and it was getting worse.

Victoria had, on several occasions, warned Glen that
he would soon be on stress leave if he carried on like
this and had suggested that he speak to someone.

Glen insisted that he was fine and that everyone had
their Achilles' heel, and then he had turned it into a
joke. 'Except for you, Victoria.'

That had given her pause, for while Glen's stress levels worried her, Victoria knew that she went the other
way and stuffed down her feelings so that no one, not

even her trusted colleague, could guess what went on inside her head.

Perhaps Glen was right and his responses were more normal, Victoria had reasoned, for there was a part of her that was perhaps a little jealous.

Not just of Glen and his ability to show emotion, but that he was part of a loving family and thought about them all the time, just as they all thought of him. Throughout the day Hayley would call and at night before the children went to bed, if able to, Glen would find the time to call and say goodnight.

'Let's just hope they're all out,' Victoria said as they got their first good look at the scene.

There was smoke billowing into the air, thick and black, as they were waved through the cordons. Some parents were being physically held back, not understanding the chaos they would create if let past.

They were guided to park behind the fire engines and they carried out their stretcher and equipment.

On a playground there were firefighters breathing in oxygen, and lines of children stood crying on a nearby playing field, clearly shocked and scared.

But they were alive and safe.

Some of the more seriously injured children were being treated on the playing field and it was then that she saw Dominic and two paramedics working on a child and draping the little body in saline sheets.

There were constant headcounts of the children taking place by the teachers but, Victoria and Glen were told, it was estimated that there were still two children in the building.

As the burnt child was being moved onto the stretcher a call went up for them to urgently move.

'Stay back.' A fire officer was pushing back the

emergency personnel. 'One of the internal structures is about to collapse.'

They were told that the next casualty, be it child, staff member or firefighter, would be for Victoria and Glen to treat and that for now all they could do was watch and wait.

There was the violent sound of an explosion followed by a deadly silence. And Dominic, who was loading one of the burn victims into an ambulance, turned and looked at the building.

There weren't just children in there; there were firefighters too.

Dominic dealt with trauma daily.

He was trained to the hilt for this and, seeing the child into safe hands, he moved fast to get back to the changing situation.

But as he ran towards the line of emergency personnel, he saw a firefighter emerge, and then, too far to do anything to halt her, he watched as Victoria started to run.

Fury ripped through him at her blatant flaunting of the rules, for it was not only Dominic that called out to her to get back.

But no, she and Glen were moving towards the firefighter and child.

With good reason though.

Victoria took safety very seriously.

They were still being told to stay back, as another explosion could often follow the first, but as practical as she was, Victoria was in the business of saving lives and she could see that this little life was ebbing fast.

The firefighter was struggling, and as Victoria approached he dropped to his knees. She could see that he, too, was injured and had given all he had to get the child out. Victoria knew help was close for him but for now she was more concerned with the child.

It was a little boy and he was bleeding profusely from a neck wound and, as he was laid on the playground, Victoria knew that time was of the essence or he would soon bleed to death. She applied pressure to the wound with her gloved fingers as Glen, who had also ignored the orders to stay back, opened a pack. He passed her some swabs but, though she tried, Victoria could not stop the bleeding. But then she found the spot and Victoria let out a long breath of relief that the bleeding had stopped.

She looked up and saw that Dominic was running over and as he approached he let rip.

'What the hell are you guys doing running forward, when the order was to stay back?'

Victoria shot him a look that said she was a bit too busy to row right now. Dominic dropped down to his knees and his silence agreed to the same as he examined the child.

'It's venous blood,' Victoria said, not moving her fingers. If it had been an artery he would have been dead before the firefighter could get him out but, even so, he was practically exsanguinated.

Glen put oxygen onto the child and Dominic inserted an IV and took blood for cross-matching. He pushed through some IV fluids while calling to Karen to run through the O-negative blood that the Mobile Emergency Unit had brought with them.

It was the most precious commodity in a major incident; O negative is the universal donor and can be given to all without cross-matching. It was used sparingly and Dominic was now grateful for a couple of earlier decisions he had made to withhold some of this most precious resource, believing those patients could wait till they got to the hospital.

This child could not wait.

'We need to get him to Paddington's,' Dominic said. 'Now.'

They were working on him on the playground and Victoria looked up to a colleague. 'Can you bring the vehicle in closer?'

Just as she looked up, Victoria saw that another child was being carried out in the arms of a firefighter. The child had red hair. That was all she could make out—and that the child was limp in the firefighter's arms. Another crew was available to take care of them and so her focus went back to her own patient.

A teacher came over and identified the child that they were working on as Lewis Evans. 'His mother's here. She's frantic.'

'Get the police to take her to the hospital,' Dominic said. 'I'll speak with her there.'

Dominic could see the redheaded child receiving care from a Rapid Response team and a doctor, and his decision was made to leave the scene and escort this patient.

It was a very difficult manoeuvre into the vehicle. Even lifting little Lewis onto the stretcher caused Victoria to lose the pressure point for a few seconds.

It was enough to know that it could not happen again.

Through the streets the ambulance blue-lighted them towards the hospital. The police had the traffic under control now and streets had been closed off so that their return journey was thankfully far speedier.

Victoria's arms ached as she knelt on the floor, and Dominic was calling ahead to Paddington's and explaining he needed a theatre held and the head-and-neck surgeon to meet them in there, when she saw Lewis's eyes flicker.

The blood and oxygen were starting to work.

'Hey, Lewis, you need to stay very still,' Victoria said. 'You're in an ambulance and we're taking you to Paddington Children's Hospital.'

Lewis didn't answer but she spoke on as if he could hear her and her voice was calm and reassuring.

'I'm Victoria,' she told him. 'You're doing so well. I know you are scared and in pain but you're going to be okay. I just need you to stay very still.'

And then she looked up and arched her neck and Dominic offered her some water.

She nodded.

He held her head steady and she took a drink and then Victoria saw the familiar building come into view but she could not relax just yet. Lewis had already lost an awful lot of blood, his heart was beating rapidly and his blood pressure was barely recordable.

'Keep the pressure on,' Dominic told Victoria, and he saw her slight eye roll—she was hardly going to let go!

The stretcher was very carefully lowered so that Victoria could keep the vital pressure sustained.

'That's it…' Dominic said, and someone helped guide her out of the back. Victoria let out a sigh, not quite one of relief, but it was good to be on solid ground and have the patient at Paddington's where he would at least stand a chance.

It was chaos outside the hospital, and security and the police were working together to keep the foyer clear for patient arrivals.

Some parents had headed straight to the hospital in a bid to find out more, as had some reporters. As well as that, there were some people who loved to have a good look at others' misfortune.

It was a relief to step inside.

They didn't turn for A&E, instead they moved swiftly through the corridors, guided by a team leader, and with relief, Victoria saw that an elevator had been held for them.

Theatre was waiting and their efficiency was amazing, so much so, that Dominic raced back down to the Accident and Emergency unit as his skills were still in heavy demand.

It was so calm in the theatre and it was just a blessing to be there.

The head-and-neck surgeon had finished scrubbing and was speaking with the anaesthetist about their approach to the neck wound.

Lewis was being given blood through both arms now and he had been given sedation before they went ahead with the intubation.

And Victoria felt dizzy.

Ignore it, Victoria told herself.

But she had been standing there for what felt like a very long time.

'How much longer?' she asked, because she was starting to see stars.

And whether it had anything to do with her complexion or voice, or just that they were ready now, the theatre nurse took over just in time.

'Come on,' Glen said.

Glen led her out of the theatre and down a corridor and Victoria bent over in the hallway with her hands on her thighs and took some deep breaths, but when that wasn't enough she sat on the floor and pulled her knees up and put her head between them.

'Do we have to go back to the school?' Victoria asked.

'No, we've been stood down,' Glen informed her. 'I'll go and find you some water.'

'Did they get them all out?' Victoria asked as Glen walked off, though she did not look up.

'I believe so,' Glen answered.

He returned a little while later and Victoria took a long, grateful drink as Glen spoke. 'Some have been taken to Riverside but most are here.'

She nodded and, having taken a drink, put her head back down. Victoria wasn't so much dizzy now but replaying the rescue in her head and questioning her decision to dash forward.

It had been instinct, she knew that, but now it was starting to hit home that it wasn't just her own life on the line.

And some time later, that was how Dominic found her.

Slumped against the wall, head between her knees, and Dominic was cross all over again with her for flouting the rules and crossing the line.

'How's the redheaded kid?' Glen asked Dominic as he approached.

'I've just brought him up for an urgent head CT and handed him over to Alistair, the neurosurgeon,' Dominic said.

He stood over her and she could feel him demand that she meet his eyes.

She looked up then and the look he gave her felt hostile, even if his voice was even.

'How bad is he?' Glen asked.

'GCS of six,' Dominic answered Glen while looking at Victoria. 'He was hiding in a cupboard.'

'Poor kid,' Glen said.

It was Glen who asked all the questions, Dominic noted, but he had one of his own, and though it was for the two of them he spoke directly to Victoria.

'Do you always ignore orders? You were told to stay back because a building had the potential to collapse.'

'I could see that the firefighter was struggling,' Victoria explained. 'And that the child was bleeding profusely.'

Victoria was starting to feel a bit better, but she was herself questioning the decision to run forward. She really didn't want to deal with Dominic right now and so she pulled herself to standing and spoke to Glen. 'Let's get back to the vehicle.'

'One moment…'

Victoria turned to the sound of Robyn's voice. Robyn Kelly was Head of Surgery and very much a part of the new drive to save Paddington's.

'Dominic, we need you to speak to the press.'

The hospital had been stretched today but the critically injured were now all in the right place and order was restoring. Speaking to the press after incidents like this was a part of the job and so Dominic nodded.

'And you too,' Robyn said, looking over to Victoria.

'Me?'

'They want a representative from all branches of the first responders,' Robyn explained, and then nodded her head towards a staff room. 'Come and see this.'

The news was on and the cameras were trained on the fire that was still burning but had been brought a little more under control.

And there, in the top right hand of the screen, was an image of Dominic and Victoria bent over little Lewis and together fighting to save his life.

'Angela Marton, a reporter, just asked the viewers to

consider how much more seriously things might have played out if Paddington's had been closed,' Robyn said. 'There are people talking about it all over talkback radio…' She looked over to Victoria. 'Finally there's some anger being generated about the merger.'

'Good,' Victoria said.

'This image is on all the channels…'

Both Dominic and Victoria did their best not to catch each other's responses as Robyn told them that they had just become the poster picture for the campaign to save Paddington's.

Robyn had to get on, and so it was Victoria and Dominic with Glen by their side who walked back through the hospital.

Glen was asking about all the injuries and Dominic was doing his best to reply, but of course his mind wasn't really on the conversation.

It was also moving on from the disaster and back to a few moments before the major incident alert had been put out.

He thought of Victoria sitting in the Imaging Department waiting room, and then he thought of her sitting slumped and pale on the floor outside the theatres.

Anyone would be feeling a bit faint, Dominic told himself. Victoria had been pushing on Lewis's neck for ages.

Then he looked over to her and he could see her staring fixedly ahead.

Once outside they walked over to the press area and Victoria spoke with her supervisor where she was given a brief.

The police would speak first, then the firefighters, followed by Dominic, and then Victoria was to speak briefly about the ambulance response.

'The last child pulled out was Ryan Walker,' she was informed. 'He's six years old.'

'Okay,' Victoria said, and she deliberately did not look over to Glen.

He had a son called Ryan and she knew he would get upset at the link.

She went and took her place in the line-up.

Yes, her mind was busy working out ways to get the angle she wanted included, but she was also acutely aware of the man who now stood next to her.

The cameras were on them as they stood side by side and she could feel his tension.

Though, this time, it was not of the sexual kind!

'We need to talk,' Victoria said as she looked straight ahead. 'Though not here.'

'Obviously,' came Dominic's rather scathing response.

She turned and looked at him, and wasn't sure if he was annoyed that they were going to be forced together as the poster image of Save Paddington's as Robyn had suggested.

Or if, somehow, he knew.

CHAPTER SIX

DOMINIC KNEW.

Or, at least, he was starting to!

He was trying very hard not to believe she might be pregnant by him, and was very determined that history would not repeat itself, and he would not be made a fool of twice.

The press conference went well. Dominic said that it had been a multifaceted effort. Victoria got in her little plug about the potential closure by pointing out that the most urgent cases had needed the proximity of Paddington's to have the best chance for a positive outcome and then they all went their separate ways.

The department was terribly busy and there was soot everywhere and the smell of smoke in the air. As well as injured children, there were staff and firefighters too but, by evening, the department was clearing and they were taken off bypass, which they had been placed on so that they could deal with the sudden influx of patients.

Dominic had been working since seven that morning, and after twelve eventful hours he should perhaps be heading for home.

Instead Dominic showered and changed into black jeans and a shirt and walked over to the Frog and Peach pub where the Save Paddington's meeting was being held tonight.

On arriving, he soon found out that the meeting had been abandoned due to the Westbourne Grove crisis and would be held in a couple of days in a lecture theatre at the hospital.

Tonight, there was too much energy for sensible conversation.

The major incident meant that the staff all needed to unwind and debrief and so it was a very noisy pub that he found himself in.

There was Victoria.

She was wearing the jeans and rust-coloured top that he had seen her wearing at the Imaging Department, and he saw she was chatting with Rosie, one of the paediatric nurses.

And… Victoria was drinking soda water.

Not that that meant anything.

He had no idea if Victoria would normally be having a drink.

The fact was, he knew nothing about her except what had taken place that night.

'Hi, Dominic, how was your holiday?' Rosie asked as he came over.

'Fine,' Dominic said.

'Where did you go?'

'Scotland.'

'Visiting family?' Rosie asked.

Dominic gave a small nod. It was easier to do that than admit that while he had hoped to go and visit his family and let bygones be bygones, he hadn't felt ready.

Dominic didn't even want to attempt another relationship until he had dealt with the rather large items of baggage left over from the previous one. But the thought of asking Victoria out had spurred him on at least to try and so he had headed for home, but in the end he hadn't been able to see it through.

It wasn't that he was being stubborn, more that he was honest and could not simply walk in as if nothing had happened until he had dealt with it in his head.

Dominic wanted a real relationship with his brother and nephew—and yes, Lorna too—and he would not be pushed, for the sake of family peace, into a false one.

So, while he had hoped to visit family and the new baby, the hurt was still there. So he had stayed in a hotel and taken some time to drive around the land that he loved, and in that time he had done a whole lot of thinking.

A lot of his thinking had been about her.

Victoria.

And now she met his eyes.

'We decided not to hold the meeting tonight,' she started to explain. 'We're going to—'

'I already heard,' Dominic said, and when Rosie drifted off to join another conversation, it was just them.

'Do you want to get something to eat?' he offered.

'I've already had something. Do you?'

'No.'

No, he did not want to try and find them a table in a crowded pub. Already Robyn was making her way over, no doubt to discuss how the interviews with the press had gone.

'Come on,' Dominic said to Victoria, because there was no chance of having an uninterrupted conversation here in the pub.

They stepped out into the street but that wasn't the ideal location either.

'We could go to mine,' Victoria offered, but Dominic shook his head.

Given what had happened with Lorna he did not want to get closer to Victoria in the least. He did not want to see where she lived and sit and have a cosy chat. 'There's no need for that,' Dominic said. 'We can say everything we need to here.'

Victoria frowned. 'Are you sure?'

'Quite sure.'

So she went ahead and told him in her usual succinct way. 'I'm eight weeks pregnant.'

And what had taken place between them was six weeks ago, but she guessed, given his qualifications, that she didn't have to tell him that they added on two weeks.

Or maybe she did, because he was giving her a somewhat quizzical look, and so she clarified things in order that there could be no doubt.

'It's yours.'

Dominic said nothing.

What was there to say?

He hadn't even thought to have that discussion with Lorna.

Dominic had trusted his girlfriend completely and look how that had turned out.

How the hell could he even come close to believing someone with whom he'd had sex with on impulse, who carried condoms and who, by her own revelation that night, had just finished with someone else.

No, he would not be fooled twice.

'I've got to reschedule my ultrasound,' Victoria said. 'I wasn't sure if you might want to be present.'

He gave a snort as he recalled the last time he'd been at an ultrasound and all that had transpired then—listening as the doctor gave the dates and asking her to repeat them, then trying to catch Lorna's eyes as she turned away.

And Victoria saw the look he gave and interpreted it correctly. 'I don't need you to hold my hand, Dominic. I meant, I accept it might be hard to believe it is yours but the ultrasound will confirm the dates for you.'

'No, it won't—you say that you're eight weeks pregnant. Well, that means they can only give parameters between five to seven days...'

'Thanks for that.' Victoria sneered at the implication.

'We used protection,' Dominic pointed out.

'I'm not about to try and convince you,' Victoria said. 'I know it's yours but I accept that you might not believe that it is,' she said. 'Whatever way, I felt that you had a right to know and now you do.'

Dominic just stood there, for once unsure what to say. She was as factual and direct as always, but he had been let down so badly before that there was no way he would be letting down his guard again.

He would be keeping his distance until he was certain.

'When the baby is born, arrange for a DNA and, if it's confirmed as mine, then we'll speak about things.'

'That's it?' Victoria checked.

'What else do you want?'

'With that attitude I don't want anything from you,' Victoria said, and walked off.

He watched her hitch up her bag and cross the street, and she was about to disappear into the underground when Dominic found himself running after her.

'Wait!' he called out.

She didn't.

Victoria stepped onto one of the escalators but she

didn't stand and let it carry her down. Instead she walked quickly but knew Dominic was fast and so he caught up with her at the bottom.

'Victoria, wait.'

'No.' It was just as busy here as it had been in the pub and so it was a hopeless place for conversation and, given his attitude, she would not be asking him again to come back to her flat. 'I'm tired, Dominic. It's been a helluva long day and right now I just want to get home and go to bed.'

He could see that she was tired and he thought of the day she had had. And he recalled the anger he had felt when she'd raced forward to grab that child.

No, not anger.

It had been fear that he had felt.

He moved her aside and she stood straight rather than lean against the wall; he put up an arm that buffeted them from the people that passed.

'Have you told work?' Dominic asked, already guessing the answer.

'Not yet,' Victoria said. 'My crewmate knows.'

'Work needs to know.' He thought of her today and the hell of that fire, and not just that—it was a dangerous job indeed. 'Victoria!'

'I'll make that choice,' Victoria said.

It wasn't really a choice; as soon as she knew she was pregnant she should tell them, but Victoria was still unable to get her head around things and had been putting it off.

'Look…' Dominic started, but she shook her head and made to leave.

'I'm not discussing this here. You were the one who chose to be told out on the street.'

He had been.

But to stop her from dashing off he told her some of his truth.

'Do you know how I know about date parameters?'

'Well, you're a doctor...'

'I know about them,' Dominic interrupted, 'because I'd been reading up on things in the baby books. A few months ago I sat in on an ultrasound with my ex and found out that the baby we were expecting couldn't possibly be mine, because I was in India at the time it was conceived. That's why I moved down to London.'

She looked at him, right at him, but instead of a sympathetic response Victoria told Dominic a truth. 'I'm not your ex.'

And then she ducked under his arm and was gone.

CHAPTER SEVEN

No, SHE CERTAINLY wasn't his ex.

Two days later Dominic sat in the back of the lecture theatre and watched as a very efficient Victoria took to the stage.

She was wearing a grey linen dress with flat pumps and her hair was tied in a loose ponytail. She was petite, but her presence was commanding and despite stragglers arriving in the lecture theatre she started the meeting on time.

'Let's get started,' Victoria said. 'It's so good to see such an amazing turnout.'

She paused as someone's phone rang out and, Dominic noted, Victoria was far from shy—instead of putting the person at ease, she glared.

'Can everyone *please* silence their phones?'

'It might be kind of important, Victoria,' someone called out, and Dominic smiled at the smart response, given the people who were in the room.

'Then put it on vibrate,' Victoria said. 'We've got a lot to get through and if we have pagers and phones going off every two minutes we shan't get very far.'

There was a brief pause as a lot of people turned their phones onto silent.

Dominic's was already off.

He had started carrying it at work, though he kept it on silent. He still did not want his personal life intruding. But now, if his parents called, which they quite often did, he would let it go to message, then speak to them during a lull in his day rather than at the end of his shift.

There still wasn't much to talk about. They opted to discuss the weather rather than face the unpalatable topic as to what their youngest son had done.

And, Dominic knew, he had taken out his malaise and mistrust on Victoria.

That was the real reason he was here tonight; he hoped to speak with her afterwards.

For now though, he listened to what she had to say.

Victoria kicked off the meeting. 'The fire has really helped showcase to people how vital an institution the hospital is.'

Robyn's hunch had proven right, and now Victoria and Dominic were the face of the Save Paddington's campaign.

The image of them came up on the screen behind Victoria and she tried not to glance over at Dominic.

He hadn't been at the other meetings, though she now knew he had been on leave. But even if she was glad of the big show tonight and for any support that could be mustered, there was one exception—Victoria rather wished he would stay away, for Dominic was a distraction that she did not need.

Then again, that's what he had done since their night together—distracted her from her life.

Even before that, she had always found herself looking out for him whenever she and Glen brought a patient into the Castle.

'The travel time is a vital point we should make,'

said Matthew McGrory, a burns specialist. He had been working around the clock with the patients from the school fire and looked as if he had barely slept in days. 'Due to the sheer volume of casualties there were some patients that were taken to Riverside, but the most severely injured children came here and were treated quickly. That first hour is vital and a lot of that time would have been lost had Paddington's not been here.'

'Indeed.' Victoria was up-front and well versed. 'And we do need to push travel time and the difference it will make to locals. However, patients come from far and wide for treatment at Paddington's. We need to promote both aspects and we need to start working out how best to do that.'

It was a call to arms meeting.

'The press is onside at the moment,' Robyn said, 'but we need to keep up that momentum.'

Rebecca, a cardiothoracic surgeon who headed the transplant team, spoke about the real issue with doctors leaving and the problems the cardiology department were facing. 'We're only able to recruit on very short-term contracts. Paddington's has always attracted world-class doctors and we can't let that change. The campaign needs to showcase the hospital in its best light.'

Ideas were building and they were starting to run with them; it was decided that the first major event to be held would be a fundraising ball.

The meeting ran for a couple of hours and Dominic watched and listened.

He could only admire Victoria.

From an initial very scattered effort, the drive to save PCH was now starting to come together.

Certainly, with the fire and its aftermath still prominent in the news, the public were starting to understand the real implications of Paddington's closing.

'Right,' Victoria said. 'I think that gives us enough to be going on with for now. Anyone who wants to carry on the discussion can—I think most of us who are not working will be heading over to the Frog and Peach.'

Phones went back on and people started heading out. Dominic made his way over to the stage.

'Well done,' he told her.

Victoria simply ignored him and packed up her computer and things in silence.

She had been on days off since the fire and hadn't seen him since the night she had told him about the baby. She certainly didn't want to see him now.

There was no getting out of it though. Dominic waited till everyone was gone and, when finally they were alone, she turned to face him and hear what he had to say.

'I want to apologise for my reaction the other night,' Dominic said.

She understood it though.

Victoria had sat bristling on the Tube but, even as she had let herself into her flat, she had been able to see where he was coming from. Dominic, especially given what he had been through with his ex, had every right to be suspicious as to whether or not the baby was his, Victoria had decided.

And she was right to hold back, but for reasons of her own that she could not think about right now.

'Dominic,' Victoria said. 'I'm pregnant from our one-night stand. Now, I accept, given what happened between us, you might assume that I drop my knickers like that...' She snapped her fingers. 'But actually

I don't. I broke up with someone before Christmas and since then…'

'I don't need your history. Victoria, I'm thirty-eight. I'm sure we're both going to have had our share of past relationships.'

And that was perhaps the moment she fully realised just how very different they were.

Victoria was twenty-nine and as for relationships…

She hadn't really had any of note.

Oh, there had been a couple of boyfriends who had lasted a few months, but she had never lived with anyone and, in truth, had never really been in love.

'Well, you shouldn't be so sure,' Victoria responded. 'I don't do very well with relationships and so I tend to steer clear of them. As I said, I broke up with someone just before Christmas, and apart from a couple of first dates that went nowhere, there hasn't been anyone since then.' No wonder the condom hadn't been up to much, Victoria thought; it had been in her purse for months. 'This year, apart from one torrid tryst in a turret, there's been no one.' And she smiled at her little tongue twister. 'I believe you were the said torrid tryst.'

'Indeed I was.'

'And I'm sorry your ex cheated and that you're not over her, but that's your issue and—'

'It's not that,' Dominic interrupted.

She raised her eyebrows and Dominic had to concede a smile, because yes, it probably sounded to her as if he wasn't over his ex. He guessed Victoria thought that he had run away to England because of a break-up, so knew he had to explain things a bit better than that. 'The person that Lorna was sleeping with was my brother.'

'Oh,' Victoria said.

And he waited for her to avert her eyes or to do what

everyone else did and move to quickly change the subject, but instead she gave a small grimace.

'Well, that's awkward!'

And he smiled a little and admitted, 'Indeed it is.'

'Are you and your brother close?' Victoria asked.

'We were.'

'And had you been going out with her for long?'

'Yes,' Dominic said.

'Were you living together?'

'Yes.' He nodded but Dominic didn't want all these questions. He was just trying to explain, a little, why he had reacted to the news of her pregnancy in the way that he had. 'I really don't want to discuss it.'

Only that wasn't quite true.

Dominic had discussed it with no one.

Everyone in his family wanted to simply move on from the uncomfortable topic and to act as if nothing had happened. Not Victoria though—she actually made him smile when she spoke next.

'You're *very* good at torrid trysts.'

'It would seem that I am.'

'Were you both sleeping with her at the same time?'

'Victoria!' His voice held a warning. 'I don't want to talk about it.'

'Fair enough.' She shrugged. 'But if that's the case, then I'm going to go for a drink with my committee.'

'Don't we have rather a lot to discuss?'

'I'll be fine,' Victoria said. 'I cope with things. So really, at this stage there's nothing much to talk about. If you want a DNA test once the baby's here, then that's fine too.'

They started to walk down the corridor but as Dominic went straight she turned to the left.

'Where are you going?'

'It's a short cut.'

Dominic didn't want the short cut; he rather liked spending time with her and, though he didn't say that, of course, it was actually nice to be walking and talking.

The short cut was an old quadrangle that he hadn't seen before and there was a glimpse of a navy sky and the scent of fresh air; Dominic guessed it would be a very welcome space to know, if working over a long weekend.

'Maybe it's not such a short cut,' Victoria added as she looked up and felt the cool evening air on her cheeks. 'More, the scenic route.'

'You really do know this hospital like the back of your hand,' Dominic commented. 'Did your father bring you here a lot?'

'Yes, there were a lot of nanny changes and so I'd be brought along until a replacement was found.'

She had been close to a couple of the nannies but they all too soon found it unbearable to work for her father and left.

It had been the same with his girlfriends, who would attempt to win over the daughter to impress the father and then would drop her like a hot stone as soon as the relationship came to an end.

Even when she had been a bit older, Victoria would come here after school or on long weekends, rather than sit in an empty house. Here at the quadrangle, weather permitting, she had done an awful lot of homework!

'What about your mother?' Dominic asked as they started to walk.

'They broke up.' Victoria gave him no more information about her mother than that. She turned and looked at him. 'I shan't let you just drift in and out of my child's life. And I'm not having him or her dropped off here just because you have to work. My baby will be at home with me.'

Dominic said nothing. If Victoria thought he would be a hands-off father, then she was wrong, but Dominic wasn't going to argue about that now.

He had something to ask her. 'I would like to be at the ultrasound.'

But Victoria had been thinking about just that over the last couple of days and immediately she shook her head. 'I don't think so. That offer has been withdrawn.'

'Can I ask why?'

'It just has.'

Dominic knew he didn't have any right to be there and so he chose not to push the issue.

For now.

They were out of the hospital and walking over to the Frog and Peach but suddenly Victoria did not want to go in.

'Are you coming?'

'No.'

She offered no more explanation than that. Victoria didn't need to give him one and was annoyed when Dominic walked after her.

'What?' she asked.

'There's surely more to discuss.'

'I don't see that there is. I'll send you a copy of the images and you can…' She shrugged. 'You can do whatever you're going to do. Measure its little crown rump length and decide if it might possibly be yours.'

Yes, she had read the baby books too.

And she walked off with more purpose this time.

It was all starting to feel terribly real.

For weeks she'd been stuffing down the possibility

that she might be pregnant; now she knew for certain that she was.

But it wasn't just the baby, or telling work that concerned Victoria.

It was Dominic MacBride himself.

She had heard his concern about her working the other night and now she could feel his slight push to be more present; she knew that it was only going to increase.

And she did not want to start relying on him.

She thought of her own mother, who had upped and left, and all the nannies and girlfriends and wives that her father had gone through.

There had been no constant in her life apart from her father and he had merely dragged her to work and palmed her off to others.

No, she did not want to start depending on a man who would no doubt soon lose interest and be gone.

She simply would not do that to her child.

CHAPTER EIGHT

DOMINIC AWOKE TO the sound of sirens in the street below.

In a decisive move, he had bought a three-bedroom apartment close to the hospital and, with the ambulance station nearby, he heard sirens often. Now, each time that he did, Dominic wondered if it might be Victoria's ambulance on its way to something.

She wouldn't even know that she had passed by his apartment, Dominic thought, as Victoria didn't even know where he lived.

They were so removed from each other's lives.

And yet they were not.

Because he thought about her all the time.

He liked her.

Or rather, he was attracted to her enormously and that didn't aide sensible thinking.

Since their liaison at Paddington's Dominic had found himself thinking about her an awful lot.

Prior to that even.

On finding out about Jamie and Lorna he had closed off from others and thrown himself into work.

Absolutely.

It had been his escape from hurt and anger, and the thought of starting again with anyone had been far from Dominic's mind.

But then she had stomped her way into his thoughts with her heavy boots and crisp handovers. Her confident smile had felt like an intrusion, yet he had found himself looking out for her.

Noticing her.

Victoria was a very different woman from any that he was used to liking.

She had intrigued him when Dominic had not wanted to be intrigued, so much so that, even while talking to a parent, he had been aware that she had been stood registering a patient in Reception. He had seen her duck behind the shelves and, later that same day, he himself had done the same and found the place to which she escaped.

And in his time at Paddington's he had escaped there a few times.

Once, when a young life had been lost, he had come from Theatre and told the parents that he had been unable to save their child.

In fact, Victoria and Glen had been the crew who had brought the patient in.

It had been the worst of nights.

His career meant that he was no stranger to death, but while all loss hurt, this one had been particularly painful.

Dominic had raced the little girl to Theatre but she had died on the operating table and telling the parents had been hell.

They had wanted her to be an organ donor and wanted her heart to go to another child.

It was their fervent wish, yet she was already dead.

Dominic had never been more grateful for the appearance of Rebecca in the interview room. She headed the transplant team and Dominic could only admire her empathy for the parents.

She had spoken with them at length and had gone through what *could* be done to give the gift of hope to another child.

Yes, she had empathy because, seeing Dominic, she had said that she would take it from here.

He had lain in the on-call room going over and over the surgery, wondering if there was anything more he could have done, while knowing that the child's fate had been sealed at the moment of impact.

Unable to sleep he had got up and it had been to the turret that he retreated, where he had looked out to a dark London night.

There, away from the constant background hospital noise, he had thought about the doctors who had fought so hard to save his brother, and accepted he had done the same for that child.

There was solace in that quiet space.

And together he and Victoria had found solace again on a very different night—the night that little William had been born.

Every sensible part of him screeched for caution and told Dominic that he could well be being taken for a ride.

Yet the sensible parts did not take into account the magic of that night, the mutual succour, for despite Victoria's denial, despite insisting her pensive mood was reserved only for the loss of the famed institution, Dominic was certain that she had been hurting for other reasons that night too.

He wanted to know Victoria some more.

Baby aside, caution aside, he wanted to know the woman behind the cool façade and it was time to do something about that.

* * *

'You've got an admirer, Victoria!'

She returned from a call-out with Glen to the light teasing of other staff. A large bouquet of gorgeous flowers was waiting for her at the station. There were freesias, which were her favourite, as well as hyacinths and other blooms. They filled the air with a rich sweet scent and all the gorgeous shades of spring were on display.

Though her heart was beating rapidly she did not show it in her expression. In fact, Victoria rolled her eyes as she opened the card, for she was quite certain who they were from.

If Dominic thought that a stunning array of flowers was going to give him a second hearing, and that she would let him in on the ultrasound, then he could not be more wrong.

But then she read the card and found out that no, she was not at the forefront of his thoughts.

'It's from Lewis's parents,' Victoria said, and she smiled as she read it. 'He was the neck injury from the fire at Westbourne Grove.'

'How is he doing?' her line manager asked.

'Apparently he's doing really well and they'll soon be taking him home.'

Victoria only knew that from the card. Unlike Glen, who checked on almost everyone, Victoria chose not to follow up on her patients.

It wasn't that she didn't care; it was more that bad news was unsettling and she had made a conscious choice not to get overly involved.

Lewis's parents had left a present for Glen too—a very nice bottle of wine that he decided would remain in his locker until they had finished nights next week, as on the Monday it would be his and Hayley's wedding anniversary.

Glen chatted about his plans for that night as they drove to their next job. 'Ten years,' Glen said. 'I can't believe it.'

Nor could Victoria envision it! 'So what are you getting her?'

'Hayley says that she doesn't want anything. She just wants…' Glen hesitated and then changed whatever he had been about to say. 'I'm getting her an eternity ring. Sapphire and diamonds.'

'That sounds gorgeous,' Victoria said. 'So what does she really want?' She looked over to Glen, who concentrated on the road ahead, but Victoria could guess exactly what Hayley wanted and Glen knew it.

'Leave it, Victoria.'

Victoria would not.

'How did you pull up after the school fire?' she asked.

'I'm fine. They got everyone out.'

Victoria knew that Glen was stressed. They had been crewmates for two years now. Though it had taken her a while to open up, even a little bit, Glen had been open right from the start.

He was friendly and laid-back and brilliant at his job, but recently things had changed.

They had been called out to a motor vehicle accident a couple of months ago and taken a very sick child to Paddington's, where she had subsequently died.

Some jobs were harder than others and Glen had taken this one very personally indeed. The little girl had been the same age as his daughter and the accident had occurred on a road that his wife often took.

It was a couple of weeks after that that Victoria had

noticed the change in him. Instead of his usual laid-back self, he was tense at times and kept calling home to check with Hayley that everything was okay.

Despite Glen's insistence that he was fine, Victoria was sure that Hayley wanted Glen to speak to one of the counsellors made available to them, but Glen steadfastly refused to do so.

She would wait for her moment, Victoria decided, and, in the meantime, keep a bit of a closer eye on him.

'Your flowers were nice,' Glen said.

'Beautiful,' Victoria agreed.

Which they were, of course, but what was niggling her was that there *had* been a thud of disappointment that the flowers weren't from Dominic and this unsettled her.

It was a busy morning and just as they were starting to think about lunch they were called out to a woman who had collapsed in a shop.

'I haven't got time to go to hospital,' the woman protested as she lay there. Her daughter was with her and was upset, and as they were transferring her mother to the ambulance, they found out that it was her ninth birthday.

'No school today?' Glen asked the little girl.

'She's goes to Westbourne Grove,' her mother said.

Victoria looked over and gave the young girl a smile. 'You're having a bit of a time of it, aren't you?'

The girl nodded. 'My friend Ryan is very sick.'

'That must be so hard for you,' Victoria said.

They took her and her mother to Riverside but once they had settled them in, and just as they were making up the stretcher, Victoria saw her father walking into the department.

He gave her a very cool look. 'Victoria.'

She gave him a small nod back and let out a breath when he had passed.

'Who's that?' Glen asked, but Victoria just gave a noncommittal shrug as if she wasn't really sure who the man who had just passed was.

She wasn't going to tell Glen that it was her father.

Glen chatted about his family all the time and, though it drove Victoria bonkers on occasion, she liked the glimpses of family life and was embarrassed by the state of her own.

They were just starting to think about lunch again when Dispatch asked if they could transfer a patient from Riverside's children's ward to the burns unit at Paddington's.

The burns unit had been stretched to capacity by the fire but a bed had opened up and a very sweet little girl called Amber was, this morning, on her way to join the others at the Castle.

'Hello, Amber,' Victoria said when she met her.

She had a deep burn on her hand, arm and shoulder that was going to require grafting. Amber became teary when she saw the stretcher.

'It's no problem,' Glen said. 'We can take you to the ambulance in a wheelchair if you prefer.'

That seemed to cheer her up and so they fetched a wheelchair and the small problem was solved, but she became distressed again when she saw the ambulance. No doubt Amber was remembering the pain she had been in the last time, and remembered the fear of the lights and sirens.

'I'm going to make you a chicken to keep you company,' Glen said, and Victoria smiled as he pulled out a rubber glove and blew it up.

He was very good with the little children and knew

how to amuse and distract them with antics, such as this one, and Victoria tended to leave that side of things to him.

Soon enough, Amber was holding her 'chicken' and seated in the ambulance, and the transfer went smoothly. As they made their way up to the burns ward she saw Dominic coming down the corridor and walking towards them.

He wasn't in scrubs; he was in a suit and tie and, to Victoria's mind, looked impossibly handsome.

Did she nod and say hi? Victoria wondered, but Dominic dealt with that—he nodded a greeting to them both and Victoria gave a brief smile back.

Glen was a bit cheeky. 'Direct Admission,' he said as they passed. 'We're taking her straight to the ward.'

'That's what I like to see,' Dominic called back.

It was just a little dig, a small exchange, but hearing his voice and dry response made Victoria smile and feel a bit hot in the face.

The burns unit was busy but they made Amber very welcome.

'Hello there.' Matthew, the burns specialist, smiled to Amber as she was wheeled in. 'I'm Matt.'

As Glen and Victoria wheeled Amber into her side room, Matthew had a brief chat with the girl's mother but she soon joined them.

'It's good to be at the Castle,' she admitted, clearly relieved and reassured to be at the famed hospital. 'Amber, you've got a couple of friends here already.'

'It's just like being back at school.' Victoria smiled.

Soon the little girl was settled and they could head off. It was incredibly warm on the burns unit as the temperature was kept high for the patients, but it made for hot work. Victoria would be very glad to get out of there, but first she had a small chat with Matt, who had spoken at the Save Paddington's meeting.

'Still being kept busy?' Victoria asked.

He nodded. 'I don't think that's going to change any time soon. I meant what I said about it being good that the fire happened so close to us. It made all the difference to some of these children. Did you bring in Simon?'

'Simon?' Victoria frowned and then shook her head.

'The little boy from the foster home?' Glen asked, because he knew about all the patients, and Matt nodded.

'No, that was another crew. How's he doing?' Glen asked while Victoria was overheating.

'I need a drink,' she said, and left them to it. Glen would stand chatting for ages and it really was terribly warm in there.

The drinks machine wasn't working but as they passed the canteen Glen nudged her.

'We'll get lunch,' he said.

And she couldn't really protest. There was no stretcher to take back to the vehicle and even if Dominic was in there Victoria knew that she couldn't avoid him all the time.

She just rather hoped that he wasn't there today.

'What do you want?' Glen asked, because they had their routine and usually Victoria would go and get a table while he went and got the food.

Except Dominic was there.

She had known the moment she stepped in, and though she deliberately didn't look over, she was aware that he was seated in the far corner chatting with a woman.

She really didn't want Dominic seeing her alone and

coming over for another 'discussion,' or request to come to the scan.

'Victoria?' Glen checked, because she hadn't answered his question.

'I'm not sure what I want,' Victoria said. 'I'll come with you.'

She chose a salad sandwich and bought a mug of hot chocolate and a bottle of water, as Glen chose tomato soup and a couple of rolls. Together they found a table, thankfully one far away from Dominic.

She drank half her water and then opened up her salad sandwich and took an unenthusiastic bite as Glen slurped his tomato soup.

'Can I ask you something, Victoria?'

'What?' she snapped, awaiting the inevitable questions as to when she was going to tell work, or whether she had told the father.

Glen had asked both regularly since he'd found out.

'Do you put butter on your peanut butter sandwiches?'

Victoria smiled. She liked their often mundane conversations and it helped take her mind off Dominic. 'Of course I do.'

'Well, Hayley doesn't. And apparently Adam has asked that when it's my turn to make the sandwiches, for me not to put any butter on.'

'Adam's nine?' Victoria checked, and Glen nodded and took another slurp of his soup. 'Well, then, I'd suggest he makes it himself if he's going to be so choosy.'

'You haven't tried getting four children to school on time, have you?' Glen sighed. 'If they all made their own sandwiches, aside from the mess that they'd leave behind, they'd never get there.'

And she conceded, because no, she'd never had to get four little people to school before.

But hopefully in a few years she'd have one little person to get there.

The pregnancy was starting to take shape in Victoria's mind and she was beginning to get excited at the prospect of being a mother.

She liked the glimpses of family life that Glen gave her.

It helped her to picture things a bit.

Glen made sandwiches for everyone if he was on an early shift. It gave Hayley a break and it worked well.

Except he'd left his behind today.

Victoria could no more imagine her father making lunch for her than a flight to the moon.

It just hadn't happened.

And they hadn't taken meals together, unless they were out at some function.

'Have you told the guy he's going to be a father yet?' Glen asked, and Victoria sighed. She was just about to tell him to mind his own business when someone answered the question for her.

'Yes, Glen, she has.'

And she stared at her half-eaten sandwich rather than at Dominic, who very calmly took a seat at their table.

'Well, this *is* awkward,' Victoria said.

'Why is it awkward?' Dominic asked. 'All three of us already know you're pregnant.' He looked to Glen. 'Did you know that the father was me?'

'I had an idea that it might be,' Glen admitted, and Victoria threw him an angry look as she realised that he had deliberately steered her into the canteen. Glen picked up his rolls and then stood. 'I'll see you back at the vehicle, Victoria.'

As he walked off Victoria looked over to Dominic. 'I'll be having words with Glen.'

'I wouldn't bother. I was coming by the station tonight to leave a message for you to contact me,' Dominic said.

'Why?'

'Because we need to speak.'

'About what?'

'Well, Glen knows...' Dominic started.

'Glen guessed that I was pregnant,' Victoria interrupted, assuming he was annoyed that others knew.

'Victoria, I'm glad that he knows. It's good that you've got him looking out for you. Mind you, he should have stopped you when there was that fire.'

'Don't interfere with my work,' Victoria said. 'He's my partner, not my line manager. I make my own choices.'

'Fair enough,' Dominic said. He was trying and failing to treat her as he would a colleague. And trying to rationalise that he had every right to be concerned if she was carrying his child.

Only, it wasn't the baby he had been thinking about on that day of the fire, because he hadn't known she was pregnant then.

He had been loading a child into the ambulance and had turned at the sound of the explosion.

He had seen her rush forward towards the firefighter.

Glen had rushed forward too.

And he had seen the firefighters going into the burning building over and over, but it had been Victoria who he had wanted to go and haul back.

Dominic knew already that she wasn't anything like the women he was usually attracted to.

And his response to her was like nothing he had known.

He had just watched her arrive in the canteen a little pink and flustered, though he had soon worked out why when he had watched her gulp down half a bottle of water—they had just come from the burns unit and boots and overalls would not have been the most comfortable things to be wearing.

And he had seen her and Glen, casually chatting as they selected their meals.

He was actually very glad that Glen knew.

'I wasn't going to broadcast the fact you were the father,' Victoria added, 'until the paperwork came in.'

'Who else knows? What about family?' he asked, worried that she had been dealing with this on her own.

'I told my father.'

'And what did he say?'

'Not very much.'

'Is he cross?'

'Cross?' Victoria checked.

'Well, because you're single?'

'I don't think he gives me enough thought to be cross. He was irritated. I asked if he could pull a few strings so that I could have the baby here at Paddington's and he did.' She closed her eyes for a moment. 'Actually, I just ran into him at Riverside.' And she told him what she could not tell even to Glen.

'We hardly even said hello to each other. We had words the other day.'

'About the baby?'

'Sort of.' She gave an uncomfortable shrug.

'I've spoken with your father on occasion,' Dominic told her, and he watched as her eyelids briefly fluttered as he said without words that he got what an awful man he was. When she said nothing he moved the conversation on.

'And your mother?'

'She's not on the scene. I've already told you that.' Victoria took a long drink of her water but then chose to continue. 'That was what my father and I had words about.'

His patience was pleasant; he waited as her eyes scanned his and she wrestled with how much to say. 'He suggested that I think very carefully whether to go ahead with the pregnancy, and that he knew firsthand how difficult it was being a single parent.' Her lips were pale and they clamped for a moment and his eyes still waited. 'He didn't really parent though,' Victoria said.

'Did you say that?'

'No.'

'So what did you say?'

Victoria flicked her eyes away and she gave a tight shrug. 'Nothing.'

And at one-fifteen, in a busy hospital canteen, Dominic knew for certain that he was about to become a father. He knew that because Victoria had just lied.

Something far more had gone on when she'd had words with her father.

And if he could tell when she lied, then the rest was the truth.

'I think,' Victoria said, 'that I'd better get used to the idea that the only person with any enthusiasm for this baby is me.'

And she looked over to him with an angry gaze while her heart waited for him to refute, to say, *No, no, I'm thrilled, Victoria*, but he just looked back at her with an expression that she could not read.

And then she amended that request from her heart

for Dominic to placate her because she wouldn't believe him anyway.

How could he be thrilled to find out that his one-night stand was expecting a baby?

Yet that was what he did—he thrilled.

There was such a pleasure to be had simply sitting here with him. There was such patience in his posture and a measured maturity to him.

Oh, what did he do to her? Victoria wondered, because she had forgotten to look away and still met his eyes.

There was an attraction between them that was so intense it was as if the rest of the people in the canteen had simply faded away.

'Would you like to go out for dinner tonight?' Dominic asked.

'Dinner?' She frowned. She had just stated that no one was very enthusiastic about the baby and he was asking her to bloody dinner. 'What sort of a response is that?'

'A very sensible one,' Dominic said.

He would not lie; he would not feign delight just to appease. 'A date,' Dominic said.

'No!'

'Just dinner,' he added, as if she hadn't turned him down. 'No talk of babies or DNA tests. We can see if we get on, see if we fancy each other.'

And she laughed.

It was such a moot point.

'That's the only thing we've got going for us,' Victoria said.

He liked her assertion.

'I think that's quite a lot to be going on with,' Dominic said. 'For a first date at least.'

CHAPTER NINE

It was quite a lot to be going on with!

Victoria had never had this feeling while getting ready for a date.

As soon as her shift was over she raced out of the station and was then chased out by Glen because she'd forgotten to take her flowers.

From there Victoria made a mad dash to the shops where, shame on her, she bought some fresh linen for the bed.

In her defence, Victoria reasoned, she had been meaning to buy some for ages and it was on sale.

Yet, she was pushing it for time and there was one reason only that she was making sure that her bedroom was looking its best!

Yes, she hadn't felt like this in for ever. In fact, it was the first time she had been truly excited to welcome someone into her home.

There was anticipation and a flutter of lovely nerves as she made up the bed, put her flowers into a vase and carried them through to the lounge. She put them on the window ledge and then headed back to the bedroom to choose what to wear. She chose her underwear carefully and then made a dash for the shower.

Dominic pulled up at the flat and, when he buzzed

and was let in, she was still in her dressing gown with wet hair.

'Sorry, we got another call-out just as we were heading back to the station…'

Which was true, but she omitted to mention the mad dash to pretty up her flat.

'It's fine.'

'I shan't be long,' Victoria said.

Her flat was tiny and really very lovely despite its very good view of trains.

It was, Dominic decided as he stood in the lounge, far more straightforward and homelier looking than its owner. There was a two-seater couch and a large chair, which was clearly her favourite, because there was a large ottoman and a pile of magazines beside it; the small shelf was crammed with paramedic procedure manuals.

It was neat but not as fastidiously so as he might have expected; it was very much a working girl's flat.

There was a gorgeous arrangement of flowers in the window and Victoria smiled to herself when she returned to the lounge to find him surreptitiously trying to read the card.

'They're from Lewis's parents,' she told him. 'The neck injury from Westbourne Grove.'

'Good.'

'I don't have a secret admirer.'

'No, you have a blatant one,' he said. 'You look beautiful.'

He made her feel just that.

Whether in boots and baggy green overalls with a messy bun, or dressed up, which tonight she was, he had always made her feel beautiful. This evening she had on a velvety, aubergine-coloured dress and black heels, and her hair was worn loose and down.

'Where are we going?' Victoria asked.

Bed, he wanted to say.

Bed, she hoped he would say.

Yet, there was so much that needed to be sorted first and it would possibly be easier to do that with a table between them.

'There's a nice French restaurant that I've heard about but have never been inclined to try,' Dominic said.

'That sounds lovely.'

Everything sounded lovely with his rich accent. He could have said they were going out for fish and chips and she'd have smiled.

She was putting in her diamond studs and she smiled as she saw him watching.

'They got us into this mess.'

'It's not a mess, Victoria. It's a baby and it will sort.'

But it still felt like a mess to her as she was so jumbled in her head. She wanted his kiss and his touch and to be just a couple going out to dinner, or deciding to hell with it and ringing for pizza later in bed. Yet they were so back to front, and he hadn't wanted to go out with her until he'd known she was pregnant.

It was a hurt that she knew, if they got closer, would only grow along with the baby.

Yes, there was an awful lot to sort out.

'Come on,' he said.

The restaurant was gorgeous and intimate and they were led to a lovely secluded table; it was so small that their knees touched, though neither minded that.

The menu was gorgeous and Victoria groaned when she saw all the lovely cheeses and raw egg sauces that she'd been told to avoid.

'When I'm not pregnant I'm coming here again and having everything on here that I can't have now!'

'Bad choice?' Dominic asked because he hadn't really given the menu a thought beforehand.

'Oh, I'm not complaining.'

She ordered coq au vin and he ordered steak béarnaise. Conversation was awkward at first, but then the food arrived.

'This is delicious,' Victoria said as she tasted her chicken. 'I make it sometimes but mine doesn't come close to this…'

'Well, it wouldn't, would it?'

She looked up. 'Why not?'

'You're not a French chef, Victoria.'

And he made her smile because he stood up to her; he challenged her. 'I could have been, had I put my mind to it—well, apart from the French bit.'

They chatted a little about the campaign to save the hospital and the fundraising ball and then she asked if he missed his old hospital in Scotland.

Dominic paused to think about it. He had been happy where he was, but working at Paddington's he was stretching his skills and really starting to settle in and enjoy it. 'More than I expected to,' he admitted. 'When I left Edinburgh, I wasn't planning on making a career move as such, yet I have. It's a great position and I doubt it would have opened up if there hadn't been the threat of closure.'

'A lot are leaving?'

Dominic nodded. 'They've just recruited a new cardiologist but I know a lot of departments are being held together with locums.'

'Was it hard to leave Edinburgh?'

'Of course,' Dominic said.

'Do you still miss it?'

He didn't really know the answer to that. Going back while on annual leave he had asked himself the same, but the fact was, he was enjoying work and had looked forward to returning to London.

He glanced over to Victoria, who had given up on her main and was waiting for his response. 'In part.'

She was scared to ask which part?

There was so much she wanted to know.

But some conversations were best had over chocolate crepes and vanilla ice cream.

Lorna and Jamie was one of them.

The food was delicious, the topic not so, but they chewed their way through both.

'Did you ever suspect there was something between them?' she asked.

'No, they only met the once...'

He swallowed and carried on.

'Every couple of years I go for a stint of working in India. I first went when I was in medical school and a few of us have kept it going. The week before I was due to go we had a get-together, and Jamie, my brother, came along. Until then he and Lorna had never met. He'd been overseas and had just got back. Well, they got on really well...'

'Clearly!'

She had spent too long chatting on the road to be shocked, Dominic guessed. And it was actually refreshing just to let it out in the open with someone who wasn't shy or coy.

'Apparently they met a few days later by chance.'

'Do you believe that it was by chance?'

She was asking the same questions that Dominic had asked himself. 'No.'

'Does it matter?' Victoria asked.

'It did to me at the time, but no, not so much now.'

And instead of saying he didn't want to speak about it, this lone wolf shared.

Once upon a time, he had discussed things with family. Not everything, of course—Dominic did not readily share his emotions—but for the most part, he and his family would generally talk. About this they could not. His parents wanted to move on and put it aside, to simply act as if it had never happened.

Victoria was the first person he had felt able to explain to about how it had all unfolded.

'When I got back from India, Lorna was throwing up...'

'Tell me about it.' Victoria groaned.

'Do you have morning sickness?'

She nodded. 'It's fading now.'

But they were not here to discuss *their* baby; they were there to find out about each other, and so she was quiet. But Dominic wanted to know how she had been faring.

'Tell me.'

'It's pretty much gone now—I just get really tired. You're keeping me up—I'm usually in bed by eight.' She gave an eye roll. 'And I've got night duty next week.'

He looked at her and there was a twist of guilt that he hadn't been there for her, that Victoria was doing it all on her own.

'Can you change your shifts?'

'I don't roll like that,' Victoria said, and then changed the subject back to what had happened with him. 'So Lorna had it bad?'

'Yes.' He nodded. 'I told her that she was very probably pregnant and she said no, that she couldn't be. I went and got a test and, of course, she was.'

'Were you pleased?'

'I don't know,' he admitted. 'I think so, but it all felt a bit rushed...'

And together they smiled at the irony of *their* situation.

'Lorna wanted to wait before we told our families.'

'I'll bet she did.'

'I told Jamie though,' Dominic said. 'We were always that close.'

'What was he like when you told him?'

'He said congratulations, but not much else.' Dominic shrugged. 'He's always been a lot more the party type than I am. I thought his lukewarm reaction was because he didn't really see becoming a father as anything to get excited over.'

'So you found out at the ultrasound?' Victoria asked, bemused. 'Wouldn't she have known you might work it out there?' It seemed very cruel to have said nothing.

'In fairness to her, Lorna had a bit of spotting so we went to the hospital, and of course they did an ultrasound. For early pregnancy the dating is very accurate. I guessed she'd be nine weeks, but she was six.'

'So you realised then and there?' Victoria asked, understanding a bit better why he had been so opposed at first to attending her ultrasound.

'I did,' Dominic said. 'I asked the doctor to repeat the dates. I honestly thought at first that she must have them wrong, but of course she hadn't.'

'What did you do?'

'We had company at the time,' Dominic answered, referring to the doctor who had been present. 'So I said nothing. Lorna kept looking away when I tried to catch her eye. The doctor said that everything was fine with the baby and when she left we had a talk. Lorna admitted that while I was away she'd met someone. She said she'd been trying to work her way up to telling me, but then when she'd found out she was pregnant, she just didn't know how to, and she wasn't sure, at that stage, whose baby it was.'

'Did she tell you then who the father was?'

'When pressed.'

'Did you suspect?' Victoria asked.

'Not even for a moment,' Dominic said. 'Even when she said that it was Jamie, I was trying to think who we knew by that name. That it must be a colleague or a friend. Even when she said, "Jamie," I didn't straight away think of him. How stupid is that?'

'Not stupid,' Victoria said.

It showed the depth of the breach of trust.

'What did you do?'

'I told her she could take a taxi and I wished her the best—not very politely though. Then I went and met with Jamie. I'd like to say I did the macho thing and we had a fight, but…' He shook his head. 'My brother had a car accident when he was ten. I was there when he nearly died. I just couldn't bring myself…'

And Victoria could see the conflict on his face; she thought of all the bloody, testosterone-fuelled fights she'd seen in her line of work and admired that he'd held back.

'Jamie was crying and carrying on like an overgrown bairn. He said that he loved her, that as soon as they saw the other, they both knew and neither knew what to do.'

And she closed her eyes for a moment, because it wasn't such a torrid tryst after all. It was really rather sad.

'Do you still love her?'

'No.'

Did she believe him? Victoria didn't know.

Did it matter?

Yes.

It did to her. But though bold in her questions about his brother, Victoria wasn't so bold with her heart.

'I said that I'd leave it to him to tell our parents.' Dominic gave a resigned shrug. 'I basically walked out on my life.'

'You've been back though?' Victoria checked.

'No.'

'But you've just been in Scotland.'

'I didn't see my family though.'

And that unnerved her.

It truly did.

That he had walked out on his life, and that even all these months later, they were still estranged.

'What about your parents?' she asked.

'We've spoken on the phone but they just want it to be put to one side. They don't want to discuss it. They just want it forgotten and for things to go back to the way they were.'

'So what were you doing in Scotland?'

'Thinking.'

And so, too, was Victoria.

All she could see was a man who had walked away. 'Weren't you the one who told me to fight for what's important?'

'I'm doing so,' Dominic responded. 'It doesn't have to be with fists.'

'I'm not talking about physically fighting, but they're your family.'

'And I'm doing my best to sort it out, but I'm not a person who just rushes in. I believe that if you say all is forgiven, then you need to mean it. I can't say I'm there yet.'

As Victoria went quiet Dominic called for the bill.

Yet it wasn't just a lull in the conversation, or that the restaurant was near to closing—her silence ran deeper.

As they drove home all she could think of was her mother, turning her back on her own family. Oh, she knew Dominic had far better reasons, but to have completely walked away from everyone he loved, for Victoria it was deeply unsettling.

All the hope of a lovely evening had been left back at the restaurant and Victoria now just wanted to be alone.

'Thanks for a nice night.'

She didn't ask him up and it did not end in a kiss.

Victoria looked at him and all she could see was a man who had abandoned everything he had professed to love.

And so she ended things with her usual lack of flare.

'I'll see you at work.'

'Victoria—'

'Let's just keep it at that,' Victoria said, and when he reached for her arms, she pulled away. 'Please, Dominic, stay back. I want to focus on the pregnancy and I just don't have space right now for anything else.'

That was the longest speech she had ever given to a man when she broke off things, but she knew it wasn't really enough.

Still, he did not push for more explanation and she was grateful for that. A kiss, or attempts at persuasion, would only further confuse her.

Victoria let herself into her flat and the gorgeous scent of freesias greeted her.

She undressed and got into the cold, new sheets and just lay there.

He had loved Lorna, she was sure of that—they had been living together, having a baby together.

Victoria ached for that glimpse of him—she truly did—but knew it was not hers to see.

They were being forced together by default.

She knew he was an honourable man and might want to do the right thing, or at the very least give it a go.

And of course Dominic had said that he no longer loved Lorna, but what if he still did?

What if that was the real reason for leaving Edinburgh so completely?

Victoria had been honest when she'd told Dominic that she didn't know how to make relationships work.

How on earth could this one?

He had only asked her out in the first place because she was pregnant.

What if Lorna decided she had changed her mind? Victoria pondered.

Or what if Victoria gave them a go and then it was Dominic who decided things weren't working out?

Victoria could not stand to fall for him only to be hurt further down the line when later he left.

And he would.

Victoria had nothing in her life to indicate otherwise.

It was safer to face parenthood alone.

She trusted only in herself.

CHAPTER TEN

SHE WAS HER usual confident self at work and did not try to avoid him.

In fact, Victoria met his eyes when she handed over patients and didn't dash off.

Perhaps she actually wanted to be a single parent, Dominic pondered.

Some women did.

He knew that Victoria was incredibly independent and she had told him that she didn't really do well with relationships.

Yet, he wanted a chance for them, and more and more he was getting used to the idea of being a father.

Not in the rush-out-and-buy-the-books way this time.

He was starting to feel the fear.

He saw her leave the department and Dominic followed her out. He knew they would be making up the vehicle and sure enough there were Victoria and Glen.

She was sitting in the back drinking tea poured from a silver flask; it was the only hint that she might be avoiding him, because in months gone by she and Glen would have come into the department to grab a drink.

'How are you?' he asked.

'Fine.' She gave him a smile and Glen made some noise about calling his wife and left them to it.

'When are you on nights?' Dominic asked.

'We start tomorrow.'

'How do you think you'll go?'

'I'll be fine.'

'Well, if you need anything, I'm on call over the weekend, so just—'

'I shan't need anything, Dominic.'

'You do need to tell work,' he said.

Yes, the fear was real and he could not stand the thought of her out on the streets at night over the weekend.

'I know what I need to do.'

She tried to end the conversation but Dominic persisted.

'What happened the other night?' Dominic asked. He had been over and over it, and the night that had started with such promise had failed for reasons that he could not grasp.

'Nothing happened.'

Exactly.

'Just because I'm not talking to my family at the moment, it doesn't mean—'

'Dominic,' Victoria interrupted him. 'What happens between you and your family is your concern. I don't want to get involved with all the ins and outs. I've got enough going on in my own life. Aside from the pregnancy, the campaign for Paddington's is getting bigger by the day.' She gave a shrug.

'What about us?'

'There's no us,' she said, and she made herself look right at him as she did so. 'Dominic, you only asked me out when you knew I was pregnant...' He opened his mouth to speak but she overrode him. 'If I'd wanted anything more than that night, then I think I'm assertive enough that I'd have asked you for a date, but I didn't. We're adults—we'll work things out closer to the baby's due date.'

And still she made herself look at him, though it was almost her undoing because she wanted to lean on him; she wanted him to tell her again that it wasn't a mess.

That it would sort itself out.

She was scared how deep her feelings were for him and was terrified to let Dominic close.

'Have you rescheduled the ultrasound?' he asked.

Victoria nodded. 'It's on Monday at ten. I'll ask them to cc you in on the images.'

'Victoria,' Glen called her. 'We've got a collapsed infant…'

She tipped her drink into the bush and replaced the lid. 'See you.'

It was a call-out to a baby who was unresponsive and the location was a hotel.

Glen drove them right up to the entrance and they loaded their equipment onto the stretcher. A member of staff greeted them and told them what was happening as she showed them up to the hotel room.

'The father called down to Reception and said to get an ambulance straight away and that the baby was very sick,' she explained. 'That's all I really know.'

They took the lift and Victoria looked at Glen, who was very quiet, as had become usual for him when it was children or babies.

The woman who had guided them up knocked on the door and, as she opened it with a swipe card, Victoria stepped in. For the first time in her career, she faltered. A gentleman greeted them in a panicked voice.

'What the hell took so long?'

For an instant she had thought that the man was Dominic.

And in that instant, she told herself that Dominic was way too much on her mind if she was starting to think that complete strangers were him.

This man was younger. It was the accent that had sideswiped her.

And also, Victoria knew, Dominic didn't panic, which this man was clearly doing.

It was all just for an instant, so small that even Glen did not notice her pause.

Just a tiny slice of time, but it was enough for Victoria to realise that this was Dominic's brother.

And so this must be Lorna.

Dominic's ex.

A tearful Lorna was kneeling on the floor beside the bed and bending over her son.

'Why were you so long…?' Jamie persisted.

'Jamie,' Lorna shouted to him to stop. 'He's turned grey! At the hospital we were told he was fine,' Lorna said. 'But I knew though that something was wrong.'

Something was very wrong.

A very small baby was lying on the bed on his back with his limbs flaccid by his side. He wore only a nappy and Victoria could see even before she reached the bed that he was grunting and struggling to breathe.

'Come on, William,' his father cried. He was frantic. 'Come on, son!'

As Glen checked the baby's vitals, Victoria administered oxygen to the infant via a bag and mask. He was breathing, but it was with effort, and so she bagged him a few times, pushing oxygen into his little lungs to assist the little one with his breathing.

As Glen attached him to the cardiac monitor she

could see from the trace and hear from the beeps that his heart was beating far too fast.

'We came down to London to bring him to Paddington's,' Jamie explained. 'My brother is a doctor there.'

And this was no coincidence, Victoria was starting to realise—they had come here to seek help for their baby.

'I know your brother,' Victoria said, and looked up briefly from the struggling infant. 'In fact,' she said to Jamie, though she was too busy to look at him, 'I thought that you were him for a second.'

She felt it better to say she knew Dominic now, rather than to say nothing. There was no time for small talk though; Victoria just felt it was better that she stated it up-front.

The baby had responded to the oxygen and was beginning to pick up; now his little hands were making fists and he was starting to kick at the air.

He went to cry and *that* was the best moment to bag him—Victoria actually saw him pink up before her eyes. In the background, she could hear them explain a little more of what had happened.

'I was feeding him and he just went all floppy,' Lorna explained.

'He's on the breast?' Victoria checked.

'For the most part.' Lorna nodded. 'He had formula yesterday while we were travelling. Sometimes he feeds well, other times it's a struggle, so I've been mixing them up.'

Little William had started to cry in earnest now and was looking a lot better than when they had first arrived.

Victoria and Glen discussed their options for a couple of moments. Inserting an IV would distress him and calling for backup wasn't required yet. Though stable now, he needed to be at the hospital if he deteriorated again, so the decision was made to transfer him as a babe in arms, the priority being to keep him from getting distressed.

They worked swiftly but calmly.

'He'll be more settled if he's held by you,' Victoria explained. As Glen watched the baby, Victoria helped Lorna onto the stretcher. Little William was placed in her arms and the monitor was laid by her legs, and soon they were in the ambulance and on their way to the Castle.

He was pinker now and looked so much better, but Victoria would relay to the staff at Paddington's just how very ill this baby had presented when they had first arrived.

'I've been so worried,' Lorna said. 'I've been saying that there was something wrong with him for weeks and everyone said I was just being neurotic.'

'You're not neurotic,' Victoria said.

Lorna started to cry, for, while it was nice to be believed, it was awful to have it confirmed that there was something very wrong with your child.

'There's been so much going on...' Lorna said.

'It's okay, Lorna,' Jamie said. 'None of this is your fault.' He looked over to Victoria. 'There's been a big family fallout. My wife's been through a lot of late.'

So they had married.

Victoria kept a very close eye on the baby and listened to the couple trying to comfort each other while so very scared for their child.

'Should we ring your parents?' Jamie asked Lorna, and she nodded. 'They're in Greece,' he added to Victoria.

'Maybe we should wait and see what the doctors say?' Lorna suggested.

Little William was a picture of contentment now, pink and warm in his mother's arms, but Victoria's eyes never left him except to glance up and see how far away they still were.

Paddington's came into view, and when there was a very sick child in your care, it was such a sight to see.

That was why so many were fighting to save it.

There were many who knew from painful experience the value of this wonderful establishment.

Little William's arrival was seamlessly dealt with, though the department was clearly very busy.

Victoria knew that even before she stepped inside because there were several ambulances in the foyer when they arrived.

It did not affect the care that William received.

Even though he was pink and crying, Victoria swiftly conveyed that this was rather more urgent than it appeared, more with her eyes than anything else, and the triage was rapid.

They were taken through to the resuscitation area and that was busy too. There must have been a vehicular incident just brought in because most of the bays were full and there was a sense of urgency all around. It was then that she saw him.

Dominic.

He was standing talking to Alistair North, a paediatric neurosurgeon, but he glanced over as Victoria came in.

And then she watched as he looked down to the stretcher and she saw his forehead furrow and his jaw tense at the sight of Lorna holding her small baby.

'Dominic!' Jamie's voice was raw as he called out to his brother. 'He's not at all well.'

And she was right about him—Dominic wasn't one to panic.

He said something to Alistair and then he came straight over.

'William MacBride,' Glen said. 'He became unresponsive while his mother was feeding him...' He relayed some more details as Victoria lifted the baby from his mother's arms and placed William in an examination cot.

'I was going to call you today,' Jamie said to his older brother, 'and ask you to take a look at him.'

'You're in the right place now.' Dominic nodded. He called for assistance, but when there was none forthcoming, he knew that these next few moments were down to him and took command. 'What's been happening?'

'He's been struggling to feed and put on weight. The doctor didn't seem too concerned and the nurse said that Lorna, well...'

'She thinks that I'm overly anxious.' Lorna spoke for herself.

'How was the pregnancy?' Dominic asked.

'It went well.' Lorna just sat on the stretcher, helpless and wringing her hands as her son was transferred from the ambulance's monitor to the hospital's. 'It's just been these past two weeks. We've been getting nowhere. Finally, I got an appointment to see a paediatrician, but it's not for a couple more weeks. In the end Jamie suggested that we bring him down to be seen by you.'

Dominic nodded but did not comment on that—he was too busy taking care of the infant and, despite the pressure he must surely be under, he did not miss a beat. He was feeling the little boy's scalp and checking his fontanelle, which Victoria knew from her own examination was sunken, a sign that he was dehydrated, and Dominic asked for more information.

'So what happened today?' Dominic asked as Victoria helped Lorna from the stretcher.

'We were at the hotel.'

'How long have you been there?'

'We got there around midnight. The journey down was fine and he had a really good night. I was starting to think we were making a fuss to have come all this way. I was feeding him and saying the very same to Jamie when he started to make all these choking noises and he went floppy.' She started to cry and Dominic nodded when Karen suggested that she find someone to take the parents to get a detailed history.

Victoria had helped Lorna from the stretcher and the anxious couple were gently led away, but at the last moment Jamie turned and came back.

'Dominic, he looks fine now, but—'

'I get that he's unwell,' Dominic said. 'Jamie…' His voice was firm. 'You need to hold it together right now. You need to keep your head.'

'I know but—'

'Come on,' Karen said, and he was again led away.

Victoria guessed that it wasn't the first time Dominic had had to tell his brother that.

The baby was listless again—even crying seemed to exhaust him—and while he lay quietly, Dominic had a very long listen to his heart.

And still she stood there.

Glen made up the stretcher and replaced the used equipment, and still she watched as Dominic took blood. Victoria stood outside as a portable chest X-ray was taken.

But then, instead of heading for the ambulance, she went back in.

'Can we get the on-call cardiologist down here,' Dominic instructed.

'Victoria,' Glen called out to her. 'We've got another job to go to.'

She knew that they had to leave.

They were extremely busy, but Victoria found herself wanting to linger and to know more.

She admired how calm Dominic was. Oh, she knew it was his job to be, but no one could even guess what he was going through right now.

There was a sense of agency to him that Victoria liked.

And then he looked up and caught her eyes and she gave a thin smile, one of support, one that said she knew how hard this was.

And he gave back a grim smile of thanks.

'We'd better go,' Glen said.

Only she didn't want to go.

For the first time she wanted to linger—unfortunately, there was no choice but to leave.

It was a long day.

An incredibly long one, and there wasn't a patient aged under sixty in sight, which meant that they didn't get back to Paddington's once.

Oh, how badly Victoria wanted to go to the hospital to find out how William was, but instead they were in and out of Riverside and nursing homes. And in a quick coffee break, where Glen rang Hayley, Victoria thought not just about little William and how he was, and not just about Dominic and how he was coping.

But about Lorna.

Victoria had had neither the time nor the inclination

to think about it when they had been dealing with the baby, but now, pausing for the first time since it had happened, she reflected on the woman that Dominic had once loved.

Perhaps he still did.

In her head Victoria had painted Lorna as some sort of vixen; in fact, she was softly spoken and pretty.

Dominic and Jamie were very similar in appearance.

Jamie, though, was expressive, not just with his emotions but with the information he shared. Oh, she knew the circumstances had been dire today and that people's reactions were often extreme when under pressure, but she just could not imagine Dominic opening up in front of someone else the way that Jamie had.

By Dominic's own admission, even when he had found out the baby wasn't his, he had stayed quiet as a doctor was present.

They were similar, yet different.

And it was the more stoic MacBride brother that Victoria very possibly loved.

It was a scary thought and one she did not want to pursue, but at the end of a very long shift she could take it no more.

'Could we stop by the Castle on the way back to the station?'

'Sure,' Glen said. He could see her tense face and was wise enough not to probe.

It had been a long day for Dominic too.

A new cardiologist had started at Paddington's and Dominic had felt a wash of relief to hand little William over, especially as Dr Thomas Wolfe seemed very thorough, if rather stern.

'He's my nephew.' Dominic had given his findings

and then started to explain the relationship he had with the patient but had immediately been interrupted.

'Then you need to step back,' Thomas had said. 'I'll be in to speak with the family shortly.'

Dominic relayed that information to Jamie and Lorna and though they had communicated throughout the day it had all been about the baby.

Lorna contacted her parents, who were holidaying in Greece, and Dominic was the one who rang his and Jamie's.

They had been very upset by the news and the call had been brief. They had soon rallied though and had called back to say that they were flying down to London and could Dominic meet them at the airport.

The underground would be far easier but their plane came in near the end of his workday and so Dominic agreed. Though he warned that he might be half an hour or so late, depending on traffic.

Then he rang his cleaner and asked her to stop by and give his apartment a quick once-over.

On top of that there were patients, of course, and near the end of a long and difficult day he looked up and there was Victoria walking towards him.

'Do you need me to come out?' he checked, assuming that she wanted him to come and assess a patient in the ambulance, as happened at times.

'No, no,' Victoria said. 'I just stopped by to see how William was doing.'

And he knew from experience that she chose not to get involved with patients, so it touched him that, for his nephew, she had made an exception.

'He's in the catheter lab at the moment. He's had a day of tests and they think he's going to need surgery.'

'Cardiac?' she asked.

'Yes.'

'How are his parents?'

'Exhausted. They're going to be staying with him overnight, of course.'

And tomorrow? she wanted to ask.

Would he be opening his home to them?

But it was not her place to ask such personal questions; Victoria had made very sure of that, so she was vague in her questioning.

'Do your parents know?'

'Of course. They'll be landing in an hour or so,' Dominic said. 'I'll be heading to the airport soon to pick them up.'

'I thought you weren't speaking.'

'We've always spoken,' Dominic said. 'We just didn't know what to talk about for a while.'

And she just looked at him as if he was speaking in a foreign language, and then she gave her smile.

'I've got to go,' Victoria said. 'Glen's waiting.'

'Okay.'

'I hope things go well.'

He watched her walk off, somehow elegant in boots and green overalls, and he did not want it left there. 'Victoria...' he called out, but she carried on walking.

She was, Dominic decided, a complicated lady.

And he wanted to understand her.

CHAPTER ELEVEN

DOMINIC RAN DEEP.

His thoughts he did not readily share and his emotions he kept under wraps.

And it took all that he had within him to keep it like that today.

He was on the phone when Jamie knocked on his office door.

'How is William doing?' Dominic asked.

'A lot better than he was this morning,' Jamie said. 'He's got a hole in his heart and he's going to be reviewed tomorrow by a cardiac surgeon to see if they'll repair it or wait.'

'Well, he's certainly in the right place,' Dominic said.

It was a phrase used often here but it was a heartfelt one and Dominic better understood it now. There was something very special about this place and he could see why Victoria and the others were fighting so hard to save it.

Little William really would get the very best care.

'Lorna can see that now. She didn't want to come down to London given...' Jamie gave a tense shrug. 'I insisted though. I wanted you to take a look at him rather than wait.'

'You did the right thing.' Dominic nodded.

'Look, about—' Jamie said, but Dominic interrupted him.

'Let's just leave it for now.'

'I don't want to leave it though!' Jamie said, his voice becoming distressed as he started to get upset. 'I'm beside myself, Dominic.'

'Listen,' Dominic said. 'For now, you're to focus on Lorna and William. That's it.'

'I need to know that you've got my back.'

'I've always had your back,' Dominic answered. 'You know that I do or you wouldn't have come down to London to have me take a look at William.'

Jamie nodded but he was impatient and wanted resolution. But Dominic would not discuss it today. 'All of that can wait,' Dominic said. 'You need to take care of your wife and son and let nothing else get in the way of that.'

'I know.'

He wanted to tell Jamie that it was time to grow up, but that took things too close to personal and it was everything Dominic knew they had to avoid for now.

'What time do they get in?' Jamie asked.

'Soon,' Dominic said. 'In fact, I need to get to the airport.'

He brought his parents back to the hospital where they fretted for a while, and then somehow the MacBrides did what families do in an emergency—they put differences aside and dealt as best they could with the new hand they had rapidly been dealt.

Most families.

He understood that look now from Victoria.

That brief look where she clearly hadn't understood what he was saying, but he wanted her to understand.

More than that, he wanted to see her.

It was late, he was tired and, yes, he had been told by her to stay back, but instead he found himself at her door.

Victoria opened it and she was wearing the same short white robe that she had been wearing the last time he was here.

She rolled her eyes when she saw him. 'It didn't go well, then?'

'What?' Dominic frowned.

'The family reunion.'

'It went very well, Victoria. I'm just here to see you.'

'Why?' she asked, and then she laughed. 'Stupid question.'

Sex was the last thing on his mind. Well, not quite, but with those three words he knew her a little bit more.

She didn't get relationships.

Not in the least.

'I'm actually here because I've had a crap day and I wanted to see you at the end of it. Are you going to let me in?'

Her flat was dark; clearly she had been about to go to bed but she let him in and turned on a side light.

He took a seat on the sofa and she sat on a chair as if they were in a waiting room.

'How are your parents?' she asked.

'Worried, but they feel better now that they've seen him. They're back at mine.'

'How's the baby?'

'He's on the cardiac unit and he's settled for the night. Lorna's staying with him.'

'Is Jamie back at the hotel?'

'No, he's staying at mine too.' He saw her eyes widen a fraction and chose to explain how it had come about. 'Jamie didn't know the way to the underground, nor about Oyster cards and things, so I offered to drop him off at the hotel. In the end I said to just check out and to come and stay at mine.'

'Are you two talking, then?'

'A bit,' he said, and then admitted more. 'Not really.'

'Then how come he's staying at yours?'

'Because he's my brother and his baby is sick, and right now the baby is the priority. The rest will have to wait.'

His voice was brusque, though he hadn't meant it to be. 'Sorry.'

'No, no…' Victoria said.

It really had been a difficult day.

'Thomas seems to think he might need surgery.'

'Thomas?' Victoria checked.

'Thomas Wolfe. He's a new cardiologist.'

'He's not new,' Victoria said, and shook her head.

'Yes, he is. He only just started at Paddington's the other day.'

'No, he used to work there years ago when I first started. He's a lovely guy.'

Dominic didn't comment; lovely wasn't how he'd describe any guy, but certainly it was not a word he'd expect to hear to describe Thomas, who he had found rather stand-offish.

Still, he didn't dwell on it.

He took in a breath and closed his eyes. It was the first time he had properly paused since he had looked up and seen Victoria walking towards him with Jamie by her side and Lorna and William on the stretcher.

'Jamie was going to call and ask me to take a look at him this afternoon…'

'I know that.'

And it was then she knew for certain that she loved him.

She didn't even have to ask what his response to that phone call would have been.

And yes, while she wanted happy reunions and for him to say that his family was fine, she was starting to understand that Dominic did not say what you wanted him to. He spoke the truth.

Having seen Lorna and Jamie for herself, she was starting to comprehend the magnitude of the betrayal.

It was a miracle, really, that Dominic had followed her into the underground that night when she had first told him she was pregnant, and that he kept coming back when so many men would have turned away.

She wanted to ask him about Lorna, how it had felt to see her today after all this time, but she knew that wasn't needed now.

'Jamie tried to talk about it,' Dominic admitted. 'But I told him that for now he has to focus on the baby. I am trying to work on things with my family, Victoria,' he said. 'But I need to do it at my own pace, not theirs.'

'I know that,' she said. 'But how can you sort it out living so far apart?'

'Because I couldn't work on it from there. Victoria, families fall out. You yourself said you've had words with your father...'

'Your family wants you to be in their lives though.' 'Doesn't he?'

'He wants me there to attend functions when he's between wives.'

'What was the row about between you?'

'I told you,' she said, but she knew she hadn't properly. 'I said I could see why my mother left him.'

'And what did he say to that?'

She shrugged.

Victoria simply wasn't ready to go there.

'Do you want a drink?' she offered.

'I do, but I have to drive.'

'I meant tea.'

'No thanks, then.'

She stood up to get him a Scotch or whatever she had to hand. 'Have a drink. I can drive you home.'

'No thanks,' he said. 'I need the car in case something happens overnight.'

She stood still. There were other solutions and both of them mentally explored them. Dominic wanted her to come back to his—he needed her tonight—but his family were all there and so he could not suggest that.

And though he wanted to stay here a while, both knew where that could lead.

Would lead.

He could see her nipples protruding through the dressing gown—life would be far less complicated if they did not so completely turn each other on.

But no, he could not stay here for the night.

'I really do need to get back home. I just wanted to stop by and tell you what was happening.'

It was nice that he had stopped by, Victoria thought, for she had been fretting about it all evening. It didn't really make sense to Victoria—after all, she had been to the hospital to see how the baby was, but she had just felt a bit sick about little William since the moment she had realised that the baby they had been called out to was Dominic's nephew.

'Will your parents worry if I keep you out late?' Victoria teased, and he rolled his eyes.

'My mother asked where I was going at this time of the night. They're driving me crazy already.'

And she smiled because it was said without malice. He put out his hand and when she took it he pulled her onto his lap.

'How are they driving you crazy?'

'Because in the twenty years that I haven't lived at home, nothing has changed. They hadn't had dinner and I suggested that we get a takeaway, as you do. But no, she wanted us all to sit down and have a proper dinner, as she calls it.'

Victoria found that her smile widened.

Oh, she loved glimpses of family life.

'Well,' Dominic continued, 'I don't really have the ingredients for a proper dinner in my kitchen, so I said I'd go shopping and of course that meant she had to come with me...'

And he was smiling now as he told her about the little shopping trip. 'Do you know how many different types of potatoes there are? Well, I do now. And for all the potatoes in the supermarket they didn't have the ones she preferred.'

'Of course they didn't.'

He let out a soft laugh and then looked to the woman on his lap and Victoria looked back at him.

She felt his hand around her waist and the warmth of his palm through the fabric. 'I'm sorry it's been such a bad day,' Victoria said.

'It's not now.'

The world and its problems were outside and waiting and he would give them all the attention that was needed. But right here, right now, the night felt kinder than the day.

'I do have to go...' he told her.

'I know that you do,' Victoria said, but she did not move from his lap and he made no move to stand.

He looked at her hair which tumbled down over her shoulders and he knew that she wore nothing beneath the robe. He looked at her mouth and then back to her eyes.

A train rattled past which told her the time. She actually liked the sound—it was like having an erratic cuckoo clock in her home but, Victoria knew, this train was the last of the night and she would not hear that sound again until just after five.

And what would her life be like then?

More complicated, Victoria was sure, because it was she who moved in for his mouth.

She tasted resistance—oh, yes, she did—for Dominic had not come here for that and did not want to muddy the waters…while, of course, also desperately wanting to.

For muddied waters became crystal clear as he tasted her kiss and it was all terribly simple after that. It had been a day of holding back and he could sustain it no more, for today *had* been hellish and now the night was not just kind, it was inviting.

Escape beckoned and he drew her in closer, hitching her up on his lap while his hands went into her hair. But Victoria pulled them down, for this was her kiss to him. And so she turned in his lap and straddled him so his hands were free to roam her.

And then he kissed her lazily as she rose on her knees to him, a kiss that simply let her lead and gladly she did. Victoria explored his mouth at her leisure as he ran his hands over her bottom and then released the tie on her robe so that it fell open.

Now his mouth was more urgent as they explored with their tongues and she knew she had never enjoyed kissing more than she did with him.

It was hungry and teasing and they shared moans of pleasure, and as his hands toyed with her breasts she was raw with need for him.

The kiss went deeper and he pulled her higher on his thighs so that she could feel him hard at her centre. She was holding his face in her hands as she kissed him and he ground her down on him.

Then she lifted higher so that he could taste her breast with warm licks, and when he pulled his mouth away, the sudden loss made her crave more.

Victoria had never wanted anyone as badly as she wanted him.

She had missed his touch and now, when there was so much to sort out, they sought the one thing that was already clear—a mutual and very deep want.

'Please...' she said while making room for his hands to free himself. Victoria could feel his breath on her breast as she held on to his shoulders. But when she could simply have lowered herself onto him, instead he ran his hand up her inner thigh and then played with her for a moment, sliding his fingers inside till she was quivering. But she did not have to ask twice for him to take her.

He eased himself inside her as she lowered herself down, and he swore with the bliss of her tight grip and told himself to hold on.

Victoria now wanted his skin pressed to hers. It seemed cruel that he was dressed, but she was so hot in his arms that all she could manage was a couple of buttons on his shirt before she gave up trying to open it.

He thrust upwards while pulling her down and the feel of him so deep inside her almost shot her into orbit.

It was raw and fast and there were hungry kisses in between, and then he turned his head to halt their kiss and slid his hips forward in the chair, taking her with him and allowing him to watch their union.

Victoria still held his shoulders and she, too, looked down. He lifted her hips and held her at his tip, then thrust just a little and the pleasure drove them both wild. She could not sustain it as she was starting to come so he pulled her hard down. She tightened and pulsed around him as Dominic came to her body's command. Relishing the heat of release, she rested on his shoulder, gathering her breath, while he moved her pliant body to extract every drop of pleasure.

Victoria closed her eyes at the bliss, while knowing she did not need to wait for morning to find out how she was feeling.

She wanted him to stay.

Victoria wanted to hole them up in her bedroom and never leave because it felt as if there were too many obstacles out there.

This love felt as though it might burst from her chest if she let it; it was just too vast to handle.

There were too many feelings that must be kept in check.

For how would he react to her barrage of questions?

Her feelings were in complete disarray.

'You need to go,' Victoria said.

She went to climb off but he did not let her. 'So you can say I got what I came for?'

He felt her short, reluctant laugh as he held her in his arms.

He was starting to know her a little too well and so she lifted her head up and looked at him.

'You do have to go.'

'I can call and tell them that if there's a problem...'

And then he hesitated because family came first, especially at times such as this, yet she had edged her way up that list. 'Come back with me.'

It was possibly the most stupid thing to say, but he was still inside her and that allowed a person to say the occasional reckless thing.

'Isn't it a bit early to be meeting the family?' Victoria said, and got off him.

'Exceptional circumstances,' Dominic retorted as he sorted out his clothes. He was annoyed at himself for pushing things, and annoyed at the contrariness of her. 'Victoria, like it or not, we're going to be parents, and trying to sort things out from a distance isn't working out too well, is it?'

'I'm on nights tomorrow,' Victoria said. 'I just want to go to bed and have a long lie-in.'

'So when will I see you?'

'At work, I guess.'

'I meant away from work. I'm not going to have our relationship dictated by how often your ambulance is dispatched to the Castle, and you kicking me out isn't exactly helping us—'

'I'm hardly kicking you out,' Victoria interrupted. 'You have a family that you need to get back to and I need to get some sleep.'

She needed him gone because she was on the edge of telling him she was crazy about him.

On the edge of asking about Lorna and how it had felt to see her again.

If he knew her—the real, insecure her—Victoria was positive that he would not want her any more.

She had never cared about anyone else in the way she cared for him, and it terrified her. She did not want to add a failed relationship between them to the mix.

'You keep asking if there's anything you can do for me,' Victoria said. 'Well, there is. Just stay back.'

'You mean that?' he checked.

'I do.'

She even held the door open for him.

So much for wanting a long sleep, because Victoria was still awake when she heard the first train of the morning clack past.

Dominic, she decided, could be as involved in their baby's life as he chose to be but she would not allow him to get closer to her.

CHAPTER TWELVE

'WHAT TIME DID you get home last night?' Katie Mac-
Bride enquired as Dominic came into the kitchen the
next morning.

Dominic, who hadn't had to answer that question for
two decades, was certainly in no mood to answer it now.

'Did you hear what your mother said?' William
prompted. He was sitting at the kitchen table, reading
a newspaper. No doubt he had got up at six and gone
out to get one, just as he did back home.

'I heard,' Dominic answered. 'I didn't make a note
of the time when I got in.'

He had tea and toast all prepared by Katie, and Dominic laughed to himself at his own suggestion last night
that Victoria should come here.

Dominic loved his parents very much but they were
straight into his business and he could only imagine a
very independent Victoria's response to his parents'
fussing.

'What time will you be back?' his mother asked as
Dominic went to leave at seven when he didn't really
need to leave until half past.

'I'm not sure,' Dominic answered. 'And tomorrow
I'm on call all weekend so I'll be staying at the hospital.'

'What about Jamie and Lorna?' William asked. 'Will you be in to visit your nephew?'

'I am going to be working!' Dominic pointed out.

'You should speak with your brother instead of avoiding him.'

'Jamie's here now.' Dominic pointed down the hall to the bedroom. 'How can I be avoiding him?'

Except deep down Dominic knew that he was.

Friday night was hell because little William had a run of atrial fibrillation and Dominic had to race Jamie back to be by Lorna's side.

Dominic sat in the waiting room on the cardiac unit and saw on the news that there was an incident at Piccadilly.

He had never felt fear watching the news until he had met Victoria.

It was hell watching flashing lights on the screen and brawls taking place and knowing she may well be in the thick of it.

And what was he supposed to do?

Did he send a text asking if she was okay and just irk her some more?

Or did he just sit there feeling ill while hoping to God she was safe?

She wasn't.

Victoria wasn't gung-ho but she could never be accused of holding back, yet as she climbed out of the vehicle to the sounds of a brawl, for the first time in her career she did hold back.

Victoria did not feel safe.

'Hey!' Glen warned the guy lying on the kerb as he lashed out with his boot. 'We're trying to help.' He looked over to Victoria. 'Can you bring the stretcher closer?' Glen said, and then he asked the police who were holding the man to get a better grip on him.

It was Victoria who drove the patient to hospital while Glen stayed in the back.

Nothing was actually said, but Victoria knew only too well that she wasn't carrying her share of the load.

Glen was lovely; he always was.

He sensed that she had lost her nerve and so he put his big body in between Victoria and the patients during a few of the trickier call-outs. But late on Sunday night, coming into the early hours of Monday morning, after attending a domestic dispute, Glen told her something.

'You need to tell work.'

'I know.'

She was on leave after this shift but she would tell her line manager about the baby this morning, when they returned to base.

And then the wheels would all be put into motion, and on her return from leave her duties would change and Victoria would no longer be operational.

'What time's your ultrasound at?' Glen asked.

'Ten.'

'You'll be wrecked,' he said because they finished at eight.

'I'll grab an hour of sleep at the station after we finish,' Victoria said.

'Is Dominic coming with you?'

'I don't want him to.'

'Let him be there.'

'Just leave it.'

She took a bite of her sandwich. She was not going to be discussing this with Glen, but also, she noted, he didn't offer to come with her this time.

Perhaps now that Glen knew who the father was, he felt that it wasn't his place to offer, but all the same, she felt terribly alone.

Victoria's job was her rock and a huge part of her identity.

She was excited to become a mother, yet it felt a little as if everything familiar was being stripped away.

How *was* she going to work and be a single mum?

Just who would be looking out for the baby on nights such as this?

Would Dominic really be there for them?

She tried to imagine him dropping over to her flat to look after their little one while she headed out, or taking the baby over to his.

How long would that last? How long till he tired of any arrangements they made or, like her father, suddenly got called into work and decided that his job was more important than hers?

Or what if he met someone else, which of course he would one day, and decide that his new family was his priority?

As her mother had done.

And then she tried not to think of the other possibility—the two of them together, knowing the odds were that they wouldn't work. He still hadn't sorted things out with his family. Even with a desperately ill baby the brothers were unable to be close.

And as for her?

Victoria had never been close to anyone.

That was her real fear—that, even with the best of intentions, he might give them a go for the sake of their baby, but that Dominic would one day tire of her and simply leave.

'How do you and Hayley make it work?' Victoria

asked, but she didn't get her answer—a call-out came and as the address was given Victoria recognised it straight away.

'That's Penny.'

They put on the lights and Glen drove skilfully through the dark London streets and soon they were pulling up at her house.

The lights were on both upstairs and down and, as they made their way up the path, Victoria saw that the front door had been left open.

'Through here.' Penny's father was on the phone trying to find out how much longer the ambulance would be, which Victoria knew from experience meant things were bad. She took a breath and went through to the lounge.

'Hello, beautiful!'

Victoria's smile was bright and no one would ever guess that Victoria's heart sank when she saw Penny.

Julia was lying on the sofa with her daughter and holding her little girl's body in her arms.

Penny's hair was loose and it was damp with sweat; her eyes were sunken and she was struggling so hard simply to breathe. Glen put on oxygen as Victoria carefully checked the little girl over.

'I'm going to use the bag to help you breathe, Penny,' Glen said, and as Penny breathed in, Glen assisted her, pushing vital oxygen into her lungs.

She was terribly hot, though as Victoria peeled back the blanket she saw that she still had on her little tutu.

Victoria chatted to the little girl, but made sure she didn't ask too many questions so that Penny could save her energy.

Her lungs were full of fluid and as Victoria inserted an IV into Penny's arm she barely flinched.

'You are such a brave girl,' Victoria said. 'I'm going to give you some medicine now and that's going to get rid of all that horrible fluid that is making it so hard to breathe.'

Penny became a bit agitated but Julia knew why. 'She doesn't like the diuretics because they made her wet herself once, but that doesn't matter, Penny.'

It did to her though.

'I've got a bed pan in the ambulance,' Victoria said, 'and we'll put lots of pads on the stretcher, so if you do have a little accident we'll have you all cleaned up before you go into the Castle.'

Penny nodded and Victoria pushed through the vital medicine.

The oxygen was helping, and with the other medications she started to calm. Soon her breathing was a little deeper, and the horrible mottled tinge to Penny's skin was starting to recede.

They needed to get her to Paddington's.

This time there was no question that she could get onto the stretcher by herself so Glen gently picked Penny up. He placed her on the stretcher and made sure that she was safely secured, and then together he and Victoria raised it up.

'Ready for the off?' Victoria said as she always did.

And always Penny nodded and smiled, or if she wasn't well enough, as was the case today, would do a little thumbs-up sign.

Today though, she spoke. 'Not...' She gasped but she couldn't finish her sentence and Julia moved to reassure her.

'We've got everything with us, Penny,' Julia said, because she always made sure that she had Penny's favourite things.

But Victoria knew that that wasn't what Penny had been trying to say.

Victoria had seen it happen in many patients—they just wanted a moment more in their home, though usually they were much older than Penny when they felt that way.

'It's okay, Penny,' Victoria said. 'We can take a minute.'

Yes, she was time critical, but the priority, too, was to cause the little girl minimum distress, and rushing her out against her wishes would only cause her to get upset. And so she stood and waited as Penny's eyes moved around the room.

And Julia understood then what her daughter had meant when she had tried to say that she wasn't quite ready to leave.

Penny wanted to take a long look at her home.

And she did.

She looked over at the television, which had been paused in the middle of a cartoon, and all of her favourite characters were frozen on the screen. Then her eyes went to the chair and then over to the sofa where she had lain and she was imprinting it all.

Penny didn't know if she would be coming home.

Julia, who was very strong and used to seeing her daughter unwell, was choking up.

'Why don't you get a glass of water, Julia,' Victoria suggested, and as Julia wept in the other room, Penny sat just taking in the memories of her home.

Glen, of course, was tearing up and Penny gave him a stern look that warned him to stop then and there.

Julia bustled back in and saw Penny's eyes linger on a photo. It looked like a holiday snap of the family at the beach. 'Shall we bring that with us, darling?' Julia asked.

Penny nodded and then rested back on the pillows and now she gave her usual little thumbs up.

She was ready.

Peter, her father, gave his daughter a kiss and told her that he was going to lock up and would see her soon at the hospital.

Once in the vehicle they alerted Paddington's to let them know they were on their way along with the details and status of the patient that they were bringing in.

Glen drove and Victoria sat in the back with Julia and Penny. There was no need for sirens as the streets were empty, but the lights were on and if needed Glen would use the siren at traffic lights or if the situation changed.

The mood was sombre.

Usually Julia would read Penny a story on the way to the hospital but she just sat there while the blue lights of the ambulance shadowed her face.

'Story…' Penny said.

'Well, let me see…' Victoria answered. And she let Julia sit quietly and gather herself for whatever lay ahead.

Victoria thought for a moment; she had told Dominic that she didn't believe in fairytales, but growing up she had loved them, just like any little girl.

She had just never had to make one up before.

Victoria thought for a moment and then she told Penny about a turret and a magic castle and a little girl who used to sneak behind the files and find her way up there. And she watched as Penny gave a faint smile so Victoria knew she must be telling the tale okay. 'There's a princess who lives there and she watches over all the babies and children.'

'Truly?' Penny gasped.

'Of course,' Victoria said. 'I told you, it's a magic castle.'

And she held the little girl's hand and told her some more and it really did seem to soothe Penny.

Her colour was terrible though and her heart was galloping, but then Penny looked up at the blacked-out windows and smiled.

Victoria glanced up too and relief flooded her as the familiar roofline came into sight.

The not-so-new Dr Thomas Wolfe was waiting for them. Victoria had been right—he had worked here. She recognised him from many years ago when she had just started to work on the ambulances, but this was no time to reminisce with him.

She was just relieved that someone so skilled was here to greet this very sick little girl.

Thomas listened to the handover as they moved her onto the resuscitation bed. He thanked the paramedics as he examined the patient and Victoria saw his expression was grim as he listened to her back and chest.

'You're doing very well, Penny,' he said to her, and he gently sat her back. She was upright in the bed as she was still struggling to breathe. The nurses worked deftly alongside him, attaching Penny to monitors and leads and pulling up the drugs and IV solutions that Thomas was calling for.

Victoria had done her job—she had delivered Penny safely to the Castle, and that had used to be enough for her. But so badly she wanted to stay and see how Penny was doing.

She actually had to prise herself away.

Maybe it was because she herself was going to be a mother that suddenly things were affecting her more.

Or maybe it was that since Dominic had come into her life she simply felt everything more acutely.

It was as if her emotions had been reset to a heightened level and Victoria felt on the edge of tears as she saw more staff running into the resuscitation room.

'I'm going to go and get a drink,' Glen said.

'Sure.' Victoria nodded and she set about making up the stretcher, telling herself to stop getting so upset, that it was just work.

Of course, Glen didn't really want a drink; his flask was in the ambulance and there was a coffee machine close by.

He walked through the department and stood in the kitchenette; he clung to the bench and told himself to take some deep breaths.

And that was where Dominic found him.

'Hi there,' Dominic said, but he got no response.

He knew that Glen's presence meant that Victoria was here somewhere, but he could see that Glen was struggling, and so, instead of heading out, he spoke with him for a while.

Dominic discovered that indeed Glen and Victoria had been at Piccadilly on Friday.

No, he didn't push for information but he guessed, and rightly so, that the weekend had taken a bit of a toll on both of them. Dominic was very grateful to this man for looking out for her.

And they spoke about the fire at Westbourne Grove and how there had been no choice really but to move forward when they had seen just how precarious Lewis's injuries were.

Then Dominic listened as Glen told him about Penny, about how bad it had been back at the house and how she had asked to stay for one lingering look.

'Poor little mite,' Glen said. 'You just can't help but compare them to your own sometimes.'

And then Glen asked him something.

'Do you remember a child we brought in…?'

And he spoke about a little girl that had been brought in a few months ago, one around the same age as Glen's daughter.

Yes, Dominic remembered it well—it was the same child that Dominic had lost on the operating table.

'I'd do anything for my children,' Glen said, 'and I just hope that for her I did the same, but I wonder if we'd just been a bit quicker extracting her from the vehicle and if we'd—'

'Glen,' Dominic interrupted.

Not unkindly.

He had gone over the very same questions about the same little girl himself, and so had the coroner.

'There was nothing that anyone could have done. Even if she had somehow been operated on at the scene, *still* there was nothing that could have been done.'

'I know that,' Glen admitted. He just needed to hear it again.

And again.

He really did need to talk it through.

'She really got to me.'

'I know,' Dominic said. 'It was awful.'

All losses hit hard, but some had the capacity for major destruction and that was what was happening with Glen.

'Victoria keeps on at me to go and speak to someone about it.'

Dominic was very glad that Victoria was on to things, and he was glad that this partnership looked out for each other.

'I think that would be very wise,' Dominic said. 'And if you do have any more questions, or talking it through raises some, then you can come and talk to me.'

Glen nodded. 'I'm just going to take a minute before I go back out.'

'Sure.'

Dominic walked out through to the department and he saw Victoria standing by the made-up stretcher, reading her phone. Dominic made his way over to her.

She felt him approach but Victoria didn't look up.

'Your colleague is crying in the kitchen,' Dominic told her, and though he kept it light he also let her know what was going on.

'I know.' Victoria looked up then and rolled her eyes. 'I'm going to politely pretend not to notice.'

But she *had* noticed, Dominic knew. Glen had just told him that Victoria had addressed this with him on many an occasion.

'Was it very grim at the house?' he asked.

'Not really,' Victoria said.

And Dominic frowned because Glen had just told him, in detail, that it had been awful—that Penny had asked for a moment to look around before they left and that Julia had become upset.

Then, as casually as anything, she told him that unless she got another call-out this morning, this would be the last time they ran into each other like this.

'I'm probably going to be working in the clinical hub—dispatch—from now on.'

'Is everything okay?'

'It's procedure,' Victoria said. 'I've got two weeks' leave, starting at the end of this shift, but when I come back I shan't be operational.'

'Good,' Dominic said. 'Well, I'll miss seeing you but I think it's better than the risk of being out there.'

'I'll still see you at the Save Paddington's meetings, I hope.' Victoria smiled.

'You shall.'

Dominic was doing his best to stay back and not crowd her.

He was finding it hell.

Maybe he should take her at face value, Dominic reasoned. Maybe he should simply accept it when she said that things did not get to her, and that she really would prefer to go through this alone.

Yet it did not equate to the passionate side she revealed at times and, he was certain, she hurt just as deeply, even if she did not show it.

He should walk away, just treat her as coolly as she said she wanted, but instead he tried another tack.

'I'm expecting a transfer from Riverside,' Dominic said. 'I've actually just been speaking with your father.'

'Lucky you,' Victoria said, and got back to reading her phone.

'What did he say to you, Victoria?' He saw her rapid blink as she deliberately didn't look up. 'When you had that row, what did he say?'

She shook her head. 'I don't want to go over it again.'

'Please do,' Dominic said. 'Of course, if it's too upsetting…'

'It's not that.' She shrugged. 'It just paints me in a rather unflattering light. He pointed out that my mother didn't just leave him.'

She didn't say it verbatim, but he could almost hear Professor Christie saying that she had left her too.

'How does that paint you in an unflattering light?' Dominic asked.

'Well, I can't have been the cutest baby.' She tried to make a joke.

'How old were you when she left?'

'I think it was just before I turned one,' Victoria said with a shrug. 'She didn't even last a year.' And then Victoria pocketed her phone and she looked right at him. 'So you can see why I don't want you flitting in and out of my child's life.' Then she thought about it. 'Not that my mother did. When she decided to leave she left for good.'

'You don't see her at all?'

'No,' Victoria said. 'I found her on social media a couple of years ago. She's got two grown-up sons. I guess they're my half-brothers.'

'Did you make contact?'

'I tried to—they all blocked me.'

'Well, I shan't be doing the same.'

'Not straight away, but you might change your mind and decide to go and live in Scotland, once you've sorted things with your family...'

'Victoria, do you remember when I told you about Lorna and you pointed out that I wasn't your ex?'

She nodded.

'Well, it works both ways—I'm not one of your parents either. I shan't be turning my back on the baby. I shall *always* be there for my child.'

Victoria already knew that.

Deep down, she always had.

After Dominic's initial poor reaction on the night she had told him, he had run after her and had been trying to get *more* involved rather than *less*.

It wasn't the baby she was now trying to protect.

It was herself.

He would be agony to lose and her heart could not take further hurt.

'What about Lorna?' Victoria said, and she silently kicked below the belt. 'Did you say that you'd *always* be there for her too?'

He didn't baulk at her question; Dominic stared her right in the eyes. 'No.'

'I don't believe you.'

'Well, you should, because half Lorna's and my problem was that I'm not very effusive.'

'Did you say you'd always be there for your brother?' Victoria asked, and that kick delivered because this time he flinched.

Not much.

She just saw the slight tightening of his lips and then he righted himself.

'I thought as much.' She shook her head. 'Thanks but no thanks, Dominic. I really do want to do this on my own.'

Dominic looked at Victoria. He was not going to force himself on someone who clearly didn't want him too close in her life.

'Victoria,' Dominic said, 'I will stay back, if that is what helps you. But with one proviso.'

'What's that?'

'If you change your mind, you're to tell me.'

'I shan't be changing my mind,' Victoria said, and then she saw that Glen was making his way towards them. 'I'll see you around.'

CHAPTER THIRTEEN

SEE YOU AROUND!

Dominic had watched her walk out and had resisted yanking her back, but really—*see you around!*

Of course he could not force her to accept his presence at the appointment, nor could he demand anything from her.

He had loathed her working on the ambulance whilst pregnant but at least it had meant that they saw each other regularly.

Now it would just be Save Paddington's meetings and they were always busy. Though there were get-togethers afterwards, there would be no real chance for the two of them to speak.

He could hardly go around to her flat, given how it had ended the last time.

Yet, he could not regret what had taken place.

That night, it had not been just the sex that had soothed. It had been the conversation and just a glimpse of peace on a tumultuous day.

And a glimpse of another side to Victoria.

He was waiting for the transfer from Riverside to arrive but that could well be hours away. Still, rather than head off and get some rest, he hung around in case

Victoria came back in, knowing that it might be their last chance to speak.

The nurses were stretched thin.

Karen was working in the resuscitation area and watching Penny while also trying to take some observations on a wriggling two-year-old. When the buzzer went over Penny's bay, Dominic stood to answer it and Karen gave a nod of thanks to him.

'Hello.'

He smiled down to Penny.

'You're not a nurse,' Penny said. She was looking a bit better and could speak in short sentences, but even that seemed to deplete her.

'No,' he said. 'I'm not, but Karen is just giving a baby some medicine and doing its obs. Can I help you with anything?'

'I want some ice.'

'I think I can manage that.'

He went and filled a cup from the dispenser and then began feeding Penny a spoon of ice chips.

'Mum's speaking to the doctor,' Penny said.

'She shouldn't be too long,' Dominic reassured. 'How are you feeling now?'

'Better.'

'That's good.'

She was a little anxious and he guessed that tonight she must have had a fright, so he did not place the cup down but instead let her get her breath for a moment and waited until she spoke again.

'A princess lives in the tower,' Penny said, pointing to the roof. 'Victoria told me.'

'That's good to know.' He smiled because it would seem that even if Victoria didn't believe in fairytales she knew how to tell them. There were so many sides to Victoria.

And he wanted to know them all.

'A beautiful princess,' Penny added, and he waited for her to take a couple of breaths before she continued. 'She watches over all the children.'

'What about the handsome prince?' Dominic asked.

'Victoria didn't mention him.'

Of course she didn't! Dominic thought as he smiled.

He fed her a few more chips of ice. He guessed that, more than ice, Penny wanted some company and so he chatted about magic and fairies and wishes that came true and, because of his accent, she asked about the Loch Ness monster and if he believed it.

'Who, Nessie?' He made it sound as if the monster was a close friend. 'My brother and I saw her one holiday many years ago.' And because he was so serious it made it more believable somehow, so Penny lay there and smiled and told him one of her wishes.

'I wish I could have ballet lessons.'

'Well, I'm sure the princess is working on that as we speak,' Dominic said, and then turned as Julia came in.

'Oh, thank you, Doctor,' she said.

'No problem.'

'What did the doctor say?' Penny asked her mother.

'That they're going to keep you here for a few days. It's her second home…' Julia added to Dominic, taking the cup of ice chips and smiling as she did so.

He could see that Julia had put on some make-up and was doing everything in her power to hide her own terrified heart.

Children often amazed him, Dominic thought, but then adults did too.

Julia had just been delivered terrible news about Penny, Dominic knew.

This wasn't going to be just a couple of nights' stay.

He had heard Thomas speaking with Karen and the news wasn't good.

A viral infection was ravaging Penny's already damaged heart and had pushed her into a dangerous level of heart failure.

'Where's Dad?' Penny asked her mum.

'He's moving the car or he'll get clamped again!' Julia said, and then she turned it into a funny story, reminding Penny how Dad's car had got clamped a couple of times.

And either the guy was out there weeping, Dominic thought, or he really was trying to sort out a car that had been haphazardly parked in the race to get to his desperately sick child.

Julia chatted and fussed, and then in came Peter smiling and waving at Penny; he came over and gave his little girl a kiss.

And Dominic watched.

You wouldn't know that they were in agony.

Unless you knew.

And suddenly Dominic did.

Victoria was hurting.

Of course she was.

And probably she hurt a bit more with each and every passing day.

He thought of Glen, idly chatting, saying how you would do anything for your children.

And the firefighters who had run into a building to save children that weren't even theirs.

Every single day it must be rammed home to her just what her mother had done.

* * *

Victoria *was* hurting.

She and Glen sat in the vehicle and Victoria got out her flask so they could have a coffee as the sun was coming up over London.

'I'm going to miss this,' Victoria said.

'You'll be back.' Glen smiled.

'I shall be,' Victoria agreed. 'But even though I'll miss not being on the road, I am ready to give it away for a while.'

Since she had found out that she was going to be a mother, she knew it wasn't just her life she was risking at times.

It wasn't the heavy lifting, more the unpredictability of some patients, which meant that once she told work that she was pregnant, Victoria would probably be moved into dispatch.

Glen had looked out for her these couple of weeks and it was time now for her to look out for him.

Of course she wasn't going to politely ignore his tears; it had just been something she'd said to Dominic.

They looked out for each other and she didn't want to leave without knowing he was taking care of himself.

'Glen,' Victoria said, 'did you see about speaking to someone?'

He nodded. 'I've got an appointment in the morning. That's why I didn't offer to take you to the ultrasound.'

'Have you told Hayley?'

'Yep,' he said. 'She's relieved,' Glen told her. 'It's our anniversary now and she said it's the best present I could give her.'

'You've got that nice wine too,' Victoria reminded him.

'And a ring.'

'How *do* you make it work?' Victoria asked him again, and this time the radio didn't go off so he thought for a moment and then answered.

'You stop being too proud for your own good.'

She guessed he was referring to a recent conversation with Hayley, and that he had finally heeded the advice and was getting himself some help.

'So we're both getting ourselves sorted after this shift,' Victoria said.

'Starting to,' Glen corrected. 'Let him be there for the ultrasound, Victoria. Whatever happens between the two of you, whether you're a couple or not, you can parent together, surely?'

Could they? Victoria pondered.

Who was she to deny her child a wonderful parent? It would have made all the difference to her.

CHAPTER FOURTEEN

THE TRANSFER FINALLY arrived and required surgery.

Dominic liked the quiet of theatre.

Some surgeons chatted or listened to music; Dominic liked quiet so he could concentrate, especially when he had been on call all weekend.

By seven in the morning his latest patient was settled on the ward. After he had done a ward round and checked on all his other patients and handed them over, Dominic was tired enough to want to go home.

But instead Dominic showered and then hung around.

He knew that Victoria's ultrasound was at ten.

But he wasn't just there for that reason; there was another thing that he needed to do.

Victoria was right to be cautious about getting involved with him.

She didn't need a man who came with baggage. He had been determined to get things sorted with his family before he approached Victoria. But then the baby had been sprung upon him and things had gone wayward for a while.

Dominic knew that the problems within his family needed to be dealt with, but more importantly, he finally felt ready.

He went to his locker and then Dominic walked through the hospital and made his way to the cardiac unit.

Some days were hard, when you were least expecting them to be.

Other days were unexpectedly not.

He walked onto the cardiac unit and there was Penny, hooked up to monitors and IVs but looking peaceful. She smiled and gave him a little wave.

Dominic waved back and then he went up to the nurses' station where Thomas stood.

'Morning,' he said.

'Good morning.' Thomas nodded.

Dominic was waiting for a nurse so he could explain that he was just here to visit, but for the moment they were all tied up so he stood at the desk.

Thomas didn't exactly invite conversation and he was back to busily writing up some notes.

'Hi, Rebecca,' Dominic said as she approached.

'Dr Scott,' Thomas greeted, and Dominic frowned at the rather formal address of her.

'Dr Wolfe,' Rebecca said, and her voice sounded strained but she pushed out her lovely smile for Dominic. 'What are you doing on the cardiac unit?' she asked him.

'My nephew's a patient here—William MacBride.'

'Oh,' Rebecca said in surprise. 'I thought the name was familiar. I'm actually here to see him.'

'I'll come back later, then,' Dominic offered. He didn't understand the tension between these two but he didn't want to make things worse. But then Rebecca declined his offer to leave.

'No, no, I need to speak with Dr Wolfe first and I have another couple of patients to see. Go ahead.'

A nurse came over then—it was Rosie—and Dominic explained why he was here and she waved him on.

Really, he could have just popped in, but he had wanted the separation, for this was not a doctor visiting.

It was a brother, a brother-in-law and an uncle that had come to visit this morning.

He looked through the glass as he approached and saw the little family.

Lorna was holding William, who was attached to monitors, but he looked rested and pink in his mother's arms.

And there was Jamie hovering over them.

Dominic could have waited until his parents arrived to drop in on them, but he had never needed the shield of his parents. He had just needed the ability to look his brother and Lorna in the eye.

Without hurt or malice.

'Hey.'

He knocked on the open door and Lorna looked up and he could see that she was startled.

Jamie stood up a touch straighter and was clearly nervous at Dominic's unexpected arrival.

'How is he doing?' Dominic asked.

'Better,' Jamie said. 'They've got him on something called beta…' He struggled with all the new terminology.

'Beta-blockers.' Dominic nodded. 'They slow the heart down and steady things.'

'I think I might need some,' Lorna said, and let out a nervous laugh as she made a feeble joke.

Oh, it seemed such a long time ago since they had been together and so much had happened since then.

'Well, you've had a very difficult time with William.'

Dominic chose his words carefully, refusing to allude to the situation between the three of them.

It was over with.

He gave her a smile and saw that she relaxed.

'I got this for William,' Dominic said, and handed over the wrapped present to Lorna.

She opened it while holding William, and with all his drips and things it took a while, but when Lorna saw what it was she smiled. It was a little Scottie dog, wearing a tartan bow.

'He's gorgeous,' she said. 'We didn't think to bring any toys with us. It will be nice to have something for his cot here.'

'Here,' Dominic said, and handed Jamie the card. Knowing how useless Jamie was with money Dominic had put in a generous cheque. It wasn't for the baby though. 'I thought you could get something for the nursery or a pusher or whatever.'

'Thank you.'

But it was the words on the card that mattered the most to Jamie and he read them again.

Dear Lorna and Jamie,
Congratulations on the birth of William.
I am thrilled to be an uncle and looking for-
ward to watching him grow up. I know you'll be
amazing parents.
Love, Dominic

And Jamie knew that his brother always meant every word.

'Do you want a hold of him?' Jamie asked, and his voice was a bit choked. 'Or maybe…' He hesitated, worried that it might be too much for his brother, but Dominic *had* meant every word.

He was ready now to be in his nephew's life.

'I'd love to hold him.'

Dominic held many babies in a day's work but he hadn't held a baby outside of that parameter, ever.

And it was very different.

William really was a gorgeous baby and had the MacBride chin and long, long hands and feet. The change of arms woke him and he opened up his eyes and gave his uncle a smile.

'You don't remember me from last week, do you?' Dominic said to him. 'Because I was sticking needles in you then.'

'He's looking better though?' Lorna anxiously asked.

'He is. And I know you must be terrified but we're a tough lot and I'm sure that he's going to be fine.' Dominic held him for a couple of moments and, as he did, it occurred to him that in the not too distant future he would be holding a baby of his own.

How could you ever walk away from your own child?

Dominic wasn't one to let his emotions run away with him, but as he looked at the little baby, he felt a choke of emotion on behalf of Victoria.

He made a choice then to be patient, a choice that he would wait for however long it took for her to trust in him.

Not just as a father.

He had far greater plans for them than that.

Dominic handed the baby back to his mother and then he shook his brother's hand.

'Congratulations,' Dominic said, and he could finally look him in the eye and smile.

'Oh!'

He turned at the sound of his mother's voice and saw the concern in his father's expression.

'I was just dropping in to see how William was doing,' Dominic explained.

'Is everything okay?' William Senior asked as he came in.

'All's good,' Dominic said. 'I'll see you back at home. And, Lorna,' he added. 'If you want a *proper dinner* or to stay at my home, then you're very welcome.' He turned to his mother. 'But I've been working all night, remember, so can you please keep it down.'

And they were back to being a family.

Dominic made his way back to Accident and Emergency. He had a coffee and killed time, watching as a nurse rolled her eyes as she did her best to hold on to her temper as she spoke with someone on the phone.

'I am sorry about that but I wasn't working last night. I'll try and find out for you.' She pressed Mute and let out a hiss. 'That man!'

'Who?'

'Professor Christie over at Riverside.'

'What does he want?'

'A transfer last night...' She shook her head. 'Don't worry, I know you're not on.'

'It's fine.'

He picked up the phone and on the other end of the line he heard the great Professor Christie berate a member of staff.

'Hello,' Dominic said. 'Dominic MacBride speaking.'

'Oh!' Professor Christie said, and he switched to charming. 'Sorry about that, I'm working with clumsy imbeciles this morning.'

He had thought about it for a long time and examined it from many angles and, in this instance, Dominic *did* know what to say.

'Well—' Dominic's voice was curt '—that might have something to do with the fact that they're working alongside an arrogant git. So,' he asked, and adopted a more professional tone, 'how can I help you?'

He saw the nurse turn with eyes wide as he heard the professor splutter into the phone.

'*What* did you just say?' Professor Christie demanded.

'Do you want me to repeat it?' Dominic calmly replied. 'Or would you like me to come over now and say it to your face?'

'Now, listen here—'

'I do listen,' Dominic said. 'I listen very carefully and I also think before I speak.'

His voice held a warning and there was silence on the other end of the line.

'Now,' Dominic said, 'what did you want to know about the patient?'

CHAPTER FIFTEEN

VICTORIA SAT IN the waiting room of the Imaging Department.

There was a television up high on the wall but Victoria was too busy replying to some emails about the next Save Paddington's meeting to watch it.

Then her phone rang and Victoria grimaced when she saw that it was her father who was calling her.

He rarely called. In fact, it was always Victoria who called him.

Perhaps there had been a change of heart, Victoria thought.

'Hi, Dad,' she said.

'Who's the father of the baby?'

'Why?' Victoria asked.

'Just tell me.'

Victoria sat there.

Her father had shown absolutely no interest in this baby and from his very brusque tone she didn't think he sounded particularly interested now.

In fact, he sounded furious as he spoke on. 'You said that he was in Scotland...'

'Why do you want to know?'

'Well, I've just had some upstart insult me. Dominic MacBride...'

Her heart was bumping against the wall of her chest. 'What did he say?'

She closed her eyes as her father repeated it.

What the hell was Dominic thinking to speak to her father like that? Dominic, who insisted his responses were measured, clearly hadn't thought this one through.

For it made a future impossible.

Any get-togethers would be fraught and tense.

And in that moment she felt as if she were about to cry, for she was mentally waving goodbye to Christmases and Easters and family celebrations and she had been trying so hard not to think of them.

'Well?' Professor Christie demanded. 'Is he the father?'

'Yes,' Victoria answered. She was cross with Dominic, even if she privately agreed with what had been said, but she did not tell her father that. Instead she told him a truth. 'And I'm very glad that he is.'

Dominic would be a wonderful father, she absolutely knew.

She was glimpsing Christmases and birthdays again, and even if she might not be in the picture, her baby would be taken care of during celebrations whenever it was in his care.

He deserved to be here.

She simply ended the call because there was another major incident occurring, but this time it was with her heart.

It wasn't just that he deserved to be there.

He would be the one she would call on if anything was wrong.

It would be Dominic's voice she would need if their baby was ill, or hot, or fussing.

Glen seemed to think it was possible but she didn't

know how to let him into the baby's life without revealing how she really felt.

Yet, he did deserve to be there.

And so, before she could talk herself out of it she sent a hurried text.

Can you come to the ultrasound?

She hit Send and then panicked because that sounded too needy, and then started to write another.

You can come to the ultrasound if you still want to.

But that didn't read right and so she didn't hit Send but then she thought of him waking to the first, as he was probably asleep and would read it and think there was something wrong.

What if there was something wrong?

She needed him here.

And then suddenly he was there.

She knew, as she always did, whenever Dominic was close. He stood over her as she stared down at her phone and then she looked up. 'You got here fast.'

'I thought I'd hang around in case you changed your mind,' Dominic said as he took a seat by her side.

He would not rush in and scare her with his feelings. That text, asking him to be here, was enough for now.

'Have you been speaking to my father?' she accused.

'Aye.'

'What did you say?' she asked, wondering if he would be vague but Dominic told her exactly.

'He was talking down to a member of his staff and one of ours. I just said he was an arrogant git. That's all.'

'So how is it going to be when you see him?' She

would not admit to the family get-togethers that she dreamed might happen one day. 'At the hospital and things.'

'I'll be civil.' He looked over to her angered face. 'Victoria, do you really think there are going to be many cosy get-togethers with me, him and the baby?'

'No,' she said, and she was struggling to keep her feelings in, because what he had said didn't bode well for any chance for them.

'But if they do happen,' Dominic said, 'then I will play the part and do the right thing, but he has to know that I know what he's like. I will not let him inflict his bloody nature on my child nor on the mother of my child. I just served him a warning today.'

His lips were taut and his words were clipped and Victoria nodded because deep down she knew that he was right.

It wasn't fear of confrontation that flooded her now; it was a wash of relief that came over her, though she tried not to show it. Finally there was someone in her corner where there never had been before, and even if he was there just to guard their child she was very glad that Dominic was on board.

'Are you nervous?' he asked.

'Are you?'

'Yes.'

And they smiled because given what had happened to Dominic, and given their short history, perhaps he should be, but Dominic nudged her and they looked up at the television.

'Look.'

It was that image of them from Westbourne Grove.

It seemed like ages ago, but it had been just a couple of weeks.

Yet so much had changed.

Images of the protestors outside the hospital came onto the screen.

The fire had been a terrible day.

It had changed so many lives, and the fight to save some of them was ongoing. Children were still desperately ill, and yet, from such a terrible event good had prevailed.

Angela Marton was now talking about the fight to save Paddington Children's Hospital and saying that Londoners did not want to lose the institution that brought hope to so many.

'I want my baby to be born here,' Victoria said.

'Our baby,' he corrected.

'So you believe me now,' she nudged.

'Victoria, the more I know you, the more I'm amazed at the speed with which you dropped your knickers.'

'Stop it!'

'It's true. That condom had probably expired.'

'So why are you nervous, then?'

'Because, like every other parent, I want our baby to be fine.' He gave her a smile. 'You do believe in fairytales.'

'I don't.'

'Penny told me about the princess.'

'How is Penny?'

'Don't worry about that now.'

'I'm not worried,' she lied. 'Just tell me.'

'She's got a virus and she's in severe heart failure.'

She thought of Penny's beautiful eyes taking in the lounge and she prayed, so hard, that she would one day be back there.

'Do you think she'll be okay?'

'I don't know, Victoria. She's got a long road ahead of her.'

'Victoria Christie.'

She stood up for the radiographer when her name was called.

'Come through.'

She was shown to a little cubicle and asked to put on a gown.

'Then go in and lie down, and I'll be through shortly,' she said.

Victoria changed and went through to the little room and got up on the examination couch, putting a blanket over her legs.

And Dominic sat by her side.

The radiographer came in then and they chatted about dates and confirmed, when she had a feel of Victoria's stomach, that indeed she did have a full bladder.

They had a little laugh, then the radiographer's pager went off and she said that she'd be back soon.

They were both very quiet.

Dominic was probably feeling sick, Victoria thought, given what had happened the last time he was in this situation.

Dominic did not feel sick.

Not in the least.

He would not be demanding a DNA test.

He knew for a fact this baby was his.

Victoria didn't *need* anyone.

Except maybe she did.

'I'm nervous.' She just came out and said it. 'What if there's something wrong?'

'Then we shall deal with it together.'

He held her hand.

Oh, she did need a handhold because it felt like silk wrapping around not just her fingers but her heart.

She started to cry.

'It will be okay,' Dominic said, and he peeled off some tissues.

'I'm just tired,' she said. 'It was a busy shift and I'm worried about Penny.'

'I know,' he said.

But it wasn't just that.

'I'm sorry I was terse with your father.'

'It's not that.'

She was glad of it now.

It was her mother.

'I love this baby so much already. I don't get how she could just leave me like that.'

'Nor do I,' he told her. 'Victoria, I shan't be doing the same.'

And Glen was right; whatever happened between them, they would do what was best for the baby.

But it wasn't just that.

It was a huge comfort to know her baby would have such a wonderful father, yet the fears about Dominic were not for her child now. They were for her own heart.

The radiographer came in and he peeled off more tissues and she pressed them onto her eyes.

'I'm enthusiastic to see our baby,' Dominic said, and that made her smile. He hadn't rushed in and said it when her eyes had pleaded for him to in the canteen.

He said it now when he meant it.

'So am I.'

And there it was.

All that fuss for something so small.

Yet so beautiful and so vital and alive.

And they weren't really listening to dates and looking at crown rump length and things.

Just watching the baby with its tiny arms and legs and even fingers and toes. It was just a moment they shared.

He looked from the screen to Victoria, and there was the flash of fresh tears in her eyes. He would never leave her, yet she didn't even know. He didn't care if it took for ever; he would get right into that guarded heart. What had happened when their baby had been made was a rare magic; he bent over and gave her a light kiss. This man could not hold back any longer!

'I love you.'

He had sworn not to push her, but he couldn't not say it. He did not want her to go another moment in this life without love.

Though because he was all stoic and Scottish, and there was someone else in the room, that was all the romance she was going to get.

It meant everything and more to hear that, but she was certain it was just the emotion of the moment. The dates matched exactly and maybe Dominic had just gotten a bit carried away.

She lay there as his hand remained over hers but those fears in her head beat faster than the heart on the screen.

It was like the world was all in this room—his hand, their baby—and she was scared for the lights to go on, for she would surely wake up alone.

And then it was over.

The images would be looked at, they were told, but everything seemed perfect, and Victoria could now get dressed.

'Thank you,' Victoria said, but she was almost scared to move because the tears were threatening.

'I'll wait in Reception,' Dominic said, but as he turned to go she started to cry.

'What are you crying over?' he asked. 'Your mum?'

It would be so easy to nod and say yes and perhaps a whole lot safer too, because she was scared to reveal herself.

Then she thought about something else that Glen had said, about not being too proud for your own good and so *this* woman met his eyes in the ultrasound room and made her confession and told him her truth.

'You,' Victoria said. 'I'm crying over you.'

'Cry *on* me, then.'

He pulled her into his arms and held her as she wept, and she told him her fears; she had so many and he dealt with each in turn.

'You might change your mind.'

'Never.' Dominic knew that he would never change his mind.

And he sounded so sure, and here in his arms she was brave enough to voice her fears for them.

'You loved Lorna.'

'Not like this,' Dominic told her. 'I've never loved like this.'

She could hear the steady beat of his heart while hers was racing, and she could feel his quiet strength.

It wasn't the first time she had cried but it was the first time she had cried in someone's arms and so she voiced her deepest fear.

'If there wasn't the baby...'

'Then you'd still be here in my arms.'

And his deep voice was soft and it felt like the truth but she disputed it all the same. 'You stayed back.'

'You askcd me to.'

'But before you knew about the baby you didn't make a move.'

'Neither did you,' he pointed out.

'I stayed back because I don't know how to make things work between us,' Victoria said.

'And I stayed back because I do.'

She frowned into his chest.

'Victoria, I told you at the start I was in the middle of something; I wasn't going to land it all on us and come into a relationship jaded and bitter. I needed to sort things out properly.'

She thought about that for a moment and then he spoke some more.

'Now I have sorted it out. I've taken the baby a present, I've had a hold and I've told Lorna she's very welcome in my home.'

'Do you still love her?' Victoria asked. 'You can't undo love.'

'Believe me, you can unravel it,' Dominic said. 'It pretty much came undone the day I found out. Victoria, I haven't been steering clear of Lorna because I have feelings for her. Not positive ones anyway. The last months have been hell, more over my family and brother, but I'll tell you this, since that night, I've thought about *you* every day.'

'Every day?'

'Every minute of every day.'

She looked up to him and she knew he was telling the truth. And that was what had been missing for ever, being thought of by another, every minute of every day.

She thought of her father and his money and occasional gifts.

And her mother who had simply walked away.

But she didn't just think about the bad things. Instead there were thoughts of Glen and how he carried his family in his heart throughout his working day.

And she was starting to believe that Dominic did the same.

'Go and get dressed,' Dominic told her, and he helped her from the examination couch. 'You need to get some sleep and so do I.'

And so she went to the ladies'.

Victoria was practical like that.

And got dressed.

Then she headed out to Reception where he was waiting and he gave her a smile as if he hadn't just rocked her world.

They took the scenic route and as they walked through the quadrangle it was as if the oxygen ratio in the air that she breathed was altered, a bit higher, the colours brighter, the air kinder.

'Thank you for being there today,' Victoria said as they came out to the ambulance foyer and she paused to say goodbye.

'Didn't you hear a word of what I said back in there?' Dominic lightly teased. 'Do you really think I'm going to let you disappear into the underground again? You're to come home with me and I'm not taking no for an answer this time.'

'What's wrong with mine?'

'I want you in my bed.'

CHAPTER SIXTEEN

AND VICTORIA WANTED to be in his bed too.

'I'm very tired,' she warned with a smile as they drove away from Paddington's.

'Victoria,' he said, 'I've been on call all weekend and you look like hell.'

She looked at him all unshaven and with dark circles under his eyes. 'So do you.'

'Good,' Dominic said, and glanced over to her, 'so you'll be able to keep your hands off me, then.'

God, but he turned her on.

His home was a large apartment, close to the hospital. They took the stairs up to his floor and, as he let them in, there were all the signs of a family in residence. Victoria was very used to coming home to her flat alone and finding it exactly as she had left it, but Dominic read a note that had been left on a table in the hall.

'I just saw them back at the hospital,' Dominic told her. 'But it says that they won't be back till this evening.'

She was too tired to look around but there was a nice feel to the place and, as she glanced in the living room, she saw two heavy-looking leather sofas with rugs over the back of them.

A stint of nights, then hanging around for the ultra-

sound and all the emotion of before, had left Victoria
so tired that she felt cold despite the warm day.

They stepped into his bedroom and she looked at the
large bed and wanted to sink into it.

'I am so going to enjoy sleeping with you,' Dominic
said as he closed the drapes and turned on a bedside
light, and she laughed.

'And I am so going to enjoy sleeping with you.'

She slipped off her clothes and got into bed. It had the
wonderful, soapy, fragrant scent of him that was now
familiar. Victoria suddenly realised that she had never
seen him naked. But she was about to get that pleasure
now, and she couldn't wait.

Dominic took off his shirt. She saw his pale skin and
the dark hair of his chest and she just lazily watched.
He undid his belt and as he undressed she saw strong
thighs and then his tumescent male beauty.

'We *are* going to sleep,' he promised, yet Victoria
wasn't so sure because she was starting to change her
mind. There are moments so special that they have to be
marked in some way, and this was one of them. So she
stretched and sighed as he climbed into bed and turned
off the light, and they lay there as a siren went past.

'Thank God it's not you out there,' Dominic said, and
he pulled her closer into him. 'Every time I hear a siren
I think of you, even before I found out that you were
pregnant. I've been so worried about you out there.'

'I will be again,' she warned, because her career was
incredibly important to her and she definitely would
be going back.

'I know that you will,' Dominic said, 'but you shan't
ever be out there again without knowing that I love you.'

And then she looked at Dominic and saw right down

to his soul, and found out that she resided there and that she had ever since their first kiss.

She lifted her face towards him and he kissed not, at first, her mouth but her cheeks and eyes and then he kissed her lips long and slow.

A goodnight kiss, even though it was morning.

The kind of *I'm not going anywhere* kiss that she had never known, and then he held her tight in his arms as they drifted off to sleep together.

For the first time they lay together to the sounds floating up from the street and the bliss of being in each other's arms. They needed no more than this right now.

It was a sleep like no other.

The end of nights and their first together ensured that it was the sweetest, deepest sleep for them both.

Victoria rolled onto her side and he wrapped around her and peace was made.

It was Victoria who stirred first. Dominic was curved into her and she was disorientated as to place and time, for the room was dark and the direction she faced unfamiliar, but she was blissfully certain of the man in whose arms she lay.

Who knows how we awaken together? she thought.

That moment when you realise someone else is present and by your side.

When respite has been taken and you awake peaceful, and there is no need for a frantic examination for you to know it is a better world.

And it was.

His hand was on her stomach and she lay with eyes open to the darkened room, half asleep, half awake and completely content. Then Victoria closed her eyes as his hand roamed the curve of her hip and he moved in closer.

Dominic kissed her bare shoulder and his hand toyed with her breast. She felt the pinch of his finger and thumb on her nipple and the nudge of him between her legs. She turned her face to him and they shared a kiss that was slow, but then both wanted more and so she rolled in his arms for just that. As she did so Dominic moved too. He held himself over her and halted her on her back, resting his elbows by her head and pushing up on his arms. She had never felt so deliciously trapped, yet so safe in love.

On so many occasions Victoria had looked down when he silently demanded that her eyes meet his, but now she looked up to his gaze. Her hand came to the back of his head and she levered herself up to meet his mouth. But it was his kiss this time and so he pressed her back into the pillows and claimed her mouth as below she parted her legs for him.

The feel of him inside her made her shiver, though their bodies were warm and still loose from sleep. His kiss was deep and intense and they moved slowly at first, revelling in the feel of togetherness and the naked heat of their skin. They simply entwined into one as they forgot they were parents-to-be and found out the couple they had now become.

Each measured thrust he delivered brought her a little more undone.

And she was his.

For all the declarations Dominic had offered, when she had given none, with each building sob that she tried to hold in, she revealed herself to him some more.

He placed his hands on the bed, either side of her breasts, and he moved up onto outstretched arms. The separation between them allowed her to lean up on the pillows as he took her, in short rapid thrusts, as she clasped his face and took his lips in a deep kiss.

It was shockingly intimate for both of them—the kissing, the feeling, the watching each other so close to the edge.

Then she closed her eyes, not to him but because the feelings were intense. He moved faster despite the slow caress of his tongue and she searched for a headboard to cling to but settled instead for his solid arms. She couldn't resist the urge to tilt her hips and take him in more deeply.

Everything gathered tight within and Victoria wanted to twist or to lift her knees, almost to shield herself from the throes of frenzy, but instead her hands moved up his arms and her fingertips pressed into his shoulders and she came hard.

And there was nowhere for her heart to hide any more.

Dominic sunk down from his arms and she accepted the weight like a raft, and for a moment they lay breathless.

She waited, but this time regret did not arrive.

'Are you going to say you've made a mistake again?' Dominic asked in that familiar wry tone.

'Well, if it is a mistake, then I intend to keep on repeating it.'

She rolled to her side and they lay staring at each other for a while.

And the feeling remained.

So she told him something she never had said to anyone. 'I love you.'

'Good.'

'And I'm sorry that I asked about Lorna.'

'Don't be, the air needed to be cleared there. We're all going to be in each other's lives. But know this— I've never felt the way I do about you with anyone else. And I tell you now, I know he wouldn't but if my brother touched a hair on your head I would kill him.'

She smiled, because it would never happen, and his voice made her shiver with delight.

'You don't fight,' Victoria pointed out.

'My love for you is savage,' he said, and as he looked at Victoria he decided that she deserved a savage kind of love.

He made her entire skin tingle, just with the stroke of his finger on her arm.

She looked deep into his eyes, and yes, he could be crabby at times, but she liked that. She liked that he did not fight and that the man she loved could never hurt another. Even when they had fought over Penny that day, he had still put the patient first.

She liked his strength and how he fought, not with fists but by holding on to what was right.

'You've been sleeping on my side,' Dominic said, and she smiled, because he made her believe in fairy-tales after all. 'I mean it,' he said, and he knelt up and leant over her. First he turned on the bedside light and then he opened a drawer.

From there he took out a little, dark, velvet box and offered her a warning. 'This isn't a ring.'

'I would hope not, given that we've only had one date.'

'Victoria,' he said in that gorgeous brogue that had her toes curl beneath the sheets. 'We are going to have many, many more. You'll be getting a ring but, for now, I want you to have these. I really have been thinking of you all the time and I hope that these will show you how much.'

He opened the box as Victoria sat up in the bed and when she looked she saw a pair of beautiful earrings. Her heart squeezed and her fingers wanted to touch them but for now she simply looked at a gift from the heart.

'They're Scottish pearls,' he told her. 'I'm lousy at one-night stands and I wanted to get you something. When I was in Scotland I saw these and while I was talking to the jeweller I found out quite a bit about them—pearls are complex things,' Dominic said. 'The oyster tries to protect itself from intruders, and from that something very beautiful is formed.'

They were golden hued and the most beautiful pearls that she had ever seen, but more than that it was the care and thought with which they had been chosen that meant so much to her.

Yes, diamonds might be for ever, but they didn't count unless they were given with love.

Those long fingers were nimble and he carefully put them in for her and, as he did, he asked her a question. 'Do you know what daunts me when I think about a future with you?'

Victoria could think of many things that might.

An unplanned pregnancy from a one-night stand, her job, her independence, to name a few, but then he broke in.

'Nothing daunts me,' Dominic said. 'I had sworn off relationships until I met you. I know we agreed to no more than what happened that night but I was always going to ask you out. I made up my mind in Scotland. I decided that once I had properly sorted things out with my family I would see if we could give things a try. If you said no, then these earrings were still for you, because what happened between us was amazing. I never thought I could trust anyone again, but I do. And the thought of a future with you thrills me.'

She put her fingers to her ears and felt the gorgeous pearls, and then she looked over to Dominic.

This beautiful, rugged man had offered her his heart and she had never been this close to anyone before.

And what he had said applied both ways, for as she looked to a future with Dominic, there was nothing that daunted.

Yes, it thrilled her, in fact.

And then as they kissed, as they lay with the world at their feet, they heard a noise. Victoria, on hearing the front door opening, pulled away and grimaced.

The day had run away from them and there were voices from the hallway. This was so not how she wanted to meet his family.

'They won't come in,' he said.

'And I can't go out.' Victoria groaned, having visions of herself being trapped hiding in his room all night.

'Why ever not?' he asked.

'What will they think?' Victoria asked, aghast at the prospect. 'I can hardly just walk out of your bedroom and meet the family.'

'Well, if you were the type for a one-night stand with a man you barely knew, then I get that it might be awkward…'

He made her laugh and she knew then that they would tease each other about their torrid tryst for ever.

He made everything fine.

Better than fine.

'I'll tell them that I've been seeing you for months,' Dominic suggested, 'which I have been.'

It was no lie. They had noticed each other right from the day they had met.

It was actually now bliss to lie in bed with him and to hear the sounds of his family outside.

'Lorna's here.' It was Dominic who grimaced a bit when he heard her voice, because though he had meant it when he had said that she could come for dinner or stay here, he knew it might be a bit much for Victoria to deal with so soon. 'Do you have a problem with that?'

'None.' Victoria grinned; after all, she was in his bed. But then she thought about it more seriously for a moment and the answer was still the same, so she shook her head. 'None.'

'Good,' Dominic said, and he rolled out of bed and started to pull on some clothes. 'Though we might keep it to ourselves about the baby for now.'

'I know that it must all feel a bit rushed,' Victoria said, thinking of how he had said he felt when he found out that Lorna was pregnant.

'Hardly rushed,' he said. 'I'm thirty-eight.'

Dominic was pulling on his jeans and she would remember that moment for ever. The moment she knew, completely, that they were meant to be.

And then he looked over and smiled as he realised the difference in his feelings between now and the last time that he had thought he was about to become a father. Still there was no need to dwell for they had moved past all that now. 'I'm just warning you,' he said, 'that when they find out they'll make an awful fuss.'

'I can't wait for the fuss,' Victoria said, and she thought of grandparents who would be thrilled at the news, and uncles and aunts and cousins and feuding brothers who had sorted things out. 'As soon as William is more stable we'll share the good news.'

She couldn't wait to get out there, but was actually quite nervous when they finally did.

The MacBrides were all in the kitchen. Jamie and Lorna and Dominic's father were sitting at the table, and his mother, a very small woman, was at the oven.

'Well, hello,' his mother said when together they walked in, and she looked a bit taken back when she saw that Dominic had company.

'This is Victoria,' Dominic introduced. 'She's been on nights too.'

'You never said that you were seeing anyone!' his mother scolded, though she smiled to Victoria.

'Well, we haven't exactly been speaking,' Dominic reminded her. 'But Victoria is very much in my life. Victoria, this is my mother, Katie.'

She met William and Katie, and Jamie and Lorna, who she had, of course, already met, but it was different this time because she was being introduced and integrated into all the main threads of this beautiful man's life.

'How is William doing now?' Victoria asked Lorna, and felt very glad that she had been up-front about knowing Dominic when they were at the hotel.

'He's doing well. Rebecca, the surgeon, doesn't seem to think surgery is necessary at this stage.'

As easily as that they chatted and Victoria understood what Dominic had meant about needing to be properly free from baggage, for there were no dark feelings harboured, no grudges and absolutely no jealousy at all.

'He's getting excellent care,' Jamie said, and then looked over to his brother. 'I can see why you want to work there—it's a fantastic hospital.'

'Is it true that it's closing?' Lorna asked.

'Not if we can help it,' Dominic said, and from the conviction in his voice, Victoria knew that she had him fully on board now in the fight to save Paddington's.

And what were the best words in the world to hear when you've woken up having been on a stint working nights and just had really good sex?

Katie MacBride said them as Dominic put an arm around her and kissed the top of her head. 'Take a seat at the table, you two. You'll be wanting a proper dinner.'

And she was entered into his fold.

Victoria had found her family.

* * * * *

FORBIDDEN TO
THE PLAYBOY
SURGEON

FIONA LOWE

To my fellow Medical Romance author,
Annie O'Neil who answered all my questions
about London so enthusiastically and speedily.
And for the laughs. Thanks! It made writing
this book so much fun.

CHAPTER ONE

ALTHOUGH CLAIRE MITCHELL had been in London for a few weeks, she still pinched herself every time she stepped out onto the streets of Paddington. For an Aussie country girl, it was all a little bit surreal—like being on the set of *Mary Poppins* or *Upstairs, Downstairs*.

Dazzling white, Victorian, stuccoed terraced houses with pillared porches and decorative balconies were built neatly around tiny central gardens. This morning as she crossed the pocket-handkerchief park, passing between two black wrought-iron gates, the ubiquitous London drizzle was cheerfully absent. Tongues of early-morning light filtered down between the tender, bright green spring foliage of century-old oaks and elms. It was a far cry from the dusty, rock-hard and sun-cracked park where she'd spent her childhood. The only shade to be found at the Gundiwindi playground had been that cast by the people standing next to her.

Walking briskly, she made her way along what would be a frantically busy road in an hour's time. Right now though, the street sweepers, bakers, newsagents and baristas were the only people out offering services to a few crazy early birds like herself. Her favourite Italian trattoria had a coffee window and Tony greeted her with a cheery *buongiorno* as he handed out six lattes, neatly stacked in a cardboard carrier. 'You bring the sunshine, *mia bella*.'

Claire smiled and gave into the irrational zip of delight she allowed herself to feel. She knew the garrulous barista flirted with every female aged two to ninety-two and that his *mia bella* meant nothing. But as few men ever noticed her, let alone tried to charm her, she accepted and enjoyed his compliments as a lovely way to start her day.

She bought a *pain au chocolat* from the bakery and balanced the bag on top of the coffees as she continued to walk towards Paddington Children's Hospital, or 'the castle' as the locals called it. A bright red double-decker bus lumbered past down the narrow road. With her free hand, she grabbed a quick photo of it on her phone and immediately sent it to her brother. He was the proud owner of the Gundiwindi garage and he adored anything with an engine. Whenever Claire saw something he'd delight in, she always sent him a photo. He always replied with either a picture of her nieces and nephews or of her parents.

Unlike herself, David loved living in the small outback town where they'd both grown up. Good at both cricket and footy, he'd always belonged and thrived and he couldn't imagine living anywhere else. She, on the other hand, had been plotting to leave since she was ten years old, desperate to escape the taunts and bullying of a small-minded town that hovered on the edge of the desert and existence.

The imposing turrets of the red-brick London hospital now loomed high above her as she approached the old ornate gates. A small group of people rugged up against the post-dawn chill clutched *Save Our Hospital* and *Kids' Health NOT Wealth* signs with gloved hands. Each morning found a different combination of people in attendance. Many were parents of current patients, but hearteningly, there were some who'd been patients themselves many years ago. Together they were united and maintained a peaceful protest presence at the gates, striving to keep alive the hope that something could be done to save the hospital from closure.

'I've brought hot coffee,' Claire called out, holding up the cardboard tray as she did most mornings. Granted, she'd only been working at the castle for a few weeks but the idea of central London losing such a vitally important healthcare provider was a terrifying thought. What if the castle had already been closed when Westbourne Primary School caught fire? The thought made her shudder. There would have certainly been deaths. Even with the hospital's proximity to the school, there'd been far too many close calls. Not everyone was out of the woods yet, including little Ryan Walker.

The stalwarts at the gate greeted her and her coffees with a cheer. 'Morning, love.'

'Early again? You still on Aussie time?' one asked.

She laughed. 'I'd be going home after a day's work if I was.'

Once she'd distributed the coffees, she ducked through the gates and strode under the decorative brick archway. Behind the beautiful Victorian façade was a modern hospital with state-of-the-art equipment and an experienced and dedicated staff. There were one hundred and fifty years of history here and she was humbled to be a part of it. When she'd received the offer of a chance to train under the tutelage of the world-renowned neurosurgeon, Alistair North, she'd actually squealed in delight, deafening the very proper Englishwoman on the other end of the line.

'Now, now, Ms Mitchell,' the secretary to the chair of the Royal College of Surgeons had said primly as if overt displays of enthusiasm were frowned upon. Then, without pausing, she'd continued to outline the terms and conditions of the scholarship.

Claire hadn't cared about her unrestrained antipodean

response. If a girl couldn't get excited about such an amazing opportunity, when could she? After all, her work was her life and her life was her work, and the scholarship was a chance of a lifetime. At the time, she'd danced down the corridors of Flinders Medical Centre telling everyone from cleaners to consultants that she was going to London.

Now, as she ran up five flights of stairs, she was almost certain that if she'd known what was in store for her at the castle, she might not have been quite so excited. When she reached the landing with the large painted koala on the ward door, she smiled. Why, when all the other wards were named after northern hemisphere birds and animals, the Brits had chosen an Aussie marsupial for the neurology ward's logo was a mystery to her but she loved that they had. It made her feel a little less like an alien in what was proving to be a very unexpected foreign land.

Despite speaking English and having been raised in a country where the Union Jack still sat in the corner of the flag, Londoners were different. The brilliant Alistair North was extremely different, although not in the often restrained and polite British way. She'd been fortunate to work with talented neurosurgeons in Australia and she understood that brilliance was often accompanied by quirks. But Mr North had taken quirk and magnified it by the power of ten. All of it left her struggling to convince herself she'd done the right thing in accepting the scholarship.

Stepping into the bright and cheery ward, she noticed with a start that the nurses' station was empty. Surely she wasn't late? Her mouth dried as she spun around to check the large wall clock. The bright, red and yellow clock hands pointed to big blue numbers and they instantly reassured her. She gave a little laugh that contained both relief and irony. Of course she wasn't late—she was never late and today she was even earlier than usual. Preparation and attention to detail was as much a part of her as breathing. It had been that way since the fateful day in grade five when her small childhood world had suddenly turned on her.

Assuming the nurses to be busy with their end-of-shift tasks, she slid into an office chair and logged on to the computer. She always read her patients' overnight reports before rounds. It was better to take the extra time, learn what had happened and to have a well thought out plan than to be caught short. Just the thought of being put on the spot with the critical eyes of the medical students and junior house officers fixed upon her made her breath come faster.

The ward cared for children with a variety of neurological, craniofacial and central nervous system disorders, including those that required surgery. Although Mr North performed many different operations, his passion was the surgical treatment of focal epilepsy. It was the reason she'd fought so hard to win the scholarship and work with him, but as her brother often said in his laconic and understated tone after everything had gone pear-shaped, 'It seemed like a good idea at the time.' Right now she was second-guessing her good idea.

While she read the reports, the daytime nursing staff drifted in, busy chatting, and the medical students soon followed. Finally, the consistently late junior house officer, Andrew Bailey, arrived breathless and with his white coattails flapping. He came to a sudden halt and glanced around, his expression stunned. 'I still beat him?'

Claire, who'd just read little Ryan Walker's 'no change' report, stood with a sigh. 'You still beat him.'

He grinned. 'I must tell my father that my inability to be on time makes me a natural neurosurgeon.'

'Perhaps that's my problem,' Claire muttered as she checked her phone for a message or a missed call from the exuberantly talented consultant surgeon who had no concept of time or workplace protocol. Nope, no messages or voicemail. She automatically checked the admissions board, but if Mr Alistair North were running late because of an emergency admission, she'd have been the one hauled out of bed to deal with it.

'I heard while you and I were slaving away here last night, he was holding court over at the Frog and Peach,' Andrew said with a conspiratorial yet reverent tone.

'That doesn't automatically mean he had a late night.'

Andrew's black brows rose and waggled at her. 'I just met the delectable Islay Kennedy on the back stairs wearing yesterday's clothes. She mentioned dancing on tables, followed by an illicit boat ride on the Serpentine and then bacon and eggs at the Worker's Café watching the dawn break over the Thames. When I see him, I plan to genuflect in his direction.'

A flash of anger swept through Claire's body so hot and fast she thought it might lift her head from her neck. *I want to kill Alistair North.* Surgery was such a boys' club and neurosurgery even more so. For years she'd gone into battle time and time again on the basis of raw talent but it was never enough. She constantly fought sexism, and now, it seemed, she had to tackle ridiculous childish behaviour and the adoration of men, who in essence were little boys. Fed up and furious, she did something she rarely did: she shot the messenger.

'Andrew, don't even think that behaviour like that is commendable. It's juvenile and utterly irresponsible. If you *ever* pull a stunt like that and turn up to operate with me, I'll fail you.'

Before her stunned junior house officer could reply, the eardrum-piercing sound of party blowers rent the air. Everyone turned towards the raucous sound. A tall man with thick, rumpled dark blond hair and wearing fake black horn-rimmed glasses—complete with a large fake bulbous nose and moustache—was marching along the ward with a little girl clinging to his back like a monkey. Behind him followed a trail of children aged between two and twelve. Some were walking, others were being pushed in wheelchairs by the nurses and many wore bandages on their heads—all of them were enthusiastically puffing air into party blowers and looking like they were on a New Year's Day parade.

'Wave to Dr Mitchell,' the man instructed the little girl on his back. 'Did you know she's really a kangaroo?'

Despite his voice being slightly muffled by the fake moustache, it was without doubt the unmistakably deep and well-modulated tones of Alistair North.

A line of tension ran down Claire's spine with the speed and crack of lightning before radiating outwards into every single cell. It was the same tension that invaded her every time Alistair North spoke to her. The same tension that filled her whenever she thought about him. It was a barely leashed dislike and it hummed inside her along with something else she didn't dare name. She refused point-blank to contemplate that it might be attraction. The entire female staff of the castle might think the man was sex on a stick, but not her.

Granted, the first time she'd seen all six feet of him striding confidently towards her, she'd been struck by his presence. Unlike herself, not one single atom of the many that made up Alistair North hinted at doubt. The man positively radiated self-assurance from the square set of his shoulders to his brogue-clad feet. He wore clothes with effortless ease, their expensive cut and style fitting him flawlessly, yet at the same time finding the perfect pitch between stuffy and scruffy. Despite his posh accent, there was also something engaging and decidedly un-British about his lopsided and cheeky grin. It wasn't a smile one associated with a consultant. It would break over the stark planes of his cheeks, vanquishing the esteemed surgeon and give rise to the remnants of a cheeky and mischievous little boy. But it wasn't so much the smile that undid her—it was the glint in his slate-grey eyes. He had the ability to focus his attention on a person and make them feel as if they were the only human being on the planet.

'Welcome to the castle, Mitchell,' he'd said to her on her first day.

As she'd shaken his outstretched hand and felt his firm pressure wrap around her fingers and travel up her arm, she'd been horrified to feel herself just a little bit breathless. Her planned speech had vanished and she'd found herself replying in her broadest Australian accent, 'Thanks. It's great to be here.'

It had taken less than a week for her to realise that Alistair North's cheeky grin almost always flagged that he was about to break the rules and wreak havoc on a grand scale. She'd also learned that his eyes alone, with their dancing smoky hue and intense gaze that made the person in their sights feel like they mattered to him like no one else, were frequently used with devastating ease to tempt women into his bed.

She conceded that, perhaps, on her first day when she'd felt momentarily breathless, she'd succumbed to the hypnotic effect of his gaze. Now, after working closely with him for weeks, she was immune to its effects. She'd spent ten years slogging her way up the medical career ladder, spending more hours in hospitals than out of them, and she wasn't about to risk it all by landing up in the boss's bed. More importantly, she didn't like Alistair North, so even if he were the last man on earth, she wouldn't be tempted.

Apparently, she was virtually the only woman at the castle with that thought. Over the past few weeks she'd been stunned to find herself sought out by hopeful women seeking information about Alistair North's proclivities, or worse still, being asked to act as go-between for disappointed and sometimes furious women whom he'd dated and then hadn't bothered to call. All things considered, from his casual disregard of the rules to his blasé treatment of women, there was no way on God's green earth or in the fiery depths of hell that she was attracted to *that man*. Not now. Not never.

The stories about Alistair North that circulated around the hospital held fable qualities. If she hadn't been working closely with him as his speciality registrar, she'd have laughed on being told the tales. She'd have said, 'They've got to be the invention of an overactive imagination.' But she did work with him. Sadly, she'd seen enough evidence to know at least two of the stories she'd heard were true so she had no reason not to believe the others. As hard as she tried to focus solely on Alistair North's immense skill as a neurosurgeon and block out the excited noise that seemed to permanently spin and jangle around him, it was impossible.

Everywhere she turned, people talked about his exploits in and out of the operating theatre. Gossip about who he was currently dating or dumping and who he'd been seen with driving into work that morning ran rife along the hospital corridors. It was as if speculation about the man was the hospital's secondary power supply. What she hated most of all was the legendary status the young male house officers gave him, while she was the one left trailing behind, picking up the pieces.

No, the sensation she got every time she was in the same space as Mr Alistair North was antagonism. The man may be brilliant and talented in the operating theatre but outside of it he was utterly unprofessional. He was stuck permanently in adolescence, and at thirty-nine that was not only ridiculous, it was sad. Most of his contemporaries were married with children but she supposed it would take a brave—or more likely deluded—woman to risk all on him. The only thing Claire would risk on Alistair North was her brain. Despite what she thought of the man, she couldn't deny the doctor was the best neurosurgeon in the country.

The little girl on Alistair North's back was now waving enthusiastically at her. Claire blinked behind her glasses, suddenly realising it was Lacey—the little girl they were operating on in an hour's time. Why wasn't she tucked up in her bed quiet and calm?

'Wave back, Kanga,' Alistair North said, his clear and precise Oxford accent teasing her. 'It won't break your arm.'

Claire's blood heated to boiling point. Did the man know that kangaroos boxed? The thought of bopping him on his fake nose was far too tempting. She felt the expectant gaze of the ward staff fixed firmly on her and suddenly she was thrown back in time. She was in Gundiwindi, standing in front of the class, with fifteen sets of eyes boring into her. She could see the red dust motes dancing in the starkly bright and uncompromising summer sunshine and the strained smile of her teacher slipping as his mouth turned down into a resigned and grumpy line. She could hear the shuffling and coughing of her peers—the sound that always preceded the one or two brutal comments that managed to escape from their mouths before Mr Phillips regained control.

Moron. Idiot.

Stop it. She hauled her mind back to the present, reminding herself sternly that she wasn't either of those things. She'd spent two decades proving it. She was a woman in a difficult and male dominated speciality and she was eleven months away from sitting her final neurosurgery exams. She'd fought prejudice and sexism to get this far and she'd fought herself. She refused to allow anyone to make her feel diminished and she sure as hell wasn't going to accept an order to wave from a man who needed to grow up. She would, however, do what she always did—she'd restore order.

In heels, Claire came close to matching Alistair North's height, and although her preference had always been to wear ballet flats, she'd taken herself shoe shopping at the end of her first week of working with him. The added inches said, *Don't mess with me*. She took a few steps forward until she was standing side on to him but facing Lacey. Ignoring Alistair North completely, and most definitely ignoring his scent of freshly laundered cotton with a piquant of sunshine that made her unexpectedly homesick, she opened her arms out wide towards the waving child.

'Do you want to come for a hop with Kanga?'

'Yes, please.'

Lacey, a ward of the state, transferred almost too easily into her arms, snuggling in against her chest and chanting, 'Boing, boing, boing.'

Claire pulled her white coat over her charge, creating a makeshift pouch, and then she turned her back on Alistair North. She strode quickly down the ward carrying an overexcited Lacey back to her bed. As she lowered her down and tried to tuck her under the blankets, the little girl bounced on the mattress.

Thanks for nothing, Alistair, Claire muttered to herself. It was going to take twice as long as normal to do all the routine preoperative checks. Yet another day would run late before it had even started.

CHAPTER TWO

ALASTAIR NORTH MOVED his lower jaw sideways and then back again behind his surgical mask, mulling over the conundrum that was his incredibly perfectionist and frustratingly annoying speciality registrar. She'd more than competently created a skin pouch to hold the vagus nerve stimulator she was inserting into Lacey Clarke. Now she was delicately wrapping the wire around the left vagus nerve and hopefully its presence would effectively minimise Lacey's seizures in a way medication had so far failed to achieve.

A bit of electricity, he mused, could kill or save a life. He knew all about that. Too much or too little of the stuff left a man dead for a very long time. What he didn't know was why Claire Mitchell was permanently strung so tight a tune could be plucked on her tendons.

Based on her skills and glowing references from the Royal Prince Alfred Hospital in Sydney and the Flinders Medical Centre in Adelaide, she'd outranked twenty-five other talented applicants from the Commonwealth. With her small steady hands and deft strokes, she had the best clinical skills of all the trainees who'd applied to work with him. She'd beaten twenty-four men to win the scholarship and that alone should tell her she was the best. Surely she knew that?

Does she though?

In his speciality, he was used to fielding egos the size of Scotland. It wasn't that Claire didn't have an ego; she did. She knew her stuff and he'd seen her run through medical students and her junior house officer with a complete lack of sympathy for any whose insufficient preparedness caused them to give incorrect answers to her questions. But he was used to trainees of her calibre thinking of themselves as 'cock of the walk' and carrying themselves with an accompanying swagger.

Claire Mitchell didn't swagger, despite the fact she had the best set of legs he'd seen on a woman in a very long time. And her shoes. Good God! Her acerbic personality was at odds with those shoes. Did she have any idea how her body moved in those heels? Her breasts tilted up, her hips swung and her calves said coquettishly, *Caress me. I promise you there's even better ahead.*

Hell's bells. He had a love-hate relationship with those shoes and her legs. Did they hint at a deeply buried wild side? Would those legs party the way he loved to party? Would he even want to party with them? *No way.* Gorgeous legs weren't enough to overcome a major personality flaw. Claire had a gritty aura of steely determination and no sense of humour whatsoever.

Given what she'd achieved so far and the fact she had a ninety-nine per cent chance of passing her exams on the first attempt—an uncommon feat in neurosurgery—she should be enjoying her hard-earned position. He doubted she was enjoying anything. The bloody woman never looked happy and it drove him crazy.

As her boss, his duty of care extended only so far as making sure she was coping with the workload and her study for her fellowship exams. However, he'd spent two years living in Australia himself, and despite both countries speaking English, pretty much everything else was different. It had taken him a few months to find his feet at the Children's Hospital and get established in a social set so he was very aware that Claire Mitchell might flounder at first. Ten days after she'd started working with him, he'd found her looking extremely downcast with what he'd assumed was a dose of homesickness. The woman looked like she needed to get out of the hospital for a bit and catch her breath.

On the spur of the moment, he'd asked, 'Would you like to grab a pint at the Frog and Peach?'

Her response had been unexpected. Her eyes—a fascinating combination of both light and dark brown that reminded him of his favourite caramel swirl chocolate bar—had widened momentarily before suddenly narrowing into critical slits. In her distinctive diphthong-riddled accent—one he really didn't want to admit to enjoying—she'd said briskly and succinctly, 'I have reports.'

'There's always going to be reports to write,' he'd said with a smile that invariably softened the sternest of wills.

'Especially when *you* don't appear to write many.'

He wasn't sure who'd been more taken aback—him, because registrars knew better then to ever speak to their consultant like that, or her, because she'd actually spoken her thoughts out loud.

'I'm sorry. That was out of order,' she'd said quickly, although not in a particularly ingratiating tone. 'Please accept my apology.'

'Jet lag still bothering you?' he'd offered by way of an olive branch. After all, they had to work together and life was easier if he got along with his trainee. So far, her standoffish manner wasn't a good sign.

At his question, a momentary look of confusion had crossed her face before disappearing under her hairline. 'Jet lag's a bastard.'

It was, but they both knew right then and there she

wasn't suffering from it. She'd spent that Friday night writing reports and he'd gone to the pub determined to forget about shoes that teased and long, strong and sexy legs. Legs that should come with a warning: Toxic If Touched. Happily, he'd met a pretty midwife with a delectable Irish lilt. The music had been so loud she'd had to lean in and speak directly into his ear. Heaven help him but he was a sucker for a woman with an accent.

Claire Mitchell now snipped the last stitch and said, 'Thanks, everyone,' before stepping back from the operating table.

Alistair thought drily that after working with her over the last few weeks, he no longer had to work very hard at resisting her outback drawl. In the weeks since she'd rejected his invitation, he hadn't issued another. As long as she did her job, he overrode his concerns that she might be lonely. Of more concern to him was why he'd been working so jolly hard at trying to get her to lighten up. Hell, right now he'd take it for the win if she looked even slightly happier than if her dog had just died.

After a brief conversation with his scrub nurse, checking how her son had fared in his school athletics competition, he left Lacey in the excellent care of the paediatric anaesthetist, Rupert Emmerson. He found Claire at the computer in the staff lounge.

'That went well,' he said, pressing a coffee pod into the machine.

She pushed her tortoiseshell glasses up her nose. 'It did.'

'You sound surprised.'

She pursed her lips and her bottom lip protruded slightly—soft, plump and enticing. His gaze stalled momentarily and he wondered how it was that he'd never noticed her very kissable mouth before.

'I'm not used to children being so hyped up before surgery,' she said crisply.

And there it was—her critical tone. *That* was why he'd never noticed her lips. Her mouth was usually speaking spikey, jagged words that could never be associated with luscious, soft pink lips. He wasn't used to being questioned by staff, let alone by a trainee who was here to learn from him. If he chose, he could make her life incredibly difficult and impact on her career, but he'd learned very abruptly that life was too short to hold grudges. As far as he was concerned, in the grand scheme of things, six months was a blip on the radar.

What baffled him though was that she obviously hadn't clashed with her previous supervising neurosurgeons or she wouldn't have got this far. He struggled to align the woman at the castle with the glowing reports that had preceded her. David Wu, a surgeon of very few words, had positively gushed about the woman, calling her intuitive, skilful and courageous. It had been his recommendation that had swayed the board to offer Claire Mitchell the scholarship.

Alistair couldn't fault her surgery but he was struggling with her personality. Take this morning, for instance. Everyone on the ward had been having fun except for Mitchell, who'd looked like a disapproving schoolmistress complete with her sun-kissed blonde hair coiled into a tight knot. Like so many of his nonmedical decisions, it had been a spur of the moment thing to call out to her to wave. The moment the words had left his mouth he knew he'd done the wrong thing. It had put her on the spot and focused attention on her. He was learning that she wasn't the type of person who welcomed the spotlight.

In his defence, he'd only asked her to join in the fun because he'd found their little patient in bed, scared and trembling. He'd scooped her into his arms hoping to reassure her, and then to take her mind off things, they'd room hopped, visiting the other kids. The parade had just happened—a combination of kids being kids, some hero worship, a packet of squeakers and a little girl needing some TLC. Now Claire Mitchell had the audacity to judge it. Judge him.

'Hyped up?' he repeated, feeling the edges of his calm fraying like linen. 'Actually, I'd call it being the opposite of terrified. Lacey's spent a week being prodded and poked. She's had an MRI and a CT scan. Hell, she was attached to the EEG for two days while we recorded epileptic events so we knew which surgery to perform.'

Despite being known around the castle for his calm and relaxed approach, his voice had developed a plummy and patronising edge. 'And after enduring all of that, you'd deny Lacey a bit of fun?'

Claire's eyes flashed golden brown. 'Of course not. I'd just plan a more appropriate time for the fun.'

Her tone vibrated with her absolute conviction that her way was the right way. The only way. He remembered how once he'd been a man of absolutes and certainties and how he'd never countenanced anything ever getting in the way of what he wanted. And hadn't fate laughed itself silly over that naïve belief? Hell, it was still chuckling.

With more force than necessary, he pulled his now full coffee mug out from under the machine. Pale brown liquid spilled down the steep white sides leaving a muddy residue. 'There's a lot to be said for spontaneity, Claire.'

Her eyes dilated as if he'd just shocked her by using her first name. 'We'll have to agree to disagree on that, Mr—' She quickly corrected herself. 'Alistair.'

Good God. Frustration brought his hands up, tearing through his hair. He'd been telling her from day one to call him 'Alistair.' She'd never called him 'sir'—probably the anti-establishment Australian in her prevented her from doing that—but she'd stuck with 'Mr North.' Every time she called him by his title he responded by calling her by her surname to drive home the point. He knew it was childish and very public school, but even so, she still didn't seem to be getting the message.

He really didn't understand her at all. Hell, he couldn't even get a read on her. Every other Australian he'd ever met or worked with tended to be laid-back, easy-going and with a well-developed sense of the ridiculous. When he was a kid, he'd grown up listening to his great-grandfather recounting the antics of the ANZACs during the Second World War—brave men who didn't hesitate to break the rules if they thought any rule was stupid. What in heaven's name had he done in a previous life to be lumbered with the only dour and highly strung Aussie in existence?

'Would you like to insert the ventricular peritoneal shunt in Bodhi Singh?' he asked, returning his thoughts to work, which was a lot more straightforward than the enigma that was Claire Mitchell.

'Really?' she asked, scrutinising him closely as if she didn't quite believe his offer.

That rankled. How was it that the woman who normally couldn't detect a joke now misread a genuine offer? 'Absolutely.'

Her mouth suddenly curved upwards as wonder and anticipation carved a dimple into her left cheek.

So that's what it takes to make her smile. For weeks, he'd been trying all the wrong things.

'Thanks,' she said enthusiastically. 'I'd love the opportunity.'

The tightness that was so much a part of her faded away under the brilliance of a smile so wide it encompassed her entire face. Along with her tension, all her sharp angles disappeared too, softened by the movement of her cheeks and the dazzling sparkle in her eyes. It was like looking at a completely different person—someone whose enthusiasm was so infectious that everyone vied to be on her team.

Pick me! Pick me!

What the hell? This was worse than a momentary thought about her gorgeous legs. Utterly discombobulated, he dragged his gaze away from her pink-cheeked face that danced with excitement, and far, far away from that come-hither dimple that had his blood pumping faster than necessary. He'd spent weeks trying to make her smile, and now that he had, he knew he must make it stop. It was one thing to wish that for the good of the patients and workplace harmony his speciality registrar be a little more relaxed. It was another thing entirely to find himself attracted to her as a woman. Hell, he didn't even like her. Not. At. All.

He'd never been attracted to someone he didn't like before, but that conundrum aside, there were many reasons why any sort of attraction was utterly out of the question. First and foremost, nothing could happen between them because he was her boss and she was his trainee. Fortunately, he knew exactly how to quash any remaining eddies of unwanted desire and kill off all temptation without any pain or suffering to himself.

'Good,' he said to her, tossing the dregs of his coffee into the sink. 'I'm glad you're on board, because I promised to have lunch with the new and very attractive burns-unit house officer. Inserting the VP would make me late.'

Her tension rode back in as fast as the cavalry into battle and her eyes flashed so brightly he needed sunglasses to deflect the glare. 'You're having lunch instead of operating?'

He gave a practised shrug—one that said, *What of it?* 'I've got complete confidence in your ability, but please, do page me if you need me.'

'I wouldn't dream of interrupting you,' she snapped.

Her previous lush mouth was now a thin, hard line and Alistair was thankfully back in familiar territory. Nothing about this Claire Mitchell was remotely attractive and his body reacted accordingly, which was to say, it didn't react at all. 'Excellent,' he said, as much to himself as to her. 'I'm glad we've got that sorted.'

Without another word, he left the room and strode towards the lifts. He'd spend the unexpected extra time with Ryan Walker's parents. It was the least he could do.

A few days later, Claire was handing out her morning coffees to the dawn crusaders at the hospital gates when she got chatting with a delightful man in his seventies. With his Cockney accent that reminded her of Eliza Doolittle's father in *Pygmalion*, he told her he'd been born 'a blue baby.'

'Me 'art's plumbing was all wrong like. Lucky for me, the castle 'ere had a pioneer in 'art surgery, otherwise I'd 'ave been dead a long time now.' Reg flicked his thumb towards the original ornate building. 'I've got a lot of love for the old girl. She gave me a chance to 'ave a bloody good life. One of me kids was born 'ere when she come early and the docs patched up the others when they broke bones. Me grandkids were all born 'ere and me first great-grand-kiddy's due on Guy Fawkes.'

'It sounds like the castle is your family's hospital,' Claire said, thinking about the affection in the man's voice.

He nodded enthusiastically. 'Too right. That's why I'm 'ere every mornin'. All us Landsburys are on the rota right down to the little tackers. If that lot in suits close 'er down, it'll be a bloody disgrace.'

Claire was about to agree when she heard her name being called. She excused herself and turned to see Victoria Christie, the petite and dark-haired paramedic who'd galvanised everyone into action by starting the Save Our Hospital committee. With rapid flicks of her fingers, Victoria was motioning her over.

Bidding Reg goodbye, Claire crossed the cobblestones with care, regretting her heels. She reminded herself that her extra height would be necessary soon enough when she did rounds with Alistair. 'G'day, Vicki.'

'Hello, Claire. How are things?'

It was a broad question that really didn't demand a truthful answer but Claire had an unexpected and utterly disturbing urge to confide in the woman about how hard she was finding working with Alistair North. The thought unsettled her. She'd never been a woman who had a lot of girlfriends, and truth be told she usually got along better with men than women—which was fortunate given she was working in a male-dominated speciality. But it was immensely competitive so any friendships that had formed were always constrained by that reality.

She'd tried friendships outside of medicine but people didn't understand the crazy hours. Her frequent failures to turn up at events due to being delayed at work frustrated them and she noticed that it didn't take long for the invitations to dry up altogether. It killed relationships too, or at least it had played a big part in her and Michael's demise.

There was more to it than just your job.

She pulled her mind fast away from difficult thoughts and concentrated instead on trying to work out why women had to run in a pack and share the most intimate details of their lives with each other. She did have two close girlfriends and she'd always considered them enough, but Emma and Jessica were in Australia juggling toddlers, babies, partners and a burgeoning women's health clinic. She missed them, and these last few weeks at the castle had thrown her for a loop. Never before had she felt so at sea in a job and she had no one to talk to about her baffling boss.

How could one man generate such disparate feelings? She lurched from admiration to antipathy and back again, although right now admiration was fast losing its gloss. In Australia, she'd worked under crusty old neurosurgeons who barely knew her name and when they did deign speak to her it was to bark out instructions. It hadn't always been a pleasant experience but at least it was predictable behaviour. They'd played by the archaic rules set down a hundred years ago and she'd just put her head down and got on with the job. So why was she struggling to do that with Alistair North?

Because he doesn't play by the rules.

And wasn't that the truth! The man drove her to the point of distraction with his lack of attention to detail outside of theatre. Sure, she was his trainee, but along with her clinical work she was carrying his administrative load as well as her own and it was wearing her down. She'd been working ridiculously long hours trying to manage the paperwork and she didn't know how much longer she could trade sleep to keep up. Last week, with an enormous sense of guilt, she'd offloaded some of it onto her house officer. Andrew had accepted it without question, because that was the system, but part of her had wanted to explain. The rest of her had overruled the idea. Since leaving Gundiwindi, she'd held her secret close so it couldn't be used against her. She'd got this far and as soon as she qualified she'd be home free.

Meanwhile, she was barely treading water with the added report load, and combined with her own exhaustion and the Pied Piper incident on the ward two days ago, she'd lost her temper. Oh, how she regretted that she'd given in to fatigue and frustration. It had been beyond unwise but what worried her even more was her current pattern of behaviour. For some reason, when she was in Alistair North's company, she lost her protective restraint.

Not once in her career had she ever spoken back to her consultant, and now with the end of her fellowship in sight, it wasn't the time to start. But as each day passed, she felt more and more like a smoking and steaming volcano ready to blow. To try and keep herself in check, she'd started clenching her fists when she felt her frustrations rising.

As a result, her palms had developed permanent dents in them. She'd discovered if she focused on the sharp digging pain she was less likely to say something she'd regret. It didn't always work and she'd clearly seen his displeasure at her criticism of his approach with Lacey. But instead of disciplining her, he'd rewarded her by letting her operate.

This unexpected offer had both stunned and thrilled her. At the time, she'd hoped it meant she'd finally passed his test of attempting to drown her under a sea of administrative work. That his offer for her to operate solo meant he'd finally recognised her clinical skills and they were entering the next phase in their working relationship. For a few delicious moments she'd floated on air and then reality had hit. His offer for her to operate had been pure expediency. The playboy had a lunch date.

That moment was the first time she'd ever doubted his professionalism. Even then, the suspicion wasn't straightforward. Back in Australia, she'd had opportunities to insert VP shunts and she was competent in the procedure. He would have known that, so the fact he wasn't going to be in the operating theatre with her wasn't exactly abandoning his patient. Yet he'd admitted to going to lunch!

So, you'll lambast him for telling the truth when he could have created excuses like your previous bosses?

Sick of the endless loop of contradictory thoughts, Claire gave herself a shake. 'Today's a new day,' she said cryptically to Victoria's question, 'with new things to learn.'

'Alistair's a generous teacher.'

'He's certainly generous,' she said, fighting the urge to purse her lips in disapproval.

Victoria laughed and her chestnut ponytail swung around her shoulders. 'Our Alistair certainly loves women. That's what I wanted to talk to you about.'

Unable to hide her astonishment, Claire blinked at the pretty paramedic. *Not you too!* If the hospital grapevine was to be believed, Victoria and Dominic MacBride were very much together. 'Oh?' she asked cautiously.

Victoria's face lit up with enthusiasm. 'You've heard about the hospital ball?'

For anyone not to have heard about the ball, they'd have to have been living under a rock. Posters graced every noticeboard inside the hospital, and outside they'd been pasted on the poster pillars along the main road. Invitations had been sent to the past and present medical and auxiliary staff and one massive wall in the cafeteria had been covered with an enormous banner declaring the Spring Fling ball to be *the* social event of the season. The chatter about it had even managed to dent the football conversations about which team would be playing in the FA Cup final in a few weeks.

'I think I may have seen a poster about it somewhere,' she said with mock thoughtfulness.

Victoria missed the joke and continued in earnest. 'It's our first major event and we're hoping to raise fifty thousand pounds. The thing is, we really need Alistair to attend. If he doesn't, it's going to affect ticket sales.'

Claire laughed and then stopped as she caught the expression on Victoria's face. 'You're serious?'

'Deadly. He told Dominic that things were—' she raised her fingers into quotation marks '—complicated, which is code for he's broken some poor deluded girl's heart once again.' She let out a long sigh. 'Why they even think they could be the one to get him to commit is beyond me. The man is Peter Pan. Anyway, we really need him at the ball because we plan to auction the seat next to him. Women will have the chance to sit next to him for one of three courses. We're also selling his dance card. Your job is to make sure he attends.'

'I doubt I can make Alistair North do anything he doesn't want to do,' she replied honestly.

Victoria shot her an understanding smile. 'Alistair was

raised right and he went to the right schools. As a result, he has a social code of conduct that he sticks to. He will go to the ball if he's your date.'

Claire's intake of breath was so sharp it sent her into a paroxysm of coughing. 'I can't ask my boss out,' she said, her voice rising sharply.

Victoria shrugged as if the fact Alistair was her boss was immaterial. 'Of course you can. We all have to do our bit to save the castle,' she said pragmatically. 'Besides, it's all about how you word the invitation. Guilt him into it if you have to. Tell him it's imperative there's a show of strength from Koala Ward. He can't really argue against the expectation that as head of the department he should be there.'

The thought of having this conversation with Alistair North was enough to make her hyperventilate. 'Victoria, I really don't think—'

'Do you know how much the community will suffer if the hospital's sold?' Victoria's hands hit her hips, elbows akimbo. 'Keeping the castle open means everything to me, to the staff and to the patients. We're expecting to raise at least a thousand pounds by auctioning off his dance card, plus all the money we'll get for selling the seats next to him.'

Oh, how she wanted to rush to the ATM right this second and withdraw the cash but the idea of eating next month took precedence. 'I can't promise you—'

'Yes, you can. And you will,' Victoria said with the sort of authority in her voice usually reserved for recalcitrant patients. She reached out her hand and gave Claire's arm a gentle squeeze. 'And all the children and families in the district will thank you.'

Claire, who towered over the brunette, couldn't comprehend how someone so petite could be such an indomitable force. 'That's blackmail,' she said weakly.

Victoria smiled. 'No. It's preventing a travesty. We're

all mucking in to save our wonderful hospital for generations to come. This is your small contribution.'

Small? If this was small, she hated to think what a big request would look like. Claire was keen to do her bit, but she knew that Victoria had just well and truly dropped her into the muck right up to her neck.

CHAPTER THREE

CLAIRE STOOD AT the end of Ryan Walker's bed and chewed her lip. She had expected the little boy to have improved much faster than this. When he'd arrived at A & E barely conscious after being hit on the head by a falling beam at the Westbourne Primary School fire, Dominic MacBride, the castle's trauma surgeon, had immediately called her and Alistair in to consult. They'd ordered a CT scan that showed Ryan had sustained a fractured skull. Fortunately, there was no displacement of bones but there was a tiny associated subdural haematoma.

Rather than rushing in with guns blazing, she'd totally agreed with Alistair's conservative treatment plan. They'd worked closely with Rupert Emmerson, the anaesthetist, who'd sedated and ventilated Ryan. Alistair had inserted an intracranial pressure monitor and she'd inserted a central line, administering a mannitol infusion to decrease any associated brain swelling from the injury. The small haematoma hadn't diminished in size but neither had it grown. As a result, Ryan remained ventilated and his condition was still in a state of flux.

Yesterday morning, in a moment of frustrated despair during teaching rounds, she'd asked Alistair if she'd missed anything. Despite the large group of students gathered around the little tacker's bed, Alistair's pewter-grey eyes had zeroed in on her as if they were the only two people in the room.

'If you've missed something, Mitchell, then so have I.'

'Shall we do another MRI?'

'He had an MRI two days ago. While his observations remain the same it's not warranted. You have to ask yourself why you're doing the test.'

Because I have to do something. Doing nothing feels like giving up.

'Surely there's another option?'

Something she'd been momentarily tempted to think was sympathy had crossed his face but it vanished the moment he opened his mouth.

'There is. We wait.'

Wait? That wasn't something. That was sitting on their hands. 'And what if he doesn't improve?'

His shoulders had risen and fallen. 'That may be the reality.'

No. 'I don't like that reality,' she'd said briskly as if being terse would change it.

He'd given her a brief sad smile before returning his attention to the group of students. 'Who can tell me the elements of the Glasgow Coma Scale?'

'I swear he squeezed my hand before,' Ryan's mother said, her voice breaking into Claire's thoughts. Louise's anxious face was lined with two weeks of worry. 'That's a good sign, isn't it.'

It wasn't framed as a question—it was a solid statement. Louise needed to reassure herself that her little boy really was showing signs of improvement when in fact he was neither improving nor deteriorating. It was the limbo that was so disconcerting and heartbreaking, especially when neither she nor Alistair could pinpoint the reason.

Claire didn't want to upset the traumatised woman but

she didn't attach the same significance to what was likely a muscle spasm. 'He's very heavily sedated, Louise.'

Claire checked his vital signs as she did twice each day. *No change.* She wrote up a drug order to override the one that was about to expire and then she turned her attention to Louise. Gunmetal-grey shadows stretched from the mother's eyes down to her cheekbones. Claire was familiar with the signs of relatives at the end of their rope.

'How are you sleeping?' she asked, despite the signs that the woman wasn't sleeping very much at all.

The exhausted mother shrugged and tilted her head towards the rollaway bed. 'It's got springs in interesting places.'

'We can get you another one,' Claire offered, having no idea if that was even possible. With all the talk of the probable sale of the hospital land and relocating the facility to one of the home counties, the powers that be weren't spending any money. If push came to shove, she'd buy a rollaway bed herself. At least it would feel like she was doing something other than this interminable waiting.

Louise sighed. 'To be fair, it's as much the disturbed sleep as anything. I wake up every time the nurses do their hourly check.'

'Would you consider taking a night off?' Claire asked carefully. She'd learned to tread very gently with families.

'I doubt I'd sleep any better at home.'

'Your GP can prescribe some sleeping tablets. Believe me, eight hours sleep in your own bed would do you the world of good.'

Louise gave her head a brisk shake. 'I want to be here when he wakes up.'

'I understand.' She pulled up a chair and sat, putting herself at eye level with Louise. 'The thing is, Ryan doesn't have to be alone. I'm sure there's someone in your extended family you could ask to give you a break? You know, so both you and Colin can get a full night's sleep.'

Louise glanced between Claire and her redheaded son, whose freckles seemed darker than ever against his porcelain-white face. A tear spilled over and ran down her cheek. 'I'm beyond making decisions. My mind feels like it's encased in a wet, London fog.'

'Then let me make the decision for you.'

She looked uncertain. 'I've never felt this exhausted in my life. It's like fatigue's not only invaded my soul but it's set up residence. All I want to do is curl up under the duvet and sleep for a week. I want to forget about the fire and how it turned my life on its head in an instant. But how can I? This is my new reality. Ryan can't leave and forget. If I go home, aren't I letting him down?'

Claire had heard variations of this story from grieving parents many times before. She gave the woman's knee a gentle pat. 'If you don't look after yourself, Louise, you risk getting sick. If you fall apart, then you'll be away from Ryan a lot longer than twelve hours.'

The enervated mother suddenly sagged as if utterly defeated by a fortnight's emotional trauma and associated sleep debt. Her weary moss-green eyes met Claire's. 'If he wakes up while I'm at home, you must call me.'

'Of course.'

'Thank you.' The woman visibly brightened. 'Perhaps my leaving will trigger him waking up. You know, like when you take an umbrella with you every day and it's always dry but the moment you leave it at home it rains.'

Claire couldn't quite see the connection.

'I've been here for days,' Louise explained, 'and nothing's changed. It stands to reason that if I leave, he'll sit up and start talking.'

A worrying sensation roved along Claire's spine and she had to resist the urge not to wince. 'Medicine doesn't really work that way, Louise,' she said gently. 'Would you like me to contact your GP about the sleeping tablets? And I can ask the ward clerk to call you a taxi.'

'Thank you. That would be great.' Louise leaned over, brushed the hair from Ryan's forehead and kissed him. 'See you soon, buddy.' She smoothed his hair back into place and then stood up. 'Promise me, Claire, you'll telephone if he wakes up.'

'I promise,' Claire said easily. 'Wild horses couldn't stop me from giving you good news like that.'

Alistair high-fived Tristan Lewis-Smith. 'Way to go, Tris,' he said with a grin.

The kid had just whooped him at virtual tennis—twice—but he didn't care. He was too busy rejoicing in the fact that the ten-year-old had been seizure free for a week. That hadn't happened in two years and it was moments like these that reminded him that what he did each day mattered. Hell, it reinforced his mantra that every single day mattered and life should be lived to the full.

He'd almost lost the opportunity to do that, and when he'd woken up in the coronary care unit, he'd vowed never to forget how life could change in a heartbeat—or the lack of one as the case may be—and how close he'd come to death. He'd been blessed with a second chance and he never took it for granted. He was thrilled to be able to give Tristan a second chance at a normal life.

'Right-oh, mate.' He pulled down the sheet and patted the centre of the bed. 'Time to tuck in and pretend to read or the night sister will have my guts for garters.'

Full of beans and far from quiet, Tristan bounced onto the bed. 'You're just saying that because you're scared if you play another game I'll beat you. Again.'

'There is that,' Alistair said with a grin. 'Hurry up. I've got somewhere I need to be.'

Tristan scrambled under the covers. 'Nurse Saunders said you couldn't stay long because you've got a hot date.'

'Did she now?' Funny that Lindsay appeared to know more about this hot date than he did. He found himself automatically tucking the sheet around the little boy, only this time an odd feeling of something akin to emptiness accompanied it.

He immediately shook it off. He had no reason to feel empty or lonely. Life was good. He had a job he loved and a spacious and light-filled apartment just off the Portobello Road that he'd filled with curios from his world travels. Three years ago, he'd added to his property portfolio and bought a pretty stone cottage surrounded by fields of lavender in Provence. When he was there, he revelled in the sensory delights of sunshine, hearty Mediterranean food and great wine. He visited at least once a month, either alone or with a companion depending on whether or not the woman he was dating was still focused on having fun. The moment a woman started dropping hints about 'taking things to the next level' she was no longer welcome in France. Or in Notting Hill for that matter.

He loved women but he didn't do next levels. It was better to break a heart in the early days, well before things got serious, than to risk shattering a life, or worse, lives. His childhood was a case in point, and furthermore, no one ever knew precisely the duration of a second chance.

Surprised by the unexpected direction his musings had taken him—he didn't do dark thoughts and he certainly wasn't known for them—he left Tristan's room and contemplated the hour. It wasn't quite eight. As it was a Thursday night there'd be a sizeable hospital crowd at the Frog and Peach and he'd be welcomed with open arms for his dart skills. Oddly, the thought didn't entice. He had an overwhelming urge to do something completely different. Something wild that would make him feel alive.

Parkour in the dark?

Alive not dead, thank you very much.

Still, parkour in daylight this coming weekend was worth investigating. He pulled out his phone and had just brought up a browser when he heard, 'G'day, Alistair.'

Astonished, he spun around at the sound of the broad Australian accent. Although he'd heard Claire Mitchell use the informal Aussie greeting with other people, she'd always been far more circumspect with him. Well, with the exception of one or two lapses. In general, he knew she tried to be polite with him and that she found it a struggle. Did it make him a bad person that he enjoyed watching her keep herself in check? The woman was always buttoned up so tightly it wasn't surprising she cracked every now and then.

Now she stood in front of him with her hands pressed deep into the pockets of her once starched but now very end-of-day limp doctor's coat. Her hair was pulled back into its functional ponytail and a hot-pink stethoscope was slung around her neck. A tiny koala clung to her security lanyard along with a small pen on retractable elastic. Her utilitarian white blouse and medium length black skirt were unremarkable except that the skirt revealed those long shapely legs that taunted him.

Her feet were tucked into bright red shoes with a wide strap that crossed her instep just below her ankle and culminated in a large red button that drew the eye. He suddenly understood completely why Victorian gentlemen had waxed lyrical over a fleeting glimpse of a fine ankle.

He scanned her face, looking for clues as to why she was suddenly attempting a colloquial greeting with him. 'G'day, yourself,' he intoned back, with a fair crack at an Aussie accent.

Behind her sexy librarian-style glasses her eyes did that milk and dark chocolate swirly thing he always enjoyed and—was she blushing?

'Do you have a minute?' she asked, quickly pushing her glasses up her nose as they continued walking towards the lifts.

'Always. Problem?'

'Um.' She surreptitiously glanced along the corridor, taking in the nurses' station that was teaming with staff. She suddenly veered left into the treatment room.

Utterly intrigued by this uncharacteristic behaviour, he followed. 'Shall I close the door?'

She tugged hard at some stray strands of her hair before pushing them behind her ears. 'Thanks.'

He closed the door and flicked the blinds to the closed position before leaning back against the wide bench. Claire stood a metre or more away, her plump lips deliciously red. He shifted his gaze and— *Damn it!* His eyes caught on a fluttering pulse beating at the base of her throat. She really had the most gloriously long, smooth neck that just begged to be explored.

That's as may be, but remember, most of the time she's a pain in the ass. Not to mention she's your trainee.

'Alistair,' she started purposefully, and then stopped.

'Claire.' He couldn't help teasing back. He'd never seen her at a loss before and it was deliciously refreshing.

She took in such a deep breath that her breasts rose, stressing the button he was pretty certain sat just above her bra line. Was it delicate sheer lace or plainly utilitarian? It was his experience that plain women often wore the sexiest underwear.

With that mouth, she's hardly plain.

As if on cue, the tip of her tongue peeked out, flicking the bow of her top lip.

His blood leapt.

She cleared her throat. 'I hope you won't take this the wrong way but…'

Trying to look utterly unaffected by her, he cocked one

brow and reminded himself of all the times she'd been critical of him. 'My sensibilities haven't stopped you from giving me your opinion before.'

This time she definitely blushed, but somehow she managed to wrestle her embarrassment under control with dig-
nity. 'True, but that was work. This doesn't exactly fall
into that category. Although I suppose it does technically
if you—'

'You're babbling,' he said, hoping it would force her to
focus. At the same time, he had an absurd and unexpected
need to rescue her from herself.

Her head jerked up so fast he was worried her neck
might snap but then she hit him with a gimlet stare. He
forced himself not to squirm as an unsettling feeling trickled through him. Did she see straight through the man he
liked to show the world? Had she glimpsed the corner edge
of the bubbling mess he kept securely sealed away?

'As the head of the department of neurosurgery,' she said,
tightly, 'I think it's important you lead by example and attend the Spring Fling.'

The Spring Fling? Surely he'd misheard. 'You mean the
neurosurgery spring symposium?'

She shook her head and once again the blush bloomed
on her cheeks. She swallowed and that damn tongue of hers
darted out to moisten her lips. This time as the zip of heat
hit him, he pushed off the bench to try and shake it off.

'I mean the fundraising ball,' she said slowly, as if the
words were being reluctantly pulled out of her.

He couldn't resist. 'Are you inviting me to the ball?'

Her eyes widened in consternation. 'No!' For a moment,
indignation spun around her before fading with a sigh and
a fall of her shoulders. 'I mean perhaps. Yes. In a manner
of speaking.'

His mouth twitched. 'It's good to know you're so decisive.'

Her chin shot up, jabbing the air. 'You can tease me all you like, Mr—Alistair, but you know as well as I do that at the bare minimum there should be a neurosurgery staff table at the ball.'

Damn it to hell. She was absolutely right but how had she found out he wasn't going? He'd been keeping that bit of information to himself, more out of embarrassment than anything else. A couple of months ago, just before Claire had arrived, he'd had a particularly tough day. He'd lost a patient—a two-year-old boy with a brainstem glioma—and for some reason he'd avoided the sympathetic eyes of his staff at the Frog and Peach. He'd hit a trendy bar in Soho instead, and in retrospect, he'd consumed one whisky too many.

It had been enough to scramble his usually accurate *crazy woman* detector. As a result, he'd allowed himself to be tempted by the Amazonian features of Lela. The thirty-year-old was a fitness instructor as well as being a part-time security guard. They'd had a lot of fun together until he'd realised her possessive streak wasn't limited to bedroom games.

He knew the ball committee had flagged the idea of auctioning off the chairs next to eligible bachelors. Usually he'd have been fine with the concept and embraced it, but he'd been worried Lela might turn up and cause a nasty public spectacle. Or worse, buy the ticket. To save himself, and the hospital, embarrassment he'd decided not to attend the ball but to make a sizeable donation to the cause instead. The only person he'd mentioned this plan to was Dominic.

Stupid, stupid, stupid! The paediatric trauma surgeon had obviously broken the bro code and told Victoria. What was it about a man in love that made him prepared to throw his friend under the bus just to stay in sweet with his lady? Now the *i*-dotting and *t*-crossing Claire Mitchell was calling him out on a perceived lack of social etiquette.

He ploughed his hand through his hair. He'd been raised on etiquette, and the irony that an Australian, with their supposedly classless society, was reminding him of his social responsibilities almost made him laugh. Perhaps he could turn this whole Lela-and-the-ball mess around and use it to his advantage.

'Let me get this straight,' he said with a lazy smile. 'You're prepared to spend an evening with me just to make sure I do the right thing?'

This time she was the one to raise an eyebrow. 'As your second-in-command, I can't expect you to attend the ball if I'm not prepared to attend.'

'Ah, yes, that sucker duty gets you every time.'

She stiffened. 'But it seems you're often immune.'

Ouch. Her words tried to scratch him like the sharp tip of a knife, but he didn't need to justify himself to her. He was very well aware of his duty. Ironically, duty had arrived in a rush just after he'd vowed to make the most of every new day that had been gifted to him. It was the juxtaposition of his life.

'None of us are immune, Claire. It's just I try to have a bit of fun too.'

She narrowed her eyes. 'And you're inferring that I don't have fun?'

Not that I've seen. 'Have you had any fun since arriving in London?'

She looked momentarily nonplussed. 'I…um…yes. Of course.'

Liar. But he was planning on having some fun with her right now and killing two birds with one stone. 'Excellent. I can certainly promise you fun at the ball. Especially considering how you've gone above and beyond the call of duty and bought the seat next to me.'

'What?' She paled, her expression momentarily aghast, and then she rallied. 'I don't get paid enough for that.'

'Brutal.' He exaggeratedly slapped his chest in the general area of his heart, his long fingers grazing the lower edge of his pacemaker. 'And here I was thinking I was your date. I tell you what. I'll pay for both of our tickets.'

'That won't be necess—'

'It's the least I can do,' he interrupted, waving away her protest. 'I imagine it was Victoria who dropped you right in it.'

She grimaced. 'You're not wrong there.'

He made a huffing sound more at the absent Dominic than her. 'The good thing is you'll be saving me from having to play nice all evening.'

Effrontery streaked across her face. 'Well, when you put it like that, I can hardly wait,' she said drily.

Her sarcasm was unexpected and delightfully refreshing and he heard himself laugh. He wasn't used to a woman viewing an evening with him as a trial. The women he dated erred on the appreciative side and often went to great lengths to make him happy. Not Claire Mitchell.

A streak of anticipation shot through him. Without realising it, she'd just thrown down a challenge. He wasn't totally convinced she was even capable of having fun and he had a sudden urge to know what she looked like when she was in the midst of a good time.

She'd smile like she did when you let her operate solo. Remember how you felt then?

He disregarded the warning that it was probably unwise to be looking forward to the ball quite this much.

'So will you be picking me—' His phone rang with the ICU ringtone, and as he pulled it from his pocket, Claire's pager beeped.

'North,' he said, answering the call just as Claire mouthed to him, 'ICU?'

Listening to the nurse on the other end of the line, he nodded at Claire and opened the treatment room door. As she walked quickly past him, her crisp scent of the sea drifted back to him and he was suddenly back on Bondi Beach when his life had been simpler and there had been few restraints placed upon it.

'We're on our way,' he told the worried nurse. Stepping out into the corridor, he followed Claire down the fire escape, taking the fastest way to ICU.

CHAPTER FOUR

CLAIRE WALKED OUT of the operating theatre, tugging her mask from her face. Her hand shook so much that her toss missed the bin and she had to stoop to pick up the mask. Even then it took her two more shots to land it.

Get a grip.

'You all right, Dr Mitchell?' Cyril, the night cleaner, asked. Apparently, he'd been working at the castle for forty years and as well as keeping the operating theatre suite clean he took a keen parental interest in the junior staff. 'You look a bit shaky.'

'Nothing a cup of tea won't fix,' she lied breezily, not trusting herself to let his concern touch her. She couldn't afford to fall apart. Not yet anyway. Not when her job was only half finished.

She walked into the doctors' lounge, which at ten in the evening was thankfully empty. She needed and wanted privacy to make this call. Picking up the phone, it took her two attempts to get the number right as her mind kept spinning off and practicing what she was going to say. As the phone rang in her ear, she concentrated on slowing her breathing and her wildly hammering heart.

'Hello,' a sleep-filled voice croaked down the line.

'Louise.' Her voice sounded unsteady and she tried to firm it up. 'It's Claire Mitchell. From the hospital.'

'Claire!' Ryan's mother's voice was instantly alert. 'You're calling me? Oh, my God,' she said half laughing, half crying, 'it's just like the umbrella story. You told me to come home and now you're calling. He's awake, isn't he? Colin, wake up. It's Ryan.'

Claire's stomach lurched so hard she had to force the rising tide of acid back down her throat. 'Louise,' she said firmly but gravely, trying to signal to the woman this call wasn't the positive one she craved. 'Ryan's not awake.'

'What?' She sounded confused. 'Then why are you calling?' she asked angrily.

Claire thought about the desperately ill little boy who was lying surrounded by all the latest medical technology. 'Ryan's condition has deteriorated.'

'No!'

Claire flinched at the pain contained in one small word.

'You said you'd call me if he woke up.' Louise's accusation was loud and clear. In the mother's mind, Claire had broken a promise to her.

'I'm sorry to have to tell you that Ryan's had another bleed. We rushed him to theatre and we've just operated on him.'

'So, this is a just a little setback? He's going to be all right?'

Claire bit her lip so hard she tasted blood. 'Unfortunately, it was a big bleed. It caused his brain to swell and it was necessary to remove a small part of his skull to ease the pressure. It's called a craniotomy.'

'He's got a hole in his head?'

The rising disbelief and trauma in Louise's voice wound through her like poison. 'The bone flap's being stored in a freezer at the hospital until the swelling in Ryan's brain has subsided. When that happens, we can reinsert it.'

'Are you saying that his brain's open to the air? That can't possibly be a good thing.'

'He'll wear a special protective helmet while the bone flap's removed.'

There was a long silence followed by a sharp intake of breath. 'He's not going to have brain damage, is he?'

This was the question Claire always dreaded. 'We won't know the exact situation until the swelling in his brain has diminished.'

'How long will that take?'

'I'm sorry, Louise, but right now I can't say. It's too hard to predict.'

She heard the sound of a duvet being moved and feet hitting the floor. 'Why didn't you see this coming? Why didn't you stop it?'

The words whipped and lashed Claire, playing on her days of misgivings that they were missing something. 'I know this is very hard for you—'

'Hard!' Louise barked down the phone, her voice so loud and outraged that Claire jumped. 'Do you have children, Claire?'

Don't play this game. You'll be the one left bleeding. Even if Louise had been a friend instead of a patient's relative, Claire wouldn't have confessed her one regret. Somehow, by pursuing the toughest medical speciality to prove to herself, Gundiwindi and the world that she was capable and intelligent, she was suddenly thirty-four, alone and with the chance of motherhood rapidly diminishing.

Alistair walked into the lounge and threw her a questioning glance as he cast tea bags into mugs.

Claire turned away from his penetrating gaze, which despite her determined efforts to stay on task had the uncanny ability to derail her concentration every single time. It both bothered and confused her. She'd always been known for her intense focus and her ability to block out all unnecessary distractions. Over the last few years, her consultants had told her that her natural attention to detail was a perfect trait for a neurosurgeon.

No one outside of her family knew that skill wasn't natural at all but borne from necessity and honed by sheer determination and bloody-mindedness. It rarely let her down. Even during what she'd considered the 'heady days' with Michael, when she'd thought he loved her, her focus hadn't faltered. However, under the assault of Alistair North's clear, iron-ore-grey eyes, it wobbled precariously.

'Louise,' she said, centring her thoughts. 'Ryan's being transferred back to ICU now. When you and your husband arrive at the hospital, Mr North and I will be here to answer all your questions. Just ask the staff to page us.'

She finished the call and slowly lowered the receiver onto the cradle. She knew she should stand up but she wasn't certain her shaking legs would hold her.

'Tough call,' Alistair commented as he opened the fridge.

'I've had better.'

'Do you take milk and sugar in your tea?'

Despite her surprise at his offer, her head fell back to rest on the couch as exhaustion caught up with her. 'Just milk.'

'You look like you could do with some sugar.'

She suddenly craved something sweet. 'Do you have chocolate?'

'Surely in the six weeks you've been here you've learned that any chocolate that enters this room vanishes in five minutes.' He rummaged through the cupboards and then gave an unexpected woot, holding up a red-and-black box. 'Will chilli and chocolate shortbread suffice?'

She had a ridiculous and overwhelming urge to cry at his unanticipated thoughtfulness. 'Awesome.'

He walked over to her carrying two mugs of tea and balancing the box of biscuits on the top of one of the mugs. 'Here you go.'

There was no sign of the teasing playboy or the supercilious consultant. In her overwrought state, she couldn't make sense of the change and that troubled her. She stuck to what she knew best: work. 'We should have done that MRI.'

Her words tumbled out loaded with blame. 'We should have done more. We caused this.'

'Hey,' he said, his grey eyes suddenly stern. 'We did not cause this. We both operated on him and we both saw exactly the same thing. This bleed was hidden by the original haematoma. That's why it wasn't showing up on the scans. On the plus side, if he'd bled anywhere else instead of in ICU, he'd probably be dead.'

Culpability pummelled her so hard it hurt and she was unable to control her belligerent tone. 'How is that supposed to make me feel better? He wouldn't have been in hospital if it weren't for the fire. We're supposed to pre-empt disasters like this. Now he's sicker than when he arrived.'

'Not necessarily,' Alistair said with frustrating logic and calm. 'The craniotomy gives him the possibility of recovery. We've done everything we can to give him a chance at the best possible outcome.' His face softened into friendly lines. 'I know this sucks, but it's just one of those god-awful things that happen sometimes.'

'I don't accept that,' she said so emphatically her hand jerked. Hot tea spilled over the rim and onto her skin. 'Ouch!'

He immediately removed the mug from her hand. 'I'll get you some ice. Meanwhile, open wide.' He shoved a shortbread into her mouth.

For reasons she couldn't fathom, she'd done as he'd asked and obediently opened her mouth. Now, more out of surprise than anything else, she bit into the soft, buttery, chocolate goodness and embraced the kick of chilli. It shocked her senses in a much-needed way and she wiped her tea-covered hand on her scrub. A large red welt with a white centre rose fast on the base of her thumb accompanied by a furious sting. Wearing surgical gloves was going to hurt for the next few days.

Alistair returned with an icepack wrapped in a red-and-white-checked tea towel. His large hand folded the pack around hers and the burn of the ice tangoed with the burn of his hand. He lifted her left hand and placed it over the pack. 'Hold that there for ten minutes.'

'Thanks.' Irrational tears threatened again along with an equally irrational sense of loss as he removed his hand. *What the hell was wrong with her?*

'Shortbread sugar starting to hit?' Alistair asked, his brow furrowed with mild concern.

Not really. Her head was spinning and she felt strangely adrift and utterly drained. It was as if a decade of fatigue had just sideswiped her. She'd been working so hard and for so long doing everything on her own, proving she was as good as or better than her peers, and fighting harder than anyone to stay on top that she wasn't used to anyone looking out for her. Right now, nothing was making sense, especially this version of Alistair who was being remarkably kind.

Her entire body sagged heavily and it took almost more effort than she had to keep herself upright. She had a ludicrous urge to drop her head onto his shoulder and take shelter there, sleeping for a week.

Have you completely lost your mind? You're at work. He's your boss and just no. *Got that?*

Aghast that her jumbled thoughts had somehow managed to get to this point, she tried squaring her shoulders in an attempt to summon up her professional decorum. Not once in her career had she ever lost control at work and tonight wasn't the time to start—especially not in front of Alistair North. No, the moment the ten minutes was up, she'd stow the ice pack in the freezer, bid Alistair a crisp goodnight and head home to bed for a much-needed sleep. Everything would make sense again after a good night's sleep.

And if it doesn't?

She'd worry about that if and when it happened.

Alistair rubbed the back of his neck, slightly bewildered and definitely disconcerted by this version of Claire Mitchell sitting next to him on the couch. Her reaction to what had been a routine craniotomy was out of proportion and out of character. When he'd first met her, he'd picked her as being meticulous, ambitious and with a 'take no prisoners' approach to work. It wasn't that she didn't care—she was indeed empathetic—but she always put the medicine first. Surely Ryan Walker's unexpected deterioration couldn't have been the first time she'd been faced with an unanswerable medical conundrum?

Whatever it was, it was obvious it had upset her greatly. As her consultant, it was his job to help her work through it. But how? He sipped his tea and pondered the matter until a possible solution came to him.

'Would it help if we took Ryan's case to peer review? I doubt they'll disagree with our treatment plan but the process will reassure you that we did everything we could.'

'Peer review doesn't have to deal with Ryan's parents,' she said, her voice cracking. Her shoulders slumped. 'Louise Walker hates me.'

Ah. So Claire Mitchell wasn't just about protocol and paperwork after all. Underneath her automaton tendencies and prickly exterior existed a regular person. For whatever reason, something about Ryan's case had got under her skin. He knew all about that. At some point in every doctor's career, one patient would touch them more than the others. 'Louise Walker is a terrified mother.'

'I know.'

Her eyes, now as round as huge saucers of warm caramel, looked at him. He got an unanticipated urge to dive right in. *That won't help matters. You don't really like her.* Baffled, he blinked and then as his vision came back into focus he saw her beseeching distress urging him to understand.

'I made Louise leave the hospital today. I insisted on it.'

He rushed to reassure her and at the same time get himself back on solid ground. 'And rightly so. The woman was exhausted.'

Her fingers plucked at invisible balls of lint on her scrubs. 'She made me promise to call her if Ryan woke up.'

Worry pulled tightly behind his eyes. 'Promises are always fraught...'

Her chin, which he'd noticed tended to tilt up sharply whenever she felt under attack, barely lifted. 'I'm not a novice.'

'No.'

'And of course I'd have called her if Ryan woke up. It was hardly an unprofessional assurance.'

Suddenly, his veil of confusion lifted. With piercing clarity, he saw exactly where this was going. He felt for her—he really did. 'When you rang Louise just before, she thought—'

'That I had the first piece of good news in two weeks.' She sucked her lips in tight and blinked rapidly. It wasn't enough to prevent a tear escaping and running down her cheek beyond the reach of her glasses. She crooked the forefinger of her uninjured hand and brushed it away.

Bloody hell. Unlike a lot of men who froze in the presence of a distressed woman, he was always moved to assist, which was why he'd already made his registrar a cup of tea. But now, seeing the usually stitched-up and almost too-together Claire Mitchell falling apart in front of him sent a visceral spike of pain into him, cramping his gut. 'Why didn't you ask me to make the call?'

Her free hand curled into a tight fist and her chin dropped towards her chest. 'You were very clear about it being my job.'

'Bloody hell, Claire,' he said softly, the words coming out on a puff of air. He felt like the worst boss in the world. 'I don't understand. You've queried me and judged my opinions more than once in the past few weeks. Why on earth did you decide this telephone call was the *one* thing you weren't going to question?'

'All I know,' she said so softly he needed to strain to listen, 'is that I've destroyed Louise Walker. I've made her pain ten times worse.'

Her head rose and her woebegone expression ate into him like acid on paper. It was as natural as breathing to put a hand on her shoulder. 'You haven't destroyed her,' he said quietly.

Her head fell forward onto his shoulder and he patted her gently on the back. 'Deep down you know that. You're just having a rough night.'

She made a muffled noise that sounded half like denial and half like a hiccough. He smiled at the very normal snorting sound coming from someone he'd thought kept a wide distance between work and her emotions. He found himself stroking her hair, the fine strands like silk against his palm. With her head now resting under his chin, the scent of cinnamon and apples drifted upwards.

Memories flooded back—a large homey kitchen warmed by the continually heating Aga, the beatific, round face of Cook and the aroma of brown sugar and butter. Everything he associated with the comfort of childhood was centred on that kitchen. Not once in his wildest dreams had he ever imagined it wouldn't always be there waiting for him when he returned home from boarding school. Twenty-six years had passed and he still missed it.

Claire raised her head, her cheeks blotchy and her eyes red-rimmed. Her gaze was fixed doggedly on the wet patch on his shirt and her small hand patted it as if the action was enough to dry it. 'Oh, God. I'm so sorry.'

The pads of her fingers warmed his skin through the fine cotton. 'No need to apologise,' he said, intending to sound hearty and encouraging, but the words came out husky as if he was suffering from a cold. 'Worse things have happened to my shirts.'

'The thing is, I've never done anything like this at work before.' She sounded utterly poleaxed. 'You must think I'm a total basket case.'

'No.' He knew he should say more. He should tell her that everyone has a bad day occasionally, that doctors are human too, and some cases have a deeper impact than others. But her heat was weaving through him and creating so much havoc that he was having trouble remembering his own name, let alone articulating anything beyond a single syllable. In a desperate attempt to regain his equilibrium, he caught her hand, encasing it in his, stopping her jerky strokes.

She stilled for a moment and stared at his white hand covering her tanned one and then, slowly, she lifted her face to his. Her liquid eyes were a mirror to her embarrassment, confusion and sorrow. Once again, he wanted to make her feel better, because anyone who worked in medicine had spent time in that dismal place and it was dangerous to linger there too long. He was about to say, 'Tomorrow's another day,' when he glimpsed something indefinable beyond the chaotic swirl of emotions. The shadows told him it wasn't new. In fact, it had the intransigent look of an indelible stain that no amount of soap, salt or methylated spirits could remove.

Was it doubt? Fear? Inadequacy? *Surely not.* But whatever it was, it hit him hard in the solar plexus and held on tight like a lasso. *Whatever it is, it's wrong. It shouldn't be part of her. It doesn't belong there.*

The need to vanquish this malignant thing and banish it from her eyes—from her soul—pulled him down towards her. His lips touched her damp cheek in a consoling kiss and the tang of salt zipped into him. He was about to pull back when her head turned and suddenly his mouth was softly touching those plump, ruby-red lips. They were soft and tear-cooled. He tasted the heady essence of bergamot.

Stop now.

He was about to pull back when her lips opened infinitesimally. He was immediately rushed by the unexpected spicy zap of chilli. Hot. Sizzling. One hundred per cent aroused woman. His breath left his lungs and for a moment he was rendered utterly still, unable to think, move or feel.

The tip of her tongue flicked against his lips so lightly and so quickly that his brain couldn't decide if it had even happened or if he was imagining it. But his body knew. Good God, it knew. He dropped his arms to her waist and hauled her in against him before opening his mouth and welcoming her in.

She came to him without a moment's hesitation, filling him completely. Her tongue explored, her teeth nipped, her heat and flavours exploded through him until he was nothing but a river of pulsating sensation. Her free hand wound its way through his hair, her fingers digging into his scalp as if she needed to hold on to something to keep herself tethered to earth.

He understood exactly. Kissing her was like being in free fall. He returned her kiss with one of his own—deep, thorough and practiced until he heard a low guttural moan coming from Claire. Usually that sound made him smile and reinforced not only that he knew exactly what he was doing but that he was the one in total control.

Not this time.

His usual measured composure with women was unravelling faster than a skein of wool in the paws of a cat. He had the strangest awareness that somehow she'd turned the tables on him completely. What had started out as a quick and reassuring kiss to console her was now a kiss that was stripping him of the protective layers he'd spent five years cementing into place.

Break the kiss. Now. Right now.

But his body overruled him again, craving what was on offer and seizing it like a drowning man grips a life preserver. He slid the utilitarian black band from her ponytail, and as her hair fell to her shoulders in a sun-kissed cascade, it released its treasured aroma of spices and apples. Golden strands caressed his face and he breathed deeply. Claire's sweet behind was now in his lap—he had no idea if he'd pulled her there, if she'd climbed in or if it was a bit of both. It didn't matter. All that mattered was here, now and her.

Her hand cupped the back of his neck, her fingers splayed. His hand, which had been gripping her hip, now slid under the loose top of her scrubs. His palm instantly tingled as it touched warm, smooth skin. He spider-walked his fingers along her spine, absorbing every rise and dip until he reached the wide strap of her bra.

He'd never considered any piece of lingerie a challenge—more like an inconvenient barrier that he dismantled easily every time. His fingers rested on the hooks and he was just about to flick and twist when Claire ripped her hand out of his and hauled her mouth from his lips. It all happened so fast that he shivered from the loss of her intoxicating heat.

Her lips, now bee-sting pouty and puffy from kissing and being kissed, gave her a sexy aura he'd never suspected even existed underneath her uptight personality. But despite how deliciously alluring it made her, it was the way her mussed hair fell softly, framing her face that got to him. It made her look younger than her years. She suddenly seemed fragile and vulnerable as if she expected the world as she knew it to end any second.

In that instant, he knew the exact direction her thoughts had taken. He was her boss and she was his trainee. Hospitals had rules about this sort of thing to protect both parties from sexual harassment charges. Without meaning to, they'd both fallen over the line together, but there was no power play happening on either side. He'd stake his life she was as surprised as he was that the kiss had even happened.

'It's okay, Claire,' he said, wanting to put her at ease, but his voice was rough, raspy and the antithesis of soothing.

'Okay?' Her voice rose with incredulity and her beautiful eyes reflected her turmoil. In a flurry of uncoordinated movements, which included her knee pressing into his inner thigh, she scrambled out of his lap as fast as if he was on fire and she was about to go up in flames too. The entire time she kept her arms outstretched in front of her as if she was scared he was going to try and touch her.

'I... This... It.' Her left hand covered her mouth for a moment before falling away. 'Nothing about any of this is okay.'

Still dazed from her kisses and with the majority of his circulating volume residing in his lap, he struggled to move beyond the basic functions of his reptilian brain. He tried a second time to reassure her. 'I meant, we're both adults.' He shrugged. 'Things happen.'

She shook her head so hard and fast that her hair whipped around her head in a golden wave. '*Nothing* happened.' Her voice trembled along with the rest of her. 'Do you understand? Absolutely nothing.'

As his blood pounded thickly through his body defying her words, both their pages beeped. The sound stopped Claire's flight to the door. 'Oh, no. The Walkers are here.'

'Right.' His voice sounded a long way away as his body lurched from lust to logic and the doctor overrode the man. Hell, he needed some time. 'I'll meet you in ICU in five minutes.'

Relief and embarrassment tugged at her cheeks. 'Yes. Good. Fine. I'll be there.' She disappeared into the corridor.

Well, that went well, Alistair. Blowing out a long, slow breath he rubbed his face with his hands and tried to fathom how something so incredible had ended so badly.

CHAPTER FIVE

'DECAF THIS MORNING, please, Tony.'

The friendly barista shot her a disbelieving look. 'Is not coffee, *mia bella*.'

She gave him an apologetic shrug. 'Please.' The last thing she needed was caffeine. It was barely seven and she was running on adrenaline. Her heart pounded, her chest was so tight breathing felt like lifting weights, she was as jumpy as a cat and she felt the telltale burn of reflux. That was always the stress marker.

Occasionally, when she thought work was going well, she'd be surprised to get the liver-tip pain telling her that her body wasn't as calm as her mind. Today, she didn't need her medical degree to know the exact cause of her extreme agitation. She'd relived the reason over and over and over last night until exhaustion had somehow managed to claim her, providing a few hours of fitful sleep.

She'd woken with a start to a foggy dawn and the weight of reality crushing down on her so hard and heavy she was surprised she wasn't lying on the floor. Real life had decisively ended a wonderful dream where she'd felt unusually safe and secure. A utopia where she'd been able to be herself without the constant and nagging worry that someone was going to find out that despite all her hard work she was always only one step away from failing. Those tantalisingly peaceful feelings had vanished a second after she'd woken. Tranquillity had been torpedoed by the visual of her nestled in Alistair North's lap, kissing him like he was the last man standing after the apocalypse.

She'd jumped her boss. *Oh, God, oh, God, oh, God.*

Hours later, she still wasn't totally certain how it had happened.

Oh, come on. Be honest. Bottom line, you abandoned your principles, you opened your mouth and took what you wanted. You sucked Alistair North's marrow into you like he was oxygen.

She barely recognised the woman she'd been last night, and she knew if it had been an option, she'd have climbed inside the man. Never before had she let go like that, giving up all thought and reason, and existing only for the streaming sensations of bliss that had consumed her. It was if she'd been drawing her life force from him. She'd certainly never kissed anyone with such intensity before.

You've never been kissed like that before.

Her mind retreated from the thought so fast she almost gave herself whiplash. Truth be told, despite her thirty-four years, her kissing experience was fairly limited. During her teenage years, her brother's footy mates had considered her far too bookish and reserved to bother trying to kiss and her peers thought she was weird for studying so hard, so when she'd left Gundiwindi bound for Adelaide Uni, she'd been a kissing virgin as well as a sexual one.

It had only taken one medical students' society party to remedy the kissing situation. She'd discovered that having a tongue shoved unceremoniously down her throat by a drunk second year had been enough. Then and there she'd determined to wait until she met someone who, A, she actually liked and, B, had some experience and panache in the art of kissing.

Michael had literally walked into her life five years later

when she'd been hiking the Milford Track in the spectacular South Island of New Zealand. After two days spent laughing and talking together, and with him proffering the occasional hand to balance her as she crossed creeks and clambered over fallen trees, he'd kissed her on the sandy shore of Milford Sound with the backdrop of the indomitable Mitre Peak.

It had been the most romantic thing she'd ever experienced. For a while, all of Michael's romantic gestures had deluded her into thinking she was worthy of love after all. When the cracks started appearing, the more she worked to shore them up, the worse things had got. His parting words still haunted her. *You're too hard to love, Claire.*

Her alarm had chosen that moment to shrill, pulling her thoughts sharply and blessedly away from the past and dragging them firmly into the present. She'd run to the shower and left the flat half an hour later, walking directly to Tony's in the ubiquitous London mist.

The barista handed her the usual half dozen coffees pressed snugly into their cardboard carrier along with one extra. 'What's this?' she asked as her left hand wrapped around the single cup.

'A proper latte, *doctore*.'

'But, Tony, I wanted decaf.'

He tapped the cup with a *D* scrawled on it. 'Is here. But you drink it and I know you wish you get your usual.'

'Thanks.' He wasn't to know that if she were any more wired she'd shatter. She handed over some pound notes but he waved them away. 'The doctors at the castle, they fix my Serena when she born with her bad foot. Sick *bambinos* need the hospital. I happy to help.'

'That's very generous of you. I know the protestors on the night shift appreciate your coffee.'

She heard the gentle clearing of a throat behind her— the British equivalent of *Hurry up*.

'Bye, Tony.'

'*Ciao, bella.* You have a good day, yes.'

A good day. Oh, yeah. It was going to be one for the ages. More than anything she wanted a time machine so she could return to last night and change everything that had happened, starting with preventing little Ryan Walker from having a large brain bleed. At least the gods were on her side today in as much as it wasn't an operating day. The thought of having to stand next to Alistair—*Mr North, Mr North, Mr North.*

You're kidding yourself if you think using his title is going to give you any protection.

It's all I've got.

That and hiding from him as much as possible. Only she knew hiding was a pipe dream. The whole point of her scholarship was to work hand in glove with the man and learn as much from him as she possibly could. Last night, she'd left the hospital the moment the difficult interview with the Walkers was concluded. In fact, she'd been the first one to leave, with a brisk goodnight to her consultant in front of the distraught parents, blocking any chance of him saying anything to her about the kiss.

The only reprieve she had today was that straight after rounds he was working from home, preparing his paper for the neurosurgery symposium.

Yesterday morning when she'd read that entry in the electronic diary, she'd rolled her eyes. In not unexpected fashion, he'd left it pretty much to the last minute to get it done. If she'd been presenting a paper, she'd have had it fully edited, bound and memorised a week ahead of time because medicine had a habit of throwing curve balls. All it took was a couple of emergencies or some staff illness to throw out a timeline. She always padded her deadlines with a lot of wriggle room, as much to allow for her own set of learning challenges as well as for external ones.

Today, however, there was no eye rolling at Alis— Mr North's laid-back procrastination, only unbridled relief. It meant the only time she had to see him today was at the ICU and Koala Ward rounds. Given they'd be surrounded by staff and students and their focus would be on patient care, how hard could that be? He was hardly going to say anything to her about last night in front of everyone and she sure as hell wasn't going to mention it. Not now. Not ever. In regards to last night, her plan was to pretend and subsequently believe that it had *never* happened. She could only hope that Mr North felt the same.

Lost so deeply in her thoughts, she was surprised to find she'd arrived at the hospital. As she distributed the coffees, she made sure to mention to everyone they were a donation from Tony's Trattoria. Chatting with the protesters and learning more and more stories about the legacy of the castle was fast becoming a favourite part of her day and she listened with delighted fascination. A woman was telling a tale about her grandfather who'd been a surgeon during the Second World War. Claire was so busy listening to how he'd risked his own life to save others by operating in the basement of the hospital during the Blitz that she lost all sense of time.

Hearing someone's watch chime the hour, she gasped. *Late!* She hurriedly excused herself, ran through the gates, pelted up the D wing stairs, flung herself through the door and arrived on Koala Ward a panting and gasping mess.

Andrew Bailey gave her a wide-eyed look. 'You okay?'

She was desperately short of breath but she dug deep and summoned up a husky 'Fine' as she tried to fill her lungs with air. At the same time, she worked on quelling the rising tide of frantic dread that threatened to swamp her like a massive wave at Coogee. Being a few minutes late for rounds with a consultant who considered ten minutes after the hour as being 'on time' wasn't an issue. Being twenty minutes later than her usual arrival time was a disaster. It meant she had no time to read and memorise the overnight reports. It meant she'd be flying blind during rounds.

Panicked, she rounded on her house officer. 'Have you read the reports?'

'Was I supposed to?' Andrew asked, half bemused and half confused. 'I thought that was the point of rounds.'

Still trying to catch her breath, she huffed loudly and caught the injured look in her generally congenial junior's eyes. He was absolutely correct—for most people that was the case. 'True, but it never hurts to be ahead of the game and impress the consultant.'

A grin broke across his round face. 'Is that why you're here early most days?'

She dodged the truth with the skill of a secret keeper. 'Something like that.'

The rumble of many feet against the linoleum floor made her turn. Alistair North was striding along the corridor with the nurse unit manager and the nursing and medical students hurrying along behind.

Claire pressed her glasses up her nose and blinked. Alistair North didn't ever wear a white coat but he generally wore one of what she'd come to realise was a selection of fine wool Italian suits. Generally, he started the day in a jacket and tie, although the ties were never serious. They were almost always prints of animated characters from kids' TV shows, which the little patients loved. Claire's favourite ties were from a fundraising range sold by the castle's auxiliary. Some clever clogs had come up with the idea of printing the children's drawings of doctors, nurses and auxiliary staff onto silk. She particularly liked the one of a doctor wearing a head torch and a big smile.

Just admit it. You like that one because it's Alistair.

Not if my life depended on it.

By late afternoon most days, he was seen on the ward

in scrubs, or if it was a non-operating day, he'd have discarded the jacket and tie. An open-necked business shirt was as casual as she'd ever seen him, but today there was no sign of a suit, nor smart casual weekend wear or even jeans. He was striding towards them wearing a T-shirt that stretched across his wide chest and perfectly outlined the rise and fall of his pectoral muscles. The shirt read *Epilepsy Warrior Run*. Her gaze instinctively dropped.

Damn. No compression tights.

Shut up! She hated the zip of disappointment that wove through her that the rest of his body wasn't delineated in fine detail by tight fabric. His running shorts, however, only came to mid-thigh, giving her plenty of opportunity to admire his taut quads.

Look up, look up, look up.

'Morning, Mitchell. Bailey,' he said with his usual nod of greeting. 'Missed the two of you at boot camp this morning.'

'Boot camp, sir?' Andrew said faintly. The rotund house officer wore the look of one who went to great lengths to avoid any sort of physical pursuit.

'Yes, Bailey. All Koala Ward staff are participating in the Epilepsy Warrior fun run. Morag—' he turned to the highly efficient unit nurse manager '—you sent the diary entry to everyone about this morning's training session?'

'Of course,' she said briskly in her thick Scottish brogue.

Claire pulled out her phone and immediately saw the reminder on her screen. Her stomach fell through the floor. She'd been so obsessed by the fact she'd landed in Alistair's lap last night and tickled his tonsils that she'd totally forgotten about boot camp.

Andrew's face drained of colour. 'Surely someone needs to be on duty on—' he read the black and purple writing on his boss's T-shirt '—the tenth. Happy to volunteer, sir.'

'Already got that covered, Bailey,' Alistair said in a tone

that brooked no argument. He swung his clear sea-grey gaze to Claire.

Be professional. She clenched her fists and willed herself not to drop her gaze. Willed herself to act as if this was just a regular morning instead of the one after her worst ever career folly. Memories of last night—of the way his eyes and then his mouth had fixed on hers—rolled back in, foaming and bubbling like a king tide.

Let it go. It didn't happen.

Oh, but it did. She had the sweet and tender bruises on her lips to prove it.

Now, faced with all six foot of him standing there in front of her wearing athletic gear and with the scent of his cologne invading her senses, it was increasingly difficult to focus on her plan to banish every delicious thing that had happened between them. *Remember the embarrassment. Remember he's your boss. That will do the trick every time.*

'It's not like you to forget an appointment, Mitchell,' he said, using her surname in the British public school way as he did occasionally. 'It's important we all attend for team spirit,' he added politely.

Despite the well-modulated parameters of his very British accent, she heard the unmistakable tone of an order. Was this his way of saying that he agreed with her that last night was an aberration? That it was a shocking mistake they both needed to forget and move on from? That it was over and done with and she needed to remember that the cohesion of the workplace team always came ahead of everything?

Please let it be so. 'We won't let you down again,' she said brightly. She sent up a plea that Alistair had caught her double meaning and knew that she understood they were both on the same page about last night. 'We're looking forward to the next boot camp, aren't we, Andrew?'

Andrew stared at her as if she'd completely lost her mind. 'Wouldn't miss it,' he said glumly.

Alistair grinned and clapped his hands together once. 'Excellent. Let's start rounds.'

As they walked towards the first bay, Morag handed Claire a tablet computer. Archie McGregor's medical history was open on the screen, but before she could silently read the first sentence, Alistair was saying, 'Lead off, Dr Mitchell.'

Eight sets of eyes swung her way. Even before her mouth had dried, her tongue had thickened and her throat had threatened to close, the words on the screen had jumbled into an incomprehensible mess. Long ago voices boomed in her head, deafening her.

Moron. That girl's a sandwich short of a picnic.

Panic eddied out from her gut and into her veins, stealing her concentration. She broke out in a cold sweat. Her greatest fear, which lurked constantly inside her and was never far from the surface, surged up to choke her. *You knew you'd get found out one day. This is it.*

No! She'd fought too hard for it to end like this. She'd set up strategies so this situation would never happen to her and she wasn't about to let years of sacrifice go to waste and have it fall apart now. Not here in London where it was too easy for people to make cheap shots at her being a colonial. Not when she was the recipient of one of the most prestigious scholarships on offer for neurosurgery. Not when she was so close to qualifying.

Think!

'Actually,' she said, shoving the tablet at her junior houseman with a hand that trembled. 'Archie is Dr Bailey's patient. He admitted him overnight.'

Andrew, who'd accepted the tablet without question, glanced at the screen. 'Archie McGregor, age seven, admitted last night post-seizure and with suspected juvenile myoclonic epilepsy. Observations stable overnight and...'

Claire wanted to relax and blow out the breath that was

stalled tightly in her chest but she didn't have any time to spare. As Andrew was fielding a battery of questions from Alistair, she was trying to calmly and surreptitiously read the next patient's history.

An hour later she was helping herself to a delicious currant bun from the nurses' breakfast platter. As she bit into the sticky sweetness, she gave thanks that she'd not only narrowly avoided disaster, she'd also survived the round. Alistair had appeared happy with both her and Andrew's treatment plans and now, emergencies excepted, her boss was gone for the day. She was thankfully home free. She had some medication charts to write up, some test results to read and then, fingers crossed, she was going to take advantage of the relative calm and spend some time in the library studying.

'Oh, good.' A very familiar voice rumbled around her, its timbre as rich and smooth as a Barossa Valley cabernet sauvignon. 'There you are.'

Shock stuck the sticky bun to the roof of her mouth and she tried desperately to dislodge it with a slurp of tea. The hot liquid went down the wrong way and she coughed violently, trying to get her breath. The next minute, Alistair's face was pushed in close to hers with his brows pulled down sharply.

'Can you get air?'

She shook her head but he misunderstood and the next minute the side of his hand sliced down between her shoulder blades like a karate chop. The snaps on her bra bit into her skin. 'Ouch.'

'Good,' he said, cheerfully reappearing back in front of her. 'I need you alive today.'

'Just today?' she said waspishly as the tangy scent of his sweat hit her nostrils. She worked hard at resisting the urge to breathe in deeply. 'I rather like being alive every day.'

'As do I. Live every day as if it's your last.'

She took a careful sip of tea. 'I've often found people who say that use it as an excuse to be selfish.'

His smile faded and a line of tension ran along his jaw, disappearing up behind his ear. 'That's a very jaundiced view of humanity.'

She welcomed the familiar antagonism vibrating between them and relaxed into it, giving thanks that everything was back to normal. 'Not at all. It's merely an observation about how some people live their lives with little thought or regard for how their actions impact on others.'

His eyes darkened and he looked as if he was about to say something when he suddenly helped himself to a currant bun. She was oddly disappointed that he wasn't going to take the discussion further. Sparring in a robust debate with Alistair North was far safer than confiding in him.

Or kissing him.

She suddenly felt stranded standing there in the small pantry. She was far too aware of him and how his mouth, which had savoured hers so thoroughly last night, was now relishing the currant bun. Too aware of how his tight behind was pressed hard against the bench and how his long, running-fit legs stretched out in front of him. She suddenly wanted to invoke the staff dress code she'd been lectured on during her orientation program.

He raised his hand to his mouth and one by one he meticulously licked the sugar from the bun off his fingers. She swallowed a gasp as her body clenched and then sighed in delight. The memory of how he tasted was burned on her brain—spicy with a hint of citrus zip. And hot. Oh-so-flaming hot.

I thought the kiss never happened so why are we doing this?

She cleared her throat. 'I best go and write up the medication changes.'

'Bailey can do that.'

'Excuse me?'

He pushed off the bench. 'Get Bailey to do the medication changes and chase up the test results. I've got some far more interesting work for you.'

A skitter of excitement whipped through her. There'd been a rumour going around that a charity in India was making overtures to the castle in regards to separating a set of conjoined twins. Being part of the multidisciplinary team from the planning stages through to the massive operation and postoperative care would be the chance of a lifetime.

'Oh?' she said, far more casually than she felt.

'We're giving a paper at the spring symposium.'

A streak of surprise was followed by a trickle of dread. 'We?' She hated that it came out on a squeak.

He nodded. 'It's the tradition across all the medical departments that the specialist registrar in his or her last year of their fellowship always gives a joint presentation with their consultant.' He scratched his head and his brow furrowed. 'Did I not mention this to you when you first arrived?'

No! 'You did not,' she said, trying to sound calm. The dread was now spinning her stomach and sending out wave upon wave of nausea. 'This is the first I've heard of it.'

'Oh, well, not to worry,' he said with a grin that held a modicum of contrition. 'Lucky it's quiet so we should meet tomorrow's deadline.'

'Tomorrow.' Her screech of disbelief could have given a sulphur-crested cockatoo a run for its money. 'But the symposium's still weeks away.'

'The papers are due tomorrow. The admin staff need time to print and bind them and prepare the handouts for the attendees.'

'We can't write a paper in a day.' She hated the squeak in her voice.

'Of course we can,' he said with all the easy confidence of someone who'd never had to think twice about reading or writing. 'Some of the best papers I've ever written have happened at that adrenaline-fuelled last-minute deadline.' Memories filled his handsome face. 'It's such a buzz to pull an all-nighter and finish as the fingers of dawn are lighting up the city.'

The very idea made her gag. 'That's not the way I work,' she countered, desperately clutching at straws. 'I mean, we don't even have a topic.'

'Of course we've got a topic,' he said, sounding amused. 'I wouldn't do that to you.'

'I guess I should be thankful for small mercies,' she said sarcastically.

'I'm sorry it slipped my mind, Claire. Your predecessor, Harry Banks, was supposed to write the paper, but as you know, he left us the moment things started looking rocky for the castle.' His face filled with kindness. 'I'm aware you like things to be ordered and just so, but believe me, stepping out of your comfort zone every now and then makes you feel alive.'

Oh. My. God. He was serious. He honestly thought he was doing her a favour. Her heart thumped so hard she was sure he must hear it. 'What's the topic?' she asked weakly.

His face lit up. 'Epilepsy surgery's the most effective way to control seizures in patients with drug-resistant focal epilepsy. I've got all the data. It's just a matter of assembling it and stringing it together with some well-chosen case studies. Don't panic. Most people prefer to attend the summer symposium on the Continent. The spring one's the smallest of the three. Think of it as a test run. If the paper's well received there, we can work it up into something bigger for *The Lancet*. Too easy.' He laughed. 'Isn't that what you Aussie's like to say?'

'Something like that,' she said faintly. The task he was

asking her to undertake would be a significant one for most people, but for her the short time frame made it monumentally huge. Hopefully, she could find a quiet corner in the library where she could spread out the data and work her way through it slowly and methodically. 'I guess I better make a start, then.'

'Excellent.' He gave her warm smile. 'Give me fifteen minutes to grab a quick shower and then meet me in my office.'

No, no, no! Working alongside Alistair risked exposing her secret and she'd do anything to prevent that from happening. With a decisive movement that said *all business*, she pushed her glasses up her nose. 'I'll work in the library.'

He tilted his head and gave her a long and questioning look. Somehow, despite feeling like a desert plant wilting under the intense scrutiny of summer noontime heat, she managed to hold his gaze.

'It makes far more sense to work in my office,' he said, breaking the long silence. 'All the data's on my computer and there'll be far fewer interruptions and distractions there.'

Fewer distractions? She stifled a groan. Her much-needed day of physical distance from Alistair North had just imploded and sucked her down with it. Now, she faced spending the working day with him in the close confines of his office. Every breath she took would carry his musky scent. The air around her would vibrate with his bounding energy and any inadvertent brush of shoulders or hands, which invariably happened when two people worked in close proximity, would only serve to remind her how amazing the strength of his toned muscles and the tautness of his skin had felt last night under her hands.

All of it was one enormous distraction, but in relative terms, her irrational attraction was the least of her worries. Her biggest problem was the challenge of hiding the fact she found data analysis and large writing tasks difficult. Under extreme pressure, it was almost impossible. If her boss discovered that, it could jeopardise her scholarship. She swallowed hard. There was only one solution—she had to get creative and make sure he never discovered her secret.

CHAPTER SIX

ALISTAIR STRODE ALONG Praed Street carrying a plastic bag containing take-away containers of Tandoori Chicken, Rogan Josh, curried vegetables and naan bread. The pungent aromas of the food made his stomach juices run and he picked up the pace. So much for a quiet day—he hadn't even managed lunch and he couldn't wait to tuck into the spicy delights.

It was eight in the evening and he'd been away from the office for hours. He hadn't intended for that to happen. In fact, when Dominic MacBride had telephoned at ten interrupting his writing day, he'd told him that a policy and procedures meeting didn't come under the banner of life or death. Today that was the only criteria that would get him to leave the office.

It was Claire who'd insisted he attend the meeting and raise the issue of referral waiting times. All had been dangerously pushed out since the staffing levels at the hospital had been decimated. 'The board needs to know their current actions are risking lives. I'd go but they won't listen to me. You've got FRCS after your name so surely that gives you more clout.'

'I doubt they can see past the dollar signs,' he'd said with a sigh, 'but you're right. It's worth a shot.'

He and Dominic had spent a frustrating few hours getting nowhere with the board and he'd been on his way back to the office when Morag called. 'Sorry, Alistair, but the Walkers are asking to see you. They're insisting upon it.'

He'd gone direct to ICU and the afternoon had rolled away from him as he'd dealt with a variety of issues. Truth be told, he should have called Bailey in to deal with most of them as they came under the banner of house officer jobs, but he'd been feeling generous. He could still remember how fraught life was as a junior doctor so he'd reinserted a central line and performed a lumbar puncture. He'd rather enjoyed the hands-on medicine, although that hadn't prevented a slight flicker of guilt that his largesse was a form of procrastination. As much as he disliked statistics, he knew he should be back in the office helping Claire with the difficult job instead of leaving her on her own to deal with it.

Given how horrified she'd both looked and sounded when she'd learned about the project, he'd been expecting to hear the return of her clipped and critical tones along with a lecture on time management each time he'd called her to notify her of yet another delay. However, on all three occasions all she'd said was, 'No worries. These things happen. Things are going well at this end.'

Ten minutes ago, just as he'd been paying for what he'd planned to be their dinner, she'd sent him a text.

No need to return to the office. Job done. Enjoy your evening.

He'd read it twice, trying to absorb the surprising and oddly dismaying text. He couldn't believe she'd finished the paper so quickly and without his help. Then again, he supposed if anyone was capable of knocking out something so complicated in a short space of time, it was probably Claire Mitchell. He'd tried to shrug off the unreasonable level of disappointment that they wouldn't be having dinner together. He'd been looking forward to returning to the office, sharing a curry, working on the paper and proving to her they were both adults and capable of being in the same room together without kissing each other.

No need for that. You've already done it.

He'd spent a restless night lurching between reliving the amazing and mind-blowing kiss and the unsettling feelings that stirred inside him whenever he recalled Claire's utterly appalled and slightly panicked post-kiss expression. As a result, he'd done his very British best at the interview with the Walkers last night and again this morning to sweep last night under the carpet and show Claire that everything was as it had been prior to the kiss. On one level he knew he should be pleased and relived that she regretted the incident. After all, they worked closely together and a fling wasn't conducive to workplace harmony, not to mention the fact it would break a dozen hospital rules. But then again, he wasn't used to anyone looking at him with such abhorrence. He felt a crazy need to prove to her that he was more than capable of respecting her wishes on the *nothing happened* front even though something incredible had taken place. He still couldn't reconcile the fact that prickly, terse Claire Mitchell could kiss a man better than his wildest fantasy.

He gave a wave to the evening protestors who were warming themselves around a brazier and then switched the take-away food bag to his other hand. For a brief moment he toyed with the idea of texting Islay Kennedy and inviting her to share the curries, but then his stomach growled. Hell, he was famished and he didn't want to delay. Taking the lift to level five, he punched in the security numbers and entered the consulting suite. After six each evening the lighting reverted to power-saving mode and the corridor was low-lit. He walked past a series of closed doors—the offices of his colleagues—and stopped in front of his, surprised by the spill of light coming from under the door. He turned the handle and stepped inside.

Holy— The first thing he saw was Claire Mitchell's sweet behind. She was leaning over his desk and the soft fabric of her dress fell in such a way that it perfectly outlined the two orbs of her cheeks. The memory of those curves pressed hard into his lap last night sent a raft of delicious sensation thrumming through him, heating his blood and making his palms itch. All he wanted to do was walk up behind her, pull her back into him and feel her pressing against hard him.

Good God! What the hell was wrong with him? This wasn't a role-play fantasy with a consenting partner. He was at work. She was his trainee and all of his thoughts were utterly inappropriate. He closed his eyes for a moment, concentrating hard on reducing his breathing from ragged to normal.

When he opened his eyes he avoided looking at the kryptonite that was her behind. Instead, he noticed her bare left foot was flat on the floor, her right knee was pressed into the seat of a chair and she was leaning over his desk. Her sun-gold hair had fallen free of its usual black band, cascading in shimmering waves across her shoulders. She held her arms outstretched in front of her, taking her weight on the heels of both hands, and her glasses dangled from the fingers of her left hand.

As his gaze strayed from her glasses, he noticed the paper. Papers to be exact. His entire office looked like someone had placed a fan in front of a ream of white A4 and turned it on full tilt. Pages spilled from the desk to the floor, some were stuck to the wall and others had migrated to his other desk and completely covered the green-tooled leather. Each page was filled with some sort of black printing—from graphs and tables to double-spaced words.

'Did it snow paper while I was gone?' he quipped as he quietly closed the door.

Claire swung around, shock etched deeply on her face and her colour as white as the paper. 'What are you doing here?'

'It's my office,' he said equably as he set down the take-away bag. 'More to the point, why are you here? You sent me a text saying you were finished.'

Her chin rose—a sure sign she was on the back foot. 'I thought I was done but I got caught up with a bit of tweaking.'

He snorted and swept his arm out to encompass the room. 'Tweaking? This looks like you're stuck smack bang in the mud-sucking middle.'

Something akin to panic crossed her face. 'And if I am?'

'It's exactly where I expected you to be.'

For a moment, her body went deathly still and then she abruptly shoved her glasses back on her face. 'You know?' she demanded in a voice that was half accusative and half defeated.

Know?

Then, as if someone had just poked her hard between her scapulas, her shoulders rolled back into a straight, sharp line and her nostrils flared. 'So this was deliberate? Some sort of macabre joke? Or worse? Sophisticated bullying to get back at me for last night? To put me in my place?'

Bullying? What the— He held up his hands as if a gun was being pointed menacingly at his head. 'Hang on just one damn minute, Dr Mitchell. That's a very serious accusation.'

She swept an arm through a pile of papers, sending them fluttering to the floor. 'And this is a serious setup. I can't believe how badly you want me to fail.'

Fail? His temper surged at her abhorrent claims. Every part of him screamed to carpet her here and now for insubordination and character assassination, but something about the tension pulling sharply at her features and the desolation in her eyes quelled his anger. The furious boil reduced to a slow and cross simmer. Once again he'd glimpsed those same malignant shadows clinging tightly where they didn't belong.

He sighed and dropped his arms, letting them fall loosely to his sides. 'Something's clearly upset you to make you behave like this but I'm at a loss as to what it is. When I said you were in the mud-sucking middle, I was referring to that moment in a project everyone experiences when you're suffering from information overload.'

She stared at him from behind her tortoiseshell glasses, intently studying his face. It was like she was trying to decode his words and match them up with his expression and tone of voice. He pressed on. 'That place in a project that demands you commence putting the data into a coherent form but the precise place to start eludes you.'

He tried for a wry smile. 'To be honest, I was very surprised to get your text saying you were finished. I expected you to only just be starting the narrative.'

For a moment she made no sound and then her face crumpled and a long, low moan escaped across her ruby-red lips. She sank onto the chair and dropped her face into her hands. 'Oh, God. No.'

The ragged sound carried old pain and it echoed around the quiet office before returning to cloak her in a toxic cloud. More than anything he wanted to reach out and touch her but then he remembered what had happened the last time he'd offered comfort. He decided that discretion was the better part of valour. He'd feed her instead.

As he silently dished up the food, she mumbled something, but given her faint volume, he assumed she was talking to herself rather than to him. Handing her a bowl of curry and some naan bread, he said, 'Want to tell me what's going on?'

Her hand shook as she accepted the bowl. 'Not really, no.'

'Put it this way. I was being polite.' He pulled up a chair and seated himself opposite her. 'You don't have an option.'

With a jerky movement, she set the bowl down on the desk. 'I can't eat knowing you're about to revoke my scholarship. Just do it and get it over with.'

He felt like he was watching a play where he'd missed act one and he was now totally muddled in act two. 'I haven't any intention of revoking your scholarship, although God knows why not, Claire Mitchell. Ever since you arrived, you've pushed the envelope and all of my buttons. You are by far *the* most challenging trainee I've ever worked with.'

She sucked in her lips. 'I... You...' She sighed and her head dropped. 'Sorry.'

It was the first time one of her apologies actually sounded sincere. Looking at the top of her bent head, he was still at a loss as to what was going on. 'I'm not sure you realise that you're also the most talented trainee I've ever had the fortune to work with.'

Her head rose slowly but her distinctive chocolate-brown brows had drawn down into a frown of doubt and anxiety. Yet again he was convinced she didn't come close to believing him. Exactly why, he had no idea. Nor did he understand why she was so convinced he'd been acting against her best interests. That accusation burned hot and cut deeply. In his private life he'd had women hurl accusations at him ranging from *commitment-phobe* to *heartless*, but at work he prided himself on equality and fairness. No one had ever suggested otherwise.

Looking for clues, he wracked his brain and tried to think of something he may have done or said to give her that impression. As he drew a blank, the mumbled words she'd spoken earlier suddenly sounded in his head as clear as a bell on a windless day.

Everything's falling apart just as I always knew it would.

Why, with a track record of successes, did his most talented trainee believe she was going to fail? He'd bet his last pound that whatever or whoever had caused those tormenting shadows of hers was connected to this eroding self-belief. He was determined to find the source.

'If we're to continue working together, Claire, I need to know two things. Why you texted me saying you were finished when obviously you are nowhere near, and more importantly, why you would even entertain the thought I had set you up to fail?'

From the moment Alistair had stepped into the office, Claire's heart had picked up its pace and now it was beating so quickly and erratically that she was light-headed and dizzy. She still couldn't wrap her head around how rapidly things had unravelled. Not that she'd ever been in control of the project, but she'd been convinced she was in control of keeping Alistair far, far away from the office for the bulk of the day. Except now he was here and she was backed into a corner of her own making. The only available escape route was ripping out her soul.

His words *'You're exactly where I expected you to be'* had not only left her feeling utterly exposed, they'd hauled her backwards into the dark abyss that was her school days in Gundiwindi. She hated the emotions the past always generated. When she'd combined them with her determination that no one was ever going to bully her again, she'd lashed out, only to discover Alistair had no idea about her secret. No one got away with incorrectly accusing their boss of a heinous crime without having to face the consequences. This was her Armageddon.

Everything she'd worked so hard to achieve was about to

shatter into a thousand irreparable pieces and she only had herself to blame. Lacing her fingers together tightly, she fixed her gaze on the tip of his left ear. 'I'm—' she forced the word up and out through a tight throat '—dyslexic.'

He looked utterly taken aback. 'Are you sure?' Doubt rang in his very precise accent.

'Your daughter's not going to amount to very much, Mr Mitchell.'

'Moron.'

'You're a very lazy girl. Accept that you belong in the remedial class.'

'Dumb ass.'

Against the harsh memories of the past, a bark of laughter fully loaded with derision broke out of her, raining down on them both. 'Oh, believe me. I'm more than sure. Dyslexia's been my constant companion since I started primary school.'

'But…'

Confusion shone in his eyes. A part of her wanted to hug him that he'd been clueless about her condition. The rest of her ached with embarrassment that she'd got herself into the situation where she was forced to tell him.

'I don't understand,' he finally managed to say as he ran a hand through his hair, making it even messier than usual. 'If you have this disability, how on earth have you got this far in your career?'

She shrugged. 'Sheer bloody-mindedness and a photographic memory.'

This time he laughed—a great booming sound that twirled around her with reassuring gravitas. 'Well, you do have bloody-mindedness in spades.'

She smiled weakly. 'Um, thank you, I guess.' She didn't know what else to say.

'Determination can carry a person a very long way.'

Unwanted tears pricked at the back of her eyes and she

blinked furiously, refusing to allow them to form, let alone fall. 'When you're told often enough that you're useless, it can go one of two ways.'

Respect flared on his face. 'And you chose success.'

She thought of her years of struggle and for the first time she glimpsed what she'd achieved in a new light. 'I suppose I have.'

'I'd say you definitely have.' He gave her a contemplative glance. 'Why didn't you tell me about the dyslexia?'

She tossed her head. 'I refuse to be defined by it.'

'But you are.'

His words crashed into her, making her chest cramp in twisting pain. She'd spent years proving she was no different from anyone else and she wasn't about to accept his view. 'No. I. Am. Not. You said yourself you had no idea I was dyslexic.'

'That's not what I'm talking about. All of us are an amalgam of our experiences.' The skin on his bladed cheeks momentarily tensed and then relaxed. 'You live with a learning disability. I imagine that isn't always easy.'

'No,' she said softly, appreciating his insight on that point if not on the other.

'Exactly how hard is it? Was it?'

The question made her flinch. 'I don't waste time thinking about it.'

Although a flash of sympathy lit up his eyes, his mouth straightened into a taut line. 'Perhaps not consciously, but I think it all came out to play today when you accused me of bullying.'

The sternness of his voice didn't hide his hurt and it ate into her. 'I'm sorry. I should never—'

'I don't want an apology, Claire,' he interrupted briskly. 'But I require an explanation as to why you would make that leap.'

She knew she owed him the truth but that didn't stop

her feeling as if she was about to rip herself open from the inside out. *Just do it and get it over with.* 'I grew up in a tiny outback town where sport ruled and there was no tolerance for being different. Not only was I myopic, I struggled to learn, which made me a sitting duck for cruel kids.'

'Bullies?'

'Yep.' A long sigh shuddered out of her. 'Although, in retrospect, it wasn't the kids who were the worst offenders. I had an ally in my brother, who was a well-respected football player. He stomped on anyone who stole my glasses and pinched my books. By the time I left primary school, I had amassed a lot of one-liners. A clever putdown confused most of the boys who were all brawn and no brains.'

'I can imagine,' he said with a knowing smile. 'I can see where you honed your acerbic skills.'

Her cheeks burned with embarrassed heat as her mind spun with confusion. She'd been so rude to him and yet here he was actively listening and trying to understand. As much as she disliked talking about her life prior to university, she wanted to honour his interest and hopefully hold on to her job.

'The saying "Everything's there but it's wired differently" is my brain. Spelling and reading have always been a challenge. I had trouble linking the sound of a word to the letters on the page. When I was little, there was no reading recovery program and as the years went past I slipped further and further behind.

'I was accused of being lazy and not putting in the effort. Teachers took to saying, "You're nothing like your brother," and it was easier for them to label me the difficult child. Mum and Dad tried to help but as I was frustrating qualified teachers, it wasn't surprising that my parents eventually accepted what they'd been told. Eyes were constantly rolled in class when I struggled to read out loud and I never gained my pen licence. By the end of primary school, nothing was expected of me. Everyone assumed the moment I turned fifteen, I'd leave school.'

His leaned forward slightly. 'What changed?'

'A guardian angel called Strez.' She smiled and gave a self-deprecating laugh. 'Mr Strezinski. He was a Polish migrant who spoke four languages. I have no idea how he landed up at Gundiwindi High or why he agreed to teach typing and woodwork. Fortunately for me, I took both subjects. He saw something in me no one else did. He lent me audiobooks so I could hear the English texts while I read along. Without having to agonise over every word, I could hear the themes and analyse the text. He suggested I type my assignments.'

Her heart swelled as it did whenever she thought of Strez. 'I'll never forget the day I got a B+ on an essay. I was both over the moon about the mark and white with fury that I had to prove to the teacher I hadn't plagiarised the work. Strez helped me devise strategies, like chewing gum, to help me focus and using headphones to block out extraneous noise. Most importantly, he was the one person who truly believed in me.'

Alistair nodded and a lock of hair fell forward. He brushed it aside. 'He sounds like a true mentor.'

She looked up into his eyes, which in the low light were the colour of silver moonbeams dancing on water. 'He changed my life. Without his help, I'd never have passed Year Twelve, let alone got into medicine. He released me from all of Gundiwindi's preconceived ideas.'

His brow's rose questioningly. 'But not, I think, from its legacy.'

She considered the statement. 'I've never thought about it in those terms. You may have a point.'

This time he gave a bark of laughter. 'There's no *may*, Claire. I see it in your eyes. There's a part of you that still believes you're that struggling little girl.'

'That's because I am.' The words shot out before she could catch them back. *Idiot!* She hated feeling so vulnerable in front of him. 'You're the first person outside of Gundiwindi to know I'm dyslexic. I only told you to try and save my job.'

A sympathetic look similar to the one he'd shown her last night flashed across his face. For a moment she yearned for a touch of his hand and immediately thought better of it. She couldn't trust herself not to lean in and repeat last night's kiss, and *that* was totally out of the question.

He moved abruptly, picking up her curry from the desk and pressing it on her. 'Eat this before it goes cold.'

She gratefully accepted it, having discovered that not being fired on the spot had revived her appetite. She was suddenly ravenous. Using the garlic naan, she scooped up some curry and savoured the subtle flavours.

'Part of me can understand why you've kept it quiet,' Alistair said. 'Medicine's fiercely competitive with a take-no-prisoners approach.'

'And I learned that hard lesson in the Gundiwindi playground. Never expose a weakness or you get trampled. Like anyone with a secret, I've gone to great lengths and become very good at hiding it. Today was no exception.' She huffed out a breath and looked him straight in the eye. 'I didn't want you here working alongside me. I couldn't risk you seeing how I have to read things twice to decipher them and once more to memorise them.'

His high forehead creased into deep lines. 'So that's why you told me you'd completed the job. You wanted to keep me away.'

She nodded and he added drily, 'Well, that answers my question as to why you were so unexpectedly conciliatory about my extended absence today.'

She gave an apologetic shrug. 'When you arrived back here and said you expected me to be in the mud-sucking middle, I thought you'd deliberately given me this task to expose my biggest weakness and my worst fear.'

Understanding rolled across his face. Ruefulness followed immediately, settling in the lines around his mouth and eyes. 'My general dislike of statistics combined with my procrastination became your worst nightmare.'

'The project isn't the nightmare.' She hurried to reassure him. 'It's the short timeline.'

He helped himself to more Tandoori Chicken. 'So what I've interpreted as officious organisation is in fact one of your coping strategies?'

She nodded slowly. 'I need time to read and memorise. I can't leave anything to the last minute.'

'And I leave everything to the last minute.'

'Why is that when it must make things more difficult for you?' she asked, genuinely interested.

A muscle in his cheek twitched unexpectedly. 'Because life's far too short to spend so much time doing stuff I don't enjoy.'

And there it was again—his selfish streak. A strand of disappointment wound through her with more intensity than she cared to experience. What did it matter to her if he was a fully paid up and card carrying member of the *live for today and for me* club.

'The first thing I did when I qualified was activate the fine tradition of all consultants and dump the bulk of the boring paperwork onto my trainees.' He suddenly winced and rubbed the back of his neck. 'Hell, Claire. No wonder we've been crossing swords. I've exhausted you.'

Guilt slugged her. 'I should have told you I was struggling, but now you know why I didn't.' She gave him an apologetic shrug. 'All of the above. The thing is, in my previous positions I've never had to deal with quite so much paperwork. Brain surgery is so much easier than reading and writing. As for public speaking, I fear death less.'

He laughed. 'Dyslexia aside, you're not alone there.' His expression sobered. 'Despite—or perhaps because of—your dyslexia and the type of brain you have, you're an excellent neurosurgeon.'

Gratitude flowed through her and for the first time she actually accepted and believed in the compliment. 'Thank you. Surgery's spatial and kinaesthetic learning.'

'The practical component is, but what about all those years of lectures?'

'Like I said, I have a visual memory. Just don't ask me to write anything quickly or my *"p"*s will become *"b"*s and vice versa, along with a lot of other words spelt backwards. Oh, and never get me to navigate because I can't follow a map, and don't expect me to identify left or right without making my left hand into an *L*.'

He grinned. 'I'll remember that.'

She watched his open and friendly face and saw kindness reflected there. Other consultants would have summoned security to march her off the premises for her earlier behaviour. Although she'd hardly enjoyed his insistence she tell him about her dyslexia and school days in Gundiwindi, she appreciated it because it had saved her job. Sure, the man had a selfish side but how could she have ever thought he was shallow? Or that he wanted her to fail?

'Claire, I meant what I said about you being best trainee I've ever had. I can teach you and make you even better, but if we're going to make this work, we need to be a team. We need to be on the same page.'

Her heart added a beat. 'I came close to throwing away my chance, didn't I?'

'Put it this way. You're lucky you're so talented and that I'm so easy-going.' He gave her a wink as he set down his now empty bowl, wiped clean with the bread. His face settled into serious lines. 'Is there anything else you're finding difficult about working with me?'

Her mouthful of curry stalled mid-swallow as their shared kiss flashed like a neon light in her mind.

He means aside from the fact your body goes on hyper-alert whenever you think about him. Aside from the fact you kissed him senseless.

She cleared her throat. 'Ah, no. Um, well, not that I can think of right at the moment.'

His eyes did that intense staring thing that made her feel as if he could see down to her soul. 'Are you sure?'

'Absolutely,' she said, trying to sound cool, calm and detached instead of a quivering mess of liquid lust. 'But I give you my word that I'll discuss any problems with you if and when they arise.'

A wide and reassuring smile broke across his face and she saw immediately why his little patients and their parents trusted him implicitly. Almost everything she'd ever believed about Alistair North had just been turned on its head.

'I'm glad we've had this conversation. It's important we're on the same page and it's going to make the ball a much more enjoyable evening.'

The ball. Her stomach flipped. So much had changed between them since she'd insisted he attend the ball and he'd turned the tables on her by buying her ticket. Thank goodness she'd already told Victoria to seat her on the opposite side of the ten-seat table from Alistair. The width of the table meant conversation between them would be impossible.

Seriously? You're worried about conversation? Be worried about the close proximity of a bloke who will rock a tux.

'Indeed,' she somehow managed to say and sound professional.

'Excellent. Consider this conversation your first staff assessment, which, by the way, you've passed. I'll get around to writing up your report, but first, I have a paper to write before nine tomorrow morning.'

An hour ago she'd have been tempted to take a crack at the chaos his procrastination had caused him, but given how generous he'd been to her that would be grossly unfair.

He scratched his head and blew out a sigh as he took in the sea of papers. 'Where to start exactly,' he said quietly as if he was thinking out loud.

As wonderful as the idea of sleep was, she'd have to be blind not to notice the dark rings under his eyes. She didn't have a monopoly on a sleep debt and to walk away now and leave him dealing with the project after he'd just gone beyond what was expected of an understanding boss wasn't something she could do.

'To the uninitiated it looks like a mess but I promise you there's a system.'

'I believe you, but thousands wouldn't,' he said with a laugh in his voice. 'Were you able to draw any conclusions from the data?'

'I was.'

'Thank goodness.'

This time she laughed. 'I'll tell you what I discovered, if you convert it into flowing words that are spelt correctly.'

'You're on.' He opened up a new document on his computer. 'And there's a silver lining to all of this, Claire.'

'There is?'

'Sure.' He gave her a bone-melting smile. 'At the end of a long night, we'll be rewarded with a perfect view of dawn breaking over London.'

She tried not to think about the fact that she had a perfect view in front of her right this minute.

CHAPTER SEVEN

LONDON HAD PUT on a warm, starlit evening for the Paddington Children's Hospital fundraising ball and from the balcony overlooking the Thames the scent of gardenias wafted on the air. The evening was in full swing—the dance floor was crowded, some potential couples seeking a quiet tête-à-tête lingered on the curve of the elegant art nouveau staircase and the liveried staff busily cleared away the remnants of the main course.

The opulence and grandeur of the nineteenth century Paris salon–styled ballroom was equally matched by the massive floral arrangements of white roses, gardenias and hydrangeas as well as by the crowd. Alistair was used to seeing his staff in their PCH uniform or scrubs. He was used to seeing Claire in her utilitarian white blouse, black skirt, white coat and with her hair pulled back in a ponytail. He sure as hell wasn't used to seeing her in a full-length ball gown with her hair piled up onto her head in a way that emphasised her long and slender neck. A neck that just screamed to be kissed.

Many of the women wore strapless dresses exposing acres of skin and generous cleavages that drew and glued the gazes of most of the men in the room. Usually, he'd have enjoyed the spectacle—hell, he'd probably have toyed with the idea of later in the evening burying his face deep into their pillow softness—but not tonight. Somehow, Claire, in her high-necked sleeveless gown with its beaded bodice and full skirt, was sexier than all of them put together. The combination was doing his head in and the irony of the evening wasn't lost on him either.

Two weeks ago when he'd insisted on bringing Claire to the ball it had been a personal challenge to see if the buttoned-up woman with the acerbic tongue was capable of enjoying herself. Back then his plan had been to crack her façade, get her to smile and, as her boss, show her that there was more to life than just work. Fate, however, had thumbed its nose at him again.

Of all people, he knew better than most how life could change in a heartbeat. Or, in his case, a lack of one. With that information etched onto his heart and soul it stood to reason that he should have anticipated how much could happen in two weeks. He had not. Tonight, he was faced with the reality of change.

For starters, there'd been *that* kiss neither of them was acknowledging and then they'd had their frank conversation in his office. Since that night, the stressed-out and snarky woman he'd thought was Claire had almost vanished. Tonight, in her place, was a woman he barely recognised inside or out.

Since he'd learned about her dyslexia and they'd pulled a companionable and constructive all-nighter on the paper for the symposium, the two of them had reset their working relationship. Now that he understood her struggles with the written word, he'd taken back the lion's share of the report writing, leaving her with an amount she assured him she could handle. With more sleep, the dead weight of hiding a secret being lifted and a workload she could manage, Claire Mitchell's general demeanour had softened. In the last fourteen days, without even trying, his professional respect for her work and his admiration for what she'd achieved against steep odds had tipped the scales. He liked her.

That's not a crime, he told himself before his subconscious could berate him. *I liked her predecessor, Harry, too.*

But you didn't kiss him.

He had no comeback to that. All he knew was that if Claire was going to the same lengths as he was not to act on the wide current of attraction that arced between them every time they stepped into each other's orbit, then she was well down the road to insanity. This thing between them lived and breathed. It flickered and flared like firelight and it tantalisingly danced and sparkled like sunshine on water. No matter how hard he tried to ignore its pull, it never completely disappeared. It was playing merry hell with his concentration.

When he was alone, his thoughts were full of her and when they were together at work he was like a cat on a hot tin roof. Simple things like the brush of fingers on his hand when he passed her a pen or when he accepted her offer of a cup of coffee took on cataclysmic proportions. Any inadvertent touch set off rafts of sensation that tumbled over and over each other, racing along his veins until he was on fire with a thirst for her that couldn't be slaked. His body, which craved release, ranted at him all the time to *just do it*.

It took more willpower than he'd ever imposed upon himself before not to throw caution to the wind, spin her into his arms and kiss her senseless. Hell, just the other day during surgery she'd reached over him and to avoid an inadvertent touch he'd pulled back so fast that he'd upended a tray of sterilised instruments. The scrub sister was yet to forgive him.

He wasn't used to holding back. Hell, what was the point when the future couldn't be predicted and any day may well be his last. He'd always acted on intoxicating zips of attraction between him and a woman. If Claire had been any other woman and she'd kissed him with that same intense abandon, he knew without a doubt they'd have spent the rest of the night burning up the sheets. Instead, they'd shared the oddest fortnight, lurching from strict professional courtesy to relaxed moments of friendship. All the while the unacknowledged attraction simmered so strongly between them that he didn't know if he was coming or going. Tonight was no exception.

'Oh. Hello,' Claire said with a friendly—if slightly hesitant—smile as she passed him walking back from the dance floor.

Strands of her golden-blonde hair had escaped from the pile atop her head, her cheeks were flushed pink and her contact-lens-covered caramel eyes were almost obliterated by her dilated ebony pupils. She looked like she'd just been tumbled onto her back and ravished. His blood dived to his groin and he grabbed a glass of water from a passing waiter, drinking it down fast to stifle a groan.

'It's warm, isn't it?' She took a proffered glass of water too. 'I've danced with Dominic and Matthew but thank goodness I only have to dance with Andrew once. My toes couldn't take much more.'

'Hmm,' he managed, frantically channelling thoughts of the icy cold streams in the Scottish Highlands where his father had started teaching him to fly-fish. Thoughts about the effect the chilly water always had on his body.

Although he'd paid for her ticket to the ball, he hadn't spent very much time with her this evening, which was both a good and a bad thing. She'd refused his offer to pick her up and drive her, insisting instead on meeting him here. When he'd arrived, he'd looked for her but he'd soon been absorbed into a group so by the time he reached their allocated table and discovered that Victoria had seated them on opposite sides of the large round, it was too late to do anything about it.

He'd spent the entrée and main course flanked on one side by a chatty physiotherapist and on the other side by the ward pharmacist. Both were perfectly delightful and interesting women and on another night he'd have probably enjoyed their company immensely. But tonight, every time he'd heard Claire's tinkling laugh—yes, the woman had actually laughed—he'd wanted to lunge across the table and throttle Duncan MacKinnon.

If anyone was going to make Claire laugh, it was going to be him. If anyone was going to show her how to have fun, it should be him, except he hadn't had the chance. The moment the meal had finished, the dancing had started and Victoria had sold him off like he was meat on a slab. He'd danced for an hour straight, fending off a dozen invitations from sexy and beautiful women. It both surprised and worried him that he hadn't been tempted by any of them. What the hell was wrong with him?

You know exactly what's wrong with you. Ethics and blue balls.

'Does Victoria know you're hiding behind the aspidistra instead of being out on the dance floor?' Claire asked with a teasing glint in her beautiful eyes.

This time he gulped champagne. From the moment he'd first laid eyes on her tonight, he'd recognised that off-duty Claire was a very different woman from Dr Mitchell. Out from under the mantle of responsibility and the pressures of her dyslexia, the need for her to control everything had faded. If anything, tonight she had a look of wonder about her, as if she couldn't quite believe she was at the ball and she was absorbing every moment. None of it was helping him control his libido in any shape or form.

'I'm not hiding. I'm taking a break.'

She laughed. 'Poor, Al. What a tough gig, having beautiful women throw themselves at you.'

Al? 'You have no idea,' he said tightly, thinking about

the battle that currently raged inside him. The beautiful woman he wanted wasn't throwing herself at him, and unless she did, he couldn't have her.

Lighten up, mate. Forcing himself to smile just like he'd been doing all evening, he said, 'But one must do one's bit to help save the castle.'

'You Brits break me up,' she said, laughing. 'Keep calm and dance on?'

'Something like that,' he said, thinking that he hadn't known calm since he'd kissed her.

'Victoria, Rosie, Matt and Robyn have done an amazing job pulling this together. Apparently, their photo's going to be in the paper tomorrow, so hopefully donations will flood in.' She gazed up at the ceiling with a starry-eyed look, taking in the intricate plasterwork and gilt. 'All of this is so far removed from the Gundiwindi Mechanic's Institute hall I keep thinking I'm dreaming it.' She swung her gaze to his. 'Did you know that Anna Pavlova once danced here and that Fred Astaire danced on the roof with his sister?'

He loved the awe that wove across her face and he had a crazy desire to try and keep it there and never let it fade. 'How do you know all this?'

'I stumbled across a photographic exhibition,' she said enthusiastically. 'Once, there was a leopard in this stunning Belle Époque room. Can you imagine?'

'Well, us crazy Brits like to shake things up a bit now and then,' he said with a grin.

'Alistair.' A voice with an Irish lilt called his name from the dance floor. A Cornish accent followed it. 'Come dance with us.'

'Yes, do,' a chorus of accents from around the British Isles sang across the ballroom.

The Koala Ward nurses were excelling at having fun, but the last thing he wanted was to be back in that pawing crush. He smiled at Claire. 'I wouldn't mind seeing those photos.'

'You're just saying that to avoid the tipsy nurses.'

Absolutely. 'As a Londoner, I think it's imperative I catch up on the history of this esteemed establishment.'

She gave an exaggerated eye roll and a lightness shot through him. 'Exactly where do I find this exhibition?'

'Downstairs. You cross the foyer, go left at reception, take the first right and there's a set of double doors—' She laughed. 'It's probably just easier if I show you.'

Yes, please. He stepped back, allowing her the space to move past him and then it was just good manners to rest his hand lightly on the small of her back to guide her as they negotiated their way across the crowded room.

'Alistair, old man,' Lionel Harrington, a retired paediatric surgeon, called out to him with a definite slur in his voice.

Claire slowed and Alistair leaned forward, saying quietly into her ear, 'Keep going or we'll be stuck with loquacious Lionel for the next half an hour.'

She immediately picked up the pace, walking determinedly against the crowd who were now returning for dessert. Instead of summoning a lift, she picked up her skirt and with a smoothness of motion that belied her high heels she almost sailed down the stunning staircase.

He had a flash of Cinderella running away from the Prince and he hurried down after her. He automatically turned towards the foyer but she grabbed his hand and pulled him through a door and down a corridor. It wasn't decorated in quite the same grand style as the rest of the hotel and he had a sudden thought. 'Are we allowed back here?'

Her hand paused on the door handle of a set of double doors and her eyes danced. 'Put it this way. There's no sign saying that we're not.'

He laughed, loving that she was living for the moment. She immediately shushed him. Using what he assumed was the staff entrance, he followed her into a large room. Large crates, ladders and other equipment were scattered around the room and half of the space was hung with framed photographs of various sizes.

He picked up a flyer that had spilled from a box. 'It says it opens on the fourth.'

'How lucky are we to get an advanced peek,' she said, eyes shining as she tugged him towards an enormous black and white photo. 'Ta-dah!'

He did a double take. 'Is that a five-foot cake balanced on an elephant that's standing on a gondola?'

'I know, right?' she said, laughter lacing her voice. Dropping her hand from his arm, she peered forward to read the information plaque next to the photo. 'And it says it was lit by four hundred paper lanterns.'

He had to fist his hand so as not to snatch hers back. 'I'm quite taken with the twelve thousand carnations and the swans.'

She shook her head in amazement. 'I can't even wrap my head around such extravagance.'

Side by side they wandered slowly up and down the room taking in the photos of famous people. Bogart and Bacall, and Marilyn Monroe, represented Hollywood royalty. There was a very young Christian Dior surrounded by five models dressed in intricately beaded ball gowns. Personally, he didn't think any of them looked as amazing as Claire.

'Here's one for you,' he said, pointing to a portrait of the famous Australian soprano, Dame Nellie Melba. It was taken when she was young and she was pressing a fan coquettishly to her cheek. 'The hotel's chef invented peach Melba to honour her triumph at Covent Garden.'

Claire laughed. 'I bet it was far more extravagant than

the Gundiwindi pub's best efforts of some canned cling peaches served with half-melted ice cream.'

'You forgot the raspberry sauce.'

'There's raspberry sauce in peach Melba?'

'Good heavens,' he said with faux shock. 'What sort of Australian are you if you don't know that?'

'Obviously a dessert-ignorant one. I guess I'll be forced to remedy the situation.'

He had a sudden flash of her mouth closing around a spoon and slowly sucking ice cream off it. He was abruptly very hot and finding it hard to breathe. Tugging at his collar, he loosened his bow tie.

One of the last photos in the collection was taken during the Second World War. 'I can't imagine dancing while the bombs fell,' Claire said softly.

He could. Dicing with death was a way of life for him with his unreliable heart. 'Why not enjoy yourself to the very last?'

She gave him a sideways look. 'More of your live-for-the-moment mantra?'

'Sure. Just like we're living for the moment now.'

A small frown creased her forehead. 'I hardly think sneaking in here is very dangerous.'

'Oh, I don't know…'

She tilted her head, looking at him from those glorious eyes of hers. Her perfume, which always reminded him of sunshine, summer days and freedom, pulled at his restraint. So help him, he should have stayed upstairs and danced with the giggly nurses instead of coming down here with her. But here they were, alone for the very first time this evening, and all he wanted to do was wrap his arms around her. He wanted to haul her in against him, feel her body pressed against the length of him and lose himself in kissing her until nothing else existed but their touch.

You know you can't do any of it.

He never prevaricated or second-guessed anything but this was new territory for him. This was Claire and he was her boss. Until she gave him a sign that she felt exactly the same way he did, that she would welcome his touch, nothing could happen.

'How can this possibly be dangerous,' she said briskly with a hint of the terse Claire from two weeks ago.

He knew her well enough to recognise the tone she used when she was stressed. Was it because she could feel this thing leaping and writhing between them, desperate to be satiated? *Please*. He gazed down at her and said softly, 'I think you know exactly how dangerous it is for us to be alone in this room.'

Alistair's impossibly deep voice flowed around Claire like dark, melted chocolate—decadent, enticing and blissfully sinful. She knew exactly how dangerous it was for her to be standing mere millimetres away from him and his rock-hard body. A body her fingertips had committed to memory just over two weeks ago and itched to touch again.

You had a plan. Why didn't you stick to it?

So much had happened between them since the evening she'd invited him to the ball and all of it made her head spin. Back when she'd issued the invitation, all he'd been to her was an infuriating and exasperating boss. Since then, she'd seen more sides to him than a polygon. When she combined it with *that* kiss, it made him—for her at least—the most dangerous man in London. It didn't matter how great he'd been about her slightly unhinged behaviour around the Walker case or his empathy and practicality about her dyslexia, or that she now recognised in him values and ethics that she admired. No matter how much her body ached to touch his again, they were still in the power dynamic of boss and trainee.

To that end, she'd gone to great lengths to protect herself

from doing something she'd regret at work. Tonight, she'd had a simple and foolproof plan for the evening—never be alone with Alistair. She'd known that outside of the protective framework of the hospital and their defined roles she might be tempted, so she'd strategised for it. She'd started by politely refusing his offer of a ride to the hotel and until now she'd only talked to him in the ballroom surrounded by three hundred people.

Why in heaven's name had she brought him down here?

She blamed the dress and the hotel. Tonight was like stepping out of her prescribed life and into a magical world of pretend. It had started the moment she'd stared disbelievingly at the woman who'd faced her in the bedroom mirror. She'd hardly recognised herself. The boutique owner on a little road just off Oxford Street deserved a medal for convincing her to buy this frock. The little girl from dusty Gundiwindi had ridden to the ball in a London black cab, which in her book was as amazing as a pumpkin carriage being drawn by white horses. The moment the hotel's doorman had swept open the cab's door and she'd stepped onto the green carpet, she'd been treated as if she was someone special. Someone who mattered. That was her ambrosia.

The opulence and grandeur of the surroundings had called to her and she'd been like a kid in a lolly shop. She'd gone exploring, making her way noiselessly along thickly carpeted corridors and peeking behind closed doors. When she'd stumbled into the half-hung exhibition, she'd been so excited about discovering the living history of the luxurious hotel that she'd wanted to share it with someone. It had totally messed with her plan. So here she was, alone with Alistair, and although his hands were by his sides and not a single cell of their bodies touched, the electricity that buzzed and fizzed between them could light up London and the home counties.

For the first time, the look in his eyes was unguarded.

The professional interest that usually resided in the grey depths whenever he looked at her—a glance that occasionally morphed into moments of a friendly gaze—had vanished. In its place, the flames of unadulterated lust burned brightly. Danger and desire swirled with an intoxicating pull.

Her body responded to it, leaping with a need to match his. Fleetingly, she wondered why he'd dropped his guard. Why now?

It's this hotel. This dress. This night. None of it's real life.

Exactly. So take what's on offer because it will vanish with the dawn.

She swallowed and dug to find her voice, not quite believing she could be so daring. 'You once accused me of not having fun. This hotel, with all of its stories, almost demands I step outside of my real life and do something outrageous for a night.'

His eyes flashed silver. 'It would almost be disrespectful not to honour the hotel's reputation as a host to many clandestine lovers.'

Tingling delight swooped through her and she was dizzy with the idea that he wanted her as much as she wanted him. But memories of Michael, along with a deep-seated need to protect herself and her scholarship, made her say, 'This has nothing to do with work. What happens in the hotel stays in the hotel.'

Tension coiled through his body, radiating from the jut of his jaw and out across the square set of his shoulders, but still he didn't move to touch her. 'I promise you, Claire. It won't spill into our work world. It's your decision. If you have any doubts…' His husky voice cracked. 'Are you absolutely certain you want this?'

Her heart rolled oddly at the concern in his question and she plucked at the organza of her full skirt. After working with him for weeks she recognised him to be an honourable man. She trusted him and knew that he'd never coerce her or use this night against her. She met his gaze. 'Tonight's all about fantasy, right?'

He made a low growling sound in the back of his throat. It made her feel strangely powerful and she rose on her toes to kiss him. For two long weeks she'd replayed the juxtaposing touch of his mouth on hers—soft and firm—and the searing heat of his lips that lit her up from the inside out. She couldn't wait another second for his taste to invade her.

Knowing his mouth was millimetres from hers, she closed her eyes and leaned in. Her lips hit air. As disappointment whipped her, Alistair grabbed her hand. He pulled her so fast towards the double doors that she almost tripped. 'What are you doing?' she asked, frantically trying to keep her balance.

'What the hell do you think I'm doing?' He wrenched open the door.

'I thought you were going to kiss me.'

He stopped and gently cupped her cheeks, his palms warm against her skin. 'If I kiss you here, Claire,' he said raggedly, 'I won't be able to stop.'

The little girl inside her squealed, twirled and clapped her hands. 'Really?'

'Yes, really.' He dropped his forehead to gently rest against hers. 'I've wanted to kiss you from the moment I saw you across the other side of the crowded ballroom. I'm not ruining this fantasy of ours by getting charged with indecent exposure. We're getting a room.'

'But Marlene Dietrich apparently—'

But he was already towing her across the foyer towards the reception desk. With one arm clamped firmly around her waist, keeping her tightly pressed against him, he said in a crisp, polite and plummy voice, 'We'd like a room for the evening.'

The receptionist—his name badge said he was Daniel—

didn't bat an eyelid. Nor did he ask about their luggage or lack of it. 'These functions can be quite exhausting, sir. I'm sure you'll find everything you need in Room 613.' After running Alistair's credit card through the machine he gave them a wallet containing two key cards. 'Just insert the card into the lift, sir, and press six. Enjoy your evening.'

At that precise moment Claire developed a fondness for what up until now she'd always considered starchy, British manners.

'Thank you,' Alistair said as he turned her and briskly marched them both to the lifts.

The journey to the sixth floor was interminable with the lift stopping at almost every floor. Their slow progression added to her frustration that Alistair was holding firm to his resolve that he wasn't going to kiss her until they were inside the room. 'You're crushing my hand.'

'Sorry.' He gave her a tight and apologetic glance before dropping her hand and hitting the number six button another three times.

She used the tortoise-like passage of time to slip off her shoes. When the lift doors finally opened on their level she picked up her skirt and her shoes, stepped out into the corridor and ran. Just as she'd found their door, Alistair caught her around the waist with his left hand and with his right he inserted the card into the lock with a quick in-out action.

'You've done that before.'

'Never with quite the same level of desperation,' he said with an ironic edge. He pushed open the door.

Together, they tumbled into the room, and as the door clicked shut quietly behind them, he kissed her.

Unlike that first time in the lounge, there was nothing slow about this kiss. It held two weeks of frustration and tightly leashed lust that now spilled into her with an urgency that chased along her veins. As it scooped up her desire and merged it into a molten ball of need, it detonated bursts of wonder. The explosions lit her up until her body was a pleasure dome of sensation and her legs threatened to buckle out from under her.

In a sea of organza and tulle she fell back onto the king-size bed, bringing Alistair down with her. Her hands tugged at his bespoke jacket, pushing it off his shoulders, and as he shrugged out of it his mouth didn't leave hers. Somehow, despite the fact his kisses had reduced her body to a puddle of vibrating need and her mind to mush, she managed to get her fingers to work. She undid the buttons of his waistcoat and popped the studs on his shirt and collar. Finally, after clawing at a flurry of white material, her palms pressed against hot skin, corded tendon and rock-solid muscle. *Bliss.*

As she ran her hands across his chest she heard herself make an involuntary moan. Alistair pulled his mouth from hers and gazed down at her with a wide grin on his face. 'Having fun?'

Her cheeks burned and she reminded herself that as much as he wanted her for his own enjoyment, she wanted him. He was hers for this night and it would be silly to waste precious time by being embarrassed. 'You bet I'm having fun,' she said, lifting her head and laying her mouth over his left nipple. She flicked out her tongue, tasting the hard nub, and then she sucked him into her mouth.

He gasped and his entire body flinched. 'Vixen,' he muttered, and as she laughed his hands moved frantically across the bodice of her dress. She could barely feel his touch through the detailed beading and corsetry and her laugher faded. She wanted his hands on her skin. His mouth on her skin. She wanted—

'Bloody hell,' he said through gritted teeth. 'I'll get gravel rash from all this beadwork.'

'The zipper's on the—' She suddenly had a face full of organza and tulle, but before she could fight the material, Alistair's mouth nipped gently at the tender skin of her inner thigh.

'Oh.' She gasped and writhed in delight as his tongue flicked and his mouth sucked, all the while moving closer and closer to her hot and aching centre. Her breath came short and sharp as the delicious assault continued and it wasn't until silver spots flickered behind her eyes that she flipped the skirt over and panted, 'Need. Air.'

He extricated himself. 'I was just having fun,' he said with a wicked glint in his eye. 'Just like you.'

Laughing, she sat up. 'In the fairy tales, they never mentioned how the Princess got out of her gown for the Prince.'

'Going on history and the lack of underwear back then, I think the Prince just pulled up the skirts and helped himself while the Princess lay back and thought of England.' As his fingers found the tag of the dress's zipper, he kissed her gently. 'But I want to see and feel all of you.'

'So do I.' She reached for his belt and as her hand brushed his erection she suddenly flashed hot and cold. *Contraception.* 'You've got a condom, right?'

He paled. 'No.'

'What?' Panic and surprise took her voice up an octave. 'I thought you—'

'Never leave home without one?' He grimaced. 'Don't believe all the hospital gossip, Claire. This—' he flicked his long, dextrous fingers between them '—is an unexpected gift.'

His lack of a condom was in a way gratifying—he hadn't planned on having sex with anyone else—as well as devastating. They might not be having sex this evening after all.

'Mind you,' he said tightly as he strode to the bathroom. 'It might be a gift that doesn't get fully unwrapped.'

No. As she jerkily pulled open the bedside drawers on both sides of the bed, she heard him muttering, 'Bloody hell. There's enough shower gel here to wash an army.'

She reached into the second drawer expecting her fingers to touch a book but instead she felt a plastic case. 'Alistair.'

He stuck his head out of the bathroom, his messy hair wild from the ministrations of her fingers. 'What?'

'Apparently, in the tradition of a hotel that's infamous for catering to the rich and famous, there's an aptly named "fun pack."' Laughing with delight, she waved it at him. 'Daniel wasn't wrong when he said we'd find everything we need. It's all here, plus breath mints.'

'Thank God for British ingenuity and organisation.' He walked back to the bed and the mood lighting cast tantalising shadows on his naked chest. 'Now,' he said with a sly grin, 'let's get you out of this dress.'

He made short work of the frock, freeing her in less time than it had taken her to pour herself into it and then he was gazing appreciatively at her new French lace bra and matching knickers. She sent up a vote of thanks to the sales assistant who'd encouraged her to buy them, despite the fact she'd spent far too much money.

'Don't think I don't appreciate lingerie, because I do,' he said, his eyes fixed on the demi-bra. 'It's just, right now I'd appreciate it more off you than on.'

With a proficiency she didn't want to examine too closely, he quickly divested her of her underwear. Attempting to match him, she unhooked his trousers and pushed his pants and underwear down to his ankles. He kicked them off and a thrill spun deep down inside her at the glorious sight of him before her—delineated pecs, washboard-flat abdomen, the tantalising trail of dark blond hair that arrowed down to the prize, which jutted out towards her, erect and ready.

I caused that, she thought in wonder, but before another thought could form, he'd killed the lights and was pulling her down onto the bed, rolling her into him in a tangle of limbs. His mouth honoured her, starting with her lips and then trailing along her jaw and down her neck before his tongue traced the hollow in her throat.

She shivered in delight, never having known such delicious sensations, and as much as she wanted to run her hands up and down his back and feel him too, she didn't want a moment's distraction from revelling in his touch. Besides, his mouth had closed around the aching and tingling flesh of her breast. An arrow of need darted deep, sharp and erotic, lifting her hips to his and bucking against him. Seeking him. Sliding her slick and ready self against him.

He groaned and raised his head. 'If you want me to go slowly, that's not the way to encourage it.'

'Fast, slow, I don't care.'

'God, Claire,' he ground out. 'I'm serious.'

'So am I.' Her heart hammered. 'Ever since that kiss I've—'

'Wanted this so badly I can't even think straight,' he said hoarsely.

'Yes.' She breathed out the word. 'Oh, yes.'

From the lights of the city that cast shadows in the room, she saw the agony of holding back glowing deep in his eyes. Her body thrummed so fast with need that her muscles quivered, desperate to close around him. She pulled her hands out of his grasp and picked up one of the distinctive blue squares. 'We've got more than one condom and we've got the night.'

'In that case, who am I to argue?'

She kissed him as she slid the condom along his silken length. Reminding herself this was her fantasy, and that he was hers to use for her pleasure, she rolled him over onto his back.

He rolled her straight back, capturing her hands again. 'I've fantasised for a long time about your legs wrapped high around me.'

She was awestruck. 'You have?'

'Do you have any idea what those shoes you wear do to me?' His voice was hoarse.

'I can put them on if you want?'

'Next time.' His voice was hoarse.

She gripped his waist with her legs, crossing her ankles above his back and he entered her tantalisingly slowly. Millimetre by millimetre, in and out, gently gaining depth until he filled her completely, she was almost screaming with frustrated pleasure. An unexpected sob left her lips.

He instantly tensed and concern pierced the fog of lust in his eyes. 'Are you okay?'

She tightened around him. 'I'm more than okay.'

It had been such a long time since she'd had sex. Since she'd experienced bliss quite like this.

It's never been like this.

Her hips rose as she matched his rhythm, welcoming the length of him stroking her. She wanted to kiss him but sensation was taking over and her head thrashed from side to side as ecstasy built. The noise of their panting breaths fell away as the edges of her mind started to blur. Nothing existed except his touch and the addictive bliss that drove her on, promising euphoria. Her body spun ever upwards—twirling, rising, seeking and craving the ephemeral delight.

With a shout of wonder, she was lifted high out of herself, shattering into a thousand shards of silver that rained down all around her. As she fell back to earth, he jerked over her, crying out her name. As she raised her head to kiss him, she tasted salt and the joy of her own tears.

CHAPTER EIGHT

ALISTAIR COULDN'T STOP grinning but he knew he had to wrestle down the desire to beam from ear to ear before he arrived at the castle. If he didn't, his joie de vivre would invite nudges, winks and comments from all the usual suspects—like the porters who'd say, 'You're looking happier than you deserve to, guv.'

And he was happy. Ridiculously happy, but no one at the castle could know the reason for his good spirits. Especially not Robyn. As head of surgery, she'd have his guts for garters and the Royal College of Surgeons would be none too pleased either if they got a whiff of anything untoward. Not that either he or Claire considered what had happened between them to be anything other than marvellous.

After making love twice—the first time hot and explosive, the second time deliciously slow but oddly more intense—they'd fallen asleep. He'd woken to find her head on his chest and her hair strewn all over his body. Normally when he had sex with a woman, he tended to leave her bed soon afterwards, but with Claire's words—*one night*—clear in his mind, along with being in the neutral territory of the hotel, he'd fallen asleep and had slept surprisingly well.

He blew a few strands of her hair out of his mouth and nose, but his tickling breath must have woken her. She'd opened her sleep-filled eyes and a moment later—the exact second she'd remembered where she was—they'd dilated into pools of caramel sauce. It was as natural as breathing to stroke her hair. 'Good morning.'

She smiled, although it held hesitancy at the edges. 'Hi.' She raised her head so she could see the bedside clock and then gasped. 'No. Nine-fifteen? This is a little awkward.'

It should have been very awkward but for some reason it wasn't.

'Why?'

She sat up quickly, pulling the sheet with her. 'Oh, you know.' She gave an embarrassed laugh. 'With the dawn comes the unforgiving light.'

He laughed. 'You look deliciously sexy and sleep rumpled to me. I tell you what. We can always keep the curtains closed and pretend it's still the night.'

Two hot-pink spots appeared on her cheeks and she groaned. 'Is that a polite way of saying I have the remnants of last night's makeup halfway down my cheeks and wild and crazy bed hair?'

He thought she looked beautiful. 'Nothing that a shower won't repair,' he'd said, kissing her gently. 'Tell you what. Let's have a shower and some breakfast before we open the curtains and concede the night's over.' She stared at him for a long moment, her face giving away nothing. A stab of disappointment pierced him. 'Or not.'

She blinked a few times before making a sound that was half laugh and half discomfiture. 'Um… Al.'

All his life he'd been called Alistair and it was rare that anyone ever shortened it. If they did, he promptly corrected them, but there was something about Claire's accent, and the intimacy the contraction implied that kept him silent. 'Yes?'

'The dawn also brings reality. My disposable contacts are long gone and I don't have my glasses. Everything's out of focus. To be honest, I can't see much further than my fingertips.'

He laughed and pulled her in close. 'You don't have to see, Claire. Just feel.'

'Is that an invitation?'

'Could I deny a half-blind woman anything?'

She smiled the smile of a woman who'd just been given a box wrapped up in tissue paper and a bow, and she slid her hands up into his hair. Her fingers delved deep, firmly exploring his skull.

'Are you taking up phrenology?' he quipped.

Her fingers moved forward to his forehead. 'With this prominence, you'd be considered benevolent.'

'That's definitely me.'

She raised her brows as if disputing his claim, but the look in her eyes didn't match it. She continued her exploration, slowly tracing the orbit of his eyes before the stubble on his cheekbones slowed the progression of her fingertips. She traversed the length of his nose, drawing a little circle on the tip and then she outlined his lips and traced his jaw. As her fingers left a spot, she kissed it.

He relaxed into her light and gentle caresses and his mind slid away from all thought, sinking blissfully into the sensations and absorbing every single one of them. She moved her hands to the column of his neck and using both thumbs in a soft massage she swept outwards from the centre until she reached the base of his throat.

His now languid body pressed heavily into the mattress and his mind emptied, conscious of nothing except the pleasure of her touch. Her fingers were drawing delicious small and continuous 'e's along both of his clavicles, moving slowly but surely out towards his shoulders.

A shot of adrenaline pierced his languor and he thrust out his left hand, immediately capturing her right. He had no problem with Claire, the woman, touching him, but

Claire, the doctor, was another matter entirely. He sure as hell had no desire to talk about what she was about to feel and instantly diagnose with her fingers. She'd ask questions—questions he didn't want to answer—and not only would it summarily end her delicious exploration of him, it would end their magical time together on a sour note. He had no intention of allowing that to happen.

Thank goodness she couldn't see very well. He pressed her hand to his mouth and kissed it before using his tongue to tickle her palm. She laughed and the musical sound surrounded him before sliding under his skin. As it trickled along his veins, he had the strangest sensation—something that made him feel different somehow—but with a beautiful and naked woman sitting astride him, he didn't pause to give it any thought.

Very slowly, he sucked one of her fingers into his mouth before releasing it and turning his attention to the next one. With each flick of his tongue, he felt her thighs tense and relax against his own and felt himself harden against her. As he released her pinkie finger he pressed her hand on his belly with her fingers splayed downwards.

She shivered and without hesitation she took the bait exactly as he'd hoped she would. Her attention was focused far from his shoulder and her fingers and mouth explored him until he begged for mercy. She rolled a condom on him and he rolled her under him.

Afterwards, they'd shared a tub and he'd cradled her back against him, keeping her hands firmly away from his chest. They'd blown bubbles of bath gel like little kids, delighting in the rainbow of colours as the bubbles floated above them. Food had followed and he'd consumed the largest breakfast he'd eaten in a very long time. He'd been unable to convince her that kippers were a treat.

'Bacon is a treat,' she'd said, savouring two poached

eggs. 'Pancakes and maple syrup are a treat, but oily smoked fish? Not so much.'

'All that omega-3 is good for your joints and helps ward off Alzheimer's.'

'You forgot to mention reducing the risk of heart disease and stroke.'

He hadn't forgotten at all. His failure to mention the top two health risks had been deliberate. Not that omega-3 could have prevented his cardiac condition, but it could help stave off other complications.

'I prefer to get my daily dose of omega-3 from nuts.' With a theatrical shudder of her white-bathrobe-clad shoulders, she pushed the plate of kippers back towards him. 'Be my guest and eat mine.'

'Well, if you're forcing it on me...' He'd speared it with his fork before enjoying the fish on hearty seed-laden toast.

'Perhaps kippers are a bit like Vegemite,' she said reflectively.

'How so exactly?' he asked, wondering about the connection between the ghastly black stuff Australians loved and the cold-water fish.

'To enjoy either of them, perhaps you have to be raised on them from an early age.'

'You might be right,' he said with a grin. 'I ate kippers a lot growing up. They were Cook's favourite breakfast food.'

Her coffee cup stalled halfway to her luscious mouth. 'Cook?' She blinked. 'You grew up with a cook?' Her disbelief rode across her face and settled in her startled and out-of-focus gaze.

He regretted the slip of his tongue. What the hell had made him mention Cook? Trying to shrug away all the disparate emotions that always hit him when he thought about Englewood, he said with feigned easiness, 'We lived in the country.'

She laughed. 'And that's your explanation? In Australia,

living in the country and having a cook are not automatically connected. Next you'll be telling me you had a nanny and you went to boarding school.'

'Guilty on both counts, I'm afraid.'

'And it keeps happening,' she said, sounding slightly bewildered.

'What keeps happening?'

'Me, feeling like I've stepped into the middle of an English novel from my childhood.' She slathered jam onto a croissant. 'I grew up in a town ringed by red dust. I'm the daughter of a mechanic and a secretary. My mother was an anglophile and she read me all the classics like *The Secret Garden*, *Wind in the Willows*, all the Roald Dahl stories and, of course, A. A. Milne. The idea of having a cook and a nanny was the stuff of stories, but you actually lived it. Tell me, did you have a secret garden?'

'There was a walled garden, but it wasn't very secret.' He gave a wry smile. 'My father used to tease my mother that she only married him for the garden. She certainly loved it and my earliest memories are playing hide-and-seek with her there.'

Claire's eyes lit up. 'Do your parents still live in the great house in the country?'

He tried to stave off the flinch but it came anyway. Not for the first time today, he gave thanks that Claire was extremely short-sighted without her glasses. 'No. Dad died when I was thirteen. Due to a complicated family will, we had to leave.'

'Oh.' Her hand shot out and rested over his. 'I'm sorry.'

'It was a long time ago,' he said, sliding his hand out from under hers and refilling their coffee cups.

She frowned. 'Thirteen's a tough age to lose your father.'

Yes. 'Fortunately, I had some excellent housemasters at school.'

She rubbed her temples and he swooped into action, needing to prevent her from asking anything else about his father. 'Headache?' he asked.

She nodded at him with a resigned smile. 'As wonderful as all of this has been, I need to get home to my glasses.'

'In that case…' He rose and pressed a button. The curtains smoothly opened to reveal a Sunday full of sunshine. They both squinted into the light.

'Oh, God,' Claire suddenly moaned. 'I have to go out into broad daylight in an evening gown.'

'No, you don't.' He pulled her to her feet and kissed her hair. 'I've bought us both a souvenir to remember our night.'

She grimaced. 'I'm not sure wearing the hotel bathrobe home is any less incriminating than the dress.'

'O ye of little faith,' he said, tucking some damp strands of her hair behind her ear. 'We're leaving wearing a set of monogrammed hotel gym gear.'

'They sell that?' She laughed. 'I love this hotel.'

He'd agreed with her.

That had been nineteen hours ago. The last words she'd said to him before she hopped into a cab were, 'See you at work, Mr North.'

'Morning, guv,' one of the porters greeted him as he entered the hospital.

'Morning, Amos.'

'Heard you had a good weekend.' The porter tapped his nose as if he was privy to some private information. Alistair tensed for moment but relaxed when Amos said, 'Saw your photo in the paper with that pretty nurse Ms Hobbes.'

'It was my job to dance with all of the nurses,' he said easily, telling the truth. 'And I went home alone.'

Disappointment flashed across the man's face. 'That's too bad, guv. Next time, eh?'

Alistair grinned and kept walking. When he arrived on Koala Ward, his team were waiting for him, including Claire. He knew she would have arrived half an hour ago to read the files.

She gave him the same quietly restrained smile she'd given him for the past two weeks—well, at work anyway. With her hair pulled neatly back in a ponytail, a fresh white coat and glasses perched on her nose she looked exactly the same as she'd always looked. Rising to her feet, she picked up her stethoscope and swung it around her neck. The bell came to rest on the V of her blouse and it snagged his gaze. Immediately, the memory of a sheer lace bra that left little to the imagination hit him so hard his blood swooped to his groin.

'Morning, Mitchell. Bailey.' His normal greeting sounded strained and he cleared his throat. 'I want an update on Ryan Walker.'

'He's not triggering the ventilator yet,' Claire said as a small frown made a V on the bridge of her nose. 'We're continuing with the treatment of sedation, ventilation and parenteral nutrition.'

'That's all we can do at the moment,' Alistair said. 'Right, Bailey, your turn.'

After the ward round finished and he'd spoken to the Walkers, he ducked into the nurses' tea room and grabbed a cheese and ham croissant. He needed the fuel before a busy morning in outpatients. He'd just brushed the last crumbs off his fingers when Dominic MacBride telephoned him.

'We need you and your registrar down here for a consult. Sooner rather than later if possible.'

'On my way.'

As he ran down the stairs, he was surprised to meet Claire on the third floor. 'On your way to A & E?'

She's hardly going to the circus.

She nodded. 'Yep.'

He opened his mouth to say, *I had a great time with you*, which was what he usually said to a woman he'd slept with and wanted to see again. He promptly swallowed the words, remembering he'd promised her what had happened wouldn't spill into their work world. Right now, they were clearly at work. He frantically sought for something else to say but pulled up blank.

What the hell was wrong with him? He was British, for heaven's sake. He'd been raised on polite small talk. It was a relief to arrive at the ground floor. He pushed open the heavy fire door for her. As she slipped past he breathed in deeply, drawing in her scent that reminded him so much of summer days on the Côte d'Azur. The tang of grapes, the softness of lavender and the refreshing fizz of lemon shot through him and he had to fist his right hand so as not to wrap it around her waist.

In the corridor, he fell into step next to her when Claire's brisk pace suddenly faltered. She abruptly stepped sideways as if she was avoiding something and bumped into him, knocking him off balance. He automatically gripped her hips to steady himself. As he did so, he noticed a man standing stock-still in the middle of the hallway staring straight at him and Claire.

It took him a moment to recognise who he was, but as his hands fell away from Claire, he realised it was Thomas Wolfe. He hadn't seen the paediatric cardiologist in years, so why the hell was he staring at them as if he'd just come face to face with his worst nightmare?

The painful intensity of Thomas's gaze gave Alistair pause, and without thinking he glanced over his shoulder. Rebecca Scott, the transplant surgeon, stood behind them, her face pale and tight.

'North. Mitchell.' She gave them a brisk nod of acknowledgment before striding past them. Without saying another word, she skirted around Thomas Wolfe and exited the corridor.

For a moment Thomas didn't move. Alistair was about to break the uncomfortable silence with a 'Good to see you again, Thomas,' when the man spun around, punched open the large plastic doors to A & E and disappeared.

'Wow. ' Claire's face was full of curiosity. 'Who was that?'

'Thomas Wolfe. He's a cardiologist. Worked here years ago. I got a memo this morning saying he's back. God knows why when the storm clouds of closure are hanging over the castle.'

'That's as may be,' Claire said thoughtfully. 'But something pretty big's going on between him and Rebecca. If looks were a loaded gun, one of us would be dead by now.'

'They used to be married.' He blew out a long sigh. 'Guess it must have been a messy divorce.'

'That's an understatement,' Claire said with a shiver. 'It's a perfect example of why people who work together shouldn't…'

Her cheeks pinked up, reminding him of how she'd looked two nights ago. More than anything he wanted to kiss her. 'Get married?' he said quickly, before she could say, *Have sex*. 'I absolutely agree with you, but surely that doesn't preclude enjoying each other away from the hospital.'

'I think we demonstrated that was possible.' Her clipped tone was at war with her expression.

'Then why are you sounding like it was a science experiment where we proved a hypothesis?'

She gave him a rueful smile. 'We agreed to one night.'

A spark of hope lit through him. 'We can always agree to one night again. Hell, we can agree to one night as many times as we wish.'

'Alistair,' she said sadly. 'That spontaneous woman on Saturday night wasn't the real me.'

He wouldn't accept that. 'I think that woman's always been very much a part of you.'

'You're just saying that so I agree to another night.'

'I'd love another night with you, but what I said isn't a line.' He really wanted to touch her but they were standing in a busy corridor and she deserved better than becoming the next topic on the hospital grapevine. 'I think that impetuous and risk-taking woman's been hampered by your dyslexia and buried by its secret.

'But it's not a secret any more, and more importantly, not everything in life can be planned.' He was intimate with the truth of that statement. 'Nor should it be because overplanning can deny you opportunities.'

He held his breath and waited for her to disagree or tell him to go to hell but she didn't say anything. Instead, she shoved her hands deep into the pockets of her white coat and rocked back on her fire-engine-red heels.

When she met his gaze again, the whirlpool in her eyes had stilled to a millpond. 'So, you're suggesting that outside of work I could benefit from some more practice at being spontaneous.'

He grinned, delight lighting through him. 'I'd be very happy to help you.'

'In that case,' she said with a tinkle in her voice, 'I'll be in touch.'

'When?' He tensed as the needy word left his lips. The moment was utterly foreign to him. He wasn't the one who ever asked a question like that—it was the domain of all the women he dated.

'When I'm feeling impulsive.' A momentary flash of lust mixed with promise in her beautiful eyes. And then it was gone and she was pushing her glasses up her nose and turning away from him saying, 'They're waiting for us in A & E.'

He watched her walk towards the plastic doors feeling slightly discombobulated. She'd just done to him what he'd done to so many women before her. He didn't like it one little bit.

CHAPTER NINE

CLAIRE SLIPPED OUT of bed and took a moment to watch a sleeping Alistair gently snoring. She smiled at him tucked up in pyjamas, finding it odd that he always wore them or a T-shirt in bed. She put it down to a British idiosyncrasy.

Padding out of the room, she pulled a throw rug around her shoulders, sat on the couch and reluctantly opened her computer. The recently unleashed woman who was living for the moment reprimanded her.

You have a man in your bed other women would fight you for. Why aren't you in there with him?

Because I've been having so much fun the last three weeks I'm behind with studying.

Pffp!

The pleasure-seeking woman pouted, sat down and crossed her arms as if she was taking part in a sit-in demonstration.

You've still got time.

Claire visualised the calendar and wasn't as convinced. Ever since she'd made that first booty call to Alistair on the Monday night after the ball, they'd met at least three nights a week. Sometimes she called him and sometimes he called her, but either way, they always seemed to end up in her flat rather than his. She was working on not letting that bother her, because this thing they shared was just sex. Did it really matter whose bed they tumbled into?

She'd gone into this affair with her eyes wide open. Her goal was to loosen the reins on her need to control everything in her life and to practise some spontaneity. And it was paying off—she'd definitely improved. Of course, she'd never be as laid-back as Alistair was at work but she was giving him a run for his money outside of it. They were having fun and enjoying each other and that's all it could be. Even if Alistair hadn't been the perennial bachelor everyone knew him to be, she wasn't easy to love.

Claire forced her attention to the podcast about endovascular coiling of an aneurysm, but as the professor's words droned on, her mind drifted. *Why is he a bachelor?* That thought had been popping into her mind more frequently of late, especially after days like yesterday. Alistair had texted her just as she'd finished handing over to Andrew at noon. She and her junior house officer were sharing a Saturday shift and she'd worked the morning. *If you're free, I've got a plan.*

As his plans so often occurred under the cover of darkness and involved them being horizontal, she'd been a bit stunned when he'd picked her up saying, 'I thought it was time you were a tourist.' He'd pointed the car towards the Thames and half an hour later she was standing in a pod on the London Eye. As the cantilevered observation wheel slowly rotated, she'd taken in the awe-inspiring view with her very own tour guide.

'This is amazing. I'm so excited I don't know where to look first.' Her back was snuggled into Alistair's chest and he had his arms wrapped firmly around her.

'Start with the easy and close stuff. There's Big Ben and the House of Commons.' He lifted his right hand and pointed. 'That big block of flats is Buckingham Palace and closer to the river is Horse Guards. That big column—'

'Nelson in Trafalgar Square.'

'Well done. Now cast your eye beyond the bridge and what can you see?'

'Our favourite hotel.' She smiled a secret smile and tilted her head back until he was looking down at her with a sexy gleam in his eyes. A delicious shiver roved through her, setting off tiny fires of desire. 'That was a great night.'

He kissed her and she started to turn into him before she realised they were sharing this pod with strangers. 'It was one of my best nights,' he said throatily before reverting back into tour guide mode. 'Keep your eye on the river and you can see Tower Bridge and the Tower of London.'

She could see their familiar shapes but it was a modern building that caught her eye. 'What's that glass and black steel building?'

'The Gherkin. It's office space and apparently its design style is neo-futuristic.'

Claire laughed. 'Looks more like a rocket to me. I think I prefer the older buildings.'

It was a gloriously sunny day without a skerrick of the famous London fog. She could see for miles. 'Where were the Olympics held?'

'Stratford.' He pointed in the direction.

'And where did you grow up?'

He didn't instantly respond. It seemed to her that a tiny gap had just opened up between their bodies, interrupting what had been one continuous head-to-toe touch.

He eventually said, 'It's further than the eye can see.'

'Show me the general direction.'

The gap closed and his warmth was once again trickling through her without any little darts of cool air. 'My mother lives in Little Wilbraham.' As the pod dropped in height he pointed in the same general direction as Olympic Park. 'It's a tiny little village south-east of Cambridge.'

She remembered him telling her he and his mother had

been required to move house when his father died. 'Has that been home since you were thirteen?'

'I've always considered it more Mother's house than mine.'

'Why?'

Did she remarry? Did you feel usurped? Did you clash with your stepfather?

She found herself hoping he'd reveal something so she could flesh out the vague sketch she'd drawn in her head of his childhood. Currently, he knew a lot more about the child she'd been than she knew of him.

'I suppose it's because I spent more time at school than I ever spent at Rose Cottage,' he said reflectively. 'We always spent part of the summer abroad, and once I'd finished school and went up to Oxford, it become a place I visited on short stays. Home's my flat in Notting Hill.'

The flat she'd never been invited to.

He suddenly spun her around in his arms and gazed down at her, his grey eyes dancing with anticipation. 'Are you ready for your next surprise?'

'There's more?'

'Of course there is. You deserve a London day out and it's my privilege to provide it.'

Her heart suddenly wobbled rather precariously in her chest. She kissed him quickly, forcing herself to concentrate on how warm his lips felt against her own rather than how very close she was to the edge of a cliff and a flashing orange danger zone sign.

Hand in hand, they'd exited the pod and walked back to the car, before re-crossing the Thames and making their way to Hyde Park. Alistair had produced a wicker basket complete with a rug, china plates and cups, champagne glasses, silver cutlery and cotton napkins. They'd picnicked in style by the Serpentine, sipping champagne, feasting on Scottish smoked salmon inside crusty buttered bread and peeled quail eggs and cheese. As they ate, they talked about the books they'd read, music they enjoyed, current political scandals and the many differences yet shared similarities between their two countries.

When Claire was almost certain she couldn't eat another thing, Alistair had delved back into the basket and with a 'Ta-dah!' produced two slices of chocolate and salted caramel layer cake and a Thermos of hot water to make tea. After they'd licked their fingers of every trace of chocolate and were utterly replete, they'd both fallen asleep in the treasured London sunshine.

Of all the times they'd spent together, yesterday afternoon had felt the most like a date. When Alistair had suggested they head home, she'd almost said, 'To your flat?' What had stopped her?

She thought about it and she couldn't get past her gut feeling that the question would have caused awkward tension. She hadn't wanted to ruin what had been a perfectly lovely afternoon. When it came to talking about himself and his family, he seemed surrounded by a taut reserve that doubled as a permanent *Approach with Care* sign. So she hadn't pushed that they go to his flat. Instead, she'd agreed with him that heading home to Bayswater was a great idea.

In the glowing cerise and violet fingers of the setting sun that streamed through the window, they'd made love. *No, you had sex.* Sex was their thing—their selfish, living for the moment thing—when they lost themselves in pure pleasure and in each other. He always started by gently pulling her hair out of her hairband and removing her glasses and then he'd kiss her long and leisurely until every part of her quivered like a taut string under the ministrations of a bow. Each time they had sex, she determined yet again to keep her glasses on because Alistair didn't require soft focus in any shape or form. She ached to see all of his perfection in sharp relief, but the moment he kissed her, she lost all coherent thought, her glasses vanished and she found she didn't care at all.

As darkness had settled over the flat, declaring the day truly gone, and the lights had flickered on both inside and out, he'd pulled on his shirt and she'd prepared herself for his goodbye. Instead, he'd said, 'I make a mean omelette.'

'Do you?' she'd asked, tracing a line from his hand, along his forearm and up towards his shoulder.

'I do.' He captured her arm and pulled her to her feet. 'Come on. You can be my sous chef.'

He hadn't been exaggerating his skills—he did indeed make a fabulous omelette. After eating the savoury delight, they'd cuddled up on the couch—she with her head on his chest, he with his arm looped casually around her—and he'd made stealth moves on her popcorn. The entire afternoon and evening had been scarily normal. Anyone outside on the street who'd paused to peer in through the window would have thought they were a regular couple.

We are so not a couple. Couples share more than sex.

They shared stories, and although she'd told him about her dyslexia and growing up and he'd certainly mentioned that his father had died when he was young and he'd spent his adolescent years at boarding school, there was something in the way he'd revealed the information that told her it was just the tip of the iceberg. And yet he was a kind, generous and thoughtful man, so why was he still a bachelor?

And just like that, she was back to where she'd started and nowhere near close to knowing what made Alistair North tick. *There's a reason for that. And he doesn't want you to know it.*

This thing they shared was nothing more than a hedonistic fling. She knew she was just another woman in a long line with many before her and just as likely many more after.

It's fine. I'm using him to practise being spontaneous and impetuous.

Then why do you want to see his flat? Why do you want to know where the estate with the walled garden is? Where he spent his childhood? Why do you want to discover the date of his birthday and if he's a good son to his mother?

I don't want that. I only want his body.

A sound not dissimilar to hysterical laughter sounded faintly in her mind and she shoved the ear buds harder into her ears. She restarted the podcast and this time she listened intently to the lecturer as if he was the only voice in the world.

An hour later she felt a tap on her shoulder and she glanced up to see Alistair standing behind the couch, freshly showered and fully dressed. She pressed pause on the podcast as a sigh of disappointment rumbled through her. She'd have loved him to be padding around her flat wearing nothing more than a towel looped low on his hips so she could watch the play of bunching muscles dancing under his skin. But the man was always pulling a shirt on and covering up.

'Good morning.' With a sexy smile, he bent down and kissed her full on the mouth. 'You're up early for a Sunday.'

The shimmers and tingles from his kiss spun through her, making her feel far more alive and happy than she could remember. 'Exams are less than six months away.'

A slight frown pulled down his brows. 'I've been distracting you.'

She pressed her hand against his cheek. 'In the best possible way.'

He kissed her again but this time it was devoid of the usual intoxicating heat. Instead, it was infused with gentleness and something else she couldn't place. 'I'll leave you to get on with it.'

Despite knowing that she needed to spend the day studying, she was filled with a disproportionate sense of despondency. She was about to say, 'Thanks for yesterday,' when he said, 'I'll go and grab some fresh clothes and return with pastries and coffee from Tony's. Then I'll quiz you on...' He squinted down at her screen.

'Aneurysms.' Somehow, she managed to pluck the word out of her stunned mind.

He nodded, his face full of empathy. 'Tricky buggers, aneurysms.' Then he kissed her on the top of her head and said, 'Back soon,' before disappearing out the door.

As it clicked shut behind him, she stared at it, trying to make sense of what had just happened. Alistair had offered to help her study.

So? Nothing odd or unusual about that. He's a neurosurgeon.

But there was everything odd and unusual about it. Consultants didn't help their registrars study—that wasn't in the job description.

Neither was having sex.

The sex has nothing to do with work.

And it didn't. They'd both kept the two utterly separate. During work hours they didn't text or call each other and when they were alone they were too focused on enjoying each other to talk about work. But this offer to help her study came on the back of yesterday's generosity and thoughtfulness. It made her heart lurch dangerously close to the rickety safety rail balanced on the crumbling precipice.

If she wasn't careful, she was at very great risk of falling in love with Alistair North. Not only wasn't it part of the plan, it was exceedingly hazardous. Loving Alistair wasn't an option because she risked far more than just her job—she risked her heart.

As she recommenced the podcast yet again, the droning voice of the professor seemed to whisper, *It's too late.*

* * *

Alistair stood at the scrub sinks looking out through the glass and saw the broad back of Matthew McGrory bent over a trolley. As the plastic surgeon straightened and the porter wheeled the patient into the operating theatre, Alistair glimpsed the serious burn to the child's face.

Matthew then came barrelling through the double doors, his athletic build making short shrift of the plastic doors. 'Hello, Alistair,' he said in his gentle Irish brogue so at odds with his rugby player bulk.

'That burn looks nasty,' Alistair said as he lathered up his arms. 'How did it happen?'

'He's one of the Westbourne Primary School kids. Name's Simon Bennett.' Matthew flicked the taps on with his elbows. 'Poor bloody kid. It's tough enough that his parents' drug habit came ahead of him and that he's basically growing up in foster care, without the added burden of disfigurement by a facial burn.'

'You using spray-on skin?'

He nodded. 'Aye. It's phenomenal and that burn is much improved. Today I'm debriding an infection on his arm. It's best done in theatre. Rupert gives him a light GA and it minimises his pain.'

'The fallout of that fire's still haunting us,' Alistair said, thinking of Ryan.

'It is,' Matthew said quietly, 'but it also proved how much the castle's needed here in central London.' He rinsed off his arms. 'By the way, the fundraising committee owes you a debt of thanks. It was good of you to let Victoria sell off every part of your night to raise money.'

'No problem.'

'Did you at least meet someone you liked? Someone to have fun with?'

Alistair immediately thought of Claire and how much fun they'd had—were still having. He opened his mouth to give the usual quip—a standard shared between two men who have no desire to be tied down—but the words stuck in his throat. He put it down to his promise to Claire to keep their affair secret and out of the hospital.

'Mr North,' a nurse interrupted. 'Patient's under and we're ready when you are.'

'On my way,' he said, stepping back from the sink with both arms raised and a silent vote of thanks to the nurse.

'No rest for the wicked, eh?' Matt said, a friendly glint in his eyes.

None indeed.

Claire paced outside the lecture theatre, clutching her notes and the accompanying USB stick that held her presentation. As she walked, she concentrated on keeping the rolling nausea at bay. The day she'd dreaded had arrived and she was about to stand up in front of her peers and their consultants.

'I've arranged for us to present first,' Alistair had said to her two days ago at the end of a long operating list. 'After all, neurosurgery's the elite surgery and deserves top billing.' What he didn't say, but was clearly implied was, 'That way you get the presentation over and done with early and you can relax and enjoy the others.'

His discretion and kindness had just about undone her. He knew how much standing up in front of people terrified her and he'd done his best to try and minimise her trauma. It had taken everything she had not to throw her arms around him there and then in front of the theatre staff and shower him in kisses of gratitude. Instead, she'd said a brisk, 'Sounds like a plan,' from behind her surgical mask and hoped he saw her thanks clear in her eyes.

His eyes had twinkled as he'd said, 'Don't be late, Mitchell.'

The scrub nurse had laughed. 'Alistair, that's the pot

calling the kettle black. You could take a leaf or ten out of Claire's book.'

Andrew Bailey, surrounded by a crowd of other junior house officers, walked past Claire and gave her the double thumbs up. He was clueless to the fact she was working very hard on keeping from throwing up the piece of toast and black tea she'd only half managed to finish at breakfast. Despite having committed the presentation to memory, she'd been up since five a.m., going over it *one more time* at least five times more.

She checked her watch. Where was Alistair? *Please don't be late today. Please.* The previously full corridor was now empty as everyone had entered the lecture theatre to take their seats. The toast hit the back of her throat and she gagged, forcing it back down.

What was wrong with her? This was even worse than the last time she'd had to present in Australia. Back there, no one had known about her dyslexia and she'd not only laboured under keeping it a secret, she hadn't received any support from her consultant. Today she was secure in the knowledge of Alistair's respect and understanding and yet she was desperately close to throwing up. It didn't make any sense. Then again, nerves rarely did.

Closing her eyes, she tried to focus on long, slow deep breaths so she could harness some desperately needed calm.

'Are you ready, Claire?' Alistair's voice sounded quietly behind her.

Her eyes flew open and she spun around as frustration and relief tangoed fast in her veins. 'You're late!'

He checked his watch. 'I'm a minute early.'

'A minute isn't early,' she heard herself screech. 'It's barely on time.'

He raised his brows. 'Have you ever known me to be a minute early?'

Against the noise of her thundering heart booming in

her ears and the agitation of her mind, she clearly heard, *No, not once*. He'd made a huge effort for her. Her heart lurched and she completely let go of the pretence that she liked him but didn't love him. It streamed away like the rush and gurgle of bath water racing down the drain. When Alistair made gestures like helping her study and arriving early, it was impossible not to feel her love for him fill up her heart and spill over into her soul.

Joy and heartache collided, crashing together in her chest. *I truly love him.*

'However, if you're going to stand here arguing the point with me, we will be late,' he said with envious ease, infuriating logic and absolutely no idea of her inner turmoil.

Her unwise love for him mixed in with her fear of public speaking, spinning her stomach like a tumble dryer. 'I think I'm going to throw up.'

'Nonsense, you're going to be fine,' he said with British exactitude. 'You're prepared. You know the work inside out, and if the worst happens, which it won't, I'm right there beside you.' He stretched out his arm towards the door and gave her a reassuring smile. 'Shall we go in and dazzle with them our findings?'

Claire didn't know if she was happy or sad that the symposium was over. Alistair, true to his word, had stood next to her but there'd been no need for him to step in—she hadn't faltered once. On Alistair's flippant but sound advice, she'd pictured the audience naked and it had helped. Whether it was that, her preparation, Alistair's presence or a combination of the three, it had carried her past her terror.

For the rest of the day, she'd floated on a sea of praise. Robyn Kelly, the head of surgery, had sought her out at lunch to congratulate her and strongly urged her to submit the paper for consideration at the international neurosurgery conference. Andrew had pumped her hand so enthusiastically that her shoulder still ached and she'd overheard Dominic MacBride telling Alistair that he wished his specialist registrar was as switched on as Claire.

Her boss had quipped, 'Of course she's brilliant. I taught her.' The man she loved had said quietly to her during the applause, 'Well done. We'll celebrate tonight.'

It was the first time he'd ever referenced their affair at work and rather than sending rafts of anxiety thudding through her, a warm glow of anticipation spread instead. When she stacked up all the little acts of caring he'd shown her over the past weeks, was his breech of their pact part of a growing affection for her? She hugged the thought tight as she closed her heart and mind to the warning. *He's known as the playboy surgeon for a reason.*

The afternoon sped by quickly with a full outpatients' clinic and now it was six in the evening. She'd called by Koala Ward to check for any outstanding IV orders and medication updates, and thankfully all was quiet. Her stomach rumbled, the noise reminding her that she'd not really eaten very much all day. This morning's nauseous nerves had killed her appetite and most of lunchtime had been spent fielding congratulations, leaving no time to eat. She'd munched on an apple during the dash to outpatients. It wasn't surprising she was now famished.

As she was rostered on until nine, she needed to stay close to the hospital but the thought of the cafeteria food suddenly made her feel queasy. Decision made, she grabbed her bag and said to Morag, 'I'm just popping over to the Frog and Peach to grab some dinner.'

'I'm glad you're accepting the house officers' invitation.' The older woman gave her a motherly smile. 'There's more to life than work, Claire.'

'I'm a specialist registrar with exams looming,' she said with a wry smile. 'There is no life outside of work.' But as she spoke the words, she knew them to be a lie. Over the last few weeks, she'd most definitely had a life outside of the hospital. 'Page me if you need me.'

'I'm sure we'll cope without you for half an hour or so. I recommend the pulled pork nachos. They serve it with their famous pale ale barbecue sauce. It's delicious.'

'Thanks for the tip.' She didn't bother to mention that Andrew had invited her for a drink at the end of her shift, not dinner. Although she appreciated the offer, the moment she could get away for the night she was heading straight home.

Home to Alistair. As she crossed the road to the pub, she felt the grin of pleasure stretch across her face and her body leap in anticipation. He'd messaged her about a late supper featuring chocolate sauce. As much as she liked licking chocolate sauce from the top of ice cream and cake, she had a fervent desire to lick rich, dark chocolate sauce off Alistair.

Her cheeks immediately heated at the thought and she laughed. Six months ago, she could never have imagined herself being so sexually adventurous but practising being spontaneous was paying off in spades. *It's not that. It's Alistair.* And she knew it to be the truth. She'd had boyfriends before and there'd been the year with Michael, but no one had ever made her feel as accepted, safe and loved as Alistair. It meant she had no need to hold anything back and as a result she'd thrown herself heart and soul into this affair. She was utterly and deliciously in love.

Earlier in the day when she'd realised she loved him, gut wrenching worry had pulled at her, but not now. She'd gained an odd sort of peace in the knowledge that she loved him. Instead of trying to plan and control everything, instead of telling him how she felt or trying to find out if he felt the same way, she was just going to savour the feeling and the evening. After all, what did Alistair always say? Live every day as if it's your last.

The pub was a glorious historic building that had been in continuous operation since being built in 1823. Claire always laughed when she was told it was a young pub— it was still older than the oldest pubs at home. In typical English style it featured dark wooden panelling, ambient lighting, comfortable chesterfield couches and a dartboard. The noise from the Thursday night crowd came out to meet her as she stepped across the threshold and much of it was emanating from a spirited game of darts between the junior house officers and the hospital porters. Not surprisingly, the porters were winning.

She was depositing her dripping umbrella in the umbrella bin when a waitress walked past balancing four plates of delicious-looking food. She breathed in the aroma of meat, battered fish, chicken and cabbage and her stomach suddenly lurched, vanquishing her hunger. She gagged and her hand flew to her mouth. She gulped in air but the kitchen door opened again and this time the sight of the food had her turning and dashing into the ladies'.

A rotund woman in her forties glanced up from applying lipstick. 'You all right, love? You look a bit peaky.'

Claire didn't dare open her mouth until she was inside the cubicle. When she did, her stomach heaved its meagre contents up into the bowl. When there was nothing left to vomit, she flushed the toilet, closed the lid and then sat shakily on the closed seat, feeling sweat beading on her top lip and under her arms. The rest of her shivered.

A tap came on the door. 'You all right, love?'

Claire raised her head from her elbow-propped hands. 'I will be. Thanks for asking.'

'Was it sumfink you ate? The food 'ere's usually top-notch.'

'I've hardly eaten anything today,' she said, thinking about this morning as she opened the door of the stall. 'I woke up feeling nauseous but that was because I was nervous about work.' She flicked on the taps and splashed her face with water.

'I think it's probably more than just nerves, love. Either you've got a bug or a baby.' The woman laughed as she checked her hair in the mirror. 'Every time I was pregnant, the smell of fried food and cabbage always did me in.'

'I can't possibly be pregnant,' she said, thinking how she and Alistair had always used condoms.

The woman handed her some paper towels and her expression held a worldly air. 'Unless you've 'ad your tubes tied, love, or you're not getting any, there's always a chance of being up the duff. My old man 'ad the snip and nine months later I 'ad me third. At least you can find out fast these days. There's a pharmacy across the road.' With a final check in the mirror, she turned and walked back into the pub.

Claire stared at herself in the mirror. A pale face with dark rings under her eyes stared back. Surely she'd just picked up a bug? She worked with children and earlier in the week there'd been a minor outbreak of gastro on the ward. Even with best practice of hand washing, it only took one child to sneeze or cough on her to transfer the infection. That had to be the culprit of the nausea and vomiting. She couldn't possibly be pregnant—she'd had a period just a couple of weeks ago.

You had a light period.

I've been burning the candle at both ends.

A flutter of panic filled her and she forced it down. She was being ridiculous and letting an off-the-cuff comment by a stranger put the wind up her. Feeling sick and off-colour all day had a perfectly reasonable explanation. She was understandably tired because she hadn't slept well worrying about the presentation. This morning's nausea had been stress and she'd vomited just now because she was overhungry and exhausted. Or she'd picked up a virus. Either way, she was *not* pregnant.

However, the pharmacy the woman mentioned would sell jellybeans and electrolyte solution, both of which were good for gastro. She left the bathroom and retrieved her umbrella. Just as she stepped back out into the rain her phone buzzed with Koala Ward's number. Sam Riccardo was fitting. The jellybeans would have to wait.

CHAPTER TEN

CLAIRE LAY IN the dark bedroom snuggled up with Alistair in a languid fog of bliss. The champagne he'd bought sat unopened in the fridge next to the untouched celebration cake and the chocolate sauce. It wasn't that she didn't appreciate his efforts—she did, very much indeed. It was just that once she'd stepped into the flat, into his arms and he'd told her how amazing she'd been this morning before proceeding to nuzzle her neck and tell her the things he'd been wanting to do with her all day, they'd both lost interest in the food and the drink.

Her phone rang, bringing reality back into the room. With a groan, she rolled over to the bedside table and picked up the glowing device. 'It's the hospital.'

'I thought you were off-duty?' Alistair stroked her hair.

'I am.' She swiped the screen, silencing the ring tone. 'Claire Mitchell.'

'It's Andrew.' Her junior house officer's voice came down the line sounding decidedly shaky.

'You sound dreadful. What's up?'

'I've got a temperature and I've been throwing up for an hour. I need to go home but I'm on call tonight. I've rung three other people but two of them have the same bug and the other is covering for one of them. My patients are stable but can you cover if needed?'

Gastro. Andrew has gastro. She gave herself a virtual high five. 'Sure. Tell the ward and the switchboard and then go home.'

'Sorry, Claire.' He made a gagging sound. 'Got to go.'

He rang off abruptly, and although Claire knew she should be sympathetic, she started to laugh. It bubbled up on a wave of deliverance, and although she tried to stop it, that only seemed to intensify the feeling. Tears streamed down her cheeks, her belly tightened and her whole body shook as she was utterly consumed by amusement and abject relief.

Alistair gave her a bemused smile before rolling her under him. His warm grey eyes stared down at her. 'What's so funny?'

'Andrew's got gastro.'

He frowned at her, his expression confused. 'And that's funny how?'

She wiped her cheeks on the sheet and tried to curb her laughter. 'It's not funny for him.'

'But it is for you?'

She smiled up at him, eager to share the joke. 'I threw up tonight at the Frog and Peach and a random woman in the bathroom asked me if I was pregnant. Of course I knew the suggestion was ridiculous but just for a short time I was a little rattled. But Andrew has gastro and quite a few other castle staff have it too. So you can see why it's funny.'

She expected him to laugh with her and then tease her about being obsessive but instead his face tightened along with the rest of his body. He rolled away from her.

'I don't think the idea of you being pregnant is funny in any shape or form.'

She gave a wry smile. 'It was really more like a momentary possibility than an idea.'

'Jeez, Claire.' He suddenly grabbed his shirt, pulling it on jerkily before he reached out and switched on the lamp.

'That's semantics. You know that both scenarios would be a total disaster.'

Would it? A tiny part of her thought being pregnant might be the most wonderful thing to ever happen to her. Her practical side conceded that a pregnancy right now wouldn't be ideal but there was something in the aristocratic way he'd said 'disaster' that made her spine tingle.

'We're two adults having sex, Alistair. Contraception has been known to fail. Although we both know it's small, there's always an inherent risk.' She gave a light laugh. 'You're the one who's always saying not everything in life can be planned.'

He swung his feet to the floor. 'Children are the one exception.'

For someone who was impetuous, it seemed an odd thing to say. She sat up and pressed her hand gently against his back. 'But you're so great with kids. I'd like to think that if we'd had an accident and I was actually pregnant, we'd be a team.'

He lurched abruptly to his feet, moving away from her so quickly that her hand was left hanging in the air. 'A team? As in parents?' Incredulity dripped from the words, landing on her like scalding water and blistering her skin. He shook his head so hard that strands of his thick hair rose off his head. 'No. That is *never* going to happen.'

His emphatic words struck her with the biting sting of an open-handed slap and her heart cramped so tightly it was hard to breathe. Michael's words, which had faded to silence over the last few weeks, roared back loudly and in surround sound. *You're too hard to love, Claire.*

'I see,' she said grimly, feeling the sudden need to cover up. Pulling on her pyjamas, she stood, pointing a shaking finger at him accusingly. 'So basically, I'm good enough for you to screw but I'm not good enough to be the mother of your children.'

He flinched and his face pulled into a grimace. 'I didn't say that. Don't put words in my mouth.'

'I'll just use the ones you inferred, then, shall I?'

'Claire.' His usually tender voice now spoke her name on a warning growl.

'Fine,' she said bitterly, hugging herself to try and stop the shaking. To try and silence the insidious voice of relationships past. 'Tell me exactly what it is that you're saying.'

He sighed, the sound patronisingly reasonable. It was the same sound people used when they believed they were dealing with a difficult person. 'Why are we arguing about a hypothetical situation? You're not even pregnant.'

Because you started it. The common childhood expression burst into her brain but the feelings behind it were anything but childish. 'Because if I was pregnant, we'd need to have this conversation.'

'This is crazy, Claire. It's all about *ifs* and *buts* and it's not worth our time.'

But suddenly it was very much worth her time because she'd glimpsed something that scared her. 'What if I was pregnant?'

'You're not.' The words quivered with barely leashed restraint.

'No, but what if I was?' She scanned his face, trying to read it. 'What would you say?'

He suddenly looked wary. 'Would it matter?'

'Of course it would matter.'

He stared at her as if she was someone he didn't recognise. 'Are you telling me that if you were pregnant, you'd want to keep it?'

It. The pronoun battered her like a barrage of needles piercing her skin with sharp and biting stings. How could one tiny word emote so much? How could two innocuous letters combined draw such a precise line in the sand and place them clearly on opposite sides? To her, a pregnancy was a longed-for baby and the reactivation of a dream she'd believed to be covered in dust. To him, it was just an amorphous *it*.

'Of course I'd want to keep it.'

Horror and bewilderment streaked across his face. 'Why?'

She didn't have to think twice. 'Because it would be our child. Because I love you.'

He went deathly still and his handsome face lost its healthy colour, leaving behind a tinge of yellowy-green. 'You don't love me, Claire.'

The softly spoken words fell like the blow of a hammer. They shattered any remaining delusional daydreams she may have been clinging to and they shattered her heart. 'I think what you meant to say was that *you* don't love me.'

He started pacing jerkily around the small room. 'This thing we've been sharing is fun, Claire. It's not love.'

She wasn't prepared to lie. 'For me it's been both.'

His hand tore through his hair and his face crumpled. 'Good God, Claire. No.'

She hated the crushing waves of despair that rolled in on her, bringing with them all the reminders that no matter what she did, or how hard she tried, it was never enough to be loved. Her breath came in short jerky pulls and she felt as if she was folding in on herself and collapsing down into a dark pit of hopelessness.

Her legs trembled like jelly to the point she reached out to the wall for support, but then her knees suddenly locked. Like a life preserver being thrown from a ship to a drowning person in a choppy sea, she saw and heard a collage of moments spent with Alistair.

You're a very good neurosurgeon.

It's your decision. If you have any doubts at all...

Don't believe all the hospital gossip, Claire.

Are you okay?

I think that spontaneous woman's always been very much a part of you.

I'm right there beside you.

You deserve a London day out and it's my privilege to provide it.

It was one of my best nights.

Her mouth dried in shock. She may not have a vast experience of men, but she'd lived with Michael. During their year together all he'd done was find fault with her in so many ways and, oh, how he'd loved to tell her. She worked too much. She studied too much. Her friends were boring. She micromanaged their lives. She was inflexible. She stifled him with her need to control every minute detail. The list had gone on and on.

Right there and then she realised with the clarity of a fine-cut diamond that Michael had only considered their relationship in terms of himself. None of it had been about her, her feelings, her wants or her needs. Yet in a few short weeks, Alistair had considered her and cared for her in more ways than Michael had managed in a year.

Did Alistair love her but not recognise what he felt as love?

The thought snuck in and took hold, sending down a deep and anchoring root. If that was the case and she took her hurt and walked away now just to avoid the possibility of further pain, she might be abandoning an opportunity for happiness.

And if he doesn't love you?

Isn't it better to have tried and failed than to never have tried at all?

Yes. No. I'm scared.

It can't be worse than it is already. It might even be better. Fight for him. Open his eyes.

Tugging at the base of her pyjama top, she sucked in a deep breath. 'Actually, Alistair, the answer is yes. I do love you. I didn't intend to fall in love and the fact that I have lies squarely at your feet.'

'What?'

'You've only got yourself to blame.'

Bewilderment hovered over every part of his lean frame. 'What the hell are you talking about?'

She mustered an attempt at a smile. 'You've been so kind to me. You care.'

'Well, of course I bloody well care.' He agitatedly rubbed his stubble-covered jaw with his palm. 'I care for every woman that I date. That doesn't mean I've loved any of them. It doesn't mean that I love you.'

Her armour pinged with the hit but she pressed on. 'Will the world end if you admit that you love me?'

'Look, Claire,' he said in a voice she'd heard him use with junior staff at the hospital. 'You've got this all wrong. Somehow you've tangled up professional courtesy and mentoring with the fun we've been having. I can assure you, none of it is love.'

A distance she'd not seen before took up residence in his eyes. 'I'm not looking for love, Claire. I thought we were both very clear on that topic from the start. I've got a great career and a good life. I've got a flat in Notting Hill, a house in Provence and I can do what I want when I please.'

She pushed her glasses up her nose and stared him down. 'You forgot to mention the German sports car.'

'Exactly,' he said as if he thought she was being helpful. 'It's not designed for a baby seat. When you add up everything I have, why would I want to tie myself down by getting married and becoming a father?'

You're thirty-nine. Why wouldn't you want to?

'It's an impressive list of possessions,' she said, trying to sound calm, when in reality desperation was clawing at her. 'There's just one flaw with your argument. Your job, your houses and your car won't love you like a family.'

His eyes immediately darkened to the steely colour of storm clouds bursting with rain and tinged with the red of outback dust. 'Like your family loved you?'

The attack was swift and lethal but as the pain seared her she somehow scrambled to tell the truth. 'My parents loved me, Alistair. They just didn't know how to help me.'

He grunted as if the explanation made no difference. Suddenly it was her turn to see everything through a red haze. 'I think that comment has far more to do with you than with me. Your father died when you were at a vulnerable age and your mother packed you off to boarding school. Is that love?'

'Don't you dare presume to think you know anything about me and my family.'

Anger radiated off him with the ferocity of a bushfire and she almost raised her hands to try and ward off the scorching heat. His reaction spoke volumes and she'd stake her life she was close to whatever it was that had him placing possessions ahead of people. 'The reason I don't know anything is because you won't tell me,' she said as calmly as she could. She reached for his arm. 'You helped me, Alistair. You listened and you didn't judge. Let me return the favour. Please let me help you.'

He spun away from her, breaking their touch. 'I don't need any help. Unlike you, there's nothing wrong with me.'

Visceral pain ripped into her, stealing her breath and spinning the room. The past tried to rise up and consume her but it stalled. Without a shadow of a doubt, the man who'd just hurt her so comprehensively wasn't the man she knew and loved. That man had always respected her. He'd given her opportunities and choices. Out of the work environment they were equals, so what the hell was going on now?

He's hurting.

But exactly what was hurting him and why, she had

no idea at all. Whatever it was, it was old and gnarly with deeply tangled roots. It lived inside him, and the more she pushed to get close, the more it would lash out and slice her until all that was left of her was a bleeding mess of heartache and pain. She'd be the one left suffering.

Self-preservation knotted inside her. She'd worked too hard to allow him to destroy her fledging self-confidence and the irony of that thought wasn't lost on her. It had been Alistair's acceptance of her that had taught her to value herself. She jutted her chin. 'I never took you for a coward, Alistair.'

As he pulled on his trousers and slipped his feet into his shoes, his mouth tugged down at the edges, thinning into a hard line. It accentuated his cheekbones, making them blade-sharp in his face. 'I was perfectly fine before I met you, Claire. I'll be perfectly fine when I walk out this door.'

He quickly grabbed his wallet, phone and car fob before storming past her. 'Of all the women I've ever fooled around with, I thought you were the one who truly understood because you put work ahead of everything. Us having sex was all about you learning to be spontaneous and having some hard-earned fun.' He laughed bitterly. 'And you were doing so well. I thought you were more like me after all.'

She jerked her chin high. 'You mean emotionally shutdown and hiding behind a collection of possessions?'

He threw her a filthy look, which she met head-on and batted straight back at him. 'Believe me,' she said cuttingly, 'I'm not that sad.'

Stalking to her front door he hauled it open. In the brief moment before he slammed it shut, the sound of tyres squelching on a wet road and the distant toot of a train drifted into the flat—the sounds of a perfectly normal London night. Only none of this came close to normal. This was the end of friendship, hopes and dreams.

The door closed with a thwack and a thick wave of silence rolled inside, enveloping her. Alistair was gone. He'd left her without so much as a backwards glance. He'd also left her love—abandoning it casually on the couch, on the bed and on every surface in the flat. It lingered in the air she breathed and the sense of loss overwhelmed her. She sank to the floor and let her tears flow.

'Morag!' Alistair roared through the closed door of the unit manager's office. His day was going to hell in a hand basket and it wasn't even ten o'clock in the morning.

Things went to hell last night.

But he wasn't spending any more time thinking about how things between him and Claire had gone pear-shaped so quickly and so unexpectedly. He'd spent the dark wee hours consumed by it, trying to work out how he'd missed the telltale signs. Good God, he had a thesis in detecting signs from women wanting marriage and babies but he had missed the clues. Claire was just like all women and she wanted what he couldn't give her. 'Morag!'

Her dark-haired head appeared around the door thirty seconds later. 'Did it slip your mind that you can walk the twelve steps from here to the nurses' station if you wish to speak with me?'

'Humph,' he grunted as he opened a filing cabinet drawer. 'I'm going to France.'

Surprise crossed her face. 'When?'

An hour ago. 'Tonight if I can get a booking on the Eurostar. Where the hell are the leave forms?'

Morag walked calmly into the office, smoothed her uniform and sat down. 'Alistair, didn't you read the memo from the board?'

He riffled through the neatly labelled manila folders. 'Which one? They've been coming in thick and fast ever since the proposed merger with Riverside.'

'The one where they cancelled all leave requests because we've barely got enough staff to keep operating as it is.'

He didn't care about any of that. He had to get out of the castle and he had to get out now. He needed the space and serenity that Provence always offered him. He needed to find his equilibrium. He desperately needed to find the solid foundations he'd rebuilt his life on after almost losing it five years ago. 'Surely that doesn't include consultants.'

She gave him a pitying smile. 'I know it's a rarefied atmosphere up there at the top of the tree, but this time you have to slum it down here with the rest of us. The board isn't paying for annual leave and nor is it paying for covering staff. France will have to wait until your next three-day weekend.'

I can do what I want when I please. His haughty statement from last night came back to bite him. *You know your job never allows you to take off at a minute's notice. Your weekends in France are blocked out at the start of each year.*

He closed his eyes to the spotlight on the fact he did plan some things. 'If the board's not spending any money, then what about this rumour that Robyn's flying in some hotshot Italian paediatrician?'

'The duke?' Morag grinned. 'Apparently they've been good friends since medical school. He's coming as a PR favour to Robyn and using his own coin.'

He sighed, seeing his out closing fast.

'Besides,' Morag continued, 'even if the board was approving leave you couldn't go today. Both Bailey and Mitchell are down with gastro along with three of my nurses.'

Claire's not in. He hated the relief that he didn't have to face her today. Hell, he shouldn't need to feel relief. She'd been the one to move the goalposts on him and change every single rule of their game. If she hadn't done that, if she hadn't pushed him about babies and about his fam-

ily, then he wouldn't have needed to speak. He wouldn't
have said the unforgivably cruel thing to her that fear had
driven out of him.

Hell, he could still see her beautiful but tortured face
every time he closed his eyes. It made him sick to his stomach. He wanted to apologise to her but if he did she'd expect an explanation from him as to why he'd said what he
said. That would immediately take them back to square
one, more arguing and even more distress. He'd survive
but he wasn't sure she would. He didn't want to risk it. He
couldn't bear to hurt her all over again.

No, it was better to say nothing and make last night the
clean break. She'd nurse her pain into a fulminating rage
towards him, which would grow into hatred and loathing.
The result would be abhorrence, which would keep her far,
far away from him. He expected her letter of resignation
to arrive in his in-box by the end of the working day. All
in all, it was the best possible outcome for both of them.
With his condition and his family history, he couldn't offer
her marriage and babies and she deserved to be free to find
someone who could.

His mind threw up a picture of a faceless man and a flash
of bright green light burst behind his eyes. He squeezed
them shut against blinding pain and automatically rubbed
his temples with his forefingers.

'Is there anything I can help with, Alistair?' Morag
asked, her usually taciturn tone softening.

A new heart. 'No. There's nothing for it but to get out
there and be junior house officer, registrar and consultant
all rolled into one.'

'Be extra meticulous with hand washing,' Morag said,
following him onto the ward. 'We don't need anyone else
getting this bug.'

CHAPTER ELEVEN

CLAIRE MUNCHED ON dry biscuits and reread a list she'd started at three a.m. when she hadn't been able to sleep. That had been twelve hours ago and no matter which way she came at it, she couldn't get the list to clearly state what she willed it to. What she wanted more than anything was to jump online and book a flight back home to Australia. She wanted to put seventeen thousand kilometres between her and Alistair and the constant reminder that he didn't love her. She tried to find some reassurance in the fact he didn't love someone else either, but that only made her feel desperately sad for him. For some reason he seemed hell-bent on not allowing himself to love anyone.

The thought of spending another three months working side by side with him most days made it hard to breathe but the thought of giving up her scholarship and returning home a failure was worse. She'd fought so hard for the scholarship and the prestige that went with it, and besides, she still had things to learn. Trying to explain to her family why she'd given up London when she'd talked excitedly about it for months would take more energy than she could muster. Trying to talk her way around the fact she'd left the tutelage of Mr Alistair North at job interviews back in Australia would be equally hard. The panel would give her uneasy looks and ask the hard question, 'Why, when you were so close to qualifying, did you throw this opportunity away?'

When she heard the truth embedded in the words—*I'm putting a broken heart ahead of my career*—she knew what she had to do. Right now, in the detritus of her personal life, her career was the only thing she had left to hold on to and guide her. The scholarship lasted ninety more days, less if she subtracted her rostered days off. She sipped her lemon and ginger tea and sat a little straighter. She could do this. She would do this. In fact, she'd start as soon as she stopped throwing up.

Actually, she hadn't thrown up since last night, and although she'd felt a little nauseous this morning, it had passed by ten and she'd wolfed down a big breakfast. She'd be back at work bright and early in the morning but meanwhile she'd check her roster and count the actual number of days she had left at the castle. Opening her calendar on her computer she looked at the whole year displayed in four neat columns. Blue denoted today, green was days off, yellow was payday, purple was when her rent was due each month, brown was the fast approaching date of her exams and red was her period.

All of it made for a heartening and colourful display that was balm to an organised person's soul. Just glancing at the planner made her feel secure and slightly more in control. Who needed spontaneity? There was no pattern to it, which by its nature was not at all reassuring. Cross-referencing with her roster, she clicked her mouse and added in her days off for the next six weeks.

Job done, she sat back and enjoyed seeing the patterns all the different dots created. She suddenly lurched forward closer to the screen and adjusted her glasses, blinking at a red dot. Her period had been due on the tenth. She knew for a fact it hadn't come on that date. It had come earlier but she'd been too busy being spontaneous to realise quite how early it had come.

And it was very light.

Her stomach rolled. *Implantation bleed.* The thought she'd dismissed so easily yesterday was a lot harder to shift today. Was what she thought was a light dose of gastro not gastro at all? Was she pregnant? Was what would constitute Alistair's disaster and her not unwelcome surprise a reality?

Or not. It wasn't like her period was always clockwork regular. There'd been times when it was a bit hit and miss, and after all, she'd moved continents and was working long hours in a stressful job. Plus, they'd always used condoms and to her knowledge no condom had broken.

There was that one time you straddled him before the condom was on.

She bit her lip. Was that all it took?

Her contraceptive lectures reverberated in her mind. *Oh, yes, it actually took less.* She tasted blood. If she was pregnant, Alistair had made it very clear to her that he didn't want to have a child with her.

It's not you, she promptly reminded herself, determined not to let past beliefs pull her down. She knew that all the way to her soul. Alistair didn't want to have a child with anyone. *So why does he work with kids?* So often, people who didn't want children were uncomfortable around them and avoided them as much as possible. Alistair not only worked with them, he was relaxed around them and he had the special skill of being able to calm a sick and terrified child. He'd ace fatherhood so why didn't he want children?

No answer was obvious and none made any sense. She couldn't help but wonder if all of it was connected to losing his father. She was intimately acquainted with childhood beliefs getting tangled up in adult lives and skewing them. Alistair had helped her see that in her own situation but he wasn't allowing her to help him. He refused to let anyone get close enough to offer any insight.

She was under no illusions. The reality was that if she were pregnant, she'd be embarking on the difficult but rewarding path of a single, working mother.

And if you're not pregnant?

I'll be relieved.

An empty feeling ringed with sadness tumbled through her, leaving an ache everywhere it touched. She gave herself a shake. Of course she'd be relieved if she wasn't pregnant. She had to be, didn't she?

'Argh!' The sound reverberated around the flat. There were too many *what-ifs* on both sides of the argument. There was only one definitive way to end this constant circular process and find out for certain if she was pregnant or not. Grabbing her phone, her keys and her handbag, she dashed out of the flat.

Yesterday, Alistair had welcomed the extra workload generated by Bailey and Cla—Mitchell's absence as it meant he hadn't had to think about anything other than work. Not that he needed to think about anything other than work right now, he reminded himself crossly, swiping the air savagely as he played solo virtual tennis in the quiet Koala Ward's lounge.

He'd spent the evening playing with the kids but they were all tucked up in bed now having been hustled away by the night nurse who liked the order of routine. He should have gone home then but the thought of an empty flat had kept him in the lounge playing game after game. He was determined to beat the machine. Determined to get thoughts of Claire out of his head.

Damn it, she wasn't the first woman he'd broken up with. She wouldn't be the last.

Other breakups didn't touch you. This one has.

He refused to acknowledge that. Hell, he'd dated other women for longer than he'd dated Claire so he had no reason to be affected by this breakup. The two of them wanted different things out of life. She had a choice in wanting a family, but he did not. End of story. Move on. Find someone else to have fun with. It wasn't like there weren't plenty of candidates to fill Claire's place.

Just this morning, he'd been called down to do a consult in the cardiothoracic ward, and while he was trying to locate the child in question, he'd come across Maddie, the pretty and chatty physiotherapist he'd sat next to at the ball. She was working with Penelope, the cute little girl with the sunny disposition who'd been in and out of hospital all her life. She'd become one of the cute-as-a-button, tug-at-the-heartstrings faces of sick children in the *Save Paddington's* campaign. Her photo, along with others, was on posters and billboards all around town.

Penelope, who was wearing a pink tutu, lay with her head and chest tilted downwards while Maddie's cupped hands postured and percussed her patient's chest, loosening mucous and easing the child's breathing.

'Hello,' Penelope said with a big smile. 'You're not one of my doctors.'

He smiled at her precociousness. 'I'm Alistair. I'm a brain doctor.'

The child considered this. 'My brain works really well. It's my heart and lungs that don't work so good.'

'Hello, Alistair,' Maddie had said with a wide smile as if she was protecting him from a difficult reply. 'Where have you been hiding lately? I haven't seen you since you stole my bread roll at the ball.'

'Oh, I've been busy,' he said, feeling oddly self-conscious. Part of him wanted to say, *With Claire.* 'You know how it is.'

'I do.' She smiled again and this time her chocolate eyelashes fluttered at him. 'But all work and no play makes for a very boring life. I'm a big fan of breaking up the work with a bit of fun. I've heard you're of a similar mind?'

You bet I'm having fun. Claire's throaty voice filled his head and he found himself comparing Maddie's flirting green eyes with Claire's studious yet sexy caramel ones. The physiotherapist's came up lacking. 'I better go and find Olivia McDermott,' he'd said, backing quickly out of the room.

A few short weeks ago he'd probably have taken Maddie up on her offer. *Before Claire.* Feeling warm, he loosened his tie and took another swipe at the virtual ball, thrusting his arm out hard and fast. Now, it was officially *After Claire*, except the damn woman was still at the hospital. All day yesterday he'd waited for her resignation to ping into his in-box, planning to expedite her leaving as quickly as possible. It hadn't arrived. The first thing he'd done when he'd hauled himself out of another fitful night's sleep this morning was to check for the email. It still hadn't come.

Despite that, he'd been stunned an hour later when he saw her standing next to Bailey, waiting for him on the ward. Her oval face had been slightly paler than usual but determination had squared her shoulders, rolling down her spine and spearing through her gorgeous—ridiculous— high heels to plant her firmly in place. All of it had said, *I'm not going anywhere.* It had rendered him momentarily speechless.

He hated that she'd said, 'Good morning, Alistair,' before he'd been able to give his usual nod and greeting. From that moment, he'd felt as if he was on the back foot for the rest of the round and that she'd been directing the play. Hell, even Bailey, who looked like death warmed up, had been less distracted than him.

At the end of the round when everyone had scattered

he'd found himself asking her quietly, 'Are you sure you're well enough to be back at work?'

'Absolutely,' she'd said with a return of the crispness that had been such a part of her when she'd first arrived from Australia. Then she'd looked him straight in the eye and added, 'I plan to make the most of my remaining seventy-two working days here at the castle.'

His mouth had dried at her announcement that she wasn't leaving. She was going to be at work five days a week for the next three months and he couldn't do a damn thing about it. But he knew women and a jet of anxiety streamed through him. 'You do know that your staying makes no difference to us?'

Her eye roll was so swift and strong that the floor felt like it had moved under his feet. 'No need to worry, Alistair. You made your feelings abundantly clear. Besides, I learned from the master on how to clearly separate work and play without any inconvenient overlaps. I'm here because it's the best place for me to learn. Everything else is immaterial.'

And he *was* the master, so why in heaven's name did his mind keep slipping back to the fundraising ball and the subsequent nights they'd shared. *Because it was good sex.*

This time his subconscious gave an eye roll.

If it was just about the sex, why do you treasure the laughter and time shared on the picnic by the Serpentine? Why did you watch a chick-flick with her on the couch? Why did you spend whole nights at her flat? You've never done that with a woman before.

Anger stirred and he swiped the air again with an even harder thwack, sending the virtual ball scudding back across the screen. It suddenly looked out of focus and he blinked to clear his fuzzy vision. Was it rather warm in here? He threw off his tie without missing a point.

Remembering fun times with Claire didn't mean anything more than that he liked her and enjoyed spending time with her. When had that become a crime?

And what do you fondly remember doing with McKenzie, Islay, Rebecca, Eloise and Leila? Shall I go on?

Shut up.

He served with gusto, slicing through the air so hard his arm hurt. Sweat beaded on his brow. He leaped around the lounge, volleying the virtual ball, determined to beat the damn machine.

Will the world end if you admit that you love me?

Claire's distinctive voice with its rising inflection was so loud in his head she may as well have been in the room with him. *Yes, damn it. It will.* He couldn't love her because if he did, then his carefully constructed new world—his post-ironman world—would tumble in on itself and bring with it all of the old pain. Pain he'd already endured once before. Pain he didn't intend to deal with again and he sure as hell wouldn't inflict it on anyone he loved.

And you love her.

The reality hit him so hard he felt light-headed and the room spun. The game buzzed at him, telling him he'd missed a shot. He started over, serving fast and faulting. He blinked away double vision, suddenly feeling unbelievably tired and cloaked with an overwhelming sense of fatalism. What did it matter if he loved Claire? Nothing good could come of it so there was no point telling her. He'd survived worse and he'd survive this. In seventy-two days she'd be gone.

'Alistair?'

Heat and cold raced through him at her voice but he didn't turn. Instead, he kept playing despite feeling that with each shot it was increasingly difficult to raise his arm. 'Claire?'

'Is it possible to add Harrison Raines to tomorrow's surgical list?'

'Fine.' He took another swipe with the plastic racquet and the room listed sideways. He staggered, fighting to stay upright.

'Are you okay?'

'Fine.' But the word echoed in his head. He didn't feel fine at all. The edges of his mind filled with grey fog. The racquet fell from his hand and he reached for the back of the couch to stop himself from falling.

Terror gripped him. Memories assaulted him. It had been a long time but he knew this feeling. He tilted sideways.

'Alistair!' Claire yelled his name as he fell.

After that everything was a blur as he slipped in and out of consciousness. He heard the thud of shoes on linoleum. Felt Claire's hand on his throat, seeking his pulse. Heard her say, 'God, his pulse is twenty-eight.' He recognised Bailey's voice yelling to get the crash cart.

'Alistair.' Hands shook him. 'Al. Do you have pain?'

Claire's beautiful face floated above him and he tried hard to fix it so it was still. He couldn't manage it.

Was this it? Had his borrowed time come to an end? *No!* He didn't want to die, but he already felt disconnected from his body as if he was on the outside and looking down on everyone frantically trying to save him. With a monumental effort he tried again to bring Claire's beautiful face into focus. Behind her sexy thinking-woman's glasses, her eyes burned with terror and pain. He wanted to change that.

It was suddenly vital to him that his last word to her wasn't a terse, 'Fine.' He didn't want her to remember their last real conversation when he'd cruelly said, 'Unlike you, there's nothing wrong with me.' Oh, the irony.

'Claire.' His voice sounded far, far away but she must have heard him because she lowered her head to his.

'It's okay, Al,' she said frantically. 'I refuse to let anything happen to you. You're going to be okay.'

He wanted to lift his hand to her cheek and feel her

soft skin against his but he lacked the strength. 'I…
Love… You.'

The last thing he heard before his hearing faded was her
choking cry and then everything went black.

CHAPTER TWELVE

As CLAIRE STARED at the contents of the St John's Hospital vending machine, she knew down to the tips of her toes that she never wanted to relive the last few hours ever again. *Not quite.* She smiled as she dropped coins into the machine. She'd happily relive hearing Alistair say quietly but clearly, 'I love you.' Was there anything more truthful than words spoken by a man who thought he was dying? She didn't think so. He loved her and she'd been right about that; however, it brought cold comfort when she'd been desperately worried she might never have the opportunity to hear him say them again.

Selecting orange juice, cheese and biscuits, and chocolate, she sent up another vote of thanks that by a stroke of luck or, as Thomas Wolfe had said to her, due to 'the mountain of unrelenting paperwork' that he'd still been at the castle at ten-thirty last night. Not only had he accompanied Alistair in the ambulance, he'd been very generous to her. As she wasn't family, without his consideration she'd have been denied any information about Alistair's condition and certainly not been allowed in to see him. Not that she'd seen him yet, but she lived in hope. Meanwhile, Thomas had reassured her that the surgery had gone well.

Along with Alistair's collapse had come a lot of answers to unasked questions. Why he was so hell-bent on living for the moment, although it seemed an excessive response to his condition. Then again, who was she to judge?

She unwrapped the thick and gooey chocolate-coated caramel bar and just as she bit into it a nurse walked over and enquired, 'Dr Mitchell?'

'Thaff's me,' she stuttered, using all her facial muscles to haul her teeth out of the caramel.

The nurse caught sight of her food stash and shot her a sympathetic smile. 'You got the five a.m. sugar drop? I get it too. Always feel a little bit nauseous at this time of the day.'

Claire nodded, still battling the quicksand-like properties of the caramel.

'Mr North's just waking up now,' the nurse continued. 'As his mother isn't due to arrive until midmorning, Dr Wolfe said you could sit with him.'

Bless you, Thomas. 'Thank you.'

They walked the length of the ward from the waiting area to the nurses' station and the nurse pointed to the door opposite. 'He's in there. I'll be in shortly to do his observations.'

Claire opened the door and stopped abruptly just inside. Alistair, always so vital and full of life, lay semi-upright in the narrow hospital bed. A sheet was pulled up tightly to his waist and a white hospital gown took over from there covering his torso to his Adam's apple. His face held slightly more colour than the cotton but not by much. Wires connecting him to the monitor snaked out from under the gown along with the IV that was connected to a pump that buzzed and purred. The rhythmic beep of the monitor, representing each life-giving heartbeat, broke the silence of the room.

Although she'd seen similar scenarios over and over since her first hospital visit as a medical student all those years ago, this was the first time someone she loved lay connected to all the high-tech machinery. Her heart beat faster in her chest and it took every gram of self-control she had not to rush over and throw herself at him and say, 'You scared me so much.'

Besides the very unwise idea of body slamming anyone who'd just undergone surgery, she knew that words like *You scared me* and *Never do that to me again* were not going to work in her favour. Alistair loved her but that hadn't stopped him walking away from her once before. She wasn't giving him a single excuse to do it a second time.

Walking slowly, she sat herself in the chair by the bed and slid her hand into his. He stirred, his head turning, and his eyes fluttered open. 'Welcome back.' She smiled, squeezed his hand and added softly, 'I believe you love me.'

Alistair's mind fought the pea-soup fog that encased it as he watched Claire's mouth move. Then her words hit him and everything rushed back. The virtual tennis. His dizziness. His almost certain belief that he was dying.

I love you.

His hand immediately moved to his left shoulder, his fingers frantically feeling for the small box-like device that had been part of him for the last five years. The shape and scar he'd hidden from Claire. All he could feel was adhesive tape and discomfort.

'It's gone,' Claire said matter-of-factly. 'Thomas removed it.'

He didn't understand. If Thomas had removed his pacemaker he'd be dead. But he couldn't be dead because he could feel the warmth of Claire's hand and the softness of her skin against his. 'If it's gone, what's keeping me alive?'

'The world's smallest pacemaker. It's wireless, and it's sitting snugly in your right ventricle doing its job perfectly.'

'Wireless?' He knew he sounded inane but he was struggling to piece everything together.

She nodded and squeezed his hand again. 'Tell me. Exactly how long had you been playing virtual tennis when I arrived to find you on the verge of collapse?'

He thought back and automatically scratched his head, noticing the IV taped to the back of his hand. 'I'm not sure. Some of the kids wanted a tournament so I organised it and I played too. We started before dinner and kept going until Sister Kaur hustled them off to bed. I suppose I stayed a little bit longer after that.'

She made a sound that was half a groan and half despairing laugh. 'Alistair, that adds up to about five hours.'

He shrugged and the stitches in his shoulder immediately pulled. *Ouch.* 'So? I had the time. It's just swiping a plastic bat through the air. It's not like I was lifting weights for hours on end.'

She dropped her head for a moment before lifting it and pushing her glasses up her nose. She gazed at him, her eyes full of love and affection with a hint of frustration. 'I know it wasn't weightlifting or rugby but substantial repetitive action for that length of time isn't recommended for people with pacemakers.'

The events of the evening came back to him and he started joining the dots. 'I should have gone home but I was procrastinating. I didn't realise how long I'd been trying to beat that bloody machine.' *I was too busy thinking about you.* 'Did I damage a lead?'

'Thomas will explain it all to you but he thinks it's more likely you exacerbated a fault. The good news is your new pacemaker's titanium. There are no leads and the battery and pulse generator are all combined into one tiny device the size of a pill.'

He glanced at the monitor and saw the perfect run of sinus rhythm. 'It's working.'

'It's working very well indeed.' She winked at him. 'So now. Back to the fact that you love me.'

The relief at being alive took a hit from reality. God,

how was he going to get out of this situation without hurting her? Without hurting himself. 'I thought I was dying.'

She didn't flinch and she didn't break her gaze. 'I know.'

A long sigh shuddered out of him. 'Now that you know all about my secret time bomb, you can understand why me loving you doesn't change a thing.'

She pursed her lips. 'I disagree. I think it changes everything.'

He threw his arm out towards the monitor and the pump. 'You saw me collapse. You worked on me. You know I could die at any moment and I refuse to put you through that.'

'So, what? We just live miserable lives apart and when I die before you at ninety, then you'll realise what a dumb idea this is?'

He pulled his hand away from hers, needing to break the addictive warmth that promised what he couldn't have. 'I'm not going to live until ninety.'

'You don't know that.'

But he did. 'Claire.' He sighed again. 'You deserve a long and happy life with someone who can give you healthy children. Someone who will be around to see them grow up. I can't promise you either of those things.'

Her mouth pursed. 'The pacemaker overrides your SA node's propensity not to fire. With that sorted and without pesky leads getting in the way of your—' she made quotation marks with her fingers '—"live for the moment" obsession of playing virtual tennis for five hours, then the odds are in your favour to live a long life.'

He dropped his gaze, wishing it were that simple.

Suddenly two deep lines carved into her intelligent brow. 'It's not just the pacemaker, is it?'

Every other time she'd pressed him for information he'd been able to deflect or walk away. Today was different. He wasn't just physically trapped in a hospital bed hooked up to equipment; he was also trapped by his declaration of love.

'This is something to do with your father, isn't it?'

His heart raced. 'Why did I fall in love with a MENSA member,' he muttered darkly.

She gave a wry smile and raised his hand to her lips. 'Because I'm good for you and you're good for me.'

And he recognised the truth in her words but it wasn't enough to convince him that he should drag her down with him. 'Dad dropped dead at forty-seven from a myocardial infarction.'

'That's young.'

'Exactly. It dramatically changed my life and my mother's. We didn't just lose Dad, we lost our home and everything familiar. My grief-stricken mother retreated into herself and it took her a long time to tread a new path without him. She did the best she was capable of doing but I ended up fatherless and half motherless for many years. I wouldn't inflict that on any child.'

He'd expected her to offer soothing murmurs but instead she asked perfunctorily, 'Did he have an arrhythmia like you?'

'Not that we knew, but given he just dropped dead with no warning, it's safe to assume that he did.'

She frowned. 'So, no episodes of dizziness? No pacemaker?'

'No,' he said irritably. 'I thought I'd established that. He was fit and healthy and then he was dead.'

She ignored his terse tone. 'How old was his father when he died?'

'Seventy-five.'

'Heart attack?'

'No. Tractor accident.'

'Alistair, have you ever read your father's autopsy report?'

He was getting sick of the interrogation. 'Of course not. I was a child.'

'Exactly,' she said emphatically, her eyes suddenly shining. 'You were a kid.'

'You're not making any sense.'

'Okay.' She tucked some hair behind her ears. 'Do you remember when I was telling you about my fabulous mentor, Strez, and how he freed me from Gundiwindi's preconceived ideas? You said, "But not from its legacy."'

He didn't know where she was going with this but he did remember the conversation. He answered with a reluctant, 'Yes.'

'I think you're suffering from a legacy too.' She leaned in closer. 'Even though you're now a qualified medical practitioner, the trauma of losing your father at a vulnerable age has blinkered you to the facts. I think you've made a massive non-scientific leap that connects your father's early death with your heart block. The result is an erroneous belief that you'll die young too.'

'It's not unreasonable—'

'It is. The statistics don't support it. Thomas told me you have a two per cent chance of dying from your heart condition. That's way better odds than crossing Piccadilly Circus at rush hour.'

Her words beat hard against his belief that he had a faulty heart just like his father. A belief cemented by the crusty cardiologist who'd said five years ago, 'You can't fight genetics, son.'

'That may be but it doesn't rule out me passing on a faulty heart to a child.'

'And I could just as easily pass on my dyslexia.'

Frustration bit him. 'That's completely different.'

'Yes, it is.'

Her acceptance surprised him and he studied her. She

immediately speared him with an intense look that belied her words and made him squirm.

She continued briskly. 'We don't know yet if your condition's inherited or if there are other factors. Want to tell me exactly what happened five years ago?'

He sighed. 'I was working really long hours and training for an ironman competition when I had my first episode of heart block.'

'Athlete's heart syndrome?'

'Yes and no. It's complicated.'

'You need to talk to Thomas and get all the facts, but I know for certain that my dyslexia's inherited. My grandmother and great-grandfather never learned to read. There's a chance a child of ours may have learning challenges.'

A child of ours.

The thought tempted and terrified him in equal measure. He fought back. 'Why don't you get this?' he asked tersely. 'Dyslexia's not a life-threatening condition.'

She folded her arms across her chest. 'It is if it's not treated.'

He snorted. 'No one ever died of dyslexia.'

'People with low self-esteem and no hope die every day,' she said softly, the message in her words sharp and clear.

'We wouldn't allow things to get to that,' he said quickly, stunned by his strong need to protect a child that didn't even exist. 'We'd be on the lookout for any signs of dyslexia. We'd make sure they had access to early intervention. They'd get all the help they needed to thrive.'

'Of course we would,' she said evenly. 'And in exactly the same way, we'd get be on the lookout and get an early diagnosis and intervention for any child of ours who had a cardiac arrhythmia.' A smile wove across her lips. 'I think that's called checkmate.'

'Claire,' he heard himself growl. 'It's not that simple.'

'Alistair,' she sighed. 'It really is. With your pacemaker,

your heart's pumping life through you just as it's been doing without error for the last five years, but you're not taking full advantage of what technology's offering you. You can let irrational fear continue to rule your life and keep everyone at arm's length or you can take a chance, embrace love, accept some low-level risk and share your life with me.

'The choice is yours.' Without waiting for him to reply, she rose to her feet and left the room.

Her words filled his head, duelling with his long-held beliefs about his life and the decisions he'd made long ago. Not once in five years had he ever questioned them. Hell, he'd accepted his fate and got on with his life, so why was he even considering what she'd said?

Because you've never been in love before.

How could it be so simple and so bloody complicated? Claire painted a picture of a life with her and children—a life he wanted badly, but either way he risked hurting her.

'Alistair.' Thomas Wolfe strode energetically into the room wearing a grey suit, a crisp white shirt and a pale blue tie. He'd obviously been home and acknowledged the new day with fresh clothes. Only the shadows under his eyes hinted that perhaps all wasn't quite as it appeared. 'Good to see you're awake.'

Alistair grimaced. 'I hear I have a state-of-the-art pacemaker.'

'The silver bullet.' Thomas's eyes lit up. 'It's a great invention. And you can play as much virtual tennis as you want, although at thirty-nine, your shoulder might object.'

Alistair sat up a bit higher. 'You're not that far behind me, old man.'

'Indeed.' Thomas's smile was wry. 'The good news is your cardiac enzymes and ECG are both normal. Your groin will feel a bit sore for a few days and you can't walk until tomorrow, but other than that, you'll be feeling yourself again very soon. No need to let this hiccough slow you down.'

'Hiccough?' He heard the disbelief in his voice.

'It's unfortunate the lead became damaged but you were close to a battery replacement anyway. In a way, you did yourself a favour. This pacemaker is a huge leap forward in the treatment of heart block, and apart from not being able to go scuba-diving or joining the armed forces, your life's your own.'

Was it? Immediately, Claire's accusation that he'd made a massive non-scientific leap about his condition burned him. 'My father died suddenly at forty-seven.'

'Of an MI?'

'I always assumed.'

Thomas checked the tablet computer in his hand. 'Your cholesterol's low, your blood pressure's in the normal range and you don't smoke. All of it puts your risk factor for an MI as very low.' He rubbed his neck. 'Your father could have died of an aneurysm or numerous other things. If it was an MI, then I think you've inherited your mother's heart genes. If you can get hold of your father's medical history, I'd be happy to take a look. Meanwhile, you having problems is not something I'd be betting any money on.'

Again Claire's voice sounded loud and clear in his head.

You can let irrational fear continue to rule your life and keep everyone at arm's length or you can take a chance, embrace love, accept some low-level risk and share your life with me.

A feeling of lightness streaked through him almost raising him off the bed and he stuck out his right hand. 'Thank you, Thomas. You have no idea how much I appreciate your straight-talking.'

'Any time.' Thomas shook his proffered hand. 'I'll see

you in the morning before you're discharged but any other questions just call me.' He turned to leave.

'Thomas, before you go, can I ask you a favour?'

One of the hardest things Claire had ever done was walk out of Alistair's hospital room yesterday morning but she'd felt it was her only option. It was that or hit him over the head in frustration. Or beg. She certainly wasn't going to beg. The old Claire may have begged but Alistair had taught her that she didn't need to beg anyone for anything. The lesson wasn't without irony.

Still, she'd been sorely tempted to beg but she'd fought it. In her mind, two things were very clear. The first was that Alistair loved and valued her. The second was that if they were to have any chance at happiness, Alistair had to come to his decision freely and not be cornered or cajoled into committing to her. She also knew that his love for her was a big part of the problem. He didn't want to hurt her and yet by protecting her from life—from his life—he was hurting her ten times over.

'How's the boss?' Andrew asked as they stripped off their surgical gowns.

'If he takes his doctor's advice, he'll be back at work next week.'

'So we can expect him here tomorrow, then.' Andrew winked at her. 'I imagine he's got women lining up to look after him so perhaps he will stay away for the week.'

A bristle ran up Claire's spine. 'The man needs to rest, Andrew.'

He grinned. 'Sure. But hey, what a way to rest.'

Claire hit him with the folder she was holding. 'Go and check your patients in recovery.'

He held up his hands in surrender. 'Yes, Mum. On my way.'

She walked to the doctors' lounge and made herself a

late-afternoon snack to keep her energy levels up. She was eating a plate of cheese and biscuits when her phone rang. 'Claire Mitchell.'

'Thomas Wolfe, Claire. As Alistair's indisposed, I was wondering if you could help me out.'

'Ah, sure. Do you have a patient who needs a neuro consult?'

'In a manner of speaking. He's a high-profile private patient and coming here's difficult with the…um…'

'Picket line,' she supplied as her thoughts roved to a possible celebrity child.

'Exactly,' Thomas said firmly. 'They're sending a car. What time suits you?'

'I'll be free in an hour.'

It suddenly occurred to her that perhaps it was a royal child, but as she opened her mouth to ask, Thomas was already saying, 'Excellent. I'll get the porter to buzz you when the driver arrives.'

'Can you give me some de—?' The line went dead. She waited for him to call her back or send a text but nothing came. A skitter of excitement raced through her at the idea of a very top-secret patient. At least it would take her mind off Alistair.

The car wasn't a limousine nor did it have any distinctive crest or signage on it, so Claire wasn't able to glean any clues about the mystery patient from her transport. When she'd quizzed the driver he'd replied that he wasn't at liberty to disclose who'd ordered and paid for the car.

Despite the evening traffic, the drive was thankfully short and soon enough she was standing on the porch of a Victorian town house with a royal-blue door. She rang the recessed brass bell and waited, her curiosity rising and her stomach churning. She probably should have eaten more before coming. She listened intently for footsteps. About thirty seconds later she was still listening. She was about to ring the bell again when the door opened.

Her stomach rolled and she felt her eyes widen. 'Alistair?'

He stood in front of her wearing faded jeans and a button-necked light wool jumper that lit his grey eyes to a burnished pewter. His hair was its usual messy chic and the addition of a five o'clock stubble shadow on his cheeks made him sexier than ever.

'You're not a celebrity child.'

A momentary look of confusion crossed his face. 'Ah, no. Was I supposed to be?'

'Thomas led me to believe…' Actually, Thomas hadn't given any details at all. She'd jumped to those conclusions all on her own. 'Never mind. You've been discharged,' she said, stating the obvious and trying to keep calm when all she wanted to do was hug him tightly. 'You've got your colour back,' she said crisply.

'I feel pretty good. How are you?' A familiar frown creased his brow. 'You look tired.'

She wanted to bask in his concern for her but she'd done that before and it hurt too much. Now, far too much was at stake. 'Yes, well, it's been a big few days.'

He gave her a wan smile. 'It has. Please come in.' He stepped back from the doorway so she could enter but as she passed him she could smell his delicious shower-fresh scent and her heart raced.

She immediately tried to slow it down. The only thing being at his house meant was that he wanted to talk to her. What he planned to say would either cause the crack in her heart to break open for good or it would heal it.

'Go through.' He indicated she walk the length of the hall and she was very aware of the noise her heels made clicking against his polished floorboards. It echoed into the strained silence.

She entered a large, light-filled space that combined a

kitchen, dining area and family room that opened out onto a walled garden. The evening was warm and the sweet perfume of wisteria drifted in through the open French doors. So this was his house? It wasn't the soulless stainless steel and chrome bachelor pad she'd imagined. If anything, it looked of a style and design that was ripe to be filled with the children he was too scared to have.

'I thought we could sit outside?' he suggested politely.

From the moment he'd opened the front door he'd been the perfect host, and if he were going to continue in the same vein when there was so much at stake, she'd go mad. With a shake of her head, she set her handbag down on the dining table next to a vase overflowing with roses, scented lilies, daisies and hypericum berries. They were a beautiful arrangement and most likely get-well-soon flowers, although she wondered at the pink and mauve colour palette for a man.

'I'm a firm believer of ripping a sticking plaster off fast.'

His brows drew down. 'Sorry?'

'Alistair.' His name came out on a sigh. 'I don't want to go through the charade of you offering me a drink and something to eat and then breaking my heart. Just do it now and get it over and done with.'

He looked disconcerted as if they were actors in a play and she'd just gone off-script. He pulled out a chair for her.

'I don't need to sit down if I'm leaving in a minute.'

He rubbed the back of his neck and glanced out towards the garden before looking back at her. 'You're not making this easy.'

She shrugged. 'I didn't think that was my job.'

'No.' He drew in a deep breath. 'I love you, Claire.'

She steeled herself against the thrill that traitorously stole through her. 'I know you do. But for us those three words are hardly reassuring.'

'I'm sorry, Claire…'

Her heart quivered and she found one hand clutching the edge of the table and the other curling around her belly as it lurched and rolled.

'I've been a fool and…'

What? His words began to penetrate her fog of despair. She clawed back her concentration and watched him carefully.

His eyes held sorrow. 'If I had my time over I'd have handled everything differently. I'm standing here before you now begging you to take a chance and risk sharing your life with me.'

For a moment, her astonishment seemed to almost stop time and then her heart leapt at his words—her words. He was saying to her exactly what she'd said to him in the hospital. 'You want to embrace love?'

He reached out his arms. 'I want to embrace love. I want to embrace you and a life together.'

More than anything in the world, she wanted to rush into his arms but something—survival—kept her rooted to the spot. 'And children?' She asked the question softly, barely daring to speak the words out loud for fear they would bring her world crashing down on her again.

'Yes.' He nodded slowly. 'That is, if we're fortunate enough to have them. You're right, Claire. If our kids face challenges, we'll be there with the resources to help.'

Relief and joy—so sweet and strong—surged through her making her sway but still she held herself back from the security of his arms. It was important to her—to them both—that she understood exactly how he'd got to this point. 'What happened to change your mind?'

'You happened.' He stared down at her while his left hand stroked her hair. 'Five years ago, when I collapsed and got the pacemaker, I saw it as a second chance at life. I also believed it came with a very big condition. I couldn't risk having kids and there are very few women out there who don't want the full package of marriage and children. So I focused on work and having fun. When a woman tried to get too close, I broke things off. It was always that easy until I met you.'

'I've always been difficult,' she said, half joking and half serious.

A slow smile broke over his handsome face. 'You're the most wonderfully difficult woman I've ever had the pleasure to know. You're also the only woman I've ever fallen in love with. It threw me so completely that I've behaved abominably.'

The only woman I've ever fallen in love with.

All those beautiful women who'd preceded her and yet it was her—the woman with the learning challenges and a lifetime of idiosyncrasies—she was the one he loved. He wanted to share his life with her come what may. Make a future with her.

Tears pricked the back of her eyes and she raised her hand to his cheek, welcoming the feel of his stubble grazing her palm. 'You were scared.'

'I can't believe how close I got to losing you.' His voice cracked and he cleared his throat. 'Thank you for coming to the hospital and talking sense to me.' His forehead touched hers. 'Thank you for loving me.'

She blinked rapidly as her legs trembled. 'Thank you for loving me.'

His arms wrapped around her, pulling her in so close and tight she could barely breathe. 'Claire?'

'Yes.'

He set her back from him so he could see her face. 'Will you do me the honour of becoming my wife?'

His proposal stunned and thrilled her and she found herself struggling to speak. 'I... That's...I... Yes,' she finally managed to splutter out. 'Yes, yes, yes.'

He grinned at her, his face alight with love. 'Thank

goodness for that.' Cupping her cheeks in his hands, he tilted her head back and kissed her with firm, warm and giving lips.

She sighed into him, letting him take her weight and absorbing the solid feel of him against her. His touch and feel radiated love, support and infinite generosity. When he eventually broke the kiss, he said, 'By the way, these flowers are for you. A peace offering for my stupidity. I don't mind if you throw them at me.'

She gave an unsteady laugh as she tried to unpack everything that was happening—how hopelessness had been turned on its head to become happiness. 'I can't throw them at you. That would be a waste. They're too beautiful.'

'So are you.' He kissed her again. 'Will you come outside into the garden? Please.'

The entreaty in his voice made it impossible to deny him. 'I think it's probably safe for me to do that now.'

He grinned and gripping her hand he tugged her across the room and out into the garden. A silver champagne bucket stood on a table and protruding from it was the neck of a bottle of champagne with distinctive gold, orange and black foil. A platter of antipasti covered in a fine net cloth sat beside it along with two champagne flutes.

He gave her a sheepish look. 'I'd planned to propose to you out here. I wanted to do my very best to make it as romantic as possible. Make it something you'd remember.'

His love and care circled her in warmth. 'And I went and threw a spanner in the works. Sorry.'

He laughed. 'Hey, I still got the girl so I don't mind at all.' He removed the foil covering on the top of the champagne bottle and then his long, surgical fingers popped the cork. The fizzing liquid quickly filled the fine crystal glasses.

When he'd set the bottle back into the ice bucket, she

stepped into his arms and ran her hands through his hair. 'You've got more than just me.'

He gazed down at her. 'In-laws, you mean? My mother's keen to meet you, and we can take a trip to—'

She pressed her fingers to his lips as she shook her head. 'I don't mean my family. I mean our family.'

He looked increasingly bewildered so she took pity on him. 'It turns out I didn't have gastro.'

His eyes widened into silver moons. 'You're pregnant?' Hope and awe tumbled from his whispered words.

'Six weeks.' She couldn't stop a broad smile despite knowing she needed to urge caution. 'It's still early days and you know that anything could hap—' She gave a squeal of surprise as her feet suddenly left the ground.

Alistair spun her around and around, his face alight with sheer delight. 'You're amazing. This is amazing.'

She threw back her head and laughed, revelling in more joy than she'd ever known. The circular motion eventually caught up with her and she suddenly gripped his shoulders. 'Feeling sick.'

He stopped abruptly and set her down on the chair. 'Sorry. Drink this.' He picked up the champagne and then laughed and put it down again. 'I'll get you something else.'

When he returned a short moment later the world had stilled on its axis and she was feeling a little better. She accepted the glass of apple juice he'd poured into a champagne glass.

Squatting by her side, he picked up his champagne flute. 'To my darling Claire, for opening my eyes and giving me back my life.'

She leaned in and kissed him, her heart so full it threatened to burst in her chest. 'To my darling Alistair, for opening my eyes so I can appreciate my strengths and skills.'

'You're most welcome.' He grinned up at her. 'Someone wise once told me that we're good for each other.'

'And don't you forget it. I love you, Alistair North.'

'I love you too, Claire Mitchell. Here's to a life lived to the full. To facing challenges head-on and to the joy of children.'

She thought about what they'd taught each other. 'To enough routine to make life enjoyable and enough spontaneity to keep it fun.'

They raised their glasses and clinked. 'To the future.'

And then he kissed her and she knew she was home.

EPILOGUE

'DO YOU THINK international travel with children comes under the heading of spontaneity and fun?' Alistair asked with a wry smile as he tramped along a wide, golden sand beach with a baby carrier on his back.

Claire laughed as she adjusted the baby carrier on her own back. 'Nothing about travelling with babies and all of their associated gear can be called spontaneous.'

'Their creation, however, was both spontaneous and fun,' Alistair teased as he slid his hand into hers and squeezed it.

'It was.' She leaned in and kissed him on the cheek. She was more in love with him now than on the day she'd said, 'I do,' in the beautiful stained-glass chapel at the castle and she was absolutely stunned that it was even possible. 'Bringing the twins to my homeland is fun.'

The twins—a boy and a girl now eleven months old—squealed in delight. Thrashing their arms wildly, they touched hands now that their parents were walking close enough so they could reach each other from their carriers.

Claire breathed in the fresh, salty air and felt peace invade her bones. She enjoyed London but she loved Australia and its wide-open spaces more. She couldn't quite believe she—*they*—were here in Queensland. The last nineteen months had been momentous. Two weeks after Alistair had proposed, he'd accompanied her to the routine pregnancy ultrasound. As she lay on the table with her hand encased in Alistair's, excitement on hearing the baby's heartbeat had turned from joy to shock and back to joy again when they'd heard two heartbeats.

'Twins? But how?' she'd asked inanely.

Alistair had laughed. 'Any twins in your family?'

'Dad has twin brothers.'

'There you go,' he'd said, kissing her on the forehead. 'Now this is the sort of inherited condition I can get behind.'

Being pregnant and studying for her exams had been tough but with her study regime and Alistair's help—both practical and emotional—she'd passed. The good news had arrived just before she'd gone into labour. A paediatrician had been on hand at the birth to check for any cardiac irregularities but both children were declared to have healthy hearts. Their six-month check-ups had all been normal and they were kicking goals on all their developmental milestones, although Claire noticed Emily did things just that little bit earlier than Noah. It was typical girl power.

Parenthood had brought with it both joy and delight along with exhaustion, but she and Alistair were used to functioning on limited sleep courtesy of years of working in hospitals. It didn't faze them too much. They'd become experts at walking the floor, bouncing the pram and driving around London in the wee small hours, all sure-fire ways to get unsettled babies back to sleep. The biggest surprise—and the most appreciated—had been Alistair's decision to cut back his work hours so he could be around more for hands-on help. Claire, loving motherhood but missing work, took up the two days a week that Alistair had dropped. It was a perfect solution. Just recently, with the twins close to their first birthday, they felt they'd found their groove and had decided to bring them out to Australia to meet her parents as well as taking a well-earned beach holiday.

At the prospect of the twenty-four-hour journey, Alistair had said, 'We're either brave or stupid.'

'We're both,' she'd said, kissing him with gratitude. 'And I love you for it.'

A pacific gull and a cormorant swooped over the gently breaking waves and then dived, probably having just spotted a school of fish and dinner. The sun, now a vivid orange ball of fire, dropped low to the horizon, shooting out fingers of red and yellow flames that lit up the scudding clouds. Claire felt the chill in the breeze for the first time.

'We should probably take them home.'

'Dinner, bath, bed?'

'For us or them?' she teased.

His eyes darkened just the way she liked. 'Twins first and then us.'

'I'll hold you to that.' They turned around and walked back towards the beach access track. Not able to hold back her sigh, she said, 'I can't believe we've only got one day of our holiday left.'

'What if we stayed?'

She laughed and gave him a gentle elbow in the ribs. 'You're just procrastinating because you don't want to face the flight back to London.'

'Well, there is that,' he said with a grin, but then his expression sobered. 'I'm serious, Claire. What if we stayed and worked in Australia? I enjoyed my time in Sydney as a registrar so I know what I'm in for. I've loved this holiday and I love this country. Your mother's besotted by the twins—'

'There's not a big call for neurosurgeons in Gundiwindi,' she said, thinking of her dusty hometown.

'True, but there is in Brisbane. The city's only a few hours' drive away for your parents, which is a lot closer than London. Plus, your dad's talking about retiring closer to the coast.'

'Is he?'

'He told me they'd been looking at properties in the hinterland.'

Her mother had mentioned something in passing along those lines but she hadn't thought anything of it because she couldn't imagine her father ever leaving Gundiwindi. The idea of having her parents closer for support was very tempting, as was the opportunity for the twins to grow up with grandparents. 'But what about your mother?' she asked, trying to be fair. 'If we stay here, then she misses out.'

'You know as well as I do Mother's not really a natural at being an extra-pair-of-hands type of a grandmother. She prefers children when they're older. We'll Skype her each week and buy a big house with a large guest room and an en-suite. She can fly out anytime she wants to visit. But I can pretty much guarantee she won't do that until they're at school.'

Anticipation and excitement started to bubble in her veins. She stopped walking and turned to face him. 'You've really thought about this, haven't you?'

'I have.'

'What about our friends and colleagues? The castle? Won't you miss the old girl?'

'Paddington's always going to have a place in my heart, because it's where I met you. But times change and we need to change with them.'

She'd never asked him to consider moving to Australia because they'd met in London. 'You'd really do this for me?'

'It's not a hardship, Claire. Yesterday, when you were at the beach with your parents, I made enquiries at Brisbane's public and private hospitals.' He stroked her face. 'Would you like to go into private practice with me in Brisbane, Ms Mitchell?'

Marvelling at how lucky she was to have him in her life,

she didn't have to think twice. 'Yes, please.' Throwing her arms around her neck, she kissed him, welcoming the future and all it had to offer.

* * * * *

MUMMY, NURSE... DUCHESS?

KATE HARDY

To my fellow PCH authors, who made writing
this such an enjoyable experience.

CHAPTER ONE

Paddington Children's Hospital

THE REDBRICK BUILDING loomed before Leo in the street; the turret, with its green dome, reminded him so much of Florence that it was almost enough to make him miss Tuscany. Then again, London had felt more like home than Florence, ever since he'd first come to study medicine here as a teenager.

As the car pulled to a halt, Leo could see Robyn Kelly waiting outside the hospital gates for him, her curly blonde hair gleaming brightly in the sun. When the Head of Surgery had asked him to come to Paddington to help out in the aftermath of the fire that had ripped through a local children's school, of course he'd said yes. Robyn had taken him under her wing when he'd been on his first rotation and had been feeling just a little bit lost; back then, he'd appreciated her kindness. And he'd also appreciated the fact that she'd seen him as a doctor first and a duke second, treating him as part of the team rather than as a special case.

This was his chance to pay just a little of that back.

There was a small group of protestors standing outside the gate, holding placards: 'Save Our Hospital' and 'Kids' Health Not Wealth'.

Which was one of the reasons why his contract was temporary: Paddington Children's Hospital was under threat of closure, with a plan to merge the staff and patients with Riverside Hospital. Not because the one-hundred-and-fifty-year-old hospital wasn't needed any more—the fact that the place was full to overflowing after the recent fire at Westbourne Grove Primary School proved just how much the hospital was needed—but because the Board of Governors had had a lucrative offer for the site. So, instead of keeping the hospital as an important part of the community, they planned to sell it so it could be turned into a block of posh apartments. The Board of Governors had already run staff numbers down in anticipation of the merger, to the point where everyone was struggling to cope.

Leo's lip curled. He'd grown up in a world where money didn't just talk, it shouted, and that disgusted him. It was the main reason why he was drawn to philanthropic medicine now: so he could give some of that privilege back. So when Robyn had explained the situation at Paddington's to him and said they needed someone with a high profile to come and work with them and get the hospital's plight into international news, Leo had had no hesitation in agreeing. It was a chance to use the heritage he loathed for a good cause.

Even though he knew the waiting photographers weren't there to take pictures of the protestors, Leo intended to make quite sure that the protestors and the placards were in every single shot. The more publicity for this cause, the better. So, right at this moment, he was here in his role as the Duke of Calvanera rather than being plain Dr Marchetti. And that was why he was meeting Robyn outside the hospital gates in the middle of the morning, instead of being two hours into his shift. This was all about getting maximum publicity.

He took a deep breath and opened the door of the sleek, black car.

'Your Highness!' one of the photographers called as Leo emerged from the car. 'Over here!'

Years of practice meant that it was easy enough for him to deflect the photographers with an awkward posture, until he reached Robyn and the protestors. Robyn had clearly primed the picket line, because they crowded behind him with their placards fully visible; there was no way that any photograph of his face wouldn't contain at least a word or two from a placard. And then he shook Robyn's hand, looked straight at the cameras and smiled as the bulbs flashed.

'Is it true you're coming to work here?' one of the journalists called.

'Yes,' he said.

'Why Paddington?' another called.

'Because it's important. The hospital has been here for a hundred and fifty years, looking after the children in the city. And it needs to stay here, instead of being merged with Riverside Hospital, outside the city,' he answered.

'Moving the patients to Riverside means the kids will have better facilities than at this old place,' one of the journalists pointed out.

'State of the art, you mean?' Leo asked. 'But when it comes to medicine, *time's* the most important thing. You can have the most cutting edge equipment in the world—but if your patient doesn't reach those facilities in time, all that fancy stuff isn't going to be able to save a life. It'll be too late.'

The journalist went red and shuffled his feet.

'You don't need flashy equipment and modern buildings

to be a good hospital,' Leo said. 'You need to be *accessible*. What would've happened to the children of Westbourne Grove Primary School if Paddington had been closed? How many of them wouldn't have made it to those lovely new buildings and all the state-of-the-art equipment at Riverside in time to be treated?'

He was met with silence as the press clearly worked out the answer for themselves.

'Exactly. And I'm very happy for you all to quote me saying that,' he said softly. 'Talk to these guys.' He gestured to the protestors, knowing from Robyn that several of them had been treated here years ago and others had recently had their own children treated here. 'Find out their stories. They're much more interesting and much more important than I am.'

'I think you made your point,' Robyn said as they walked into the hospital together.

'Good,' Leo said as she led him in to the department where he was going to be working, ready to introduce him to everyone. 'Paddington's is an important facility. An outstanding facility. And I'll do everything I can to help you publicise that.'

Rosie Hobbes stifled a cynical snort as she overheard the Duke of Calvanera's comment. Who was he trying to kid? More like, he was trying to raise his own profile. Why would someone like him—a rich, powerful playboy—care about the fate of an old London hospital?

She knew he'd agreed to come and help at Paddington's because he'd trained with Robyn, years ago; but it was still pretty hard to believe that an actual duke would want to do a job like this. Who would want to work in a hospital that was currently full to the brim with patients but badly understaffed because the Board of Directors hadn't replaced anyone who'd left, in line with their plan to move everyone out and sell the place?

Especially a man who was so good-looking and seemed so charming.

Rosie knew all about how charm and good looks could hide a rotten heart. Been there, done that, and her three-year-old twins were the ones who'd nearly paid the price.

Thinking of the twins made her heart skip a beat, and she caught her breath. It had been just over a year now, and she still found panic coursing through her when she remembered that night. The threats. The dead look behind that man's eyes. The way he'd looked at her children as if they were merely a means to getting what he wanted instead of seeing them as the precious lives they were.

She dug her nails into her palms. Focus, Rosie, she told herself. Freddie and Lexi were absolutely fine. If there was any kind of problem with either of the twins, the hospital nursery school would've called her straight away. The place was completely secure; only the staff inside could open the door, and nobody could take a child without either being on the list as someone with permission to collect a child, or giving the emergency code word for any particular child. Michael was dead, so his associates couldn't threaten the twins—or Rosie—any more. And right now she had a job to do.

'Everything all right, Rosie?' Robyn asked.

'Sure,' Rosie said. Her past was *not* going to interfere with her new life here. She was a survivor, not a victim.

'I just wanted to introduce you to Leo,' Robyn continued. 'He'll be working with us for the next couple of months.'

Or until something even more high profile came along, Rosie thought. Maybe she was judging him unfairly but, in her experience, handsome playboys couldn't be trusted.

'Leo, this is Rosie Hobbes, one of our paediatric nurses. Rosie, this is Leo Marchetti,' Robyn said.

'Hello,' Rosie said, and gave him a cool nod.

He gave her the sexiest smile she'd ever seen, and his dark eyes glittered with interest. 'Delighted to meet you, *signora*,' he said.

Rosie would just bet he'd practised that smile in front of the mirror. And he'd hammed up that Italian accent to make himself sound super-sexy; she was sure he hadn't had an accent at all when he'd walked onto the ward with Robyn. She should just think herself lucky he hadn't bowed and kissed her hand. Or was that going to be next?

'Welcome to Paddington's, Your Highness,' she said.

He gave her another of those super-charming smiles. 'Here, I'm a doctor, not a duke. "Leo" will do just fine.'

'Dr Marchetti,' she said firmly, hoping she'd made it clear that she preferred to keep her work relationships very professional indeed. 'Excuse me—I really need to review these charts following the ward round. Enjoy your first day at the Castle.'

The Castle? Was she making a pointed comment about where he came from? Leo wondered. But women weren't usually sharp with him. They usually smiled back, responding to his warmth. He liked women—a lot—and they liked him. Why had Rosie Hobbes cut him dead? Had he done something to upset her?

But he definitely hadn't met her before. He would've remembered her—and not just because she was tall, curvy and pretty, with that striking copper hair in a tousled bob, and those vivid blue eyes. There was something challenging about Rosie. Something that made him want to get up close and personal with her and find out exactly what made her tick.

She hadn't been wearing a wedding ring. Not that that meant anything, nowadays. Was she single?

And why was he wondering that in any case? He was here to do a job. Relationships weren't on the agenda, especially with someone he worked with. He was supposed to be finding someone suited to his position: another European noble, or perhaps the heir to a business empire. And together they would continue the Marchetti dynasty by producing a son.

Right now, he still couldn't face that. He wasn't ready to trap someone else in the castle where he'd grown up, lonely and miserable and desperate for his father's approval—approval that his father had been quick to withhold if Leo did or said anything wrong. Though what was wrong one day was right on another. Leo had never been able to work out what his father actually wanted. All he'd known for sure was that he was a disappointment to the Duke.

He shook himself. Now wasn't the time to be thinking about that. 'Thank you,' he said, giving Rosie his warmest smile just for the hell of it, and followed Robyn to be introduced to the rest of the staff on the ward.

Once Rosie had finished reviewing the charts and typing notes into the computer, she headed on to the ward. Hopefully Dr Marchetti would be on the next ward by now, meeting and greeting, and she could just get on with her job.

Why had he rattled her so much? She wasn't one to be bowled over and breathless just because a man was good-looking. Not any more. Leo had classic movie-star looks: tall, with dark eyes and short, neat dark hair. He was also charming and confident, and Rosie had learned the hard way that charm couldn't be trusted. Her whirlwind marriage had turned into an emotional rollercoaster, and she'd promised herself never to make that mistake again. So, even if Leo Marchetti was good friends with their Head of Surgery, Rosie intended to keep him at a very professional distance.

She dropped into one of the bays to check on Penelope Craig. Penny was one of their long-term patients, and the little girl had been admitted to try and get her heart failure under control after an infection had caused her condition to worsen.

'How are you doing, Penny?' Rosie asked.

The little girl looked up from her drawing and gave her the sweetest, sweetest smile. 'Nurse Rosie! I'm fine, thank you.'

Rosie exchanged a glance with Julia, Penny's mother. They both knew it wasn't true, but Penny wasn't a whiner. She'd become a firm favourite on the ward, always drawing special pictures and chattering about kittens and ballet. 'That's good,' she said. 'I just need to do—'

'—my obs,' Penny finished. 'I know.'

Rosie checked Penny's pulse, temperature and oxygen sats. 'That's my girl. Oh, and I've got something for you.' She reached into her pocket and brought out a sheet of stickers.

'Kittens! I love kittens,' Penny said with a beaming smile. 'Thank you so much. Look, Mummy.'

'They're lovely,' Julia said, but Rosie could see the strain and weariness behind her smile. She understood only too well how it felt to worry about your children; being helpless to do anything to fix the problems must be sheer hell.

'Thank you, Rosie,' Julia added.

'Pleasure.' Rosie winked at Penny. 'Hopefully these new drugs will have you back on your feet soon.' The little girl was desperate to be a ballerina, and wore a pink tutu even when she was bed-bound. And Rosie really, really hoped that the little girl would have time for her dreams to come true. 'Call me if you need anything,' Rosie added to Julia.

'I will. Thanks.'

Rosie checked on the rest of the children in her bay, and was writing up the notes when her colleague Kathleen came over to the desk.

'So have you met the Duke, yet?' Kathleen fanned herself. 'Talk about film-star good looks.'

Rosie rolled her eyes. 'Handsome is as handsome does.' And never again would she let a handsome, charming man treat her as a second-class citizen.

'Give the guy a break,' Kathleen said. 'He seems a real sweetie. And his picture is already all over the Internet, with the "Save Our Hospital" placards in full view. I think Robyn's right and he's really going to help.'

Rosie forced herself to smile. 'Good.'

Kathleen gave her a curious look. 'Are you all right, Rosie?'

'Sure. I had a bit of a broken night,' Rosie fibbed. 'Lexi had a bad dream and it was a while before I got back to sleep again.'

'I really don't know how you do it,' Kathleen said. 'It's tough enough, being a single mum—but having twins must make it twice as hard.'

'I get double the joy and double the love,' Rosie said. 'I wouldn't miss a single minute. And my parents and my sister are great—I know I can call on them if I get stuck.'

'Even so. You must miss your husband so much.'

Rosie had found that it was much easier to let people think that she was a grieving widow than to tell them the truth—that she'd been planning to divorce Michael Duncan before his death, and after his death she'd reverted back to her maiden name, changing the children's names along with hers. 'Yes,' Rosie agreed. And it wasn't a total lie. She missed the man she'd thought she'd married—not the one behind the mask, the one who put money before his babies and his wife.

She was busy on the ward for the rest of the morning and didn't see Leo again until lunchtime.

'I believe we'll be working closely together,' the Duke said.

She rather hoped he was wrong.

'So I thought maybe we could have lunch together and get to know each other a bit better,' he added.

'Sorry,' Rosie said. 'I'm afraid I have a previous engagement.' Just as she did every Monday, Wednesday and Friday when Penny was in the hospital.

He looked as if he hoped she'd be polite and invite him to join her in whatever she was doing. Well, tough. This wasn't about him. It was about her patient. 'I'm sure Kathleen or one of the others would be very happy for you to join them in the canteen,' she said.

'Thank you. Then I'll go and find them,' he said, with that same charming smile.

And Rosie felt thoroughly in the wrong.

But Leo had already turned away and it was too late to call him back and explain.

Why was Rosie Hobbes so prickly with him? Leo wondered. Everyone else at Paddington Children's Hospital had seemed pleased that he'd joined the team and had welcomed him warmly. Everyone except Rosie.

Did she hate all men?

Possibly not, because earlier he'd seen her talking to Thomas Wolfe, the cardiology specialist, and she'd seemed perfectly relaxed.

And why was he so bothered when she was just one member of the team? Wherever you worked, there was always a spectrum: people you got on really well with, people you liked and people you had to grit your teeth and put up with. He was obviously one of the latter, where Rosie was concerned, even though today was the first time they'd met. He knew he ought to just treat her with the calm professionalism he reserved for people who rubbed him up the wrong way. But he couldn't help asking about her when he was sitting in the canteen with a couple of the junior doctors and two of the nurses.

'So Rosie doesn't usually join you?' he asked.

'Not when Penny's in,' Kathleen said.

'Penny?'

'You must've seen her when Robyn took you round,' Kathleen said. 'One of our patients. Six years old, brown hair in plaits and the most amazing eyes—grey, with this really distinctive rim?'

Leo shook his head. 'Sorry. It doesn't ring a bell.'

'Well, you'll definitely get to know her while you're here. She has heart failure, and she's been in and out of here for months,' Kathleen explained. 'She's a total sweetheart. Rosie's one of the nurses who always looks after her. When she's in on a Monday, Wednesday or Friday, Rosie spends her lunch break reading her ballet stories.'

'Because the little girl likes ballet, I presume?' Leo asked.

'Lives and breathes it. And also it gives her mum or dad a break, depending on who's taken the time off to be with her,' Kathleen explained.

'So Penny's special to Rosie?'

'She's special to all of us,' Kathleen said. 'If you've seen any drawings pinned up in the staff room or the office, nine times out of ten it'll be one of Penny's.'

'Right.' Leo wondered why Rosie hadn't told him that herself. Or maybe she'd thought he'd have a go at her for being unprofessional and showing too much favouritism to a patient.

He chatted easily with the others until the end of their lunch break, then headed back to the ward. The first person he saw was Rosie, who he guessed had just left her little patient.

'So did Penny enjoy her story?' he asked.

Colour flooded into her cheeks. 'How do you know about that?'

'Kathleen said you have a regular lunch date with her when you're in.'

'It gives Julia and Peter—her parents—a chance to get out of here for a few minutes to get some fresh air,' she said. 'And it isn't a problem with Robyn.'

So she *had* thought he'd disapprove of the way she spent her lunch break. 'It's very kind of you,' he said. Was it just because Penny was a favourite with the staff, or did Rosie maybe have a sister who'd gone through something similar? It was too intrusive to ask. He needed to tread carefully with Rosie or she'd back away from him again.

'She's a lovely girl.'

'Maybe you can tell me about her after work,' he said. 'I hear there's a nice pub across the road. The Frog and...?' He paused, not remembering the name.

'Peach,' she supplied. 'Sorry. I can't.'

Can't or won't? he wondered. 'Another previous engagement?'

'Actually, yes.'

Another patient? He didn't think she'd tell him. 'That's a shame. Some other time.'

But she didn't suggest a different day or time.

He really ought to just give up.

A couple of his new colleagues had already made it clear that they'd be happy to keep him company if he was lonely. It could be fun to take them up on their offers, as long as they understood that he didn't do permanent relationships.

Except there was something about Rosie Hobbes that drew him. It wasn't just that she was one of the few women who didn't respond to him; his ego could stand the odd rejection. But she intrigued him, and he couldn't work out why. Was it that she was so different from the women he was used to, women who swooned over him or flattered him because he was a duke? Or was it something deeper?

It had been a long time since someone had intrigued him like this. Something more than just brief sexual attraction. And that in himself made him want to explore it further—to understand what made Rosie tick, and also why he felt this weird pull towards her.

Tomorrow, he thought. He'd try talking to her again tomorrow.

Rosie was five minutes late from her shift, and the twins were already waiting for her with their backpacks on. They were singing something with Nina, one of the nursery school assistants, who was clearly teaching them actions to go with the song. Rosie felt a rush of love for them. Her twins were so different: Lexi, bouncy and confident, with a mop of blonde curls that reminded Rosie a little too much of Michael, and yet other than that she was the double of Rosie at that age. And Freddie, quieter and a little shy, with the same curls as his sister except mid-brown instead of golden, and her own bright blue eyes; thankfully he hadn't turned out to be Michael's double. Rosie was determined that her children were going to know nothing but love and happiness for the rest of their lives—and she really hoped that they wouldn't remember what life had been like when their father was around.

'Mummy!' The second they saw her, Lexi and Freddie rushed over to her and flung their arms round her.

'My lovely Lexi and Freddie.' Rosie felt as if she could breathe properly again, now she was back with her babies. Even though she loved her job and she knew the twins were well looked after in the nursery school attached to the hospital, she was much happier with them than she was away from them.

'So what have you been doing today?' she asked, holding one hand each as they walked out of the hospital.

'We singed.' Lexi demonstrated the first verse of 'The Wheels on the Bus,' completely out of tune and at full volume.

'That's lovely, darling,' Rosie said.

'And we had Play-Doh,' Freddie added. 'I maked a doggie. A plurple one.'

Rosie hid a smile at his adorable mispronunciation. 'Beautiful,' she said. She knew how badly her son wanted a dog of their own, but it just wasn't possible with their current lifestyle. It wouldn't be fair to leave a dog alone all day; and she couldn't leave the twins alone while she took the dog for the kind of long walk it would need after being cooped up all day, and which the twins would be too tired to do after a day at nursery school.

'We had cookies,' Lexie said.

'Chocolate ones. Nina maked them. They were crum— crum—' Freddie added, frowning when he couldn't quite remember the new word.

Crumbly? Or maybe a longer word. 'Nina made them,' Rosie corrected gently, 'and they were scrumptious, yes?' she guessed.

'Crumshus!' Lexie crowed. 'That's right.'

The twins chattered all the way on the short Tube journey and then the ten-minute walk home. They were still chattering when Rosie cooked their tea, and gave them a bath. Although Freddie was a little on the shy side with strangers, he strove to match his more confident sister at home.

And Rosie was happy to let them chatter and laugh. She'd worried every day for the last year that their experience with Michael's associate had scarred them; but hopefully they'd been too young to realise quite what was going on and how terrified their mother had been.

Once the twins were in bed, she curled up on the sofa with a cup of tea and a puzzle magazine. A year ago, she would never have believed she could be this relaxed again. Some things hadn't changed; she was still the one who did everything for the twins and did all the cooking and cleaning. But she no longer had to deal with Michael's mercurial mood swings, his scorn and his contempt, and that made all the difference. Being a single parent was hard, but she had the best family and good friends to support her. And she didn't have Michael to undermine her confidence all the time.

Various friends had hinted that she ought to start dating again. Part of Rosie missed the closeness of having a partner, someone to cuddle into at stupid o'clock in the morning when she woke from a bad dream. But she'd lost her trust in relationships. Good ones existed, she knew; she'd seen it with her parents and with friends. But Rosie herself had got it so badly wrong with Michael that she didn't trust her judgement any more. Trusting another man, after the mess of her marriage, would be hard. Too hard. Plus, she had the twins to consider. So she'd become good at turning the conversation to a different subject rather than disappointing her well-meaning friends and family, and any direct suggestions of a date were firmly met with 'Sorry, no.'

Just as she'd rebuffed Leo Marchetti this evening, when he'd suggested that they went for a drink in the pub over the road after work.

Had she been too hard on him?

OK, so the guy was a charmer, something that set all her inner alarm bells clanging. On the other hand, today had been Leo's first day at Paddington's. The only person he knew at the hospital was Robyn, so he was probably feeling a bit lost. Guilt nagged at her. She'd been pretty abrupt with him, and it wasn't his fault he'd been born with a Y chromosome and was full of charm. She needed to lighten up. Maybe she'd suggest having lunch with him tomorrow.

But she'd make it clear that lunch meant lunch only. She wasn't in a position to offer anything more. And, if she was honest with herself, it'd be a long time before she was ready to trust anyone with anything more. If ever.

CHAPTER TWO

'YOU'RE IN CLINIC with Rosie, this morning,' Kathleen said to Leo with a smile when he walked onto the ward. 'It's the allergy and immunology clinic.'

'Great. Just point me in the right direction,' he said, smiling back.

Hopefully Rosie would be less prickly with him today. And if they could establish a decent working relationship, then he might be able to work out why she drew him so much, and he could deal with it the way he always dealt with things. With a charming smile and a little extra distance.

He looked through the files while he waited for Rosie to turn up.

'Sorry, sorry,' she said, rushing in. 'I was held up this morning.'

'You're not late,' he pointed out, though he was pleased that she didn't seem quite so defensive with him today.

'No, but…' She flapped a dismissive hand. 'Has anyone told you about today's clinic?'

'Kathleen said it was the allergy and immunology clinic, so I'm assuming some of these patients have been coming here for a while.'

'They have,' she confirmed.

'Then at least they have some continuity with you,'

he said with a smile. 'Are you happy to call our first patient in?'

Their first patient was an eighteen-month-old girl, Gemma Chandler. 'The doctor asked me last time to keep a food diary with a symptom chart,' her mother said.

'May I see them, please?' Leo asked.

She took it out of her bag and handed it to him; he read the document carefully. 'So she tends to get tummy pain, wind and diarrhoea, and sometimes her tummy feels bloated to you.'

Mrs Chandler nodded. 'And sometimes she's come out in a rash on her face and it's been itchy. It's really hard to stop her scratching it.'

'There are some lotions that help with the itch and last a bit longer than calamine lotion,' Leo said. 'I can write you a prescription for that. And you've done a really good job on the diary—I can see a very clear link between what she's eating and her symptoms.'

'It's dairy, isn't it?' Mrs Chandler bit her lip. 'I looked it up on the Internet.'

'The Internet's useful,' Leo said, 'but there are also a lot of scare stories out there and a lot of wrong information, so I'm glad you came to see us as well. Yes, I think it's an allergy to dairy—more specifically lactose intolerance. What that means is that Gemma's body doesn't have enough of the enzyme lactase to deal with any lactose in the body—that's the sugar in milk. What I think we need to do is try an exclusion diet for the next fortnight to confirm it. So that means I'd like you to check the labels for everything and make sure there's no milk in anything she eats or drinks. If you can keep doing the food diary and symptom chart, we can review everything in a fortnight.'

'We can give you some information leaflets about substitutes and vitamin supplements,' Rosie said. 'You can give Gemma rice milk instead of cow's milk, and sun-flower margarine instead of butter.'

'Gemma's meant to be going to her cousin's birthday party, next week.' Mrs Chandler sighed. 'So that's going to be difficult—she won't be able to have any of the sand-wiches or any of the cake, will she?'

'You could do a special packed lunch for her,' Rosie suggested. 'And I'm sure if you tell your family and friends, they'll help you work things out.' She handed Mrs Chandler a leaflet. 'Eating out with a toddler can be tricky enough, but having to take a food allergy into account can make it seem overwhelming.'

Was she talking from personal experience? Leo wondered. Or was it because she'd worked with so many pa-tients in the allergy clinic? Not that he could ask without being intrusive, and he didn't want to give Rosie any ex-cuse to back away from him.

'There are some good websites on the back of the leaf-let for helping you to find places where they offer dairy-free options,' Rosie said.

'Thank you,' Mrs Chandler said.

'And we'll see you and Gemma again in a fortnight to see how things are. If her symptoms are better,' Leo said, 'I'll refer you to a dietitian so you can get proper support with a long-term exclusion diet. And in the meantime, if you have any questions or you're worried about anything, give us a call.'

Mrs Chandler nodded. 'Will she ever grow out of it? I've heard that some children do.'

'We really can't tell, right now,' Leo admitted. 'I think this is something we'll need to take one step at a time.'

Once the Chandlers had gone, while Leo was writing up the case notes, Rosie got out the next patient's notes. 'Sammy Kennedy. He's a sweetheart.'

'What's he seeing us about?' Leo asked.

'He has CAPS.'

Cryopyrin-Associate Periodic Syndrome. Leo knew it was an auto-inflammation disorder where the immune system was overactive and caused prolonged periods of inflammation, rather than the body producing antibodies against itself. 'That's rare,' he said. 'About one in a million. Actually, I've only seen one case before.'

'Sammy's my only case, too,' she said. 'Most patients with CAPS in the UK have Muckle-Wells Syndrome, and that's the variant Sammy has.'

'Tell me about him,' Leo invited. Sure, he could read the file, but this way he got the chance to interact with Rosie. And he liked how quick her mind was.

'He's eight years old and he's been coming here for nearly a year. He comes to clinic with his mum roughly every eight weeks. We check his knees and ankles and do bloods to measure the inflammation levels, and then we give him an injection of the drug that keeps his MWS under control,' she explained.

'That's the drug that blocks interleukin 1β, yes?' he checked.

'Yes,' she confirmed. 'The treatment's still new enough that we don't know the long-term effects, but we're hoping that it will stop more severe problems developing as he grows older.'

'Such as deafness?'

'Exactly,' she said. 'Are you ready to see him now?'

He nodded. 'Absolutely.'

Rosie went out into the reception area and came back with Sammy and his mother.

Leo smiled at them. 'Hello. I'm Dr Marchetti—you can call me Dr Leo, if you prefer. And you're Sammy?'

The little boy nodded.

'Tell me how you're doing, Sammy,' Leo invited.

'Sometimes I have good days, and sometimes I get bad days,' Sammy said, shrugging.

'OK. What happens when you have a bad day?'

'Mum says it's a flare-up. It affects my tummy, my knees and my head. I get a rash, and it's always at night.' Sammy grimaced. 'Show him, Mum.'

Mrs Kennedy took out her phone and showed them a picture of the nettle rash on Sammy's stomach.

'How often do you get flare-ups?' Leo asked.

'Every couple of weeks. But it's not been so bad, lately.'

'Are you happy for us to examine you?' Leo asked.

Sammy gave him a rueful smile. 'I know the drill. You ask me questions, look me over, take blood and then give me the injections.'

'That's a pretty good summary,' Leo said, smiling back.

'I don't like the injections,' Sammy said. 'They sting and they make my skin sore. But I guess it's better than the rash.'

'A lot of people don't like injections, so you're not alone there,' Leo said. 'Is there anything you'd like to add or ask, Mrs Kennedy?'

'We're getting to be old hands at this, now,' she said. 'It's fine.'

Between them, Rosie and Leo examined Sammy, and she took a blood sample. Then Leo administered the drug.

Sammy flinched.

'I'm sorry it stings,' Leo said.

'It's all right,' Sammy said, clearly trying to be brave.

'I have something for you,' Rosie said. 'That is… Unless you're too old to have a lolly for being brave?'

Sammy grinned when he saw the red and white lolly. 'As if I'm going to turn down a lolly. Especially when it's in my team's colours!'

'You're a football fan?' Leo asked.

Sammy nodded. 'I'd like to be a footballer, but my CAPS is going to get in the way a bit, and I don't want to let my team down. But I guess I could be a scientist when I grow up and invent a needle that doesn't hurt when you give someone an injection.'

'That,' Leo said, 'is a brilliant idea, and I think it deserves something extra.' He produced another red and white lolly. 'Don't tell Rosie I raided her lolly jar,' he said in a stage whisper.

Sammy laughed. 'See you in a couple of months, Dr Leo.'

'See you,' Leo returned with a smile.

When the Kennedys had left, he looked at Rosie. 'Sammy's a nice kid.'

'He is,' she agreed. Then she paused. 'I was a bit abrupt with you yesterday. Sorry. So, um, I was wondering, would you like to have lunch with me today? Just as colleagues,' she added hastily.

Again he glanced at her left hand and saw no sign of a wedding ring. Did she really mean having lunch together just as colleagues, or did she feel the same pull of attraction towards him that he felt towards her?

It might explain why she'd been so prickly yesterday; she might be just as spooked by her reaction to him as he was by his reaction to her. Though quite where they went from here, he had no idea. What he'd seen of Rosie so far told him that she was very professional—straight-talking, yet deeply caring towards her patients. He liked that. A lot.

But he also had the strongest impression that Rosie Hobbes wasn't the sort to have a casual fling. Which meant she was off limits, because he wasn't looking for something serious and long-term.

'Just as colleagues,' he agreed.

Once they'd seen the last patient at the clinic, they headed for the canteen. Leo noted that she chose a healthy salad and a mug of green tea—not that his own sandwich and coffee were *that* unhealthy. But Rosie clearly looked after her health.

'So how are you settling in?' she asked when they'd found a table.

'To the hospital or to London?'

'Both, I guess.'

'Fine,' he said. 'The staff all seem really nice here, and I trained in London so I feel pretty much at home in the city.'

'That's good.'

There was a slightly awkward silence, as if she didn't really know what to say to him next. It might be easier to keep the conversation going, Leo thought, if he asked her to tell him more about Paddington Children's Hospital and its predicament.

'Obviously Robyn told me about the Board of Directors and their plans, when she asked me to come and work here,' he said, 'so I understand why we're so short-staffed at the moment. But I gather there was a fire at a local school which made things a bit trickier?'

She nodded. 'It was about a month ago. The fire started in the art department, apparently. I'm not sure if it was a broken heater or something that caused the initial fire, but some of the paper caught light.'

'And everything else in an art department tends to be on the flammable side,' he said.

'Exactly. It was pretty scary. The school did what they could to get the kids out, but we were overflowing with patients suffering from everything from smoke inhalation to burns. Simon Bennett had severe facial burns; he's due for some reconstruction surgery, so he's in and out for check-ups at the moment, poor lamb.' She winced. 'And then there's little Ryan.'

'Ryan?' he asked.

'Ryan Walker. He was one of the last to be rescued. The poor little lad was hiding in a cupboard. He heard the firemen when they'd put the fire out in his classroom and came out of the cupboard, but then a beam snapped and hit him on the head.'

'He's lucky to be alive, then,' Leo said.

She nodded. 'But the poor little mite was very badly hurt. He had a craniectomy the other day. Right now he's under sedation and has a helmet on to protect him until the surgical team can replace the skull flap.'

'Poor kid,' Leo said.

'I know. But just think—if we'd been moved to Riverside,' she said softly, 'he wouldn't have made it. And the same's true for Simon.'

'So you're fighting for the hospital to be saved.'

'Victoria's set up a committee—actually, Quinn, Simon's foster mum, is on the committee. We've got protestors outside the gates twenty-four-seven. Though you already know that,' she said. 'You were photographed with them yesterday.'

And the photographs had since been used all round the globe. 'Might as well make the press do something useful,' he said dryly.

'Do the press hound you all the time?' she asked.

'Off and on. It depends if it's a slow news day—but they're rather more interested in the Duke than in the doctor.' He paused. 'Is that why you said about a castle yesterday?'

'Castle?' She frowned for a moment, and then her expression cleared. 'It's what all the staff call the hospital, because of the turrets.'

'Oh.'

She stared at him, looking slightly shocked. 'Hang on. You thought I was having a dig about you being a duke?'

'We didn't exactly get off on the right foot together yesterday,' he pointed out.

'No—and I guess I was a bit rude to you. Sorry.'

He appreciated the apology, though he noticed she didn't give him any explanation about why she'd been so abrupt with him.

'For the record,' he said, 'I did grow up in a castle. And I can tell you it's not all it's cracked up to be. For starters, castles tend to be draughty and full of damp.'

'And full of suits of armour?'

He smiled. 'We do have an armoury, yes. And I have been thinking about opening the place to the public.' Which might give his mother something more immediate to concentrate on, instead of when her son was going to make a suitable marriage and produce an heir to the dukedom.

'But I really don't understand,' she said, 'why a duke would want to be a doctor. I mean, don't you have to do loads of stuff for the dukedom?'

'I delegate a fair bit of it,' he said, 'and I have good staff.'

'Which again makes you different from any other doctor I've met.'

He wondered: was that different good, or different bad?

'I don't know anyone who has staff,' she said. 'Anyone at all. In fact, I don't even know anyone who hires a cleaner.'

'Guilty there, too,' he said. 'Obviously I know how to use a vacuum cleaner, but there are a lot of other things I'd much rather do with my free time.'

She said nothing.

'I want to be a doctor,' he said softly, 'because I want to make a real difference in the world.'

'Can't you do that as a duke?'

'Not in the same way. I don't want to just throw money at things. It's not enough. I want to make the difference *myself.*'

'From the way you talk,' she said, 'anyone would think you don't actually like being a duke.'

He didn't.

'Let's just say it's not what everyone thinks it would be like—and plenty of people see the title first and not the man.'

She reached out and squeezed his hand in a gesture of sympathy. His hand tingled where her skin touched his, shocking him; he was used to being attracted to women, but he wasn't used to having such a strong reaction to someone and he wasn't quite sure how to deal with it.

She looked as shocked as he felt, as if she'd experienced the same unexpected pull. 'Sorry. I didn't...' Her words trailed off.

Didn't what? Didn't mean to touch him? Or didn't expect to feel that strong a physical reaction?

He had the feeling that she'd find an excuse to run if he called her on it. 'No need to apologise. It's nice that you understand,' he said. 'So have you been working at *this* castle very long?'

'For nearly a year,' she said.

'Where were you before?'

'The other side of London, where I trained.'

He noticed that she hadn't actually said where. Why was so she cagey about her past?

He'd back off, for now. Until he'd got his head round this weird reaction to her and had made sense of it. And then maybe he'd be able to work out what he wanted to do about it. About *her*.

* * *

On Wednesday lunchtime, Rosie disappeared, and Leo remembered what Kathleen had said to him: Rosie read to Penny every other day, when she was in. Not quite able to keep himself away, he found himself in the corridor outside Penny's room. Rosie's voice was clear and measured as she read the story, and every so often he could hear a soft giggle of delight from Penny.

'Rosie's so lovely with her,' a voice said beside him.

He looked round; the woman standing next to him looked so much like Penny that there was only one person she could be. 'You're Penny's mum, yes?'

'Julia.'

'Dr Marchetti,' he said, holding out his hand to shake hers. 'Although your daughter isn't one of my patients because I'm not a heart specialist, I work with Rosie, and Rosie told me all about Penny.'

'Rosie's such a lovely woman. So patient. And it's so kind of her to read to Penny in her lunch break.'

'I think you'd probably have a queue of staff there, if you asked,' Leo said. 'From what I hear, Penny's a firm favourite. And her kitten pictures are pinned up in the staff room—they're adorable.'

'Aren't they just?' But behind her smile Julia's eyes were sad. 'I'm sorry, I'm probably keeping you from a patient.'

'It's fine,' Leo reassured her. 'But if there's anything you need?'

'Rosie's there,' Julia said. 'But thank you.'

'I'll let you get on.' He smiled at her, and headed back to his office to prepare for his next clinic. But all the same he couldn't get Rosie out of his head.

Thomas propped himself against the desk where Rosie was sitting. 'Obviously I've read the file, but you've seen

Penny more than anyone else this week. How do you feel she's doing?'

Rosie grimaced. 'There doesn't seem to be any change in her condition this week, even though we've been juggling her meds as you asked us to do.'

'So it's not working. I'm beginning to think that the only way forward for her now is a transplant.' He sighed. 'Julia's in today, isn't she? I'll ask her to get Peter to come in as well, so I can talk to them together.'

It wasn't going to be an easy conversation, Rosie knew. 'Do you want me to be there when you talk to them?'

He shook his head. 'Thanks for the offer. I know you've been brilliant with them, but this is my responsibility. It's going to come as a shock to them.'

'You know where I am if you change your mind,' she said gently.

'Thanks, Rosie. I appreciate it.'

Thomas looked almost bruised by this, Rosie thought, but he clearly wasn't going to let anyone close enough to support him. She remembered how it had felt when things with Michael had gone so badly wrong, so she wasn't going to push him to confide in her. But it was always good to know that someone could be there for you if you needed that little bit of support. 'Thomas, I'm probably speaking out of turn, but are you OK?'

'Sure.' He gave her an over-bright smile which clearly underlined the fact that he wasn't OK, but he wanted her to back off.

'Uh-huh,' she said. She didn't quite have the nerve to suggest that maybe he could talk to her if he needed a friend. 'I guess I'll see you later, then.'

He nodded, and left the nurses' station.

Rosie hated this situation. Whatever way you looked at it, someone would lose. She really hoped that Penny would get the heart she needed; though that would also mean that a family would be bereaved, so it kind of felt wrong to wish for a heart. The best of all outcomes would've been if Penny had responded to the drug treatment, but it wasn't to be.

And poor Julia. Rosie could imagine how she'd feel if she was in Julia's place, worried sick about Freddie or Lexi and knowing that they might not be able to get the treatment they needed so badly. Despite the misery of her life with Michael, he had given her the sheer joy of the twins. She had a lot to be thankful for.

But now wasn't the time to dwell on that. She had a clinic to do.

Leo happened to be checking some files at the nurses' station when Rosie walked over. He could see that she looked upset, and the words were out of his mouth before he could stop them. 'Do you want to go for a drink after work and tell me about it?'

She shook her head.

'Don't tell me—a previous engagement?' he asked wryly.

'I'm afraid so.'

'A chat in the ward kitchen, then.'

'Thanks, but I have obs to do.'

'Thirty minutes,' he said, 'and you can take a five-minute break—and I'm not pulling rank, before you start thinking that. You look upset and I'm trying to be supportive, just as I would with any other colleague who looked upset.'

She looked surprised, and then rueful. 'All right. Thirty minutes,' she said. 'Thank you.'

While she was doing her patients' observations, he finished his paperwork and then nipped out briefly to Tony's

Trattoria, the place across the street that he'd been told sold decent coffee, to buy two cappuccinos.

He'd half expected Rosie to make some excuse not to see him, but she arrived in the staff kitchen at the same time as he did.

'Thank you.' She smiled as he handed her one of the distinctive paper cups. 'Someone told you about Tony's, then?'

'Decent Italian coffee? Of course—and it's much better than the coffee in the hospital.'

'We have instant cappuccino here in the ward kitchen,' she reminded him, gesturing to the box of powdered sachets.

'That stuff isn't coffee, it's an abomination.' He smiled back at her. 'So are you going to tell me what's wrong?'

Her beautiful blue eyes filled with sadness. 'I was talking to Thomas earlier. It's Penny.'

He frowned. 'What about Penny?'

'We've been juggling her meds all week and it's just not working.' She shook her head in seeming frustration. 'Thomas says we're probably going to have to look at a transplant, so he's going to do an assessment. But even if she's on the list there's no guarantee she'll get a heart. It could be anything from days, to months, or even more than a year before a suitable heart is available, and it feels horrible to wish for a heart for her because it means that another family's lost someone they love.'

'But at least they have the comfort that their loved one has saved a life by donating their organs after death,' he said softly. 'And you're thinking a heart might not arrive in time?'

'You know that one in five cases don't. Those are really big odds, Leo. And she's such a lovely little girl.'

'Hey.' He gave her a hug. Then he wished he hadn't, because holding her made him want to do more than that.

Right at that moment, he wanted to kiss her tears away—and then kiss her again and again, until he'd made her forget her worries.

When he pulled back slightly and looked her in the eye, her pupils were so huge that her vivid blue irises seemed more like a narrow rim. *So she felt it, too.* He looked at her mouth, and ached to find out for himself how soft and sweet it tasted. He shifted his gaze and caught her looking at his mouth, too. Could they? *Should* they?

He was about to give in to the impulse and dip his head to hers when she pulled away. 'Sorry. It's not appropriate to lean on you like that.'

Leo knew she was right. Except he was the one who'd behaved inappropriately. 'The fault's all mine,' he said. 'I guess it's being Italian that makes me—well...'

'Hug people?' she finished.

'Something like that.' But he wasn't ready to let things go. 'Are you sure I can't take you to dinner tonight?'

'I'm sure. Thank you for the offer, but no.'

And yet there was a hint of wistfulness in her face. He was sure he wasn't just being a delusional, self-absorbed male; but why did she keep turning him down whenever he asked her out? If she'd said that she was married, or in a relationship, fair enough. He'd back off straight away. But she hadn't said that, which made him think that it was some other reason why she kept saying no. But he could hardly ask anyone else on the ward without the risk of becoming the centre of hospital gossip, and he loathed gossip.

Maybe he'd just keep trying and eventually he'd manage to wear her down. Because he really liked what he'd seen so far of Rosie Hobbes, and he wanted to get to know her better. And he wanted to work out why she attracted him so strongly, what made her different from the usual women he dated.

* * *

'Thanks for the coffee and sympathy,' Rosie said. 'I'd better get on.'

'See you later,' he said.

The problem was, Rosie thought, Leo Marchetti was actually *nice*. She'd been on ward rounds with him a couple of times now and she'd seen that he was lovely with both the kids and their parents. A couple of the mums had tried to flirt with him, but he'd stayed totally professional and focused on the children. And he'd been especially good with the more worried parents, explaining things in a way that stopped them panicking.

She was tempted to take him up on his offer of dinner out. Really tempted.

Except she wasn't in the market for a relationship, and it wouldn't be fair to date anyone until she was ready to trust her heart again. And nothing could really happen between her and Leo. He was a duke and moved in the kind of social circles that would never see her as his equal; and, after her experiences with Michael, she refused to put herself in a position where anyone would treat her as second class. It couldn't work, so there was no point in thinking about it. Besides, she already had the perfect life: two gorgeous children, a brilliantly supportive family and a job she adored. Wanting more—wanting a partner to share that with—was just being greedy.

Plus, her judgement was rubbish when it came to men. She'd fallen hook, line and sinker for every lie that Michael had told her.

So she needed to keep thinking of Leo as just another colleague. Yes, he was attractive; and she was beginning to like him a lot. But that was as far as it could go.

CHAPTER THREE

On Friday morning, Leo was talking to Rebecca Scott, the transplant surgeon, on the ward. 'Rosie tells me that Thomas is putting Penny on the transplant list.'

Was it his imagination, or did Rebecca freeze for a second when he mentioned Thomas's name? Rebecca and Thomas were always very professional with patients, but he'd noticed that they never shared a smile or any personal comments with each other, the way they did with other staff members. He had a feeling that something was definitely going on—or maybe something had happened in the past.

He knew all about complicated relationships. He was careful to keep his own as simple as possible, so the women he dated didn't have any expectations that he wouldn't be able to live up to. But, whatever the differences were between Rebecca and Thomas, it was none of his business. As long as everyone on the team was kept informed about any issues with their patients, nothing else mattered. He needed to keep out of this.

'Yes.' There was a flicker of sadness in her eyes, quickly masked. 'Are you settling in to the hospital OK?'

'Yes, thanks.' Clearly Rebecca wanted to change the subject. Well, that was fine by him. The last thing he wanted to do was accidentally trample over a sore spot.

'Everyone's been very welcoming and I haven't had to sit in a corner on my own at lunchtime.'

She smiled. 'That's good. Well, I'm due in Theatre, so I'll let you get on. But give me a yell if there's anything you need.'

'Thanks. I will.'

Rosie spent her usual Friday lunchtime reading to Penny and talking about kittens and ballet. She knew Thomas had talked to Peter and Julia about putting their daughter on the transplant list, and gave Julia an extra hug at the door. 'We're all rooting for her, you know. We're not supposed to have favourites but our Penny's special.'

A tear trickled down Julia's cheek and she clearly couldn't speak.

'It's OK,' Rosie said softly. 'I'm a mum, too, so I know exactly how I'd feel in your shoes.'

'We really appreciate you reading to her,' Julia said.

Rosie smiled back. 'No problem. My two are more into dinosaurs than anything else at the moment, but when Lexi's older I'm sure she'd enjoy the kind of stories I've been reading to Penny.'

In the middle of the afternoon, she was at the nurses' station, writing up notes, when Leo came over and handed her a paper cup of cappuccino. 'Good afternoon. I brought you something to help you write up your notes,' he said.

'That's really nice of you, Leo, and I love the coffee from Tony's,' she said, 'but that's the second time you've bought me coffee this week and now I feel in your debt. Which makes me feel uncomfortable.'

'There's no debt.' He paused. 'Or maybe you could buy me a coffee after work, if that would make you feel better.'

Buying him a coffee to make them even would make

her feel better, but she absolutely couldn't do anything after work. 'Sorry. I can't.'

'Or come out with me for a pizza at the weekend,' he suggested. 'We can go halves and you can buy me a coffee then.'

How easy it would be to agree to have dinner with him.

And it worried Rosie just how much she was starting to like Leo Marchetti. He was kind, he was great with patients and parents and staff alike, and he was beautiful to look at with those dark, expressive eyes and a mouth that promised sin.

It would be so, so easy to say yes.

But how did she know that she wasn't going to be repeating her past mistake and fall for someone who made her heart beat faster but would let her down when she needed him? Leo seemed a nice guy on the ward—but would he be different in a relationship that wasn't strictly professional? Would he turn out to have feet of clay?

There was one way to find out. She could agree to one date. Then, if Leo took one look at the twins and ran for the hills, she'd know she'd been right about him all along. And she was pretty sure that he would leave her alone once he knew she was a single mum of three-year-old twins.

'All right,' she said. 'But, as you've been buying me coffee, *I'll* take *you* out for a pizza.'

He blinked, looking slightly shocked that she'd actually said yes. 'When?'

'Tomorrow night.' Before her nerve broke.

'OK. That's good. I'll pick you up,' he said. 'What time?'

She frowned. 'Hang on. I thought I was taking you out for pizza? Shouldn't I be the one picking you up?'

'Change of plan. I'm taking you out for dinner,' he said.

So once she'd agreed to something, then he changed

the goalposts? Well, Leo would find out the hard way that her goalposts weren't changeable. Her children came first. And that wasn't negotiable.

'Six o'clock, then,' she said, and wrote down her address for him.

'And your phone number? In case of emergencies and change of plans?'

She wrote that down, too.

'Thanks. I'll text you later so you have my number.'

'OK.'

'I'll let you get on,' he said. But before he walked away, he touched the back of his fingers briefly against her cheek—and every nerve-end sizzled at his touch. Just like Wednesday afternoon, when he'd hugged her and then he'd been at the point of actually kissing her. Worse still, she'd been thinking along the same lines.

This really wasn't good.

Rosie had to force herself to concentrate on the paperwork until the end of her shift, and then she headed down to the hospital nursery school to pick up the twins. Right at that moment, she wasn't sure if she'd just made a huge mistake in suggesting going out to dinner with Leo.

But it would settle things once and for all: she was pretty sure he'd look at the twins, make some charming excuse and scuttle off. And then he'd never ask her for another date. She'd be off the hook.

Leo could hardly believe that Rosie had actually agreed to a date.

Six o'clock seemed a little early for him to pick her up, but maybe they could go for a drink before they went out to dinner. He caught Robyn at the end of his shift. 'Just the person I wanted to see.'

'Something you need at work?' she asked.

He smiled. 'No—everything's fine and I'm really enjoying working here. This is personal. I was wondering if you could recommend a nice restaurant locally.'

'Oh, is your mother coming over to stay?'

He shook his head. 'Right now Mamma's a little frail, so I'd rather she stayed in Tuscany where she can be looked after properly.' He squished the faint feeling of guilt that really he ought to be the one keeping an eye on his mother, as her only child and a qualified doctor. But he specialised in paediatrics, not geriatrics, so she was getting better care than he could give her. And he called her every day when he wasn't in Tuscany; he wasn't neglecting her completely.

'So do you mean somewhere romantic?' Robyn teased.

He actually felt himself blush. 'Yes.'

She mentioned a couple of places and he made a note of them on his phone.

'Dare I ask who the lucky woman is?'

He smiled at her. 'Now, now. A gentleman doesn't tell tales.'

She laughed. 'Leo, you might be a gentleman, but you'll date her twice and be utterly charming, and then you'll end it before she has a chance to get close to you.'

'I date women more than twice,' he said. He knew she was teasing, but he also knew that she had a point. He never had let a woman close to him, since Emilia. Maybe he ought to leave Rosie well alone.

The problem was, he didn't want to. She drew him, with that odd mixture of warmth and wariness. He wanted to get to know her better and understand why she drew him like this. And, if he was honest with himself, she was the first woman since Emilia who'd made him feel this way. Which was another reason why he should just drop this: the last time he'd felt that incredible pull towards someone, it had gone badly wrong.

When he got home, he booked the table at one of the restaurants Robyn had suggested. But, the next day, he couldn't settle to much; he was too filled with anticipation. It made him feel a bit like a teenager again, though the teenage Leo Marchetti had ended up with a heart so broken that he'd had to escape from Rome to London before he could mend himself. He'd never want to go through his teens again, with all that uncertainty and that desperation to please someone who constantly changed the goalposts and made the young Leo feel that he'd never be able to match up to expectations. And he didn't have to ask anyone's permission to date someone.

He shook himself. His father was dead and Leo was comfortable in his own skin now. He knew who he was and what he was good at—and he didn't have to please anyone but himself.

Late that afternoon, he drove to Rosie's and parked his low-slung two-seater convertible on the road outside her house.

She answered the door wearing understated make-up and a little black dress: very different from how she usually was at work, with no make-up and a uniform.

'You look lovely,' he said, and then felt like a fool when she raised one eyebrow.

'Not that you don't usually look lovely,' he said, feeling even more gauche. Which was weird, because normally he was relaxed with women. He *liked* their company. Why was he so awkward with Rosie?

She smiled. 'Thank you for the compliment. Come in.'

He stopped dead in the doorway when she ushered him into the living room and he saw two small children playing with a train set on the floor. The brown-haired boy and golden-haired girl were clearly Rosie's children, as they had her bright blue eyes and her smile. And they looked to be around the same age, so he guessed that they were twins.

He couldn't see a babysitter anywhere, unless maybe someone was in the kitchen or something.

And the penny dropped when he looked at Rosie's face.

She'd invited him to pick her up here, expecting him to take one look at the children and make a run for it.

That really smarted. Had his reputation already spread through the hospital, if she thought he was that shallow?

Then again, maybe she'd been badly hurt by the twins' father. Until he knew the full story, he shouldn't judge her the way she'd obviously misjudged him.

'So that's dinner for four?' he asked.

She shrugged, and lowered her voice so the children couldn't hear. 'I come as a package, Leo.'

'It would've been useful to know that.'

'So you could back off earlier?'

She was really that sure he was so unreliable? Or had someone made her believe that about all men? 'No,' he said. 'So I could've brought a four-seater car with me instead of a two-seater.'

Colour flooded into her face. 'Oh.'

'I would be delighted to take you all out,' he said, keeping his voice as low as hers, 'but either we need to use a taxi or—if you have appropriate seats—your car. Is there any particular place the children like eating out?'

Leo wasn't running away.

And he'd asked where the twins liked eating out, not where she liked eating out.

He was putting her children first.

Shame flooded through Rosie. She'd misjudged him. Badly so. Every single assumption she'd made about him had been based on Michael's behaviour, and that wasn't fair of her. OK, so the hospital grapevine said Leo dated a lot, but she hadn't heard anything about him leaving a trail of broken hearts behind him. It was possible to be good-looking and be a decent human being as well. She knew her experiences with Michael had made her unfairly judgemental, but it was so hard not to just leap in and make assumptions.

'Thank you,' she said, feeling like an ungrateful monster. 'Are you sure about this?'

'The children are obviously dressed up, ready to go out,' he said. 'I'm not going to disappoint them.'

'I said I'd take them out,' she admitted.

'So how were you going to explain me to them?'

'You're my colleague. You popped in to tell me something about the hospital, and you couldn't come for a pizza with us because you're already due somewhere else.'

He raised an eyebrow. 'So you really did think I'd take one look at the children and scuttle away.'

'Yes, and I apologise. I was wrong to judge you on someone else's behaviour.' She closed her eyes briefly. 'I'll explain later, but I'd prefer not to discuss it in front of the twins.'

'All right. So shall I cancel our table while you book us a table somewhere that the twins like?'

This was way, way more than she deserved. 'Thank you,' she said. She'd already booked the table; but, sure that he wouldn't join them, she'd booked it for three rather than for four. It wouldn't take much to change that. 'And I'm sorry.'

Leo said nothing, just gave her a grave little nod that made her feel about two inches tall.

Leo walked back into the hallway and called the restaurant to cancel his booking. Once he'd ended the connection, he waited for Rosie to finish her own call, then followed her into the living room and crouched down to the twins' level. 'Hello. I'm Leo.'

The little boy refused to look at him, but the girl smiled at him. 'I'm Lexi. My name starts with a *luh*, like yours.'

'Delighted to meet you, Lexi.' He shook her hand, then looked at the little boy. 'And you are…?'

The little boy dipped his head and looked up shyly.

He had Rosie's eyes, Leo thought, huge and piercing and beautiful.

'He's Freddie,' Lexi said.

Did he always let his sister do the talking for him? Leo wondered. 'Delighted to meet you, too, Freddie,' he said, and held out his hand.

But the little boy looked wary and refused to take his hand.

Was Freddie wary of all men, or just of him? Leo wondered. Given that there was no evidence of the twins' father, had there been some kind of super-bitter divorce? It would perhaps explain why Rosie had been so quick to judge him harshly—and maybe the twins' father was the person she'd referred to when she'd talked about judging Leo on someone else's behaviour.

'I work with your mummy at the hospital,' he said.

'We go to school at the hospital,' Lexi said.

'School?' They looked a bit young to be at school.

'Nursery school,' Rosie explained.

That made a lot of sense. Now he understood why she rushed off at the end of every shift and had consistently refused to meet him after work: she needed to pick up her children straight after work.

'How old are you, Freddie?' he asked.

The little boy said nothing, and Lexi—clearly the more

confident of the two—nudged him, as if to say, *Answer the man*.

'Freddie's a little bit shy,' Rosie said.

'Mummy says don't talk to someone you don't know,' Lexi said.

'Quite right,' Leo said.

'But you know Mummy, so we can talk to you,' Lexi added.

'Three,' Freddie said reluctantly. 'I'm three.'

'I'm three and a little bit,' Lexi said. 'I was borned before Freddie.'

Leo had to hide a smile at both her charming grammatical mistake and the importance of her tone. 'So you're the older twin, Lexi.'

Freddie seemed to have a burst of confidence, because he said, 'Mummy's taking us out. We're having pizza for tea.'

'And I'm going with you,' Leo told him.

'Why?' Lexi asked.

'Lexi, that's rude,' Rosie warned.

'It's fine,' Leo reassured her. 'I'm coming with you because your mummy's very kind. I haven't worked at the hospital for very long and I don't know many people, so she thought I might be lonely this evening and said I could maybe come for pizza with you. If that's all right with you both, Freddie and Lexi?'

The twins looked at each other.

'So Mummy's your friend?' Freddie asked.

'She is,' Leo confirmed, not quite daring to meet Rosie's eyes. Friendship definitely didn't describe their relationship. But it would do for now.

'Then you're our friend, too,' Lexi said. Her smile was so much like Rosie's that it made Leo's heart feel as if it had just flipped over. Given how wary Rosie had been with him, it wouldn't be surprising if her children were just as nervous with people. Yet Lexi had seemed to accept him almost instantly.

'Are you coming to the park with us?' Freddie asked.

'We're not going to the park tonight, Freddie,' Rosie said.

'Tomorrow?' Lexi asked hopefully.

'We'll see. But we need to go for pizza now, so we have to put the trains away.'

Freddie stuck out his lower lip. 'But we want to play trains when we get back.'

'We'll see,' Rosie said. 'For now, we need to put the trains away before we go out. Shall we have a race and see who can put the track away fastest?'

'Me!' Lexi said.

'Me!' Freddie echoed.

Between them, they dismantled the wooden track and put it into a large plastic lidded box. Leo held back, watching them. Rosie was strict with her children rather than spoiling them, insisting that they clear up and have good manners. But he was also pretty sure that Rosie Hobbes would never, ever starve her children of love. In her case, firm went with fair, and he'd just bet that she told the twins every day—several times—that she loved them.

How different his own childhood had been. His mother had spoiled him but had never stood up for him, and his father had been cold and manipulative, seeing Leo firstly as the future Duke and only secondly as his child. The child who constantly disappointed him.

He pushed the thoughts away. Now wasn't the time to dwell on that.

'Do you mind me driving?' Rosie asked Leo when she'd strapped the children into their car seats.

'No.'

She grimaced. 'Sorry. Judging again. I don't mean to.'

'Any man who has a problem with a woman driving,' Leo said softly, 'needs to get a life.'

Which made her warm to him even more.

The children insisted on singing all the way to the pizza place; Rosie knew she was being a coward by letting it give her the excuse not to make small-talk with Leo, but right now she felt so wrong-footed.

She made each child hold her hand on the way in to the restaurant; once they were seated, with Lexi next to him and Freddie opposite, Leo asked the children, 'So is this your favourite place to eat?'

'Yes! We love pizza,' Lexi said.

'Me, too,' Leo said, 'because I was born in Italy, where pizza comes from.'

'Where's Italy?' Lexi asked.

Rosie was about to head her off, knowing that her daughter could ask a million questions and then a million more, but Leo took out his phone and pulled up a map. 'See that long, thin country there that looks a bit like a boot? That's Italy. And I come from here.' He pointed out a region to the north-west of the country.

Tuscany. The part of Italy Rosie had always wanted to visit. She and Michael had planned a tour of the area, stopping off at Florence and Siena and Pisa—but then he'd had to cancel their holiday because he was starting a new job. More like, she thought grimly, he'd gambled away the money he'd been supposed to use for their flights and hotels, and she'd been too naive to realise. She'd believed every word he'd said.

'Are the houses pretty?' Lexi asked.

'Very pretty.' Leo pulled up some pictures to show her. 'See?'

'That one looks a bit like the hospital,' Lexi said, ''cept it's yellow, not pink.'

'Are there castles in Italy?' Freddie piped up.

'There are castles,' Leo said, and found some more pictures. 'In Italy we call a castle a *palazzo*.'

'*Pal—*' Freddie began, and stopped.

'*Palazzo*. Like a palace,' Leo said. '*Pal-at-zo*.'

'Pal-as-o,' Freddie repeated, not quite getting it, but Rosie noticed that Leo didn't push him or mock him. Instead, he was actually encouraging the little boy to talk.

'Are there princesses in the castle?' Lexi asked.

'The waitress is here, Lexi. We need to tell her what we want to eat,' Rosie interrupted gently.

'Dough balls,' Lexi said promptly.

'Dough balls, what?' Rosie reminded her.

'Dough balls, please,' Lexi said.

'Me, too, please,' Freddie said.

'That's three for dough balls, please,' Leo said.

Rosie smiled. 'Four for dough balls, please, two small *margherita* pizzas for the children, a four cheeses thin crust for me and…' She paused and looked at Leo.

'A *quattro stagioni* thin crust for me, please,' Leo said.

Lexi's eyes went round. 'What's a cat—?' She stopped, looking puzzled.

'*Quattro stagioni*,' Leo said. 'It means "four seasons" in Italian, and each quarter of the pizza has a topping of food you find in each season. Do you know what the seasons are?'

'Like spring,' Rosie prompted when Lexi was uncharacteristically quiet.

Lexi shook her head.

'That's OK,' Leo said. 'Spring's when the daffodils and bluebells come out, summer's when it's hot, autumn's when all the leaves turn gold and fall off the trees, and winter's when it's cold and snowy.'

Of course Leo was good with kids, Rosie thought. He was a paediatrician and spent every working day treating children. It stood to reason that he'd be good with children outside work, too. But she appreciated the way he'd explained the concept simply and without fuss, rather than dismissing Lexi's question or ignoring her.

Lexi continued quizzing Leo about Italy while they were waiting for their meal, and even Freddie started to come out of his shell when Leo started asking him about his favourite trains. He also helped Freddie cut up his pizza without making a big deal of it, and Rosie felt the barrier round her heart start to crack.

This was what she'd always thought having a family would be like.

Except Michael hadn't wanted that. She and the children simply hadn't been enough for him. And OK, she could deal with the fact that maybe he'd made a mistake in choosing her as his life partner; but how could he have turned his back on his children? All this time later, it still hurt.

Leo was used to dealing with children at work, but very few outside. And he was surprised to discover how at ease he felt with chatterbox Lexi and shy Freddie.

Every so often, he glanced across at Rosie, to check that she was comfortable about the way he was chatting with her twins, and he was amazed to see that she actually looked relaxed—something he most definitely wasn't used to seeing from her at work.

Leo didn't do relationships; Robyn's teasing assessment had been very close to the mark. Yet he found himself drawn to this little family. And he was actually enjoying himself, answering Lexi's barrage of questions and trying to tempt Freddie out of his shell.

This was the kind of childhood he wished he'd had. Where his father might have cut up his meals for him without making a big deal about it, rather than making him eat his meals on his own in the nursery until he was old enough to know which knife and fork to use, and use them without spilling anything. Where his mother would have helped him decorate his whipped ice-cream sundae with sprinkles and jelly beans, not minding if anything spilled on the table or on her clothes. Though he had a feeling that she'd been acting on his father's decisions rather than her own; if you were fragile and you were married to a bully, it would be easier to agree with him than to risk a fight.

You couldn't change the past.

But maybe, he thought, his future could be different.

And maybe it didn't mean having to find himself a 'suitable' noble bride and producing an heir to the dukedom. Maybe it was about finding the life and the family that he wanted.

Maybe.

CHAPTER FOUR

AFTER THE MEAL, Rosie drove them back to her house.

It would be rude not to invite Leo in for coffee; but she was pretty sure that he'd make an excuse not to come in. Although he'd been lovely with the children, tonight hadn't been the romantic date for two he'd been expecting, and she wouldn't blame him for feeling just a bit disgruntled with her. When she'd planned this evening, she'd thought it was the best way of making him understand she wasn't interested in a date; but now she could see how stupid and selfish she'd been. She should've just told him straight.

Except a little part of her *had* wanted to date him.

And Leo Marchetti made her feel seriously flustered.

'You're welcome to come in for coffee,' she said, 'but I quite understand if you need to get going.'

His dark eyes were unreadable. 'Coffee would be lovely, thank you.'

Oh, help. He wasn't rushing away as fast as he possibly could. This felt as if she'd leaped out of the frying pan and into the fire.

'I'll put the kettle on, if you don't mind waiting while I put the children to bed?' she asked as she closed the front door behind them.

'I don't want to go to bed,' Lexi said.

'It's bedtime now, Lexi,' Rosie said firmly. 'And if you want to go to the park tomorrow, you need to get enough sleep tonight. I'll read you a story.'

'I want Leo to read me a story,' Freddie said. 'He's my friend.'

'Leo…' She paused, trying to think up a reasonable excuse.

'—would be delighted to read you a story,' Leo cut in gently. 'Do you have a favourite story, Freddie?'

'Dinosaurs!' Freddie said, and charged up the stairs.

'Thank you,' Rosie mouthed to him.

Once Rosie had brushed the children's teeth and Lexi and Freddie were in their pyjamas, cuddled beneath their duvets, Leo sat on the panda-shaped rug on the floor between their beds, holding the book that Freddie had picked out.

'*One* story,' Rosie said, and kissed them both. 'I'm going to put the kettle on for Leo and me to have coffee. Night-night. I love you, Freddie. I love you, Lexi.'

'Love you, Mummy,' they chorused. 'Night-night.'

In her small galley kitchen, Rosie could hear Leo reading the story. She loved the fact that he actually put on different voices for different dinosaurs; but part of her wanted to cry. This was something the children had really missed out on; although their grandfather often read to them, it wasn't quite the same as having their father read them a bedtime story every night.

Being a parent sometimes felt like the hardest, loneliest job in the world; although her parents and her sister were brilliantly supportive, it wasn't the same as having someone with her all the time. Someone to help make the decisions.

Once Leo finished the story, he sang a lullaby to them. Rosie didn't recognise the words and was pretty sure that he was singing in Italian, but he had a gorgeous voice. It was something that Michael had never bothered doing, and he'd actually smashed the CD of children's songs she'd bought for the car because he said it annoyed him and he couldn't put up with the twins caterwauling the same song over and over again.

Michael.

She was going to have to tell Leo about Michael. She'd promised him an explanation and she wasn't going to back out; but it wasn't a pretty story and even now she felt sick about how poor her judgement had been.

She busied herself making the coffee until she heard Leo come down the stairs. 'Thank you for reading to them—and for singing a lullaby. That was really kind of you.'

'No problem,' he said. 'They're nice kids.'

'Thank you.' She added milk to her own mug, then handed him the other. 'It's instant,' she warned, 'but it's decent instant coffee.'

'"Decent" instant coffee? I'm not entirely sure there is such a thing,' Leo said with a smile, 'but thank you.' He glanced at the drawings held to the outside of the fridge with magnets. 'I like the pictures.'

'The pink one is Lexi's and the yellow one is Freddie's. They feel about dogs the way that Penny at the hospital feels about kittens,' Rosie said ruefully. 'Nearly all their pictures are of puppies.'

'But you don't have one?'

She shrugged. 'I'd love one. But it wouldn't be fair to leave a dog on its own all day.'

Which was why he didn't have a dog, either. He took a sip of the coffee.

'Is it as bad as you thought it would be?' she asked, looking slightly worried.

Yes. Not that he was going to tell her that. 'It's drinkable.'

'But you'd prefer proper coffee?'

He shrugged and smiled. 'I'm from Tuscany. We Italians take our coffee seriously.'

'I guess.' She looked awkward. 'Well, come through.'

He followed her into the living room. Like her kitchen, it was tiny; yet it was also cosy, and there were photographs of the children on the walls, from what was clearly their very first picture in hospital through to a more recent-looking one that he assumed had been taken at the hospital nursery school.

And there were lumps of clay on the mantelpiece that were clearly meant to be dogs. Leo couldn't remember his parents ever displaying his artwork. Then again, maybe dukes and duchesses weren't supposed to put their young children's very first clay models among the Meissen and Sèvres porcelain.

'I enjoyed tonight,' he said. And he was surprised by how much he had relished the feeling of being part of a normal family.

'I'm afraid the twins can be a bit full-on,' she admitted, 'especially when Lexi starts chattering away. She really could talk the proverbial hind leg off a donkey.'

'She's lovely,' he said, 'and it's good that she's confident.'

'Probably because she's the elder twin—well, by all of fifteen minutes—and girls' language seems to develop faster than that of boys. Though I worry about Freddie,' she said. 'He's so shy.'

'Lots of young children go through a shy phase.' They could pussyfoot around the subject for ever, or he could push her just a little bit to find out why she'd been so sure he would walk away as soon as he saw the twins. 'Until tonight, I had no idea you had children.'

'Or you would never have asked me out?'

'That isn't what I said.'

'No. Sorry.' She sighed. 'And I'm really sorry I misjudged you. And I misled you. It was wrong of me.'

He might as well ask her outright. 'Who hurt you so badly, Rosie? Who broke your trust?'

She grimaced. 'Michael. My ex.'

'Freddie and Lexi's father?'

She nodded. 'I owe you the truth. But not everyone at work knows the whole story and I'd prefer to keep it that way.'

He could understand that. He didn't exactly tell many people about his own past. 'I won't betray your confidence.'

She looked at him, her eyes a piercing blue; and then she seemed to make the decision to trust him. 'I met Michael at a party when I was twenty-two, a year after I'd finished my nursing training. He was a friend of a friend. I thought he was charming and fun when I met him, and he was the most good-looking man I'd ever met. I couldn't believe it when he actually asked me out. And dating him was like nothing I'd ever experienced before. We went to the most amazing places—Michelin-starred restaurants, VIP seats at concerts for really big-name bands, and he whisked me away to the poshest hotel in Paris for my birthday. He completely swept me off my feet.' She looked away. 'We'd been together for three months when he asked me to marry him. Of course I said yes. I'd fallen in love with the sweetest, most charming man and I could hardly believe that he felt the same way about me. He made me feel so special.'

But obviously things had gone sour.

'And then it wasn't fun any more?' he asked gently.

'He changed,' she said, 'when I fell pregnant—it happened pretty quickly and, although he told me he was thrilled to be a dad, it didn't feel like it. He changed jobs a lot. I thought it was because he was ambitious and wanted to make a good life for our children.'

Leo didn't need to ask for the 'but'.

'He started coming home later and later,' Rosie said. 'And then the bailiffs came round. Michael told me that he was taking care of the bills and the money, and it was my job to take care of the children.' She looked away. 'Except he wasn't actually taking care of the money. I had no idea at the time, but he had a gambling problem. When I finally saw our bank statement, I realised that we were in debt up to our eyeballs.' She took a deep breath. 'Gambling's an illness. I know that. And I believed in my marriage vows, being with him in sickness and in health, so I tried to support him. I found him a group that would help him beat the addiction, and a good counsellor. He promised me he'd go. That he'd stop gambling. For our children's sake.'

And it was very clear to Leo that Michael had broken that promise.

'The next time someone came round demanding money,' Rosie said softly, 'it wasn't a bailiff. Michael was in debt to—I don't know any names, but they definitely weren't the kind of people you'd want to cross. All the time I thought he was going to counselling and the support group, it turned out he was still gambling and getting into more and more debt. He'd bailed out of the support group and the counselling after the very first session. And this man…' She shuddered. 'He threatened the children. His eyes looked dead, Leo. He meant it. If Michael didn't pay the money he owed, something would happen to the children. That man looked at them as if they were just leverage, not precious little lives. There was no pity, no compassion. I've never been so scared in my life.'

'Couldn't the police protect you and the children?'

She shook her head. 'This guy didn't act as if he was afraid of the law. I threatened to call the police. He just looked at me, and he didn't need to say a word: I knew that if I reached for the phone he'd break every bone in my hands to stop me. And then probably a few more to teach me a lesson.' She grimaced. 'He said Michael had three days to pay up, or else.'

'And you didn't go to the police?'

'I did, the very second he left, but I had no evidence. I couldn't describe the man in detail, I didn't know any names, and Michael wasn't talking. And I was so scared, Leo. Not for me, but for my babies. They were only two years old, still toddlers. I couldn't risk anything happening to them.' She closed her eyes. 'I could have forgiven Michael for lying to me—but I couldn't forgive him for putting our babies in danger. I asked him why he didn't go to the support group or to counselling. He said he didn't want to. And you can't change someone, Leo. If they don't want to change, you can nag and nag and nag until you're blue in the face—and all you'll do is give yourself a headache because they won't listen or do anything different. I told him I was leaving with the children, and as he'd clearly chosen gambling over us I was going to divorce him so I could keep them safe. My parents were brilliant. They took us in until I found my job at the Castle and this flat, and could get back on my own two feet.'

'And you divorced Michael and the thugs never came back?'

She blew out a breath. 'That's the bit I regret. The bit where I think maybe I should've done more. Because he died before I could even get an appointment with the solicitor,' she said. 'He was in a car accident.'

Something in her expression told him that there was more to it than that. 'But you don't think it was an accident?'

'I don't know. He was the only one involved. Michael, a tree and a soft-top car that I found out later was about to get repossessed because he hadn't kept up the payments.' She bit her lip. 'That man said he had three days to pay up. And the accident happened the day after the deadline.'

'So you think the bad guys had something to do with it?'

'I don't have any proof. I don't know if the people he owed money to decided to make an example of him for anyone else who thought about not paying them back, or whether Michael knew he'd run out of options and he drove straight into the tree because he couldn't see any other way out of the mess he'd made. Either way, I know I should've done more to help him. The crash was on a little country road and it was hours before anyone found him.' She looked haunted. 'His legs were shattered in the crash, and he bled out. He died all on his own, Leo, thinking everything was hopeless.'

'It wasn't your fault that he died, Rosie,' Leo said. 'You tried to get him to go to counselling. You found him a support group. He chose not to go. He lied to you about it, he got into even more debt with the wrong kind of people and he put the children at risk. You can't be responsible for someone else's choices.'

'What he did was wrong, but he didn't deserve to die for it.' She dragged a hand through her hair, looking weary. 'I told the police everything I knew, but there wasn't any evidence to back it up. And the people he owed money to haven't come after me, so I guess they must have decided that his death cleared his debt.'

'Do you see anything of Michael's family?'

She shook her head. 'He fell out with them before he met me. They didn't come to the wedding, even though we invited them. They've never even seen the twins.' She swallowed hard. 'And they didn't come to Michael's funeral.'

'It must've been a really bad row.' Despite his differences with his own father, Leo had attended the funeral. He'd even sat by his father's hospital bed for twenty-four hours straight after the first stroke, hoping that they might have some kind of reconciliation and he could help his father towards recovery. But the elder Leo had been intractable, and they hadn't reconciled properly before the second—fatal—stroke.

He still felt guilty, as if he could've done more. So he understood exactly where Rosie was coming from. And he wasn't sure if it was more a need to give or receive comfort that made him put his arms round her.

That first touch undid him even more than the first time when he'd hugged her and almost kissed her. This time, the impulse was way too strong to resist.

He could feel the warmth of her body through the material of her dress and his shirt, and it made him want more. He knew he shouldn't be doing this, but he couldn't help dipping his head and brushing his lips against hers. His mouth tingled where it touched hers, and warmth slid all the way down his spine.

Rosie was still for a moment, as if shocked that he'd made such a bold move—but then, just when he was about to pull away and apologise, she slid her hand round his neck and kissed him back. It felt as if fireworks were going off inside his head.

When he finally broke the kiss, her cheeks were flushed and her mouth was reddened and full. He had a feeling that he looked in the same kind of state.

'Sorry,' he said. 'I shouldn't have done that.'

She stroked his face. 'It wasn't just you,' she said wryly.

'So what are we going to do about this?' he asked. 'I like you, Rosie.'

'I like you, too,' she admitted.

There was a 'but'. He could see it in her expression.

'But we can't do this,' she said softly. 'Right now I'm focused on my children and my career.'

'That's totally understandable,' he said. She was a single mum. Of course her children had to come first.

'And you're only here on a temporary contract. I guess you'll be going back to Italy when it's over.'

'Maybe, maybe not.' He shrugged. 'My plans are quite fluid at the moment.'

She frowned. 'But you have commitments in Italy. You're a duke.'

'And, as I told you the other day, I delegate a lot of the work. I have excellent staff.'

'But at the end of the day you're still the Duke, and you have responsibilities,' she said. 'I imagine you'll have to marry some European princess.'

'Not necessarily a princess,' he said.

'But not a commoner.'

'That was a sticking point for my father,' he said—and then was horrified to realise what he'd just blurted out.

This dismay must've shown on his face, because she took his hand and squeezed it. 'Don't worry. I'm not going to spread that round the hospital or rush out to spill the beans to the first paparazzo I can find.'

'Thank you.' And he believed she'd keep his confidence, the way he'd keep hers.

'Considering what I just told you,' she said, 'if you ever want to talk…'

'Thank you.' Though he had no intention of telling her about his past. About Emilia, the girl he'd fallen in love with in his first week at university—and how his father had disapproved of Emilia's much poorer background. Leo hadn't realised it at the time, but his father had made life hard for her behind the scenes; his father had pulled strings and made it clear that he'd ruin her life if she didn't stop seeing Leo. Emilia had resisted for a while, but in the end she'd broken up with Leo. And she'd left university, too; he hadn't been able to track her down.

He'd learned the hard way that 'love conquers all' wasn't true. He'd loved Emilia and she'd loved him, but it hadn't been enough to overcome his father's opposition. And Leo hadn't been prepared to settle for an arranged marriage without love, or to bring a child into the dysfunctional world he'd grown up in. He wanted to change things. To make a difference to the world. To do *good*. And so he, too, had left the university at Rome, and applied to read medicine in London. His father had threatened to disown him, and by that point Leo had stopped caring about trying to please someone who could never, ever be pleased. He'd simply smiled and said, 'Do it.'

His father hadn't disowned him.

And Leo had still been stuck with the dukedom.

'Tell me,' she said softly.

He shook his head. 'Old news. And you can't change the past. I've come to terms with it.'

'Have you?'

'Probably not.' He couldn't stop himself running the pad of his thumb along her lower lip, and his whole body tightened when her beautiful blue eyes went dark with the same desire that flooded through him. 'What are we going to do about this thing between us?'

'I don't know. Pretend it isn't happening, I guess,' she said. 'I have to put the children first.'

'Agreed.'

'And you're probably not going to be around for long. I can't bring you into their lives, only for you to leave as soon as they get attached to you. I won't do that to them.'

It was so easy to break a child's heart. He knew that one first-hand and still had the scars from it. 'So see me when they're not around.'

'I'm a single mum, Leo. When I'm not at work, I'm with them all the time.'

'And at work we're both busy. I won't ask you to give up your lunchtimes reading to Penny. That wouldn't be fair to anyone.'

'So we're colleagues.' She paused. 'Maybe friends.'

That wasn't enough. 'I want to see you, Rosie,' he said softly. 'There has to be a way. Tell the children what you told them today—that I'm new at work and don't know many people at the hospital. That's true.'

She was silent for so long that he thought she was going to say no. Then she grimaced. 'Leo, I'm not very good at relationships.'

Neither was he.

'I find it hard to trust,' she admitted.

Given what she'd told him about her ex, that was understandable. 'I don't have any easy answers,' he said, not wanting to brush her feelings aside and make her feel that she was making a fuss over nothing. But he didn't want to make some glib, smooth reply, either. 'I have no idea where this is going. But I like you, Rosie, and I think you might like me. So isn't it worth a try?'

Again, she was silent while she thought about it. Finally,

she nodded. 'As far as the children are concerned, you're *just* my friend from work. My friend who isn't going to be around for very long.'

'That's fair.' He paused. 'And when they're asleep... Then I get to hold your hand. To talk to you. To kiss you.'

She went very pink, and Leo couldn't resist stealing another kiss. Rosie Hobbes, now she was letting him a little closer, was utterly adorable.

'It's Sunday tomorrow,' she said, and Leo loved the fact that her voice had gone all breathy.

'So we can do something together, the four of us?'

'The park, maybe,' she suggested.

'That sounds good. Shall I pick you up or meet you there?'

'Meet us there,' she said. 'Half-past ten. I'll text you the postcode so you can find it on your satnav.'

'OK.' He stole another kiss. 'I'm going now. While I can still be on my best behaviour.'

The colour in her face deepened, and he guessed that she was wondering what it would be like if he wasn't on his best behaviour; even the thought of it made him feel hot and bothered.

'Tomorrow,' he said.

But on Sunday morning, when Leo was showering after his usual early-morning run, he realised how selfish he was being.

He'd let his attraction to Rosie get in the way of his common sense.

She was absolutely right. They shouldn't do this. She needed to put her children first. It wasn't fair for him to let her and the children get close to him, then walk away. She needed more than he could offer her—more than a fling. What did he know about a normal family life? This wasn't fair to any of them. He needed to do the right thing and call a halt.

As soon as he was dressed and his coffee was brewing, he texted her.

Sorry. Can't make it.

And hopefully by the time he saw her at work tomorrow he'd have a reasonable excuse lined up.

Sorry. Can't make it.

Rosie stared at the message on her phone.

So Leo had changed his mind about going to the park with her and the children. He hadn't even given a polite excuse, saying that he was needed at work or there was a family thing he had to sort out; he'd sent just a plain and simple statement that he wasn't coming.

So she'd been right to be wary of trusting him. OK, he hadn't bolted on seeing the twins and he'd even been really sweet with them, reading them a bedtime story and singing them a lullaby. But now he'd had time to think about it and clearly he'd realised that she wasn't what he wanted. She wasn't able to give him a simple, uncomplicated relationship; she came with baggage and a heap of mistrust. Plus, they came from such different worlds: he was the heir to a dukedom and she was a single mum of two. With all that, how could it possibly work?

She shouldn't have let down her guard last night. But instead she'd told him everything about Michael—and she'd let him kiss her.

What a fool she'd been.

Well, she'd still take the children to the park. They

weren't going to miss out on a treat just because she'd been so foolish.

Tomorrow, when she had to face Leo at work, she'd act as if nothing had happened. And she'd keep him at a distance for the rest of his time at Paddington Children's Hospital.

CHAPTER FIVE

On Monday morning, Rosie kissed Freddie and Lexi good-bye at the hospital nursery school. 'See you after work,' she said with a smile.

'Are we going to have pizza with Leo tonight?' Freddie asked.

'No.'

Nina, the children's favourite classroom assistant, raised an eyebrow. 'Who's Leo?'

Oh, help, Rosie thought. Still, at least she was here when the subject was raised—and now she could make it very clear that the man the twins had adored when he'd met them on Saturday was absolutely not going to be a fixture in their lives. 'He's a new colleague,' Rosie said. 'You know what it's like when you start a new job and you don't know anyone. There's nothing worse than being all alone on a Saturday night, so I invited him to join us for pizza.'

'Uh-huh.' Nina didn't look the slightest bit convinced.

Rosie definitely didn't want this turning into hospital gossip. 'I think he has a soft spot for one of the nurses in the Emergency Department,' she said. It wasn't true, but she hadn't been specific so it wasn't *quite* the same as spreading a rumour. She was just deflecting the attention from herself. 'So now—thanks to the twins—he knows a nice pizza place to take someone to.'

'Right,' Nina said, still not looking completely convinced.

'My shift starts in five minutes. I need to go,' Rosie said, kissed the twins goodbye again and left before Nina could quiz her any further.

And of course the first person she saw when she walked onto the ward *would* have to be Leo Marchetti.

The man she'd thought would run a mile, but had surprised her.

The man who'd sung a lullaby to her children, then kissed her until her knees had gone weak.

The man who'd then changed his mind and lived all the way down to her original expectations.

'Dr Marchetti,' she said, and gave him a cool nod.

'Ros—' he began but, at her even cooler stare, he amended his words to, 'Nurse Hobbes.'

Worse still, she discovered that she was working in the allergy clinic with him all day.

Well, she could be professional. She could work with the man and make sure that their patients had the best possible care. And she'd make quite sure that all their conversations revolved around their patients.

'Our first patient is Madison Turner,' she said. 'She's six, had anaphylactic shock after being stung by a wasp, and this is her second appointment for venom immunotherapy. Two weeks ago, she had six injections over the course of a day and she responded well.'

'Good. So today she's due for three injections,' Leo said. 'Would you like to bring her in?'

'Of course, Dr Marchetti.' By the end of today, Rosie was sure she'd be sick to the back teeth of being polite and professional, but she'd do it for the sake of their patients. And she'd be very glad when her shift was over.

When she brought Madison and her mother in, Leo

smiled at them and introduced himself. 'Good morning. You already know Nurse Hobbes. I'm Dr Marchetti—Dr Leo, if you prefer.'

'Good morning,' Mrs Turner said.

'Hello, Dr Leo,' Madison said shyly.

'Before we start, can I just check that you have your emergency kit with you,' Rosie asked, 'and that Madison had her antihistamines last night?'

'We did everything you said in your letter,' Mrs Turner confirmed.

'That's great. So how have you been doing since you came in last?' Leo asked Madison.

The little girl looked at her mum, who smiled and said, 'She's been fine. No problems. Her hay fever flared up a bit on the day we came here last, but Rosie had already told us to expect it and everything was fine after that.'

'Good. Today's going to be very similar to last time, except Madison will only have three injections instead of six,' Leo explained. 'We'll space them an hour apart, but we'd like you to stay in the department for an hour or so after she has the last one, so we can keep an eye on her in case of any allergic reactions.'

Mrs Turner patted her bag. 'We have books and a games console,' she said, 'plus drinks and snacks—nothing with nuts, in case someone else is allergic to them.'

'That's perfect,' Rosie said with a smile. 'If everything's OK today, we'll see you for a single injection next month, and then a monthly maintenance dose. Madison, Dr Leo needs to have a quick look at you and I need to take a few measurements and get you to blow into a tube for me—that's to check how your breathing is, so we're happy you're fine to have your next treatment. Is that OK?'

The little girl nodded, and between them Leo examined

her and Rosie took all the obs and did a lung function test. 'Everything's fine,' she confirmed to Leo.

'Nurse Hobbes has some special cream so the injection won't be so sore,' Leo said, and Rosie used the anaesthetic cream to numb the injection site on Madison's skin.

'Mrs Turner, if Madison has any kind of allergy symptoms between now and the next injection, we'd like you to tell us straight away,' Leo said. 'I realise you probably already know them, but I like to be clear so I'll repeat them, if you don't mind. If Madison has a rash or any itching, if she feels dizzy or light-headed or generally not very well, if there's any swelling of her face, lips or tongue, if it's hard for her to breathe or if her heartbeat's too fast, then we need to know right away.'

'Got it,' Mrs Turner said.

'Madison, can you look at the butterfly on the ceiling and count the spots for me?' Leo asked, and swiftly administered the injection before she'd finished counting.

'Seven,' Madison said.

He smiled at her. 'Good girl. Thank you. We'll see you in an hour.'

Rosie followed the Turners out to the waiting room. 'Let us know if you're worried about anything,' she said. 'And you might find that, just like last time, Madison's hay fever is a little bit worse tonight, but an antihistamine will help.'

'We're prepared for that, thanks to you,' Mrs Turner said. 'No hot baths tonight, either, and we need to just have a very quiet and lazy evening, right?'

'Right,' Rosie confirmed with a smile.

Leo noticed that Rosie was being super-professional with him. She only spoke to him when necessary between patients, and kept popping out to check on the children who, like Madison, were waiting between immunotherapy treatments. It felt as if she was avoiding him as much as she could.

He could understand why. After all, he'd been the one to back off on Sunday morning. He hadn't even given her a proper explanation, because he couldn't find the right words and he'd been selfish enough to take the easy option of saying nothing. To back away, just as he always did.

He sighed inwardly. He hadn't been fair to Rosie. He knew he ought to let her go, because he couldn't offer her a future; yet, at the same time, he was drawn to her and to the way that he'd felt as if he were part of a family on Saturday night. The whole thing threw him. He wasn't used to feeling confused and torn like this—torn between doing what he knew was the right thing and doing what he really wanted to do.

Rosie Hobbes was special. Walking away from her might be the stupidest thing he'd ever done. Yet at the same time he knew she was vulnerable; it wouldn't be fair of him to get involved with her and then walk away when his temporary contract came to an end.

The more he worked with her and saw the calm, kind way she dealt with even the most difficult and frightened of their little patients, the more he wanted her in his life.

Should he follow his heart or his head?

He still didn't have an answer by the end of the morning's clinic, but he needed to talk to her. The least she deserved was for him to apologise for backing off on Sunday and to explain why he'd acted so hurtfully.

'Ros—Nurse Hobbes,' he corrected himself. 'Can I talk to you over lunch?'

She shook her head. 'I'm reading to Penny.'

Of course. It was Monday. How could he have forgotten? 'After work?'

Again, she refused. 'I need to pick up the children.'

'Then during your break, this afternoon,' he said. 'I really think we need to talk.'

'There's absolutely nothing to say. We work together.'

But her gaze had lingered just a little too long on his mouth. He had a feeling that she was remembering that kiss on Saturday and it was confusing her as much as it was confusing him. Or was he deluding himself?

'Please,' he said softly. 'Give me a chance to explain.'

She was silent for so long that he thought she was going to say no. Finally, she nodded. 'All right.'

'Coffee at Tony's?' he suggested, thinking there might be a tiny bit more privacy there than in the hospital canteen.

'There isn't really enough time. I'll meet you in the ward kitchen,' she countered.

He could put up with the vile instant coffee; what bothered him more was that it was usually busy in the ward kitchen. 'I'd rather talk somewhere a little quieter,' he said.

She was implacable. 'That's as quiet as you're going to get.'

'Fair enough.'

To his relief, the kitchen was empty when he got there at the beginning of their afternoon break. He filled the kettle and switched it on, and had just made the coffee when she walked in.

'Thank you,' she said as he handed her the mug.

'No problem, Rosie.' Again, she skewered him with a look for using her first name. He sighed. 'If you would prefer me to call you "Nurse Hobbes", fine—but it's a bit formal for someone who kissed me back on Saturday night.'

'We all make mistakes.'

'Yes, and I made rather more of them than you did, this weekend,' he said wryly. 'Rosie.' This time, to his relief, she didn't correct him. 'I want to spend time with you,' he said. 'You *and* the twins.'

'Which is why you promised them you'd go to the park with us on Sunday, but you called it off at the last minute and didn't even give a reason?' she asked.

He raked a hand through his hair, knowing she was right to be upset with him about it. 'I wanted to go. But the three of you are vulnerable, and I don't want to lead you on.'

'It's not fair to Lexi and Freddie to let you into their lives, only for you to disappear again,' she said. 'Do you even know how long you're going to be in London? You're on a temporary contract, after all.'

'It's for a couple of months, but we might be able to extend it. If not, there are other hospitals in London.'

She frowned. 'So now you tell me that you're planning to stay in London?'

He couldn't answer that properly. 'It's possible.'

'Even so, you're a duke and I don't have even a drop of blue blood. I'm a single mum of two, and I'm just about the most unsuitable person you could get involved with.'

'You're kind, you're straight-talking and you're sweet,' he corrected, 'and I don't care about blue blood or difficult pasts.'

'You might not,' she said dryly, 'but your family might.'

'The one person who might've protested—no, I'll be honest with you,' he corrected himself, '*would* have protested, is dead.'

She looked completely confused.

He sighed. 'I trust you to keep my confidence, the way I'm keeping yours about Michael.'

She flinched, then nodded. 'Of course.'

'I didn't have the greatest time growing up.' It was the first time he'd really talked about it to anyone, and it made him uncomfortable. Like rubbing on a bruise so deep it hadn't even started colouring his skin yet. 'My father had pretty set views on life. I knew I was supposed to study for some kind of business degree to prepare me for taking over my father's duties on the estate and eventually inheriting the dukedom, and I guess I rebelled by going to university in Rome rather than nearby in Florence. I thought I'd get a bit more freedom there.'

'But you didn't?'

He shrugged. 'At first, I really thought I had. I fell in love with a girl I met in my first week there—Emilia. I thought she loved me, too. She was sweet and kind and clever, and I was so sure my parents would love her as much as I did.' He paused. 'And then I made the mistake of taking her back to Tuscany for the weekend.'

'Your parents didn't like her?'

'My mother did. My father decided that she wasn't good enough for me. So he warned her off.'

Rosie looked shocked. 'And she accepted that?'

'I didn't realise at the time how much he leaned on her. She must have resisted him at first, but then suddenly there were all these little administrative mistakes that made her life difficult—her finances were late, or her rent showed up as unpaid, even though she'd paid it and had a receipt. Her marks started dropping and her future at the university was under threat. Her part-time employer suddenly changed his mind about her working for him, and she didn't even get an interview for everything else she applied for. I didn't connect it at the time, but my father was behind it all. The longer Emilia dated me, the harder it got for her, until she did what he wanted and broke up with me. Then she left the university,' he said quietly.

'That's awful,' Rosie said.

'I tried very hard to find her—I even used a private investigator—but she went completely to ground. I had a feeling my father was behind her disappearance, so I confronted him about it.' It had been the worst row they'd ever had. The first time Leo had really stood up for himself. His father had taken it extremely badly. 'Let's just say my father epitomised everything I don't stand for. And that's when I realised that he was never going to change. He'd manipulated her and he was always going to try and manipulate me because that was who he was. I could either let him do it, or I could stop trying to please a man who'd never be pleased, no matter what I did. I might have to inherit the dukedom, but I decided I'd do it my way. I left Rome and I applied to read medicine in London—so I'd have a career where I could give back some of my privileges, instead of trying to take more.'

She reached out and took his hand. 'I'm sorry you didn't have the right support when you were younger.'

'Plenty of people have had it much worse than me. I shouldn't complain.'

'What about your mum? Didn't she try to talk your dad round?'

'My father was quite forceful in his views,' he said. 'It was easier for her to agree with him.'

'That's something I don't understand,' she said softly. 'Because I'd never let anyone hurt my children. Including their father. That's why I left Michael, and why I changed the children's names along with mine.'

'You're a strong woman,' he said. 'Not everyone is like that.' His mother probably would've liked to be, but Leo came from a line of old-fashioned men who believed that a woman's place was to shut up and agree with her husband, and a child's place was to ask 'how high?' when his father said 'jump'. And his mother's family was the same. Even the kindest heart could get beaten into submission. And sometimes words left more scars than physical blows. He could understand now why Beatrice hadn't tried to stand up to her husband.

'Not everyone has the support behind them to help,' Rosie said, going straight to the core of things. 'My family was brilliant. They backed me.'

'You're one of the lucky ones,' he said.

'Did you try looking for Emilia again when you came to London?'

'I found her before that,' he said.

The bleakness in Leo's eyes told Rosie this wasn't a story with a happy ending. 'What happened to her?' she asked gently.

'After Emilia left Italy, she did charity work in Africa. While she was out there, she caught a virus.' He looked away. 'She was too far from the medical care she needed. She never made it home.'

Rosie winced. 'That's so sad. Is that why you chose to study medicine?'

'It's one of the reasons, yes,' he said. 'Plus, everyone's equal in medicine. And it means I can give something back.'

Leo Marchetti was a good deal more complicated than she'd thought he was, Rosie realised. Despite all that privileged upbringing, he'd had his heart well and truly broken. Not just because he'd lost the woman he'd fallen in love with, but because his father sounded like a complete control freak. If he'd been so desperate to control Leo that he'd bullied Emilia into leaving, what else had he done? It sounded as if Leo's mother hadn't been able to stand up to her husband, either.

No wonder Leo was wary about families, after such a miserable childhood. No wonder he hadn't wanted any relationship to get serious. But she came with a family: how could it work out between them?

'So where do we go from here?' she asked.

'If I'm honest, I don't know,' he said. 'I understand why you don't want to get involved. I'm not exactly looking for a relationship, either.'

At least he was up front about it. 'The papers all say you're a playboy.'

He grimaced. 'The press will say anything to sell copies. Yes, I've dated a lot in the past, but I don't make promises I can't keep and I don't lie my way into someone's bed. I offer my girlfriends a good time, yes, but I make it clear that it's fun for now and not for always.'

'I have the twins to think of,' she said. 'I can't just have a fling with you because it's not fair to them. And you can't offer me more than a fling, so...' She spread her hands. 'Maybe we should just call it a day. Maybe we can be friends.'

'I don't want to be just your friend,' he said.

'So what do you want?' she asked.

'That's the thing, Rosie,' he said. 'I want you.'

His dark eyes were soulful and full of sincerity. And even though Rosie found it hard to believe anything a man told her—she'd heard too many lies to take things at face value any more—Leo had shown her that he trusted her. He'd told her things that the gossip magazines would no doubt love to know—and he was trusting her not to break the story to the press. So maybe, just maybe, she could trust him.

'My head's telling me I should back away now—that it's going to cause no end of complications if I do what my heart's telling me to do,' he said.

'What's your heart telling you to do?' she asked.

'Something different. To take a risk,' he said. 'I like you and I think you like me.'

His admission made her feel as if all the air had just been sucked out of her lungs. Yes. She did like Leo. She thought she could like him a lot. But seeing him... Would that be a huge mistake? 'So what are you suggesting?' she asked.

'That we see where this takes us.'

'We've already discussed this. I come as a package, Leo. I have two three-year-olds,' she reminded him.

'I appreciate that, and I'm including them in this whole thing. We've already told them that I'm your friend from work. Right now, they don't need to know anything more complicated than that. As far as they're concerned, you're being kind to me because I don't know many people. And, actually, that's a really good example to set them.'

Rosie thought about it. Maybe this was a way to have it all—to see Leo on more than just a friendship basis, but for the twins to think that he was just her friend.

But what if she got it wrong? What effect would it have on Lexi and Freddie if they got close to him and then he disappeared out of their lives?

On the other hand, she knew it would be good for Freddie to have another male role model in his life, even if it was only for a little while. And the Leo Marchetti she was beginning to know was a decent man. He'd be a good role model.

'No strings,' she said. 'And the children don't get hurt. They come first.'

'Absolutely,' he said.

Excitement fluttered low down in her belly. This was the first time in nearly five years that she'd agreed to date someone. And Leo Marchetti wasn't just someone: he was the most attractive man she'd met in a very long time.

'So what happens now?' she asked. 'I'm a bit rusty when it comes to dating.'

He smiled. 'It's not exactly the thing I'm best at, either. Which is how come I've got this stupid reputation as a playboy. Even though I'm not one really.' He swallowed hard. 'Since Emilia, I haven't met anyone I've wanted to get close to. Until now. Until *you*.'

Which was honest. And he'd gone a step further with her, admitting that he didn't have a clue where this was going to take them. 'Thank you for being honest,' she said. And she needed to be equally as straight with him: they didn't have a future. How could they, when their worlds were so different? 'Just so it's clear, I'm not looking for a stepfather for Freddie and Lexi.'

'So is this going to make us friends with benefits?' he asked.

'I don't know—but I think we've all been hurt enough. Just as long as we don't expect too much from each other, I guess.'

'We'll play it by ear, then, and muddle through together,' he suggested.

'OK.'

'When are you free this week?' he asked.

'I was going to take the children to the park on Wednesday, on the way home from here. You could come with us, if you like, and then have dinner with us at home afterwards?'

He smiled. 'Thank you. I'd like that very much.'

Rosie wasn't sure if she was doing the right thing or not, but maybe her sister and her parents and her closest friends were right and it was time to try again, put the past behind her. Leo had been damaged, too, and she realised now that he'd backed away on Sunday more from a fear of hurting anyone than from seeing the children as a burden. Maybe a few dates with no strings would do them both good. 'Wednesday, then. And we're both due back in clinic.'

'Indeed. And thank you, Rosie. For giving us a chance.' He leaned forward and kissed her on the cheek. It was the lightest contact, but it made her skin tingle. And she remembered how it had felt when he'd kissed her properly on Saturday.

A new beginning.

Maybe it wouldn't work out.

But they were both adults. They'd make sure that Freddie and Lexi weren't hurt; and they could try to enjoy this thing between them while it lasted.

CHAPTER SIX

ON WEDNESDAY AFTERNOON, Leo collected something he'd
stowed in his locker, then waited for Rosie outside the
hospital while she collected the twins from the hospital
nursery school.

Lexi gave him an accusing look when they stopped in
front of him. 'You didn't come to the park with us. You
said you would.'

'I know, and I'm sorry I let you down. But your *mamma*
says we can go today on the way home,' Leo said.

'Are you coming with us?' Freddie asked, looking
faintly suspicious.

'I am, if you don't mind,' Leo said solemnly. He held
out the bag he was carrying. 'I thought maybe we could
play ball. If you like playing ball?'

'I want to go on the swings,' Lexi said.

'And I want to go on the slide,' Freddie said.

'How about,' Rosie suggested, 'we do all three?'

The twins looked at each other, then at her, and nodded.

As they walked to the park, Leo was surprised and
touched that Freddie wanted to hold his hand on the way.
It gave him an odd feeling. He couldn't really remember
going to a park when he was small, even with his nanny;
whereas clearly this was something that Rosie did regularly with her children and they all looked forward to it.

Once they were at the small enclosed playground, Leo pushed Lexi on the swings while Rosie pushed Freddie.

This was all very, very domestic and so far out of Leo's experience that it scared him stupid. Though he knew that if he backed away from Rosie again, she wouldn't give him another chance. He had to damp down the fear of the unknown and the fear of getting too involved.

They headed for the slide next. It was high, and wide enough for about four people to go down at a time; Leo was slightly surprised that Rosie, who was a bit on the over-protective side where the twins were concerned, was actually letting them go on it.

'Will you slide down with me, Leo?' Freddie asked.

'What's the missing word, Freddie?' Rosie asked quietly.

'Please,' Freddie added swiftly, and Rosie gave him a thumbs-up.

'Sure,' Leo said. He helped the little boy climb up to the top of the slide and sat down next to him on the platform.

'I have to hold your hand or we can't go down,' Freddie informed him.

Leo wasn't sure whether that was Freddie's way of saying that he was a bit scared, or whether it was one of Rosie's rules to keep her children safe on the slide. Either way, he wasn't going to make a fuss about it. 'Sure,' he said, and held Freddie's hand. 'Ready?'

'Ready,' the little boy confirmed.

'After three. One, two, three—go!'

Rosie took her phone out of her bag and snapped a photograph of them on the way down, then smiled at him as they reached the bottom.

The sudden rush of adrenaline through Leo's blood had nothing to do with the slide and everything to do with that smile.

Lexi and Rosie went next, and Leo took a picture of them on his phone.

'You go down with Mummy, next,' Lexi said when they walked over to Leo and Freddie.

What could he do but agree?

At the top, Freddie called, 'Mummy, take a picture!'

'Do you mind?' Rosie asked.

He knew she wouldn't pass it to the press or make life difficult for him. 'Sure.'

Once Rosie had taken the photo and tucked her phone back into the pocket of her jeans, Lexi called, 'You have to hold hands!'

If he refused, then he'd be undermining Rosie's rule for the children—which wouldn't be fair. If he held her hand, he'd be undermining his own resolve not to get too close. Either way, this was going to be tricky.

'Ready?' Rosie asked softly.

'Yes,' he lied.

She took his hand. His skin tingled where it touched hers and he suddenly really wanted to kiss her, but he managed to hold himself in check. That was absolutely not going to happen in front of the children.

Sliding down towards the children, seeing them clap their hands with glee, made something around the region of his heart feel as if it had just cracked. And then going down the slide again with Lexi, and finally the four of them together, all holding hands and whooping at the same time... It was something he'd never done before. Something that felt really, really good.

They played ball and had another last go on the swings before Rosie called a halt. 'Time for tea,' she said.

'We're having macanoni, 'cause it's Wednesday,' Freddie told him seriously as Rosie unlocked her front door.

Leo hid a smile at the little boy's charming mispronunciation. 'I love macaroni,' he said.

'Good, because I feel a bit bad cooking pasta for an Italian,' Rosie said.

Leo laughed. 'Macaroni cheese isn't actually Italian. It was invented in England.'

'Seriously?'

'Seriously—obviously there have been pasta and cheese dishes in Italy for centuries,' he said, 'and some were even recorded in a fourteenth-century Italian cookbook called *Liber de Coquina*. There's a version in an English cookery book around the same kind of date, but the first modern recipe for macaroni cheese is actually in an English book from the middle of the eighteenth century.'

Rosie looked even more surprised. 'How do you know this? Did you study cookery or something before you studied medicine?'

'I found out in the general knowledge round at a pub quiz,' he admitted. 'Anyway, I really don't care who invented it. I like it.' He paused. 'Anything I can do to help?'

'Sure. You can help lay the table with Freddie and Lexi, and help them with the drinks,' she said. 'And if you want some wine, there's a bottle in the rack.'

'I'll have whatever you're having,' he said.

She smiled, and his heart felt as if it had done a backflip. 'I like red or white, so pick what you prefer. Oh, and we have strawberries for pudding.'

While the macaroni cheese—which she'd clearly made the previous night—was heating through in the oven, Rosie started chopping salad, and he helped the twins lay the table and put beakers out for water.

'Mummy says we're not big enough to carry a jug yet,' Lexi confided, looking slightly forlorn.

'You will be, soon,' he said, and filled the jug with

water before taking it to the table and opening a bottle of red wine for himself and Rosie.

He chatted to the twins while Rosie finished up in the kitchen, enjoying the way they opened up to him and told him all about their day, what they'd drawn and sung and glued. And it somehow felt natural to let them curl up each side of him on the sofa and teach him one of their nursery songs.

Rosie lingered in the doorway, watching Leo with her two very earnest children. Of course he was good with kids; it was his day job, after all. But she liked the way he behaved with them, persuading them to take turns and giving shy Freddie that little bit of extra encouragement so his confidence started to grow to match his sister's.

Was Leo Marchetti the one who could change her life for the better?

Or would he back away again when he realised that treating children in a hospital was very different from living with them every day?

At least they'd agreed that he wouldn't let the children get too attached to him: that as far as the twins were concerned Leo was simply her colleague and a friend, and not a potential replacement father.

She brought in the dish of macaroni cheese and served up, encouraging the twins to add salad to their plates.

'This is very nice. Thank you,' Leo said after his first forkful.

Was he just being polite? Rosie wondered. This was a far cry from his normal life. Although she was a reasonable cook, she didn't kid herself that she made anything exceptional. This was all just ordinary stuff. Very domestic. A world away from how the Duke of Calvanera lived.

Once they'd finished their pasta and demolished a large

bowl of strawberries between them, Rosie announced that it was time for bath and bed.

'But we want to stay up with Leo!' Lexi protested.

'Bath and bed now,' Rosie said firmly. 'Otherwise you'll be too tired to do anything at nursery school tomorrow morning. And I happen to know you're doing splatter painting tomorrow.'

'Yay! My favourite,' Freddie said. 'Lexi, we have to have our bath now.'

'I'll do the washing up,' Leo offered.

Rosie shook her head. 'It's fine. I understand if you need to get on.'

'No. You cooked. Washing up is the least I can do,' Leo said.

'Will you read us another bedtime story?' Lexi asked.

'Please?' Freddie added.

'That's up to your mum,' Leo said.

How could she refuse? 'If you don't mind, Leo, that would be lovely.'

He came upstairs when she'd got the twins bathed and in their pyjamas. 'So what story would you like tonight?'

'The dinosaur story, please!' they chorused.

Rosie leaned against the door jamb and watched him read to the children. He seemed to be enjoying himself, and the children enjoyed it enough to cajole him into reading a second story to them.

'Time to say goodnight,' she said gently when he'd finished, knowing that they could badger him into half a dozen more stories.

Lexi held her arms up towards him. 'Kiss goodnight,' she said sleepily.

'Me, too,' Freddie said, doing the same.

Leo glanced at Rosie for permission. Part of her felt she ought to say no—she didn't want Leo getting close to the children and then leaving. Yet how could she deprive them of that warmth—a simple, sweet kiss goodnight? She gave a tiny nod.

'Goodnight. Sleep tight,' he whispered, kissing each of them on the forehead in turn, and being hugged tightly by both twins.

'Thank you,' she said quietly when they were downstairs again. 'I appreciate you being kind to them.'

'They're lovely children,' Leo said.

Was that a hint of wistfulness she saw in his face? she wondered.

'And I enjoyed this evening. I can't remember the last time I went down a slide.'

Definitely wistfulness, Rosie thought. Leo clearly hadn't had much of a chance to visit a playground when he was young. Poor little rich boy, probably having everything his parents could buy him and yet not having a normal childhood where he was free to run and laugh and play.

'I'm glad you came with us.' She paused. 'Would you like another glass of wine?'

He shook his head. 'I left my car at the hospital.'

Which was his cue to leave. And probably the best thing, she thought.

'But I'd like to stay for a little longer, if that's OK with you,' he said.

He rested his palm against her cheek, and her mouth went dry.

It went drier still when he rubbed the pad of his thumb against her lower lip.

And then he bent his head and brushed his mouth against hers. What else could she do but slide her hands round his neck and lean against him, letting him deepen the kiss?

She was dizzy by the time he broke the kiss.

'My beautiful Rosie,' he whispered. 'Right now I just want to hold you.'

Unable to form any kind of coherent sentence, she simply nodded.

She hadn't expected him to scoop her up and carry her to the sofa, and it made her knees go weak. 'That's…' All the rest of the words went out of her head when he sat down and settled her on his lap.

'A bit caveman-like,' he finished wryly. 'But you're irresistible. You remind me of Titian's *Flora*.'

'Flora?'

He took his phone from his pocket, looked up the portrait on the Internet and handed the phone to her. 'Obviously your hair's shorter—but you're beautiful, like her.'

All curves, Rosie thought as she looked at the portrait. Michael had liked her curves until she was pregnant; then he'd considered her to be fat and unattractive.

She pushed the thought away and handed the phone back to Leo. 'Thank you for the compliment. Sorry. I don't know a lot about art.'

'I spent a lot of time in the Uffizi in my teens,' he said. 'This was always one of my favourites.' He stole another kiss. 'Tell me about your teens.'

'There isn't really that much to tell. I spent my time with my sister and friends, doing the kind of things teenage girls do,' she said. 'Trying out different make-up, doing each other's hair, talking and listening to music.' She smiled. 'And films. Monday night was cheap night when I was a student nurse, so a group of us used to go out every Monday when we weren't on placement or doing a late shift.'

'Any particular favourites?' he asked.

'We'd see anything and everything,' she said. 'Freddie and Lexi like the cinema, too. I try to take them to see all the animated films, because they're so magical on a big screen. One or other of them always needs the loo halfway through, but they love going to see a film.'

Again, he looked wistful. Clearly his parents hadn't done that sort of thing with him when he was young. 'Maybe we could do something like that at the weekend.'

'Maybe,' she said. 'So your teens were spent mooching about museums?'

'And studying. And trying to wriggle out of deadly dull functions.'

Where his father had shown him off as the heir? She sensed it was a sore spot, but she didn't know what to say. The only thing she could think of to do was to kiss him. Judging by how dark his eyes were when she finally broke the kiss, it had been the right thing to do.

She stayed curled on his lap with her arms round him, just chatting idly. Finally, he stole a last kiss. 'I'd better let you get some sleep.'

'Are you OK to get back to your car from here?'

He smiled. 'Yes, but thanks for asking.'

She had the strongest feeling that people didn't tend to try to look after Leo Marchetti very much. Maybe it was because he was so capable and efficient at work; or maybe it was because everyone assumed that the Duke's personal staff kept his life completely in order. But did anyone really see the man behind the doctor and the dukedom? 'I'll see you at work tomorrow, then.'

'Yes. Goodnight.'

Rosie was still smiling when she'd finished brushing her teeth and was curled up in bed. Just spending time with Leo had felt so good. Her children liked him, too. So did she dare to keep dreaming that this might actually work out?

On Thursday, Leo was working in clinic while Rosie was working on the ward, but he caught up with her at lunchtime.

'Had a good morning?' he asked.

'Yes and no.' She sighed. 'I was looking after young Ryan today.'

'How's he doing?'

'He's showing small signs of improvement, but he's still unconscious.' She bit her lip. 'It's really tough on his parents.'

'Do you think he's going to recover?' Leo asked.

'I really don't know. In some respects, it's kind of early days; in others, it...' She shook her head and grimaced. 'And then there's Penny.'

The young patient who was a favourite with everyone who met her. 'She's on the transplant list now?'

'Yes. And now it's a waiting game.' Rosie stared into her coffee. 'They're both so young. And, despite all the advances in medicine and the different treatments, are we really going to make the right difference to either of them?'

'Yes. Years ago, they wouldn't even have come this far,' Leo reminded her. 'But you're right. It's hard on the parents.'

'I was just thinking. If the worst happens—and I really hope it doesn't, for his family's sake—then it would be good if Ryan turned out to be a match for Penny,' Rosie said softly.

'So at least one of them would be saved?'

She nodded, and he reached across the table to squeeze her hand briefly.

'Sometimes this job is tough,' he said.

'You're telling me.' She blew out a breath. 'Sometimes I look at Penny and Ryan and Simon, and it makes me want to run down to the hospital nursery school so I can hug Freddie and Lexi really, really tightly.'

'Of course it does. You're a mum, so you have a pretty good idea of what your patients' parents are feeling.'

'I just wish I had a magic wand.'

'Me, too,' he agreed softly. 'But we're doing the best we can.' Even if it sometimes felt as though it wasn't enough.

On Friday night, Leo texted Rosie.

Do you want to go to the cinema tomorrow?
Have looked at schedules.

Nothing really suitable, was the reply.
Was she backing away from him?
His phone beeped again.

How about the aquarium?

Fine. Meet you when and where?

Tube station at ten? she suggested.

I'll be there.

She was already there when he walked to meet her. The twins jumped about in excitement when he walked up to them, and hugged him round his knees—something he hadn't expected, and another little shard of ice around his heart melted.

'We're going to see the sharks!' Freddie said.

'And the starfishies,' Lexi added. 'I love starfishies.'

Clearly this was something they were really looking forward to. It was another thing way outside his experience, but Leo found himself thoroughly enjoying the visit, and the twins' excitement was definitely infectious. He lifted one or the other up every so often so they could have a closer

look at the occupants of a tank; and he noticed that Rosie
got them to count the fish and name colours and shapes.

'How many arms does your starfish have?' he asked
Lexi.

She counted them, then beamed at him. 'Five!'

'Well done.' He smiled back at her.

There was a play area in the central hall where the
youngest children could do colouring and older ones could
answer quizzes. On impulse, when Lexi and Freddie sat
down, he crouched beside them. 'Shall I draw something
for you to colour?'

'Yes, please!' they chorused.

'A shark for you, Lexi, and a starfish for you, Freddie?'
he asked, teasing them.

'No, that's silly—it's the other way round!' Lexi said.

Freddie just clapped his hands with glee as he watched
Leo draw.

He glanced up at Rosie. Were those tears he saw in her
eyes? But why? What had he done wrong?

Once they'd finished laboriously colouring in the
shapes, they looked at Rosie. 'Can you write our names,
please, Mummy?' Lexi asked.

'Sure. Can you spell them for me?' Rosie asked. Leo
watched as both children looked very earnest and spelled
out their names phonetically; Rosie wrote down what they
said.

'Thank you, Mummy,' Freddie said, then turned to Leo
and gave him the shark picture. 'This is for you.'

'So's this,' Lexi added, not to be outdone and thrusting
her starfish picture at him.

'Thank you, both of you,' Leo said. 'I'll put the pictures
up when I get home.'

'On your fridge, like Mummy does?' Lexi wanted to
know.

'Absolutely like Mummy does,' he said with a smile.

When they walked through the shark tunnel, the twins were both shrieking with joy and pointing out the sharks swimming overhead. Rosie was smiling, but she took their hands and crouched down beside them for a moment. 'I know you're excited, but you'll scare the sharks if you keep screaming. Can we pretend to be mice?'

'But mice don't live in the sea,' Freddie said. 'They live in houses.'

'You could be a new species,' Leo said. 'Sea mice.'

The twins thought about it, then nodded and were much quieter—still pointing out the sharks but careful to whisper.

Rosie caught Leo's eye. 'Thank you,' she mouthed.

Once they were through the tunnel and Rosie had bought a new storybook about Sammy the Shy Shark, they headed out to the South Bank. They all enjoyed hot dogs from one of the street food vendors, then sat down on a bench to eat *churros* with chocolate sauce while they watched some of the street entertainers, a juggler and a woman making balloon dogs. Both children ended up with their faces covered with chocolate, and Leo made the mistake of buying them each a balloon dog before Rosie had wiped their hands and faces clear—they insisted on kissing him thank you, smearing his cheeks with chocolate.

Rosie laughed and took a photograph of them all posing with chocolaty faces before giving him a wipe from her handbag and cleaning the twins up.

By the time they were back at Rosie's, the children were worn out. They managed half a sandwich before they nearly fell asleep at the table.

'No bath tonight, I think,' she said with a smile. 'Straight to bed with a story.'

Leo helped her get the children into their pyjamas and tucked them in; again, the domestic nature and the closeness made him feel as if something was cracking around his heart.

'I didn't think about dinner tonight. The best I can offer is a takeaway,' she said.

'Which would be lovely. And I'll pay, because you fed me on Wednesday,' he said.

They shared a Chinese meal, then curled up on the sofa. 'I meant to ask you earlier,' he said. 'What did I do to upset you?'

'Upset me?' She looked confused.

'In the aquarium. You looked as if you were blinking back tears.'

'Ah. That.' Her face cleared. 'You drew them a picture of their favourite sea creatures so they could colour them in.'

She didn't say it, but he had the strongest feeling that Michael had never done anything like that. 'I didn't mean to make you cry.'

'They were happy tears,' she said softly.

'Even so, I can still kiss you better.' And how right it felt, to hold her close and kiss her until they were both dizzy.

Leo was beginning to think that this might be what he actually wanted his life to be like—a job he adored at the hospital, and the warmth and domesticity of Rosie and the twins. He just needed to find a way to square it with his duties in Tuscany. Though he knew it was way too early to be thinking about that. For now, he'd just enjoy spending time with her.

At the end of the evening, he kissed her goodnight. 'See you at work on Monday.'

'See you Monday,' she agreed. 'And thank you for today. I had a fabulous time and so did the twins.'

'Me, too,' he said.

'Oh, before I forget.' She rummaged in her handbag and brought out a tiny paper bag with the logo of the aquarium on it.

'What's this?' he asked.

'Just a little something.'

He opened the bag to find two magnets: one shaped like a shark and one like a pink starfish.

'You told the twins you were going to put their pictures on your fridge. I'm guessing that you might be a bit short on magnets,' she explained.

'I am,' he agreed. His flat was pristine, like a show house, with no little decorative touches whatsoever. The magnets and the pictures might just be the first step to turning it into a home. 'Thank you.' He kissed her again, more lingeringly this time. 'Monday.'

'Monday,' she said.

And for the first time in a very long time, Monday morning felt like a promise.

CHAPTER SEVEN

'ARE YOU BUSY at the weekend?' Leo asked Rosie on Monday evening.

'Why?'

He stole a kiss. 'It's rude to answer a question with a question.'

'I don't have anything planned,' she said.

'Good.' He paused. 'Do the children have passports?'

'Yes, though they haven't actually been abroad. Why?'

'I was just wondering—would you like to come to Tuscany for the weekend?'

She blinked. 'Tuscany? Are you...' It was suddenly hard to breathe. 'Leo, are you asking me to meet your family?'

'Yes and no,' Leo hedged.

'Which doesn't exactly tell me anything,' she pointed out.

'There aren't any strings. I need to be in Tuscany for the weekend, and I thought you and the children might like to enjoy a bit of summer sun. Plus, I've been telling Lexi that the best ice cream ever comes from Italy, and it's about time I proved it.'

'So would we be staying at your family home?'

'The Palazzo di Calvanera. Yes.' He smiled at her. 'Mamma's a little frail. Although I speak to her every day, and I know her companion will tell me if she's in the slightest bit worried about my mother's health, I like to keep an eye on her myself as well. Going to see her at the weekend will put my mind at rest.'

Of course Leo would be a dutiful son.

But Rosie also remembered what he'd told her about Emilia, the girl he'd fallen in love with at university. The girl his family hadn't considered good enough for him. Would Leo's mother decide that, as a single mum of two, Rosie was also completely the wrong sort of person for her son?

'Maybe your mother would prefer you to visit on your own,' she suggested warily.

'I'm sure she'd enjoy meeting you and the children.'

How could she explain her worries? That this was suddenly sounding really serious—as if he was starting to expect things of their relationship? Things that she might not be able to deliver? 'You and me... It's still very early days,' she said.

'True.' He drew her hand up to his mouth and kissed the backs of her fingers.

'I don't want to give your mother the wrong impression.'

'There's no pressure,' he reassured her. 'I just thought you might like to see the *palazzo*. It has an amazing rose garden. And a lake. The children will love running around the place.'

A lake. Which might not be fenced off. Which would be dangerous for the children. She pushed the thoughts away. She could run faster than they could, and she could swim. There was a more immediate danger than the one she was imagining. 'Meeting your mother—does that mean you expect to meet my family?'

'I've already met the twins,' he pointed out.

'That isn't what I mean, and you know it. This thing

between us... We agreed we'd take things slowly and see what happened.'

'Which is exactly what we're doing.'

What, when he was asking them to visit his family home and to meet his mother?

Her doubts must have shown on her face, because he said again, 'Rosie, there's no pressure. Tuscany will just be a little break for us, that's all. A chance to have some fun. And I can show Freddie the suits of armour and Lexi all the portraits of the Duchesses.'

He wasn't playing fair. He knew she'd find it hard to say no where her children were concerned. 'Supposing your mother doesn't like me?'

'My mother,' he said softly, 'will like you very much. You're honest, you're open and you're caring. And she's not bothered about blue blood.'

But his father had been very bothered indeed.

Again, her feelings must have shown on her face, because he added, 'My father would have thought you way too uppity. You wouldn't have liked him very much, either. But Mamma's different. She doesn't share his views. You'll like each other.'

'I don't know,' she said.

'If you're worried about the travelling, I'm using a friend's plane. There won't be lots of queuing at the airport or anything.'

She blinked. 'Hang on. You're using a private plane?'

'It's not as fancy as it sounds. It's quite small,' Leo said.

'My friends own *cars*, not planes.' She couldn't quite get her head round this. 'Leo, I think your world is very, very different from mine.'

'Not at heart, it isn't. And actually I was going to ask you a favour over the weekend.'

'So there are strings attached?'

'No. Of course not.' He frowned. 'You can say no. But part of my duties… The main reason I'm going back is because there's a charity ball in aid of a clinic I support, and I need to be there.'

'What kind of clinic?'

'Paediatric medicine. For children whose families can't afford to pay for treatment,' he explained.

She frowned. 'So healthcare in Italy isn't like it is in England?'

'It's actually very similar, a mix of public and private healthcare,' he said. 'Family doctors are paid for by the Ministry of Health, like they are here in England, and emergency care and surgery are both free. You pay some money towards medication, depending on your income; and if your family doctor refers you to a specialist or for diagnostic tests, you only have to pay a little bit towards it. But waiting times can be quite long, so there are private hospitals where you can pay a bit more money to see the specialist or have treatment a bit sooner.'

'And that's what this clinic is? A private hospital, except patients don't pay?'

He nodded. 'I also work there when I'm in Italy.'

He'd said that he had an interest in philanthropic medicine. Obviously supporting this clinic was part of that, Rosie thought.

'So I was wondering if you might accompany me to the ball.'

'What about the children?' Rosie asked. They could hardly go to a glitzy ball. Apart from the fact that they were too young to attend in the first place, the ball probably wouldn't start until way past their bedtime.

'I can arrange a babysitter for them,' he said.

'No.'

He frowned. 'What do you mean, no?'

'Leo, do you really expect me to leave my children in a strange place with someone I don't know?'

'It's my home, and I know the babysitter,' he pointed out. 'I think I already told you that my mother has a companion, Violetta. Her daughter Lisetta lives nearby and I'm sure she'd be very happy to babysit.'

So he hadn't even asked the babysitter yet? Then again, that was fair—he hadn't known if Rosie would say yes or no to his invitation. Even so, the whole idea freaked her. 'Leo, the point is that *I* don't know her,' she countered. 'Yes, I know it's your home, but do you seriously think I'd be happy to leave my children in a country where they don't speak the language—where *I* don't speak the language, for that matter—with someone they don't know and I don't know?' She took a deep breath. 'Look, I know I'm overprotective, but no mother on earth would agree to anything like that.'

He looked at her. 'But *I* know Lisetta. I've known her for years. Isn't that good enough?'

'How can you not see that it isn't?' Rosie asked.

Leo thought about it. Part of him thought that Rosie was being unreasonable; it wasn't as if he was asking her to leave the children with someone who was a complete stranger. He'd known Lisetta since she was small, and he knew she was kind and she was good with children. Then again, a year ago, Rosie's husband's associate had threatened to hurt the children. Of course she'd be more protective than the average parent.

'I've known Lisetta for years and I trust her,' he said. 'Of course I understand that you're worried. It's natural. But I trust Lisetta, and I hope you know me well enough to realise that I'd be careful with your children and I wouldn't expect you to leave them with just anybody. I also have a security team at the *palazzo*, so no stranger will ever get anywhere near the children. They'll be perfectly safe. I guarantee that.'

She blew out a breath. 'OK. Let's put it another way. Your mum's not in the best of health. Would you bring her over to London and then leave her on her own for the evening with someone she didn't know—someone who didn't speak the same language as her—while you went out partying?'

'It isn't partying. It's a charity ball and attending it is part of my duties to the clinic—to the estate, actually, because some of the funds for the clinic come from the estate. Anyway, my mother speaks good English, and so does Lisetta. There won't be a language barrier for the children.'

Rosie put her hands over her face and groaned in apparent frustration. 'You're really not listening to me. Would you leave your mother with someone she didn't know and you didn't know, either—say, my neighbour?'

'If you vouched for your neighbour, then yes. Your word is good enough for me.'

'And I guess in that situation your mother could call you if there was a problem. But it's not the same thing for the children. The twins won't be able to call me if they're worried. They're only three.' She shook her head. 'It's lovely of you to ask me, Leo, but I really can't leave them with a stranger, even though she's somebody you know. I just can't do it.'

'What if,' Leo said, 'we took a babysitter with us—someone you know?'

'How do you mean?'

'The twins talk a lot about Nina from the nursery school. I'd be happy to pay her to come with us for the weekend, if she's free. Obviously I'll organise things so

she flies with us and she'll stay with us at the *palazzo*.
Would that make you able to come to the ball with me?'

'I...' She looked torn.

'Rosie. Of course the children come first. Always,' he
emphasised. 'But you also need some time for you. You're
their mum, yes, and that's important; but that's not all of
who you are. You're also a person in your own right. Come
and have some fun with me. Just for a few hours. Dinner,
a little dancing. I promise you'll be home by midnight.'

'I don't speak any Italian.'

That was a much easier problem to overcome. 'I can
teach you a couple of phrases and translate for you if you
need me to, and anyway, a lot of people at the ball will
speak English.'

She bit her lip. 'Leo, I'm sorry, but this is a big deal. I
really need to think about it.'

At least it wasn't a flat no. 'All right.' He paused. 'If
you do say yes, then I'd like to buy you a dress for the occasion.'

'I'm perfectly capable of buying my own...' Her voice
tailed off as she clearly realised what the ball entailed.
'It's a formal ball. That means black tie and haute couture, doesn't it?'

'White tie,' he said.

'Which is even more posh!'

'It's not that different. A white bow tie and waistcoat
instead of a black bow tie.'

'But it's a proper tailcoat, not a dinner jacket.'

'Yes.'

She grimaced. 'If I go—and I do mean *if*—then maybe
I can hire a dress from one of those agencies that special-
ise in posh clothes.'

'Or alternatively you could let me buy you a dress. Not
because I'm trying to control you,' he said carefully—he

definitely wasn't walking in his father's shoes, 'but because you'd be doing me a huge favour and you shouldn't be out of pocket for being kind.'

'I'll think about it.' She took a deep breath. 'You said about going this weekend. That's not when the ball is, though, is it?'

'Um, actually—yes.'

She blinked. 'That's not a lot of notice, Leo.'

'I know.' He stole a kiss. 'Obviously I've known about the ball for a while. But when I originally arranged to attend it I didn't know I was going to work in London, or that I was going to meet you.'

She bit her lip. 'I'm really not sure about this.'

'Talk it over with someone you trust,' he said. 'If you decide to come with me, then maybe we can go shopping for a dress on Thursday night. Babysitter permitting, of course.'

'All right.'

'Tell me your decision on Wednesday,' he said. 'Will that give you enough time to think about it?'

'I guess so.' Though she didn't sound sure. Clearly he'd pushed her too far, too fast.

'No strings,' he said again. 'If you say no, I won't be offended. But I'd like to spend some time with you and the children.'

That evening, after Leo had gone, Rosie texted her sister.

Need some advice. Are you free tomorrow night?

Daisy rang her straight away. 'I can talk now.'

Oh, help. That didn't give her any time to think about what she was going to say. 'Uh-huh.'

'Rosie? What's wrong?'

'Not wrong, exactly.' She sighed. 'I've been, um, seeing someone.'

'Seriously? That's great! So come on—tell me everything. What's his name, how did you meet him, what's he like?'

She should've known that her sister would give her a barrage of questions. She answered them in order. 'Leo, at work, and he's nice.'

'So why do you need advice?'

This was complicated. 'Daze—I need this to be confidential, OK?'

'Now you're worrying me. Please tell me you haven't met another Michael.'

'He's about as opposite from Michael as you can get,' Rosie reassured her.

'So what's the problem?'

'He's working here on a temporary contract. He's from Italy. And he wants the children and me to go to Italy with him at the weekend.'

'This weekend? To meet his family?'

'Yes. And to go to a charity ball.'

'A charity ball.' Daisy sounded concerned. 'That's a bit flashy. Actually, Ro, that sounds like Michael.'

'It's not quite the same. The ball's in aid of a paediatric clinic that Leo supports. They treat children from families who can't afford to pay,' Rosie explained.

'Whereas Michael would've been all about the glitz and the glamour and it wouldn't actually matter what the charity was,' Daisy said dryly. 'OK.'

'I, um, neglected to tell you that he's also a duke.'

'A duke? What? So how come he's a doctor if he's a duke?'

'It's complicated. But he's a good man, Daze. The children like him.'

'Hang on. He's met the children, and you hardly know him?' Daisy sounded even more shocked.

Rosie squirmed. 'I didn't behave very well. He kept asking me out and he wouldn't take no for an answer. I said yes and met him with the twins. I, um, assumed he'd take one look at the twins and bolt. But he was good with them, Daze. Really sweet.'

'I'm trying to work this out. You've only known him a little while?'

'A couple of weeks,' Rosie confirmed.

'I'm still trying to get my head round the fact that you've let him anywhere near the children.'

'Because he'd need ten people to vouch for him in writing, and sign it in blood?' Rosie asked wryly. 'I'm not that bad, Daze.'

Her sister's silence said otherwise.

Rosie sighed. 'They think he's Mummy's friend who just started at the hospital and doesn't know many people yet, so they're being kind and being his new friends, too.'

'And Freddie actually talks to him?'

'Freddie's really come out of his shell with him,' Rosie said. 'Lexi likes him, too.' She bit her lip. 'But it's going too far, too fast.'

'Maybe not. If Freddie's talking to him that tells me the guy has to be something special,' Daisy said. 'So what's the problem with Italy and the ball? Apart from the fact that it sounds as if he only just asked you and that's not a lot of notice, I mean.'

'He wants someone he knows to look after the twins.'

'Someone you don't know. And you said no.' Daisy paused. 'Does he know about Michael and that debt-collector?'

'Yes. I'm not being overprotective of the children, am I?'

'You're pretty much a helicopter mum,' Daisy said, 'but in the circumstances it's understandable.'

'Then he suggested we could ask Nina from the nursery school to go with us, to look after the children—he's going to pay her if she can do it.' Rosie took a deep breath. 'He said he thinks we all need a bit of fun.'

'He's got a very good point,' Daisy said. 'It's way past time you had some fun in your life. You've been a single parent for a year; and Michael left you to do everything for the twins, so you were practically a single parent before that, too. The only thing you've gone to without them was your ward's Christmas meal last year, and I had to nag you into that. Go and enjoy it, Ro.'

'Really?'

'Really,' Daisy said. 'What are you going to wear?'

'It's a posh do. He, um, offered to buy me a dress.' There had been a time when she'd had several suitable dresses. She'd sold them all to help pay off the debts Michael had left her with. Nowadays, she lived in either her nurse's uniform or casual clothes, neither of which would be remotely suitable. 'That's not because he's being flashy, but because he says I shouldn't be out of pocket for doing him a favour.'

'Actually, he sounds really thoughtful. *Nice*,' Daisy said. 'When are you going shopping?'

'If I say yes, it'll be Thursday night.' She paused. 'Daze, I know it's short notice, but could you—?'

'Of course I'll babysit,' Daisy interrupted. 'And then I get to meet him when you bring him home. If I think he's a Michael in disguise, I'll tell you and you can back out. If he's not, then you can go to Italy and have some fun with him. When's the last time you went out dancing?'

'Before the twins were born,' Rosie admitted.

'So that's well over three years. Go,' Daisy said. 'And if Nina can't come with you at the weekend, I will.'

'Daze, that's…' Rosie felt her eyes film with tears.

'That's what sisters are for. You'd do it for me if I was in your shoes,' Daisy said.

'Thank you.'

'So I'll pick the children up from the nursery school at five on Thursday.'

Daisy was on the very short list of people who were authorised to pick the twins up in Rosie's absence; in accordance with the nursery school rules, Rosie had supplied photographs and code words, so she knew that it wouldn't be a problem.

'Thanks, Daze. I owe you one.'

'Just make sure you've got pizza, dough balls and strawberries in your fridge on Thursday, and we're quits,' her sister said, laughing. 'I love you, Ro. And it'll be so nice to see you having a bit of fun, for once.'

It turned out that Nina was free at the weekend and was more than happy to come to Italy with them. So on Thursday evening Rosie went shopping with Leo.

She stared at him in dismay as they reached the doors of a very posh department store. 'Leo, this place is really pricey.'

He shrugged. 'I hear their dresses are nice.'

'But—'

'But nothing,' he said gently. 'You need a dress for the ball.'

'It makes me feel a bit like Cinderella,' she muttered.

'Firstly,' he said, 'I'm not Prince Charming. Secondly, you're a first-class nurse, not a kid whose family treats her badly and turns her into a skivvy. And, thirdly, is it so bad to enjoy a little bit of glitz and glamour just for one evening?'

When the price was as high as she'd paid with Michael, yes.

'I said there were no strings,' he said. 'And I meant it.'

And she was behaving like a whiny, attention-seeking brat. He was trying to do something nice for her, and she was practically throwing it back in his face.

'Thank you,' she said, determined to make the effort so he felt appreciated.

Once she'd pushed Michael to the back of her mind, she actually found herself enjoying the evening, trying on different dresses.

'Might I make a suggestion?' the assistant asked.

'Sure,' Rosie said.

'With your hair, this one will look stunning,' the assistant said, and brought out a turquoise floor-length chiffon gown. The dress had a sweetheart neckline, and white lace and sparkling crystals adorned the straps.

'Your hair and the dress are the opposites on the colour wheel,' the assistant said. 'And I know the perfect shoes for this, too. What size are you?'

'Five and a half,' Rosie said. 'Standard width.'

'Wonderful. Leave this to me.'

By the time Rosie had changed into the dress, the assistant had brought over a pair of copper-coloured strappy high heels. They fitted perfectly.

'Would you like to show your boyfriend?' the assistant asked.

Leo wasn't exactly her boyfriend... 'OK,' she said.

The look on his face when she walked out of the changing room told her everything. And warmth spread through her when he opened his mouth and no words came out. Could she really make this clever, gorgeous man speechless?

'You look amazing,' he said finally. 'Well, you look amazing in jeans as well. But that dress is perfect.'

'Thank you.'

'But you need an evening bag as well.'

'Why?' she asked.

'For your phone,' he said. 'Because I presume you're going to call Nina on the hour to check on the twins.'

She winced; she'd sent Daisy three texts already this evening. 'Am I being overprotective?'

'A little,' he said. 'But I understand why.'

'Thank you. And I do appreciate…' She gestured to the dress.

'My pleasure. You look amazing,' Leo said again.

'Thank you. But I feel guilty about you spending so much money on me.'

'You're doing me a favour,' he reminded her. 'As I said, you shouldn't be out of pocket for that.'

Once she'd changed back into her everyday clothes, the assistant had found the perfect sequin bag to match the shoes and Leo had paid for her outfit, he took the bags, slid his free arm round her shoulders and shepherded her out of the shop. 'Dinner?' he asked. 'And I'm pretty sure you texted your sister at least twice to check on the twins, so if there was a problem we'd have been on our way back to yours an hour ago.'

'Busted,' she admitted. 'And I sent her a picture of me in the dress.'

'And she approved?'

'Very much so.' She felt the colour flicker into her face. 'She said not to rush back.'

'Dinner, then,' he said.

He found a small restaurant, and she smiled as she

glanced through the menu. 'This would definitely be too fancy for the twins. I can't remember the last time I ate out at a restaurant where I didn't check the menu out beforehand to make sure it was child-friendly.'

'Enjoy,' he said. 'And this is my treat. No arguments.'

'Thank you,' she said.

The food was amazing: crab with avocado and grapefruit, followed by pan-fried halibut on a bed of seaweed with morels and Jersey royals. She had just enough room left afterwards to share a passion fruit *crème brûlée* with him; and it was oddly intimate, sharing a dessert so that every so often their fingers brushed together.

This felt like a proper date.

The first she'd been on for years and years.

It made her feel unexpectedly shy.

'Everything OK?' he asked.

She nodded. 'You and me, on our own.'

'I enjoy being with the children,' he said. 'But it's also nice to be with you on our own, too.'

She liked the fact that he was still putting the twins first—the way their own father hadn't.

And holding hands with him across the table while they had coffee and *petits fours* felt incredibly romantic. He clearly felt the same, because he held her hand all the way home.

She paused on the doorstep. 'Given that I'll be meeting your family this weekend, would you like to meet my sister this evening?' Or was this rushing things too much?

'I'd love to meet her,' he said.

'Come in,' she said, and opened the front door.

The woman who emerged from the living room looked very like Rosie, Leo thought, with the same copper-coloured hair and bright blue eyes. Rosie didn't even need to introduce them because it was so obvious that the other woman was her sister.

'Ro, the twins are both asleep—and, no, you don't have to rush up to check on them, because you know I won't let anything happen to them.' She smiled at him. 'I'm Daisy, Rosie's big sister. You must be Leo.'

Direct and to the point. He liked that. He shook her hand. 'I'm very pleased to meet you.'

'I hear you're taking my sister to Italy for the weekend.'

'No strings, no pressure, and the children come first,' he said immediately.

'I'm glad to hear it.' She smiled again. 'Come and help me make coffee while my little sister completely ignores what I said and rushes upstairs to check on her babies. And considering she's had several text updates from me…'

'Sorry,' Rosie mouthed, and fled upstairs.

'What you're doing for her—it's nice,' Daisy said.

'But she's already been hurt by a man who swept her off her feet, offered her the good life and let her down. I think the English saying is "handsome is as handsome does",' Leo said.

Daisy nodded. 'I realise you don't plan to do that to her, or you wouldn't even be discussing it with me.'

'Life is complicated,' Leo said. 'And sometimes I think you need to grab happiness with both hands, even if you find it in a place where you didn't expect it.'

'True,' Daisy said.

'I'll be careful with them,' Leo said softly. 'All of them.'

'Good.' Daisy took the coffee from the fridge. 'That's all I ask.'

'And it's nice that she has family to look out for her.'

'You don't?'

He coughed. 'I imagine that Rosie's already told you who I am and you've checked me out online.'

'Isn't that what you'd do if you had a little sister?' Daisy countered.

'Absolutely.'

'The gossip columns say you stop at three dates,' Daisy said.

That stupid reputation. He loathed it. 'I always make that clear up front.'

'Is that your deal with Ro?'

'No,' he admitted. 'I don't think either of us expected this and, if you want me to be honest with you, we don't have a clue where this is going. We're taking it step by step. But I would never deliberately hurt her or the children. As far as the twins are concerned, Rosie's being kind and befriending me because I don't know many people in London.'

'Fair enough,' Daisy said.

'You won't have to pick up the pieces,' he assured her solemnly.

'Daze, are you grilling him?' Rosie asked, appearing in the doorway.

'Big sister's privilege.' Daisy sounded completely unrepentant.

'I'd be more worried if she didn't,' Leo said. 'It's fine. I think Daisy and I understand each other.'

'We do,' Daisy agreed. 'And I want to see this dress properly. That selfie you sent me from the changing rooms was hardly visible.'

'Bossy,' Rosie grumbled, but went to change into her new finery.

Daisy was duly impressed. 'Stunning. You know Lexi's going to say you need a crown because you look like a princess. I can't remember which one has the blue dress?'

Rosie groaned. 'Cinderella.'

'We've already established that I'm not Prince Charming and my car's not going to turn into a pumpkin at midnight,' Leo said. 'Plus you love her, Daisy, and you don't make her be a skivvy.'

Daisy grinned. 'But you have dark hair, like the original Prince Charming, and you're taking my sister to a ball. Are you going to have to wear a royal outfit with a sash and gold epaulettes?'

He groaned. 'No. I'm just a duke. It's standard white tie.'

'White tie's super-posh. Does that mean you wear a top hat? Or an opera cloak?' Daisy asked.

He laughed. 'Now you're making me sound like a pantomime villain. No. And there's no monocle, either.'

'Pity. Because I think Freddie would love to try on your top hat.'

'Freddie,' he countered, 'would much rather have a dinosaur outfit.'

Daisy smiled. 'That's true. Right. Enough grilling from me. Let's go and drink our coffee.'

Rosie seemed more relaxed around her sister, Leo noticed. And he liked this fun, teasing side of her. He rather thought that she brought out the best in him, too. So maybe this would work out, after all. And if his mother got on as well with Rosie as he thought she might, this weekend could be the start of their future.

CHAPTER EIGHT

On Saturday morning, Leo drove over to Rosie's house. They fixed the children's car seats in the back of his car, then stowed their luggage in the boot and picked up Nina.

'We're going to Italy to eat ice cream,' Lexi informed Nina, bouncing in her seat.

'And we're going to see knights in armour, with swords,' Freddie said. 'We're staying in a real castle!'

Nina laughed. 'I can see just how much you two are looking forward to it. I'm looking after you tonight while Mummy and Leo go to the charity ball.'

'Mummy looks like a princess in her dress,' Lexi said. 'It's so pretty.'

'You can tell me all about princesses and knights on the way,' Nina said, 'and we can colour in some pictures.'

'Yay!' the children chorused.

Michael had always upgraded their seats when they travelled, Rosie remembered; luxurious as it had felt at the time, it wasn't the same league as travelling with the Duke of Calvanera. Just as Leo had promised, there was no waiting around at the airport. And the plane, although small, was beautifully appointed, with deep, comfortable seats and lots of leg room.

'I still can't quite get my head around the fact that your friend owns a plane,' she said to Leo.

The children were enthralled by their first flight, especially when the pilot told them over the intercom that they could take their seat belts off. Leo took the children to the window and lifted them up so they could both see the land below.

'All the houses are tiny!' Lexi said in awe.

'And the clouds are all big and fluffy,' Freddie said.

They were overawed by seeing the mountains, too. And then finally Leo strapped them back into their seats for the descent so they could land at Florence.

Again, there wasn't a lot of waiting around. There was a limousine waiting for them at the airport, with car seats already fitted for the children. Rosie noticed that the driver was wearing a peaked cap and livery; she wondered if he was one of Leo's staff, or whether he'd just hired a car and driver for the journey.

As they headed into the hills outside Florence, Leo told the twins all about what they were seeing, and answered all their excited questions. Rosie was glad that she didn't have to make conversation, because adrenaline was pumping round her system. Supposing Leo's mother didn't like her? Would it be a problem that Rosie already had children? What if she did or said something wrong at the ball tonight and caused some kind of diplomatic embarrassment?

The nearer they got to the *palazzo*, the more her nerves grew.

And she was near to hyperventilating when the car stopped in front of a wrought-iron security gate set into a large stone wall.

'Here we are,' Leo said cheerfully. He climbed out of the car and tapped a code into the keypad set into the wall, and the iron gates swung open.

There was a long drive flanked with tall cypress trees, and then the vista opened up to show the castle itself. It was a huge three-storey building made of honey-coloured stone with a tower at one corner. The tall, narrow windows with their pointed arches were spaced evenly among the facade, and there were colonnaded arches along the ground floor. The perfect fairy-tale castle, Rosie thought.

'Is that the princess's tower?' Lexi asked, pointing to the tower.

'No, it's my tower,' Leo said. 'My study is on the very top floor and the views are amazing. I have a bedroom and bathroom on the floor below it, and a sitting room on the floor below that.'

'So are you a prince?' Lexi asked.

He smiled. 'No. You know I'm a doctor because I work with your *mamma* at the hospital.'

'But you live in a castle. You must be a prince,' Lexi said.

'I'm a duke,' he said gently.

'What's a duke?' Freddie wanted to know.

'It's a bit like a prince,' Rosie said.

'I just don't wear a crown or robes or anything,' Leo said.

'But can you make people into knights?' Freddie asked.

'No.' Leo smiled at him. 'But I can show you some knights' armour, when we go inside.'

The front door opened as they got out of the car, and an older man with grey hair and wearing a top hat and tails came to meet them.

Leo made formal introductions. 'This is Carlo, who manages the house for me,' he said to Rosie, Nina and the children.

'*Buongiorno.* Welcome to the Palazzo di Calvanera,' Carlo said, removing his hat, and bowed stiffly. 'If there's anything you require, *signora*, *signorina*, please just ask.' He looked at Leo. 'Is your luggage in the car, Duca?'

Leo rolled his eyes. 'Carlo, you've called me Leo for the last thirty-odd years. That doesn't change just because we have guests—and did you borrow that outrageous outfit from your son's theatre company?'

'I might have done.' Carlo laughed. 'Leo, you're the Duca di Calvanera. Your butler is supposed to dress accordingly.'

Leo laughed back. 'And this is the twenty-first century, so dress codes are a thing of the past. I guess I should consider myself lucky that you didn't find some outlandish livery.'

'Gio had a great costume from *Twelfth Night*. I was tempted to borrow it,' Carlo admitted. 'Except his Malvolio is much thinner than I am. I couldn't even get the jacket on, let alone done up.' He bowed to Rosie again. 'My son Gio has a theatre company in Florence. Leo helped him start the business.'

Seeing the warmth between Leo and the older man, Rosie wasn't surprised that Leo had helped Carlo's son.

'Your *mamma* is in her usual sitting room with Violetta,' Carlo said to Leo. 'I'll bring the luggage in and ask Maria to arrange refreshments.'

'Thank you.'

'Welcome home, Leo. It's good to see you.' Carlo hugged him impulsively. 'It doesn't seem five minutes since you were the same height as this little *bambino* here.' He ruffled Freddie's hair.

Freddie immediately clung to Leo's leg and stared up at Carlo, wide-eyed.

'Sorry. He's a little shy,' Rosie said.

'No matter.' Carlo bent down so he was nearer to the children's height. 'What would you like to drink? Milk? Juice? Lemonade?'

'Milk, please,' Lexi said.

'Me, too,' Freddie whispered. 'Please.'

'Welcome to the *palazzo*,' Carlo said again, and ushered them inside.

The inside of the castle was equally grand. The entrance hall had marble columns and a marble chequered floor; the walls were dark red and hung with gold-framed pictures, while the ceiling had ornate plasterwork around the cornices and a painting in the centre. Rosie glanced around to see Venetian glass chandeliers, a suit of armour holding a massive pole-axe, a marble-topped gilt table bearing a huge arrangement of roses and an enormous grandfather clock.

Lexi looked delighted. 'It's just like the prince's castle in *Beauty and the Beast*.'

'You like *Beauty and the Beast*?' Leo asked.

Lexi nodded. 'And it's Mummy's favourite because Belle teaches the prince to be kind.'

'It's important to be kind,' Leo agreed.

Was he just being kind to her and the children? Rosie wondered. Or was there more to it than that?

At one end of the hall was a massive sweeping staircase with gilded railings and balusters. Rosie could imagine the Duchesses walking down the stairs, hundreds of years ago, wearing long swishy dresses with wide skirts.

Right at that moment, she felt slightly intimidated. Even though Carlo had been very welcoming, this was way outside her normal life. She'd visited stately homes in the past, enjoying the glimpse into a world so different from her own, but now she was staying in an actual castle as a guest. A castle whose owner had kissed her until she was dizzy.

'Carlo said Mamma is in her sitting room,' Leo said. 'Come and meet her.'

Rosie took Freddie's hand and Nina took Lexi's hand, and they followed him through the corridor into the sitting room where his mother was waiting. The room had an or-

nate plasterwork ceiling, but the walls were an unexpectedly bright turquoise. The huge windows let in lots of light
and gave a view over the formal garden at the back of the
palazzo; the marble floor was covered with silk rugs, but
what worried Rosie was the furniture. The upholstery was
either old-gold velvet or regency gold and cream stripes;
the material wouldn't take kindly to small sticky hands.

'Don't touch anything,' she whispered to Freddie and
Lexi.

The twins looked almost as intimidated as she felt.

'Allow me to introduce you,' Leo said. 'Mamma, Violetta, don't get up.'

Rosie noticed the stick propped against the sofa next to
Leo's mother, and could guess why Leo had just said that.

'This is Rosie, her friend Nina from the hospital nursery school, and Rosie's children Freddie and Lexi. Rosie,
Nina, Freddie and Lexi—this is my mother, the Duchess
of Calvanera, and her friend Violetta,' Leo finished.

'*Buongiorno, Duchessa. Buongiorno,* Signora Violetta.'
Rosie made a deep curtsey, and Nina followed suit.

'*Bwun-gy-or-no,*' Freddie and Lexi said, with Freddie
bowing and Lexi curtseying and nearly falling over when
she lost her balance.

'My dears, it's so nice to meet you. And we don't stand
on ceremony at the *palazzo*. Please, call me Beatrice, and
you really don't have to curtsey to me,' Leo's mother said,
to Rosie's immense surprise. Hadn't Leo said that when
he'd brought previous girlfriends here, his parents had reacted badly? Then again, he'd also said that his father had
been difficult but his mother was sweet.

'And please call me Violetta,' Violetta added with a
smile.

'Thank you for having us to stay, Beatrice,' Rosie said.

'Yes, thank you,' Nina added.

'You are all most welcome. Refreshments, I think, Leo. Go to the kitchen and ask Maria to arrange it.'

'Carlo is arranging everything,' Leo said.

'I think you should go yourself, Leo,' Beatrice said, looking pointedly at the doorway.

Leo was a little wary of leaving Rosie alone with his mother and Violetta. Then again, his mother hadn't been the problem with Emilia, and the *palazzo* definitely wasn't the same place without his father's iron fist. His father certainly wouldn't have been happy about the changes to the sitting room from the original moody dark green to the much brighter, warmer turquoise. Or the fact that his wife spoke her mind nowadays. '*Sì*, Mamma,' he said, and left for the kitchen.

As he'd half expected, Maria greeted him as warmly as Carlo had, fussing over him. 'It's good to have you back, Leo,' she said. 'The *palazzo* needs you.' She gave him a pointed look. 'And children. This place needs the laughter of children.'

Carlo had obviously told his wife just who had arrived with Leo. 'Which is what it will have, this weekend.' And maybe Rosie's children would help to banish some of the ghosts here. He hoped.

Leo returned to his mother's sitting room, carrying a massive silver tray of tea, cake and small glasses of milk for the children, and discovered that Lexi was sitting on his mother's lap, talking animatedly about princesses and crowns. He had to hide a smile; he should have guessed that the little girl would be the one to break the ice, and that it would take about ten seconds for her shyness to dissolve into her usual confidence. Freddie, the shyer twin, was sitting next to his mother on the sofa and holding her hand very tightly.

'Carlo's taken the luggage upstairs,' he said, and deftly poured the tea.

He could see Rosie eyeing the glasses warily. No doubt she was panicking that the twins would either spill the milk everywhere or break the glasses. 'The glasses are sturdy,' he said quietly to her, 'and spills are easily mopped up. Stop worrying.'

'Freddie, Lexi, you need to sit really still while you drink your milk,' Rosie said, not looking in the slightest bit less worried.

He handed the children a glass each.

'Maria has made us some of her special *schiacciata alla Fiorentina*,' he said, gesturing to the cake. 'It's an orange sponge cake with powdered sugar on top.'

Rosie looked aghast, clearly worrying about sticky fingers.

'Leonardo spilled more crumbs over the furniture when he was little than I care to remember,' Beatrice said, 'so please don't worry about Lexi and Freddie spilling a few crumbs.'

'My daughter Lisetta, too,' Violetta said. 'She spilled blackcurrant all over that sofa over there.' She pointed to one of the regency striped sofas. 'They survive. Things clean up. Don't worry about sticky hands and spilled drinks.'

Rosie gave them both a grateful look.

The cake was still slightly warm and utterly delicious, and both children were scrupulously polite and careful, he noticed.

'Leo, why don't you show Rosie, Nina and the children round the *palazzo* while Violetta and I have another cup of tea? I'm sure Freddie will like to see our knights in armour.' Beatrice smiled at Rosie. 'I know it is the custom in Italy to drink coffee all day, but Leonardo introduced us to English tea some years ago and it's so refreshing in summer.'

'Thank you,' Rosie said.

'Knights and princesses!' Lexi said, and wriggled off Beatrice's lap, almost spilling the old lady's tea in the process.

'Lexi. Slow and calm, please,' Rosie said quietly. 'You nearly spilled Beatrice's tea just then.'

Lexi put a hand to her mouth in horror. 'Sorry,' she said.

'It's all right. Everything's exciting when you're little,' Beatrice said, ruffling her curls. 'And I think children should be heard as well as seen.'

Since when? Leo thought. When he'd grown up, the 'children should be seen and not heard' rule had been very much in evidence. The only real affection he'd been shown had been from his nanny, from Carlo—a much more junior servant in those days—and from Maria if he sneaked into the kitchens.

Then again, maybe that had been more his father's rule, and Beatrice had been as scared of her husband's mercurial temper as Leo had been. Certainly his mother seemed to have blossomed in widowhood. She was physically more frail, with her arthritis forcing her to use a stick, but mentally she seemed much stronger. Maybe his father had played the same nasty little games with her that he had with Leo, dangling the promise of love and then making it impossible to reach.

'Come with me,' Leo said, and showed Rosie and the children the other formal rooms. The dining room, with its polished table big enough to seat twenty; another sitting room; a ballroom with a slew of floor-to-ceiling windows and mirrors to double the light in the room; the room his staff used as the estate office during the week, the heavy old furniture teamed with very modern state-of-the-art computer equipment; the library, with its floor-to-ceiling shelves that Lexi announced was just like the one in *Beauty and the Beast*; the music room, with its spinet and harpsichord and baby grand piano.

Freddie gasped as Leo led them into the final room: the armoury. Suits of armour from various ages of the *palazzo* stood in a line, and instead of paintings on the walls there was a display of shields and swords.

'But that one's a *little* suit of armour,' Freddie said in awe, pointing to the child-sized suit of armour.

At the same age, Leo had been fascinated by the miniature suit of armour. His father had forbidden him to touch it, but the lure had been too great. The time Leo had been caught trying on the helmet, he'd been put on bread and water for three days for daring to disobey his father.

Well, he wasn't his father.

Deliberately, he walked towards the little suit and removed the helmet. 'This is ceremonial armour,' he explained. 'It was made for the son of one of the Dukes of Calvanera, a couple of hundred years ago. Do you want to try on the helmet?'

Freddie's eyes grew round. 'Can I? Please?'

'Sure.' Leo helped him put it on, then knelt down beside him. 'Time for a selfie, I think.'

'Me, too!' Lexi demanded.

Leo hid a grin when she swiftly added, 'Please.' No doubt Rosie had just reminded her about manners. 'Your turn, next,' he promised; and when she was wearing the helmet with the visor up he took a selfie of the two of them together.

Freddie was galloping on the spot, clearly pretending that he was a knight on a horse. Leo smiled and ruffled his hair before returning the helmet to the tiny suit of armour.

'Come and see upstairs,' he said, leading them back into the hall and up the wide sweeping staircase.

Portraits in heavy gilt frames hung on the walls of the staircase; clearly they were portraits of previous Dukes, because Rosie noticed that the fashions seemed to change and grow older, the higher they climbed. Which meant that the forbidding man in the very first portrait must've been Leo's father. Part of her wondered why he hadn't said as much; then again, the little he had told her about his father made her realise why they hadn't been close. Though she noticed that he didn't mention the next portrait up, either, which was presumably his grandfather; like Leo's father, the Duke looked stern and forbidding. Had all the Dukes of Calvanera been like that? In which case the *palazzo* must have felt more like a prison for a small child. She'd seen the expression on his face when his mother had talked about children being heard as well as seen; clearly his childhood hadn't been much fun.

The first-floor hall had a marble floor and another of the ornate painted ceilings, Rosie noticed. But the guest rooms turned out to be much simpler than the downstairs rooms; they had wooden floors and the walls were painted lemon or duck-egg-blue or eau-de-nil on the top half and white beneath the dado rail. The paintings still had heavy gilt frames, but they were of landscapes rather than people. French doors let light into the rooms, fluttering through white voile curtains.

'This is where you'll be sleeping tonight, Freddie and Lexi,' Leo said, showing them into a room with twin four-poster single beds.

'Oh, look, a princess bed!' Lexi said in delight, seeing the gauzy fabric draped at the head of one bed.

'And a prince bed,' he said with a smile, gesturing to

the other one. 'Nina, I assumed you'd like to be next door, but if you don't like the room just let me know and we can move you to one you prefer.'

'It'll be just fine, thanks,' Nina said.

'The bedrooms all have their own bathrooms,' Leo said, and Rosie peeked in to see yet more marble on the floor, but the suite was plain white enamel and the gilt towel stand was relatively simple.

The next room was clearly Rosie's, because her dress was hanging up to let the packing creases fall out.

'Again, if you'd rather have a different room, just say,' Leo said.

'No. It's beautiful,' she said, meaning it.

'Can we see the tower?' Lexi asked.

'Sure.'

Leo's rooms were very different from the rest of the house, Rosie thought. He didn't show them his bedroom, but the walls of his sitting room were white and the furniture was much more modern than in the rest of the house, and the artwork was watercolours of the sky and the sea. The room at the top was his study; the walls were lined with books, but the desk was the same kind of light modern furniture they'd seen in his sitting room, and there was a state-of-the-art computer on his desk.

'And you need to see out of the window,' he said, lifting both twins up so they could see.

'You can see nearly to the edge of the world,' Freddie said in awe.

'Well, to the hills in Tuscany,' Leo corrected with a smile.

A tour of the gardens was next.

'We've finished our tea, now,' Beatrice said, 'so we'll join you.' She struggled to her feet, waving away Leo's offer of assistance, and steadied herself with her stick. 'I'm a little slower than I'd like to be, so I'll only walk with you as far as the roses,' she said.

'Thank you, Mamma,' Leo said.

Violetta took Beatrice's other arm, and the two older ladies led the way.

As soon as they were outside, Leo crouched down to Lexi and Freddie's level. 'You know Mummy has rules at the playground? I have rules here. You can run around as much as you like on the grass, but you don't go anywhere near the lake without Mummy, Nina or me holding your hand, OK?'

'OK,' the twins chorused solemnly.

'And the same goes for the fountain in the middle of the garden. You need to stay three big jumps away from it, unless one of us is holding your hand.'

Rosie loved the fact that he'd put the children's safety first, and explained it to them in a way they could understand.

As they walked along, her hand brushed against his. The light contact made all her nerve-endings zing. It would be so easy just to let his fingers curl round hers, but that wasn't appropriate right now—not in front of her children, his mother, Violetta and Nina. She glanced at him and he was clearly thinking the same, because he mouthed, 'Later.'

Later they would be dancing cheek-to-cheek at the ball. Desire sizzled at the base of her spine at the thought of it. She could imagine walking here through this garden with him when they got home, the warm night air scented with roses. And he'd kiss her with every step...

She shook herself, realising that Beatrice was telling them about the flowers and the fountain in the centre of the rose garden.

'This is so lovely,' she said. 'Do you ever open the gardens to the public?'

Beatrice shook her head.

'Maybe you should,' Violetta said. 'It would be good for the house to have visitors. You could have a little *caffè*, too.'

'It would be an excellent idea, Mamma,' Leo agreed.

'Perhaps. We'll wait here for you,' Beatrice said, and sat down on one of the stone benches by the fountain.

Leo took them to see the lake; once they'd finished their tour of the garden, they collected Beatrice and Violetta, then sat on the terrace at the back of the house in the shade, and Carlo brought them a tray of cold drinks.

'Can we play ball?' Lexi asked.

'Sure,' Leo said, and took the children into the middle of the lawn.

'Thank you,' Beatrice said to Rosie. 'It's so good to see my son looking relaxed and happy—and I know it's down to you.'

How much did she know? Flustered, and not wanting to make things difficult for Leo, Rosie said, 'We're just friends.'

'That's not the way you look at each other, child,' Beatrice said.

Rosie bit her lip. 'I wasn't sure you'd approve of me being Leo's girlfriend. I'm not from a noble family, and I already have two children.'

'That doesn't matter—and it's a pleasure to hear children laughing here.' Beatrice looked sad. 'It didn't happen as often as it should have when Leonardo was growing up.'

Leo had said his father was difficult, Rosie remembered.

Beatrice took her hand and squeezed it. 'As a *mamma*, all you want is to see your child happy, yes?'

'And you worry about them all the time,' Rosie agreed.

'I think we understand each other,' Beatrice said softly. 'And I'm glad he brought you here.'

So maybe, if this thing between her and Leo worked out the way Rosie was starting to hope it might, his family wouldn't object…

After Leo had tired the children out playing ball, they came back to sit in the shade.

'Why don't you have a dog?' Lexi asked.

'Lexi—that's rude,' Rosie said gently.

'No, it's fine. I don't have a dog because I'm too old,' Beatrice said. 'You can't take a dog for a proper walk when you have to walk with a stick. Not even a little dog.'

'We don't have a dog because Mummy works,' Freddie said dolefully.

'Let's do some colouring,' Rosie said, hoping to head them off.

Nina took pads of drawing paper and crayons from her bag. 'You can do a nice picture of the castle,' she said.

But, as Rosie half expected, both children drew their favourite picture: a dog.

'This is for you,' Lexi said, giving her picture to Beatrice. 'It's a dog but you don't have to take it for walks.'

'And I drawed you one, too, so you have two and they won't be lonely,' Freddie said, not to be outdone.

Beatrice was close to tears as she hugged them. 'Thank you, both of you.'

'Maybe you can sing a song for Beatrice and Violetta,' Nina suggested. 'Like you do at nursery school.'

When the twins had finished their song, Beatrice smiled. 'This reminds me of my Leonardo singing songs, when he was little.'

'He singed to us last week,' Lexi confided.

'He sings a lot,' Freddie added.

'Maybe you should indulge your *mamma* and the children, Leo, and sing to us now,' Violetta suggested with a smile.

He groaned. 'I don't have any choice, do I?' But he gave in with good grace and sang some traditional Italian songs.

This felt magical, Rosie thought, but she was still aware that this opulent, privileged world was nothing like her everyday existence. So she would let herself enjoy every second of the weekend, but she would keep in the back of her mind that this was just a holiday and she shouldn't get used to it. She and the children belonged in their tiny little terrace in London, not a duke's castle in Tuscany.

'So what is the children's routine?' Beatrice asked later.

'They usually eat at half-past five or so, and then have a bath before bed,' Rosie said.

'The ball starts at eight,' Leo said, 'and it will take us about half an hour to get there.'

'It won't take me long to get ready,' Rosie reassured him.

'I'm here to take care of the children,' Nina reminded them.

'And perhaps I can read a bedtime story,' Beatrice said. 'It's been a long time since I've read a goodnight story. Too long. I miss that.'

Was that his mother's subtle way of reminding him that he was supposed to get married and have an heir? Leo wondered. Then again, maybe she was just lonely and enjoying the chance to have some temporary grandchildren. She certainly seemed to have taken the twins to her heart, which gave him hope.

'Nina, I hope you will eat with Violetta and me tonight,' Beatrice said. 'Maria has planned something special for tonight.'

Nina went pink with pleasure. 'Thank you.'

Again, it showed Leo how different the *palazzo* was now. Under his father's rule, Nina would've been banished to the nursery with the children and treated as a servant.

Maria had made garlic bread shaped like teddy bears for the children, served with pasta and followed by ice cream. And she insisted that Rosie and Leo should have some *piadinas*, toasted flatbreads filled with cheese and ham. 'You can't dance all night on an empty stomach.' She waved her hand in disgust. 'The food's always terrible at a ball, all soggy canapés and crumbly things you can't eat without ruining your clothes. You need to eat something now.'

'Thank you, Maria,' Leo said, giving her a hug.

When they'd finished eating, Nina waved Rosie away. 'I'll do bathtime. Go and get ready—the children will want to see you all dressed up, and so do I.'

Rosie knew it would be pointless arguing, so she did as she was told and then headed for the children's bedroom.

'Look! Mummy's just like a princess,' Lexi said in delight.

'A special princess,' Freddie added.

Rosie smiled. 'Thank you.'

'But there's something missing,' Beatrice said thoughtfully. 'Violetta, I wonder, can you help me?'

The two older women left the room, and returned carrying some small leather and gilt boxes.

Rosie gasped when Beatrice opened the boxes to reveal a diamond choker, earrings and bracelet.

'These will be perfect with that dress. Try them on,' Beatrice said.

'But—but—these are *real* diamonds.' Put together, they were probably worth more than she'd ever earn over the course of her entire lifetime, Rosie thought.

'Diamonds are meant to be worn, not stuck in a safe. I'm too old to go to a ball and I can't dance any more, not with my stick,' Beatrice said. 'So perhaps you can wear these for me, tonight.'

Warily, Rosie tried them on.

The jewels flashed fire at her reflection and made her feel like a million dollars.

'But what if I lose them?' she asked.

'They're insured,' Beatrice said. 'But you won't lose them—will she, Leo?'

'Of course she won't,' Leo said, entering the twins' room, and Rosie caught her breath. He looked amazing in a tailcoat, formal trousers and white tie, shirt and waistcoat.

'You have to take selfies,' Lexi said.

'I agree,' Beatrice said, and produced a state-of-the-art mobile phone. 'Use this. I will send you the pictures later.'

What could Rosie do but agree?

'Put your arm round Rosie's shoulder, Leo,' Violetta directed.

The touch of Leo's hand against her bare shoulder made desire shimmer through Rosie.

'Bellissima.' Beatrice smiled and took the photograph. 'Now off you go to the ball, and have a wonderful time.'

CHAPTER NINE

Leo drove them in to Florence in a sleek, low-slung black car—the kind of car Rosie had only ever really seen in magazines.

When she said as much, he gave her a rueful smile. 'I know I see myself more as a doctor than as a duke, but I have to admit that cars like this are my weakness. And it's the privileged bit of my life that pays for this.'

'But you don't spend all the money on yourself. We're going to a charity ball tonight,' she reminded him, 'in aid of a clinic you support financially. And Carlo said you supported his son's theatre company.'

'It's important to give something back.'

Rosie had a feeling that his mother might agree with him, but his father definitely hadn't. Though now wasn't the time to bring up the subject. Instead, she said, 'Right now I really feel like Cinderella. Is this car going to turn into a pumpkin at midnight?'

Leo laughed. 'No, but you look beautiful and this is going to be fun.'

And it was going to be just the two of them.

Well, and a lot of people that Leo knew either professionally or in his capacity as the Duke of Calvanera.

But tonight she'd get to dance with him; and for those

few moments it would be just them and the night and the music.

While Leo parked the car, Rosie called Nina to check that everything was OK. Reassured, she went into the ball, holding Leo's arm.

The hotel was one of the swishest in Florence, over-looking the River Arno. Like the *palazzo* in the mountains, the building was very old, but had been brought up to date. The ballroom was even more luxurious than the one at Calvanera, as well as being much larger; it had a high ceiling with ornate mouldings, painted in golds and creams. The floor-to-ceiling windows had voile curtains and heavy green velvet drapes; mirrors between the windows reflected even more light from the glass and gold chandeliers hanging from the ceiling and the matching sconces on the walls.

'This room's amazing,' she said.

'Isn't it just?' Leo agreed.

And everyone was dressed appropriately, the men in white tie and the women in an array of gorgeous dresses. Rosie had never seen anything so glamorous in her entire life.

A jazz trio was playing quietly on the dais at one end of the room.

'Dance with me,' Leo said, 'and then I'll introduce you to everyone.'

It had been quite a while since Rosie had been dancing, and Leo was a spectacular dancer; as he waltzed her round the room, it felt as if she were floating on air. And being in his arms felt perfect. Like coming home.

He introduced her to a stream of people, explaining that she was on the team with him at Paddington Children's Hospital in London; just as he'd reassured her earlier in the week, everyone spoke perfect English, and Rosie felt slightly guilty that all she really knew in Italian was *please*, *thank you*, *hello* and *goodbye*. Nobody seemed to mind; and, although she ended up talking mostly about medicine, she didn't feel as out of place as she'd half expected to be.

'Leo, can you excuse me for a second?' she asked after a quick glance at her watch.

'I know. You need to check on the children.' Though he wasn't mocking her; she knew he understood why she was antsy.

She went out to the terrace, where it was a little quieter, to make the call. Nina confirmed that everything at the *palazzo* was just fine—there hadn't been a peep out of either twin.

Rosie had just ended the call, slipped her phone back into her evening bag and was about to head back into the ballroom to find Leo when a man standing near to her on the terrace fell to the floor in a crumpled heap.

A woman screamed and knelt down beside the man—presumably his wife—and Rosie said to her, 'I'm a nurse—can I help?'

'Mi scusi?'

Oh, no. Just when she really needed not to have a language barrier, she'd found one of the few people here who didn't speak English.

She gestured to the man, then clutched a fist to her heart, miming squeezing, and hoped that either he or the woman would realise that she was asking if he thought he'd had a heart attack.

'Mi ha punto una vespa.' He pointed to his hand.

Vespa? Wasn't that a motorcycle? She didn't have a clue what he'd just said.

'Una vespa.' His wife mimed flapping wings.

He seemed to be having problems breathing and was wheezing; and then Rosie's nursing training kicked in as she noticed the reddened area on his hand. He'd clearly been stung, or bitten by an insect, and was having a severe allergic reaction.

'Do you have adrenaline?' she asked, hoping that the Italian word was similar to the English one.

'Adrenaline?' The woman frowned and shook her head.

Rosie grabbed her phone and called Leo, who answered within two rings. 'Rosie? Is something wrong with the children?'

'No. I'm on the terrace with a man I think is having a severe allergic reaction to a sting. He and his wife don't speak English but between us we worked out they don't have adrenaline. I need you to talk to them for me to find out his medical history, for someone to ring an ambulance and for someone to put a call out to everyone at the ball in case someone else has an adrenaline pen we can borrow.' She handed the phone to the woman. 'Speak to Leo, *per favore*?'

There were glasses on a nearby table containing ice as well as the drinks; she grabbed a tissue from her bag and gestured to the ice. *'Per favore?'* she asked the people standing round the table. At the assorted nods, she grabbed the ice, put it in the tissue and put the makeshift ice pack on the man's hand. Gently, she got him to lie back on the terrace, and talked to him to keep him calm. 'It's going to be all right,' she said, knowing that he wouldn't understand what she was saying, but hoping he could pick up on her tone.

The man's wife finished talking to Leo and handed the phone back to Rosie.

'Grazie,' Rosie said. 'Leo?'

'His name's Alessandro and hers is Caterina. He's been stung before and the swelling was bad but he didn't think to talk to his doctor about it. The last time must have sensitised him, because he's never had an anaphylactic reaction before,' Leo explained. 'I've got an ambulance on its way and I've got a call out in the ballroom for an adrenaline pen.'

'Great. Thank you. How do I say "Everything will be OK"?'

'Andrà tutto bene,' he said. 'I'll be there as soon as I've found an adrenaline pen.'

'Thanks.' She hung up and squeezed Alessandro's hand and Caterina's in turn. 'Alessandro, Caterina, *andrà tutto bene,*' she said. 'Everything will be fine. An ambulance is coming.'

'Grazie,' Caterina said, looking close to tears. She, too, talked to Alessandro; Rosie didn't have a clue what she was saying, but Caterina's tone was reassuring and she was clearly trying to be brave and calm for her husband's sake.

To Rosie's relief, Leo arrived a couple of minutes later with an adrenaline pen. While he explained to Caterina and Alessandro why Rosie had laid him flat and put an ice pack over the sting, and what was going to happen next, Rosie glanced at her watch and then administered the adrenaline.

She really wasn't happy with Alessandro's breathing, and when he was still struggling five minutes after she'd given the first injection, she gave him a second shot.

Finally, the ambulance arrived. Leo spoke to the paramedics to fill them in on what had happened; then they carried Alessandro off on a stretcher with Caterina accompanying him.

'You saved his life,' Leo said.

'Not just me. You talked to Caterina, you got someone to call the ambulance and you got the adrenaline pen.'

'But you saw what the problem was. Without you working that out, it might have been too late by the time the ambulance got here,' Leo said. He held her close. 'You, Rosie Hobbes, are officially a superstar.'

She shook her head. 'I'm just an ordinary nurse.'

'Ordinary is definitely not how I'd describe you,' Leo said. 'Caterina's going to ring me from the hospital and let me know how Alessandro gets on.'

'That's good.' She bit her lip. 'Talking of calling...'

'Of course. You need to check on the children.' He stroked her face. 'Come and find me when you're done.'

'Thank you.' She called Nina. 'Is everything OK?'

'It's fine,' Nina said. 'Honestly, Rosie, you don't need to worry. You know I'll call you if there's a problem. I have Leo's number as well as yours and that of the hotel reception, and I'm sleeping right next door to the children—so if one of them wakes up I'll hear them straight away.'

'Sorry. I do trust you. I'm just one of these really terrible overprotective mums,' Rosie said.

'Just a bit,' Nina said, though her tone was gentle. 'I hope you don't mind, but I'm not planning to stay up until you get back. Violetta has gone home and Beatrice has gone to bed, and I'm going to read in my room for a bit. So just try to relax and enjoy the ball, OK?'

'OK,' Rosie said. 'And thank you.'

She went to find Leo and relayed the conversation to him.

'She has a point,' he said with a smile. 'You need to relax and enjoy this. Come and dance with me.'

Just having him there with her made her feel better, and Rosie finally managed to relax in his arms.

As she'd promised, Caterina rang from the hospital to tell Leo that Alessandro was recovering and would be sent home in the morning, along with an adrenaline pen that he'd make sure was with him at all times.

When the music slowed and the lights dimmed, Leo

held Rosie close. And there in the ballroom, swaying to the music, it felt as if nobody else was there: just the two of them.

At the end of the evening, Leo drove them back to the *palazzo*. Although someone—presumably Carlo—had left the light on by the front door and in the hallway, Rosie was pretty sure that everyone in the *palazzo* was asleep.

'There's a full moon,' Leo said quietly, gesturing to the sky. 'And I'm not ready to go to bed yet. Come and walk with me for a while in the gardens.'

'Do you mind if I take my shoes off?' Rosie asked when he led her onto the lawn. 'I'm not used to wearing heels this high.'

'Sure,' he said, and let her lean on him while she removed the strappy high heels and placed them on one of the stone benches.

Every single one of Rosie's senses felt magnified as they walked hand in hand through the gardens. In the moonlight, the garden looked magical; beneath her feet, the lawn felt like velvet. She could smell the sweet, drowsy scent of the roses, and in the distance she could hear a bird singing.

'Is that a nightingale?' she asked.

'I think so.' He stopped and spun her into his arms. 'Dance with me, Rosie,' he whispered.

Instead of the jazz band, they had the nightingale; instead of the chandeliers, they had the moon and the stars; and there was nobody to disturb them in their makeshift ballroom.

She closed her eyes as Leo held her close and dipped his head so he could brush his mouth against hers. Every nerve-end was begging for more, and she let him deepen the kiss; his mouth was teasing and inciting rather than demanding, and she found herself wanting more and more.

'Rosie,' he whispered when he finally broke the kiss. 'I want you.'

'I want you, too,' she admitted.

'Come to the tower with me?' he asked.

'I need to check on the children first.'

'What if you wake them? Or Nina?' he asked.

'I won't.' But she needed to see them.

'OK. Let's do this,' he said softly. He scooped her up, stopping only at the stone bench to pick up her shoes, and carried her back to the *palazzo*.

He set her on her feet again and kissed her before unlocking the door and dealing with the alarm system. And then he reset it and led her to the children's room.

The night-light was faint but enough to show her that they were both curled up under their duvets. She smiled and bent down to them in turn, breathing in the scent of their hair and kissing their foreheads lightly, so as not to wake them.

Just seeing them safe made her feel grounded again.

'I'm sorry,' she whispered when they'd left the children and were heading for the tower. 'I know they're perfectly safe here and I'm being ridiculous.'

'But Michael's associate really frightened you.'

She nodded. 'It's so hard to get past that.'

'It's OK. I understand.' He scooped her up again. 'But now it's you and me. Just for a little while.'

Could she do this?

Could she put herself first—just for a little while?

When he kissed her again, she said, 'Yes.'

Leo's bedroom in the tower was so high up that he knew nobody would be able to see into the room. Moonlight filtered in through the soft voile curtains at the windows; he led Rosie over to the window, leaving the heavy drapes where they were, and pushed the voile aside for a moment. 'You, me and the moonlight,' he said, and kissed her bare shoulder.

She shivered, and slowly he lowered the zip of her dress. Her skin was so soft, so creamy in the moonlight. He turned her to face him, cupped her face in his hands and dipped his head so he could brush his mouth against hers, then pulled back so he could look into her eyes. Her pupils were huge, making her eyes look almost black.

'I want you,' he whispered. So badly that it was a physical ache.

'I want you too,' she answered, her voice slightly hoarse.

He slid the straps of her dress down and kissed her bare shoulders. When he felt her shiver, he paused. 'OK?'

'Very OK. Don't stop.'

He drew the gauzy material down further, then dropped to his knees and kissed her bare midriff. She slid her fingers into his hair. 'Leo.'

He wanted everything. Now. And yet the anticipation was just as exciting. He helped her step out of the dress, then hung the garment over the back of a chair.

She stood there before him wearing only a strapless lacy bra, matching knickers, and diamonds.

He sucked in a breath. 'Do you have any idea how sexy you look right now?'

'I just feel underdressed,' she confessed, a blush stealing through her cheeks.

He spread his hands. 'Then do something about it, *bellezza*.'

'Bellezza?'

'In my language it means "beautiful",' he explained.

'Oh.' Her blush deepened; and then she gave him a smile so sexy that it almost drove him to his knees. 'You're beautiful, too,' she whispered. 'And I want to see you.'

'Do it,' he said, his voice cracking with need and desire.

Slowly, so slowly, she removed his jacket and hung it over the top of her dress. Then she undid his waistcoat, slid it from his shoulders and draped it over the top of his jacket.

Leo was dying to feel her hands against his bare skin; but at the same time he was enjoying the anticipation and he didn't want to rush her. The tip of her tongue caught between her teeth as she concentrated on undoing his bow tie, then unbuttoned his shirt. He could feel the warmth of her hands through the soft cotton, and it made him want more. He couldn't resist stealing a kiss as she pushed the material off his shoulders and let the shirt fall to the floor.

Then he caught his breath as finally he felt her fingertips against his skin.

'Nice pecs, Dr Marchetti,' she murmured. She let her hands drift lower. 'Nice abs, too.' She gave him a teasing smile, and excitement hummed through him. Where would she touch him next? How?

And he wanted to touch her. So much that he couldn't hold himself back; he traced the lacy edge of her bra with his fingertips. 'Nice curves,' he said huskily, and was rewarded with a sharp intake of breath from her.

Her hands were shaking slightly as she undid the buckle of his belt, then the button of his trousers.

'OK?' he asked.

'It's been a while,' she admitted. 'I guess a part of me's a bit scared I'll—well—disappoint you.'

How could she possibly be worried about that? 'You're not going to disappoint me,' he reassured her. 'And I didn't plan this. Tonight really was all about just dancing with you and having fun.'

'I wasn't planning this to happen, either.' Her eyes widened. 'I don't have any protection. I'm not on the Pill.'

'I have protection,' he said. 'But I don't want you to think I'm taking you for granted.'

In answer she kissed him, and he felt his control snap.

He wasn't sure which of them finished undressing each other, but the next thing he knew he'd dropped the diamonds on his dressing table and had carried her to his bed, and she was lying with her head tipped back into his pillows, smiling up at him.

'I've wanted you since the moment I first saw you,' he whispered.

'Even though I was horrible to you?'

'Even though.' He stole a kiss. 'I don't know what it was. Your gorgeous eyes. Your mouth. Your hair. But something about you drew me and I want you. Very, very badly.'

'I want you, too,' she confessed.

She reached up and kissed him back. When he broke the kiss, he could see that her mouth was slightly swollen and reddened from kissing him, and her eyes glittered with pure desire. It was good to know she was with him all the way.

He kissed the hollows of her collarbones, then let his mouth slide lower. She gasped when he took one nipple into his mouth; he teased it with the tip of his tongue until her breathing had grown deeper and less even. Then he stroked her midriff and moved lower, kissing his way down her body and circling her navel with his tongue. He loved the feel of her curves, so soft against his skin.

'*Bellezza,*' he whispered. 'You're so beautiful, Rosie.'

'So are you,' she said shyly, sliding her hands along his shoulders.

He kneeled back so he could look at her, sprawled on his bed. His English rose. And now he wanted to see her lose that calmness and unflappability he was used to at work. He wanted to see passion flare in her.

Keeping his gaze fixed on hers, he let his fingertips skate upwards from her knees. She caught her breath and parted her thighs, letting him touch her more intimately.

'Yes, Leo,' she whispered. 'Now.'

He reached over to the drawers next to his bed, took a condom from the top drawer, undid the foil packet and slid the condom on.

Then he kissed her again and whispered, 'Open your eyes, Rosie.'

When she did so, he eased his body into hers, watching the way the colour of her eyes changed.

She gasped, and wrapped her legs round him so he could push deeper.

He could feel the softness of her breasts against his chest, the hardness of her nipples.

'You feel like paradise,' he whispered.

'So do you.' Colour bloomed in her cheeks.

He held her closer, and began to move. His blood felt as if it were singing through his veins.

'Leo.' He felt her tighten round him as her climax hit, and it pushed him into his own climax.

Regretfully, he withdrew. 'Please don't go just yet,' he said. 'I need to deal with everything in the bathroom—but I'm not ready for you to leave just yet.'

'I'll stay,' she promised.

When Leo came back from the bathroom, Rosie was still curled in his bed, though she'd pulled the sheet over herself and she blushed when she saw that he was still completely naked.

He climbed into bed beside her and pulled her into his arms. 'Stay a little longer?'

He liked just lying there, holding her, with her head resting on his shoulder and his arm wrapped round her waist. There wasn't any need to make small talk; he just felt completely in tune with her. He couldn't remember ever feeling this happy before at the *palazzo*.

Rosie and the children really fitted in, here. He'd resisted the idea of having a family in Tuscany, not wanting to subject a child to the kind of misery he'd known here. But he wasn't his father; so maybe this place could actually house a happy family.

His last thought before he drifted into sleep was that maybe he, Rosie and the twins could be a family here...

CHAPTER TEN

NEXT MORNING ROSIE WOKE, warm and comfortable and with a body spooned against hers. When she realised that she was still in Leo's bed, she was horrified. She'd only meant to stay for a little while—not for the whole night. Supposing the children had woken from a bad dream, needed her and found her missing?

'Leo. *Leo*,' she whispered urgently. 'I need to go back to my room before the children wake up.'

And she hadn't even bothered taking off her make-up last night. She probably looked like a panda this morning—a panda with a bad case of bed-head.

'With a combination of lots of fresh air and all that running around yesterday, they're probably still asleep,' he pointed out, and kissed her. 'Good morning, *bellezza*.'

Oh, help.

When he spoke in his own language to her, it made her knees go weak. And that sensual look in his eyes... Panicking, she began, 'Leo, I don't normally—'

He cut her off by pressing a finger gently to her lips. 'No apologies. Last night was last night. We didn't plan it.' He held her gaze. 'But I don't have any regrets.'

She could see by his face that he meant it.

Did she have regrets?

Yes and no.

She didn't regret making love with him. He'd made her feel wonderful. But it was way too tempting to let herself believe that this thing between them could turn from a fairy tale to real life. And she knew that couldn't happen. He needed to marry someone from his world and produce an heir to the dukedom.

'Thank you,' she said. 'But I really do have to go now.' She bit her lip. 'If you don't mind, I could do with a hand zipping up my dress.'

'I've got a better idea. I'll lend you a bathrobe,' he said. 'It'll be quicker. And I'll see you back to your room and carry your dress.'

'What if people see us?' she asked, worrying. She wasn't ashamed of what they'd done; but she didn't want people knowing about it. This was just between them. *Private.* And she needed some time to process it. To think about where they could possibly go from here. She couldn't do that if everyone knew about it.

'They won't,' he said, 'but if anyone sees me on the way back from your room I'll tell them I went outside for some fresh air before my shower.' He stroked her face. 'The *palazzo* is a little bit like a warren, and the least I can do is see you safely back to your room.'

It made sense. Otherwise she was at risk of going into the wrong room and embarrassing herself even further.

She shrugged on the fluffy white bathrobe he held out for her. It was way too big for her, but she tied the belt tightly.

He wrapped a towel round his waist, sarong-style; it looked incredibly sexy, and she had a hard job reminding herself that they were supposed to be just colleagues.

Except last night they'd been lovers.

'You need these, too.' Leo handed her the diamonds and she put them carefully in the deep pockets of his robe.

He carried her dress and shoes, and thankfully they didn't bump into anyone on the way back to her room. She put the jewels on the dressing table, then gave the bathrobe back to him.

Leo smiled and stole a kiss. 'I'll see you at breakfast, then. Do you know how to get to the breakfast room?'

'Down the stairs and then turn right?' she guessed.

He nodded. 'See you in a bit.'

Rosie hung up her dress, showered and dressed swiftly, then went into the children's room. They were just waking up and gave her the sweetest smiles.

'Mummy!' Freddie exclaimed. 'We missed you.'

'I missed you, too. I love you,' she told them both, and hugged them fiercely.

'Were there any princes and princesses at the ball?' Lexi wanted to know.

'No, but there were some very pretty dresses.'

'Did you take selfies?' Lexi asked.

'No.' She ruffled her daughter's hair. 'I need to get you both up now. We have to go down to breakfast.'

Rosie had just finished helping them get dressed when Nina came in. 'Sorry. I wasn't sure if they'd be awake yet.'

'It's fine. You're not supposed to be on duty twenty-four-seven,' Rosie said with a smile. 'I'll read them a story while you get ready, and we can all go down together.'

'That sounds good. Did you have fun last night?' Nina asked.

'Yes. The ball was great. And it really helped knowing that you were here with the children. Thanks so much for that.'

'No problem. They were angels.'

Once Nina was ready, they made their way to the breakfast room: a sunny room overlooking the terrace. Beatrice and Leo were already there.

'Good morning,' Beatrice said. 'Did you sleep well?'

Rosie didn't dare meet Leo's gaze. 'Very well, thank you.'

'Coffee, *signor, signorina*?' Carlo asked. 'And hot chocolate for the children?'

'That would be lovely, thanks,' Rosie said.

'Help yourself to pastries and *biscotti*,' Leo said.

'We tend to have a very light breakfast in Italy,' Beatrice said, 'but Maria can make you bacon and egg, if you prefer.'

'This is all perfect,' Rosie said with a smile. 'And thank you for the loan of your diamonds.' She returned the boxes to Beatrice.

'My pleasure, my dear,' Beatrice said. 'Now, tell me all about the ball.'

Rosie focused on the dancing and the dresses—but Leo had his own story to tell.

'She saved a man's life last night, Mamma,' he said. 'He was stung by a wasp and had a very bad allergic reaction. Thanks to Rosie, he made it to hospital and he'll make a full recovery.'

'It wasn't just me,' Rosie said, squirming. 'I couldn't have done it without you translating for me, and getting the ambulance and the adrenaline.'

'But if you hadn't noticed what the problem was,' he said gently, 'Alessandro might have died.' He smiled at Freddie and Lexi. 'Your mummy is amazing.'

'That's what Aunty Daze says,' Lexi confided.

Violetta arrived after breakfast; they spent the rest of the morning in the gardens, with the children running round and playing ball with Leo. A couple of times, she caught his eye and wondered if he was remembering last night, when the two of them had danced barefoot in the moonlight among the roses.

On the way back to the airport, Leo switched on his phone and a slew of messages flooded in.

He grimaced and handed his phone to her.

The *Celebrity Life!* magazine website had run a report on the charity ball last night, asking who the beautiful woman was with the Duke of Calvanera—especially as she was wearing the Calvanera diamonds. Had someone finally caught the reluctant Duke?

There was a newer story attached to it: *Angel in Diamonds*. All about how she'd been a ministering angel to a man suffering from a near-fatal allergy to wasps, and saved his life.

Oh, no.

She grimaced and mouthed, 'Sorry.'

'It gets worse,' he mouthed back, and her dismay grew when he leaned over and flicked into a second website.

The journalists had dug up her past.

Rosie Hobbes, a twenty-five-year-old mother of twins, is a nurse at the beleaguered Paddington Children's Hospital. She was previously married to Michael Duncan, who died after his car collided with a tree, leaving a mountain of gambling debts.

Rosie stared at the screen, horrified, and totally shocked that her private life had been spilled over the press so quickly.

And then the fear seeped in.

What if Michael's former associates saw all this and decided that Leo, as the Duke of Calvanera, had plenty of money? Supposing they came after him, or threatened the children again? And Leo's mother was vulnerable at the *palazzo*, being elderly and frail. Although Violetta, Carlo and Maria would be with her, Rosie knew, would they be enough to keep her safe?

She didn't even know where to start asking questions, but looked helplessly at Leo.

'My PR team is doing damage limitation,' he said grimly.

'What's wrong?' Nina asked.

'Nothing,' Rosie fibbed—then grabbed her own phone from her bag and texted Nina.

Press gossip about me, things I don't want the children to hear but you probably need to know. Am sorry I didn't say anything before.

She sent Nina the link to the two articles.

'That'll probably be a text from my mum asking if I'm going to be home for tea tonight,' Nina said when her phone beeped.

Thankfully the children were too young to read many of the words, Rosie thought.

A few minutes later, Nina texted her back.

Poor you. Not fair of them to drag it all up. You OK?

Rosie sagged with relief; at least this wasn't going to be a problem at the hospital nursery school. She also knew that Nina wasn't a gossip.

I'm fine, she fibbed. Thanks for keeping it to yourself.

Try not to worry, Nina responded. Let me know if there's anything I can do. Thanks.

Leo was busy on his phone—Rosie assumed he was dealing with his PR team—but he reached over to squeeze her hand, as if telling her that everything was going to be all right.

But the more she thought about it, the more she realised that it wasn't going to be all right. She was completely unsuitable for him. The press would bring up her past over and over and over again, and he'd be tainted by association. Beatrice had been so kind and welcoming this weekend; but right now Rosie felt as if she'd thrown all that back in Beatrice's face.

Nina kept the children occupied with stories and singing and colouring all the way back to England, so they weren't aware that anything was wrong. And thankfully they fell asleep in the car so there weren't any awkward questions.

Leo dropped Nina home first but, when he was about to turn into Rosie's road, they could see a group of people waiting at the front of Rosie's house.

'The paparazzi,' he said with a sigh.

'But how do they even know where I live?' Rosie asked, shocked.

He groaned. 'Sorry. They can dig up practically anything. I should have thought about this earlier.' He drove past her road. 'You'd better stay at mine.'

'They're probably camped out there, too,' she said. 'Maybe you'd better drop us on the next road. We can cut through the back.'

'I can't just abandon you.'

'You're not abandoning me. You're dropping us off at a place where we can walk through to the back of my house unseen.'

'I don't like this,' Leo said.

'It's the only option,' she said firmly.

'One condition, then,' he said. 'You let me know you're home safely, and you call me if there's any kind of problem at all.'

'OK,' she promised.

She woke the children. 'We're going to play a game,

now,' she said. 'We're going to pretend to be invisible, so we have to tiptoe home.'

'Yay!' Lexi said, then screwed up her face and whispered, 'Yay.'

Rosie couldn't help smiling. 'Say goodbye and thank you to Leo.'

'Bye-bye and thank you,' the twins chorused.

Thankfully they managed to get in the back door without incident, and Rosie shepherded the children upstairs. At least one of the waiting press must've seen a movement through the frosted glass panel of the front door, because the doorbell went, but Rosie ignored it.

Safely indoors, she texted Leo.

Going to put the children to bed.

Call me later, he texted back immediately.

Rosie continued to ignore the doorbell and ran a bath for the children.

'Mummy, it's the doorbell,' Freddie said. 'It might be the postman.'

'Not on a Sunday. Whoever it is can come back later,' Rosie said firmly, 'because I'm busy right now.'

The phone shrilled, and she ignored that, too—until the answering machine kicked in and a gravelly voice said, 'Mrs Duncan, you really need to answer your phone. We wouldn't want another accident, would we?'

She went cold.

Michael's associates. Nobody else would call her Mrs Duncan. But how had they got hold of her number? She'd moved from the place she'd shared with Michael, and her new number was ex-directory.

'As a children's nurse, you know how easily bones break.'

She had to suppress a whimper. That was a definite

threat. They were going to hurt the children if she didn't do what they wanted.

'Mummy? Mummy, what's the matter?' Lexi asked.

'Nothing,' Rosie lied. 'I left the radio on in my bedroom.' She turned off the taps. 'Go and play in your bedroom for five minutes while I sort it out.'

She grabbed the phone and headed downstairs so the children wouldn't hear her. 'What do you want?' she whispered fiercely.

'About time you answered us, Mrs Duncan,' the gravelly voiced man said. 'You know what we want. What Michael owed us.'

'Michael's dead, and I don't have any money.'

'But your new boyfriend does. The Duke of Calvanera.'

'He's not my boyfriend,' Rosie said desperately.

'The papers are all saying he is.'

'The papers are just trying to sell copies. He isn't my boyfriend.'

'No? I believe the Duchess of Calvanera is quite frail. Imagine a fall and a broken hip at that age,' the man continued.

They were threatening Leo's mum as well as the children?

Fear made her feel queasy. But then she remembered her promise to herself after Michael's death: that nobody would ever make her feel a second-class citizen again. These people weren't going to bully her, either. 'I'm calling the police,' Rosie said.

There was a laugh from the other end of the line. 'You think they'll be able to do anything?'

'You threatened me. I'm recording every single word you say on my mobile phone,' Rosie lied.

'A recording proves nothing. But we know where you

are. I'd advise you to talk to your boyfriend and get him to pay Michael's debts.'

The line went dead.

Oh, dear God. The nightmare that she'd thought was over had come back again. Except this time they'd been more explicit. They wanted money, or they'd hurt the children and Leo's mum.

She couldn't take that risk—but she also couldn't ask Leo to pay Michael's debts. And supposing the thugs decided they wanted interest as well? The only way she could think of to keep everyone safe was to end her relationship with Leo—and talk to the police. And even that might not be enough.

Florence had been perfect. Too perfect, maybe, because it had shown her the life she wanted. The future that maybe she could have with Leo. But the price was too high: she couldn't risk the safety of her children, Leo or Leo's mother.

She went back upstairs and chivvied the twins into the bathroom. They chattered away about the *palazzo* and the suit of armour, and Lexi was still clearly convinced that Leo was really a prince. It took three bedtime stories to calm them down. But finally the children fell asleep, and Rosie went into her own room, shutting the curtains in case the paparazzi tried to get some kind of blurry shot of her through the window.

And now she needed to talk to Leo.

It was a call she didn't want to make—a call that would break her dreams and trample her heart—but she couldn't see any other solution.

Leo answered straight away. 'Are you OK?'

No. Far from it. 'Yes.' She took a deep breath. 'Leo—we can't do this any more.' And these were the hardest words she was ever going to have to say. They actually stuck in her throat to the point where she thought she was going to choke, but finally she managed to compose herself. 'We have to end it.' Which would wipe out the threat to the children and his mother, and by extension to Leo himself. But she also knew she needed to give him an excuse that he'd accept instead of trying to solve. 'The press are going to make life too difficult. So I'd rather you didn't see me or the twins any more.'

'Rosie, this will blow over and people will have forgotten about it by the middle of the week. It's probably a slow news day.'

That was true. But she had to convince him. Tell him she didn't want the kind of life he could offer her—even though she did. 'There are photographers camped outside my house.'

'They'll get bored and go away.'

That was true, too. Digging her nails into her palm and reminding herself that she had to do this for everyone's safety, she demanded, 'When? I can't camp out here until the middle of the week. I'm due at work tomorrow and the children are due at nursery school. I can't just ring in and say we're not turning up.'

'I'll send a car and get someone to escort you in.'

'No.' Because it wasn't really the press that was the problem. Maybe he'd understand if she dropped a hint about what really worried her. 'What if Michael's associates see the papers and crawl out of the woodwork?'

'They won't,' he reassured her. 'If they do try anything, I'll have the police onto them straight away—both in here and in Italy.'

Oh, but they had already. And the police wouldn't be able to help, Rosie was sure. Michael's associates were right in that she had no proof. 'You have a security team in Italy,' she said tentatively. 'Maybe you'd better make sure they take extra care with your mother.'

'Why?' His voice sharpened. 'Rosie, are you trying to tell me they've been in touch with you?'

Oh, help. She'd forgotten how quick his mind was. Of course he'd work it out for himself that she wasn't just being overprotective—that something had happened to worry her. 'No,' she lied. 'I just think you should take extra precautions—with yourself as well as with your mother. And you need to get your PR people to make a statement to the press, saying that we're nothing more to each other than colleagues.' Even though Leo could've been the centre of her life. She had to give him up. To keep him safe.

'But, Rosie—'

'No,' she cut in. Why did he have to make this so hard? Why couldn't he just walk away, the way he normally walked away from his girlfriends? 'I've thought about it and thought about it, and this is the only way. It has to end.' It was the last thing she wanted. But there was no other way. 'It has to end *now*. I'm sorry. Goodbye, Leo.'

She switched off her mobile phone after she cut the connection, and she ignored her landline when it shrilled.

How stupid she'd been, thinking she could escape Michael's shadow. It would always be there, and would always darken anything she did. And it wasn't fair to Leo or his family to expect them to deal with it, too.

The only way out of this was to end it between them.

Even though her heart felt as if someone had ripped it into tiny shreds and stomped on it and ground it into the floor. Because she'd fallen in love with Leo. Not the Duke—yes, the glitziness of the ball had been fun, but it wasn't who Leo was. She'd fallen for the man. The man who'd been so good with the twins. The man with the huge, huge heart. The man who really cared and wanted to make a difference to the world.

She wanted to be with him. But there just wasn't a way she could do that and keep everyone safe, and it wasn't fair to make everyone spend the rest of their days looking over their shoulders, worrying that her past was going to catch up with them. All that worry and mistrust would eat into their love like woodworm, little tiny bites at a time, and eventually what they felt for each other would simply crumble and fall apart, undermined by all the worry.

So she'd tell the children that Leo had had to go back to Italy, and she'd distract them every time they asked if they could go back to the *palazzo* to see him. And she'd hope that Leo could find the happiness he deserved with someone else—someone whose past wouldn't be a problem.

And even though she wanted to sob her heart out for what she'd lost, she didn't. Because some things hurt too much to cry.

Her last call was to the police. They sent someone to interview her, but it turned out that her fears were spot on: she didn't have anywhere near enough information to identify Michael's associates.

'We can check your phone records,' the policeman said, 'but we still might not be able to trace them. They might have used an unregistered mobile to call you.'

'Unregistered?' Rosie queried.

'Pay-as-you-go, bought with cash and with no ID to link to the phone. But if they do call you again, ring us straight away.'

'I will,' Rosie said, though it just made her feel hopeless.

And, when she went to bed that night, she couldn't sleep. She was haunted by that gravelly voice and the threat to her children and Leo's mother—three people who were too vulnerable to protect themselves. Then there was Leo himself. He was strong: but Michael's associates were capable of anything. She couldn't bear to think that they'd arrange an accident for him, the way she was sure they had for Michael. And how could you fight a nameless opponent, someone who stayed so deeply hidden in the shadows?

Hopefully Leo's PR team would get the word out that they weren't an item. Then Michael's associates would realise that he wasn't going to pay them, and they'd give up—just as they had when Michael had died.

And, although it broke her heart to do it, the alternative was worse. At least this way, Leo had the chance of finding happiness in the future. This way, Leo would be safe.

CHAPTER ELEVEN

THE PAPARAZZI WERE still outside Rosie's house the next morning, albeit not quite so many of them as there had been the previous evening. Rosie was much less worried about them than about the possible repercussions from Michael's former associates, but she took a taxi to the hospital instead of using the Tube, and she had a quiet word with the head of the nursery school about the situation and to ask for an extra layer of security for the twins.

And then it was time to face the ward.

'I saw you in the news this morning,' Kathleen said cheerfully. 'Loved the dress. So when did you and Leo get together?'

'We're not together,' Rosie said firmly. 'You know what the press is like. They add two and two and make a hundred.'

'But you went to Italy with him.'

'Yes,' Rosie admitted.

'Florence is really romantic.'

'I was looking at the Italian healthcare system and what we could learn from it,' Rosie fibbed. 'We went to a ball, yes, because it was to raise funds for a paediatric clinic that the Duke of Calvanera supports.'

Given that she so rarely went out on hospital evenings out, she really hoped that Kathleen would accept the story.

Especially as most of it was true. To Rosie's relief, the other nurse simply smiled. 'Well, it was still a lovely dress.'

'Thank you,' Rosie said.

'So did you really save someone's life?'

Rosie grimaced. 'It wasn't just me. I was part of a team. And you would've done the same if someone had collapsed in front of you, wheezing and having trouble breathing, with a massive swelling on his hand where a wasp had stung him.'

'So you did save someone's life,' Kathleen said. 'Because that sounds like the beginning of anaphylaxis to me.'

'It was. Luckily he's fine now. And I'd better get my skates on.'

'You're on the allergy clinic this morning,' Kathleen said. 'With Leo.'

Rosie's heart sank. She'd known that she'd have to face Leo this week and they'd have to work together at some point, but she'd hoped for a little more time to prepare herself. To remind herself that no matter how attractive she found him, she had to put the safety of her children and his mother first.

'Nurse Hobbes,' Leo said, and gave her a cool little nod, when she rapped on the door and walked into the consulting room.

Formal was good. She could cope with that. 'Dr Marchetti.' Though she couldn't look him in the eye. Or the face, for that matter—because then she'd remember how his mouth had felt against her skin, and it would undermine her attempts to stay cool and calm in front of him. She looked down at the notes in her hand. 'I believe our first patient is Madison Turner, for the next session in her anti-venom treatment.'

How ironic. An allergy to wasps: just what had drawn the press's attention to her at the ball.

If Alessandro hadn't been stung, would she and Leo have got away with it? Or would the press still have tried to make up a story about them and Michael's associates would've crawled out of the woodwork anyway?

'If you'd like to bring Madison through, please,' Leo said, his voice cool.

When she sneaked a glance at him, Rosie realised that he was trying just as hard not to look at her. Guilt flooded through her as she realised she'd hurt him. But she hadn't dumped him because she didn't like him. Quite the opposite. She'd ended things with him solely to keep him, his family and the twins *safe*.

Not that she intended to discuss it with him. Talking about it wouldn't make things better—if he knew the full story, it might lead him to do something brave and reckless, and her sacrifice would've been for nothing. She couldn't bear to think of him being badly hurt. Or worse.

'I'll just go and get Madison,' she said.

She really hoped the tension between them didn't show, for the sake of their young patients and their parents. She did her best to be her usual professional self, and concentrated hard on getting the observations right and recording everything thoroughly. Leo barely spoke to her, except when he wanted some information from notes that she was using.

The rest of the morning's clinic was just as awkward. Rosie was glad to escape at lunchtime, and even more relieved that she had a cast-iron excuse to avoid Leo, because Monday was one of her days for reading to Penny.

'I saw your picture in the paper,' Julia said.

'It was a lot of fuss about nothing,' Rosie said with a smile. 'Any nurse would've done the same, in my shoes.'

'I didn't mean about the poor man who was stung. You were at that fancy ball with Leo Marchetti, weren't you?'

'As a colleague,' Rosie fibbed. In a desperate bid to divert Julia from the subject, she said, 'The sun's shining for once—you really should make the most of it. And I'm dying to find out what happens next in that ballet story, Penny.'

'Me, too!' the little girl said with a smile.

Thankfully Leo wasn't in the staff canteen when Rosie grabbed a sandwich and a cold drink from the kiosk before going back to the ward. But the afternoon allergy clinic was just as awkward as the morning's. She simply didn't know how to behave towards him. Friendly felt wrong, given that she'd just ended their relationship; but coolness felt wrong, too, as if she were adding insult to injury.

She was really glad when clinic ended and she was able to go down to the nursery school to pick up the twins.

'Was everything all right today?' she asked Nina, trying to damp down the anxiety in her voice. 'Nobody tried to...' *Take the twins.* She could barely get the words out.

'No. Everything was fine,' Nina reassured her. 'Is the press still hounding you?'

'I didn't go outside at lunchtime; it's my day to read to Penny,' Rosie said. Though even if it hadn't been, she wouldn't have gone outside. She planned to use a taxi to and from the hospital for the foreseeable future rather than taking the Tube, too, even though it was going to make a hole in her budget. The most important thing was that the children would be safe.

'I'm sure Leo can do something. Maybe his press team—'

'It'll be fine,' Rosie said with a smile. 'I'd better get the twins home. Thanks for everything, Nina.'

Leo was thoroughly miserable.

He missed Rosie.

And he missed the twins.

The weekend in Tuscany had been wonderful. Hearing children's laughter flood through the *palazzo*, watching the twins run around the gardens, seeing their delight in being allowed to touch the tiny suit of armour...

He'd actually felt like a father.

And, for the first time in his life, he'd actually wanted to be a father. Wanted to share his ancestral home with the next generation down. He'd loved showing Lexi and Freddie around.

Even more, he'd loved being with Rosie. Her quiet calmness. Her sweetness. The way she'd been unflappable at the ball, ignoring the fact that she was wearing haute couture and real diamonds and focusing instead on saving someone's life.

The sweetest bit for him had been dancing with her on the grass in the moonlight, just the two of them and the roses. And then making love with her. Losing himself in her. Falling asleep with her curled in his arms.

Yet ironically his home country had been the cause of their problems. If he hadn't taken Rosie to the ball, she wouldn't have caught the attention of the press.

She'd been pretty clear that it was over between them. That it had to be over, for the sake of her children. Although she'd put the blame on the press, she was obviously terrified that Michael's associates were going to crawl out of the woodwork and threaten the twins. And, for the second time in his life, Leo felt utterly powerless. The first time had been when his father had driven Emilia away, and Leo hadn't been able to convince her that he could keep her safe—that their love would be enough.

How ironic that he was in exactly the same position now. Except his family wasn't the problem: his mother had welcomed Rosie and the twins warmly, and he was pretty sure that Rosie had liked his mother, too. The problem was that Rosie was scared, and she couldn't get past the fear for long enough to let him solve the problem. Leo was pretty sure he could sort it out: a good lawyer would be able to get her an injunction. Even if she didn't know who they were, he'd be able to find out. Or his security team would.

This was crazy. He was supposed to be a doctor, a man who fixed things. Right now, he didn't have a clue how to fix this. How to make Rosie see that he *could* keep her safe. That everything would be just fine, if she'd give them a chance.

He'd just have to think harder. Work out what would be the one thing to make her trust him. But in the meantime he did what she'd asked and instructed his PR team to make it very clear that he and Rosie were absolutely not an item. And he had a quiet word with his legal and security team to see what they could find out about Michael and his associates, and to keep an eye on Rosie and the children. If the thugs really were watching her, his team would know very quickly—and he'd be able to keep Rosie and the children protected. And then maybe, once she realised that he could keep her safe, she'd learn to trust him.

Tuesday was just as difficult, Rosie found. Ward rounds, when she was rostered on with Leo; a staff meeting that spilled over into lunch and they all agreed to order in some sandwiches, so Rosie had to spend her lunch hour with Leo whether she liked it or not. She knew she had to speak to him, otherwise someone would notice the tension between them and start asking questions she didn't want to answer; but oh, it was hard. How did you make small talk with someone when you'd shared such a deep intimacy with them and remembered the feel of their skin against yours?

The worst thing was, she missed Leo. Like crazy. The children asked after him, too, wanting to know if he was coming to the park or if they were having pizza with him. Rosie was rapidly running out of excuses. And every lie ripped another little hole in her heart. If only she could be with him. If only she'd never met Michael—or if only Michael hadn't mixed with the wrong people because of his gambling problem...

But Wednesday morning brought her a different set of worries. The paparazzi and her fears about Michael's associates were forgotten when she went to wake up the twins and Freddie refused to get up.

Her son was often quiet, but he wasn't the grizzly sort.

'My tummy hurts,' he said.

And his face and hair were damp, she noticed. She sat down on the bed next to him and gently placed the back of her hand against his forehead.

It was definitely too hot.

'Does anywhere else hurt, Freddie?'

'Here.'

He pointed to his neck, and she went cold.

Had he just lain awkwardly during the night—or was it something more serious?

The first thing she needed to deal with was that temperature. And then she'd better call work to say that she couldn't come in, and the nursery school to say that the twins wouldn't be in today.

She grabbed the in-ear thermometer from the bathroom cabinet, along with the bottle of infant paracetamol. A quick check told her that her instincts were right: Freddie had a fever. 'I've got some special medicine to help you feel better,' she told Freddie, and measured out the dose. 'And I think you need to stay in bed this morning. If you're feeling a little bit better this afternoon, we'll all cuddle up on the sofa with a blanket and we'll watch *Toy Story*.' It was Freddie's favourite, guaranteed to cheer him up.

'I'm hot, Mummy,' he said.

'I know, baby.' She kissed his forehead. 'I'm going to get Lexi dressed, and then I'm going to bring you some juice.' It would be gentler on his stomach than milk. 'Do you want some toast? Or some yoghurt?'

He sniffed. 'No.'

'All right. I'll be back in a minute. Love you.'

'Love you, Mummy.' His lower lip wobbled, and a tear trickled down his cheek.

Once she'd got Lexi dressed, Rosie made her daughter some breakfast and grabbed the phone. Work was able to get agency cover for her, and the nursery school confirmed that a couple of children had gone down with some sort of tummy bug. Probably tomorrow both of them would be down with it, she thought wryly.

She'd just gone up to Freddie when he suddenly stiffened, twitched, and his eyes began to roll.

Oh, no.

'Freddie? Freddie?'

He didn't respond, and then the seizure began in earnest.

Pretend he's not yours. Pretend he's a patient, she reminded herself, and let her nursing training kick in. She glanced at her watch as she put him in the recovery position. OK. This was the first time he'd ever had a seizure—and he had a high temperature. Given his age, this was a perfectly normal thing.

As long as it lasted for less than five minutes.

She kept half an eye on him and half an eye on her watch. When the timing of the seizure reached seven minutes, she knew he needed better medical attention than she could give him at home. Given the time of day, it would be quicker for her to drive him to Paddington Children's Hospital herself rather than call an ambulance.

'Lexi, Freddie's not very well and we're going to take him in the car,' she said.

Somehow she managed to get both twins out to the car.

There were a couple of paparazzi loitering outside. 'Rosie!' one of them called. 'What's wrong?'

'My little boy's ill,' she said, pushing past them. 'Can't you find something better to do with your time than hassle me? I need to get him to hospital. Now!'

'Can we help?' the other one asked.

'Just go away. *Please*,' she said. She strapped the children into their car seats and hooked her phone up to her car's stereo system so she could make her phone calls safely. As soon as they were on the way to the hospital, she called the ward. 'Kathleen? It's Rosie. I'm bringing Freddie in with a febrile seizure.'

'Right. We'll be ready,' Kathleen said. 'Take care and we'll see you in a few minutes.'

'Thanks.' She cut the call and called her mother; to her relief, her mother answered on the fourth ring, and agreed to meet her at the hospital and take Lexi back home with her.

Just please, please let Freddie be all right, she thought grimly, and headed for the hospital.

'Was that Rosie?' Leo asked.

'Yes,' Kathleen confirmed.

'And she said that Freddie's ill?'

'Febrile convulsions.'

'I'll take the case,' he said.

'But—'

'I'm a doctor,' he said softly. 'And that comes before anything else. I'll look after Freddie.'

Though when Rosie appeared in the department, a couple of minutes later, carrying Freddie and with Lexi trotting along beside her, she didn't look particularly pleased to see him.

'I'm on duty. Treating children is my job,' he reminded her, taking Freddie from her and carrying the little boy over to one of the side rooms.

'Will you make Freddie better, Leo?' Lexi asked as he laid the little boy on the bed.

'I'll try my best,' he promised. Obviously Rosie hadn't had anyone who could look after her daughter at extremely short notice; at the same time, he needed to distract the little girl so he could find out exactly what symptoms Freddie had. 'Lexi, can you draw a picture of a dog for Freddie while I talk to your mummy, please?'

She nodded solemnly, and he gave her some paper and a pen.

'My mum's going to pick her up from here. She's on the way,' Rosie said.

'Not a problem,' Leo said gently. 'Kathleen said Freddie's had febrile convulsions. Can you give me a full history?'

'I'm probably overreacting,' she said, but he could hear the underlying panic in her voice. 'Freddie had a high temperature this morning, and he said his tummy and his neck hurt.'

A sore neck and a high temperature: that combination could mean something seriously nasty.

Clearly she was thinking the same thing, because she said, 'I checked and there's no rash.'

Though they both knew it was possible to have meningitis without a rash.

'I've given him a normal dose of infant paracetamol,' she said. 'It hasn't brought his temperature down. And then he started fitting.' She swallowed hard. 'Neither of the twins has ever had any kind of fit before. I know he's of the age when he's most likely to have a febrile seizure, but it went on for more than ten minutes.'

'And you did exactly the right thing bringing him in. You're a paediatric nurse, so you know it's really common and most of the time everything's fine.'

But he could see in her expression that she was thinking of the rare cases when everything wasn't fine.

'It could be a bacterial infection causing the temperature and the fit,' he said. 'Not necessarily meningitis: it could be a urinary tract infection, an upper respiratory tract infection or tonsillitis, an ear infection or gastroenteritis.'

She dragged in a breath. 'But it could be meningitis—you know a rash isn't the only sign.'

He nodded. 'Did Freddie have a vaccination for meningitis C?'

'Yes, at twelve weeks and again at a year,' Rosie confirmed.

'Again, that's a good sign,' he said gently. Small children didn't always get the classic triad of meningitis, but it was worth asking. 'Apart from saying his neck's sore, has he shown any signs of confusion, or a dislike of bright lights?' When Rosie shook her head he continued, 'Has he had any pains in his legs? Are his hands and feet cold, or has he said they feel cold?'

'No.'

'Again, that's a really good sign.' He checked Freddie's temperature, heart rate and capillary refill, and looked in his ears. 'Did he show any signs of pallor before the fit, or has there been any change in the colour of his lips?'

'No.'

'That's good.' But Leo also noted that Freddie wasn't smiling, and he was very quiet. Was that because the little boy had gone back into his shell or simply because he wasn't feeling well?

'I'm going to take a urine sample for culture,' he said. 'Given what you've told me, I'm not going to take any risks and I'll treat him for suspected meningitis until I can find out what the problem is. I'll need to do a lumbar puncture.'

Rosie went white.

How Leo wanted to hold her. Tightly.

But right now it wasn't appropriate. He needed to be a doctor first. 'You know the drill,' he said, 'and you also know it takes a couple of days to get the test results back, so I'll need to admit him to the ward. I'll start him on antibiotics and I might put him on a drip if I'm not happy with his hydration. I'll give him antipyretics as well, so I need you to tell me exactly when you gave the last dose, and I'll need you to sign the consent form.'

'All right,' Rosie said.

There was a knock on the door and an older woman stood in the doorway. 'Rosie?'

'Thanks for coming, Mum.'

Even if Rosie hadn't spoken, Leo would've known exactly who the older woman was; she had the same bright blue eyes as Rosie and her hair would've been the same colour years ago. Rosie was clearly trying her best to keep it together in front of the twins, but Leo could see the strain in her eyes.

'Mrs Hobbes. I'm Dr Marchetti—Leo,' he said.

He could see the moment that the penny dropped. Yes, he was *that* Leo. 'Take care of our Freddie,' Mrs Hobbes said quietly.

'I will,' he promised.

'Lexi, are you ready to go with Nanna?' Rosie asked.

The little girl nodded. 'Freddie, I drew you a doggie to make you better.' She handed the picture to her twin and gave the pen back to Leo.

'Mum—before you go.' Rosie lowered her voice, as did Mrs Hobbes, but Leo caught every word they said. 'Just be careful. Michael—those men...'

Mrs Hobbes looked grim. 'Have you told the police?'

'They said to call them if I got another call. But just... Be careful, Mum.'

'She'll be safe with me,' Mrs Hobbes promised. She turned to Lexi. 'Come on, sweetie. We'll go back to my house now, and Mummy can text us to let us know how Freddie is.'

Lexi took her hand and left the room beside her grandmother.

Leo really wanted to talk to Rosie about Michael's associates, but it would have to wait; he needed to treat Freddie first. But then he'd deal with the situation. Because now he knew exactly why Rosie had ended things between them—and he had a pretty good idea why she hadn't told him the full story.

'Freddie, I'm going to take a little bit of fluid from your back so I can do some tests,' Leo said. 'I've got some special cream, so it won't hurt.'

'Promise?' Freddie asked.

'Promise,' Leo said solemnly.

'Will you sing me a song?'

If it would distract the boy, it was a great idea. 'Sure I will, while Mummy holds your hand,' he said, and sang Freddie all the nursery songs he knew in Italian and English while he performed the lumbar puncture.

'All done,' he said, and then he saw that Rosie was crying. Silently, but the tears were running down her face.

Ah, hell.

He couldn't just ignore it.

He wrapped his arms round her.

She pulled away. 'This isn't appropriate.'

'Yes, it is,' he said softly. 'You're my colleague, you're on your own and you're upset. I'm not an unfeeling monster who can walk away from that, regardless of whatever else might have happened.'

She leaned her head against his shoulder for just a moment, as if wishing that she really could rely on him, then pulled away. 'I have to be strong, for Freddie's sake.'

'But you don't have to be alone,' he reminded her. 'I'm here. Any time you need me.' And he wanted her and the twins in his life. For good.

He wasn't going to put pressure on her now, but once Freddie was on the mend they could discuss it. In the meantime he would just be there for her. No strings, no talking. Just there.

'Rosie—I heard what you said to your mum.'

She looked away. 'It's not your problem.'

'I can help. Right now you've got more than enough on your plate. Let me take some of the burden.'

'I can't.'

He sighed. 'There aren't any strings, if that's what you're worried about. Look, it's my fault that they've been in touch with you. If you hadn't come to Italy with me, the press wouldn't have heard about you, and Michael's associates wouldn't have contacted you. So, actually, it *is* my problem.'

She looked utterly miserable. 'I need to concentrate on Freddie.'

'Exactly. Let me deal with this so you can concentrate on him instead of worrying.'

She looked torn, but finally she said, 'All right. And thank you.'

He hated the way she sounded so broken and defeated. But, once Freddie was on the mend, she'd have that layer of worry removed. In the meantime he'd do his best to support her. And he'd solve her problem with Michael's associates.

The following two days were the worst forty-eight hours of Rosie's life. It was hard to keep Freddie's temperature down, and even though he was on antibiotics she worried that it really might be meningitis. If she lost him…

Leo kept a close eye on Freddie, and he also brought in sandwiches and coffee for Rosie.

'I can't eat,' she said.

'You have to, if you want to be strong for Freddie.'

But she couldn't face eating anything, not when she was so worried. And she didn't want to leave her little boy that night, so Leo made sure she had blankets and fresh water.

'I'll stay with you,' he said.

And how tempting it was. The idea of being able to lean on him, having someone there to support her. But she'd ended it between them. She couldn't be that selfish. 'No. You're on duty. You need a proper sleep.'

'I've done my time as a junior doctor. I can sleep in a chair.'

How she wanted to say yes. 'Thank you, but we'll be fine.'

'OK. Call me if you need me.'

At three in the morning, she thought about what he'd said. She was bone-deep tired, but how could she possibly sleep when her little boy was so sick? And it wouldn't be fair to call Leo, just because she felt alone and helpless. He'd offered, and she knew he'd be there within minutes if she called him. But it just wouldn't be fair of her.

Her eyes felt gritty from lack of sleep the next morning. And then Leo walked in with a paper cup of coffee from

Tony's, fresh pastries and a pot of prepared strawberries, raspberries and blueberries.

She stared at him, unable to pull any coherent words together.

'Eat,' he said. 'I'm pulling rank as your senior colleague. You need to eat.' He glanced down at the sleeping child. 'I'm not leaving until you've eaten at least half the food and drunk that coffee.'

She knew he meant it. And although he didn't make her talk to him—he spent his time looking through Freddie's chart—having him there did make her feel better. Less alone.

'Better?' he asked when she'd managed to force down the fruit and one of the pastries.

'Better.'

'Good. Go and have a shower.' He produced a toothbrush and toothpaste. 'Hospital shop, before you ask. It'll make you feel a bit more human. I won't be going anywhere until you're back.'

'If he wakes—'

'—then I'll tell him where you are. Stop worrying.'

Gratefully, she took a shower and cleaned her teeth. Although she didn't have fresh clothes, just the shower and cleaning her teeth made her feel better. And the fact that Leo cared enough to do that for her, even though she'd dumped him…

She scrubbed the tears away. Not now. She had to stay strong.

'Thank you,' she said when she got back to Freddie's bedside to discover that he was still asleep.

'Any time. Hopefully the antibiotics will start to make a difference today. I'll drop by later,' Leo said.

And he was as good as his word. He called in twice to

see how Freddie was doing. He also made her go out for a walk at lunchtime while he sat with Freddie.

'But—'

'But nothing,' he cut in gently. 'This is what you do for Julia. Let me do the same for you.'

'What about the press?'

'What about them? I'm a doctor first and a duke second. I couldn't care less about what the press thinks. You, Freddie and Lexi are the important ones here,' he told her. 'And Freddie knows me. He knows I'll do my best for him.'

She couldn't fault Leo as a doctor. He'd been meticulous with all the children they'd treated together, and he'd kept a really close eye on Freddie.

'But, just so you know,' he added, 'I've spoken to my PR team. They're dealing with the press and you don't have to worry any more.'

Maybe not about the press. But medicine was another matter: small children could become very sick, very quickly. And there was still the issue of Michael's associates.

As if he guessed at the fear she'd left unspoken, he said, 'I've also spoken to my security team and my lawyers. They've talked to the police here and they've been doing some investigations of their own. We know who they are. There's an injunction in place now, and my security team is keeping an eye on you, so nobody can get anywhere near you, Lexi or Freddie. You're *safe*.'

She couldn't take it in. Any of it. Everything felt like a blur. He knew who they were? But how? How had his team managed to find out who Michael's associates were, when the police hadn't been able to help her?

'Right. Out,' he said, gesturing to the door. 'Go and get some fresh air.'

Rosie did as she was told, her feet practically on autopilot. She wandered aimlessly round the streets outside the hospital, but all she could think of was Freddie. Her little boy. Was he going to be all right?

Unable to bear being away from him any longer, she went back in to the ward, only to find Freddie holding Leo's hand and Leo telling him some story about castles and magic suits of armour.

'Mummy.' Freddie gave her a half-smile and relief washed through Rosie. Was he really getting better? Or was this a slight recovery before he got worse?

There was a knock on the door, and Julia leaned round the doorframe. 'Hi. I won't stop—but Penny heard that Nurse Rosie's little boy wasn't very well, so she's done a drawing for him.' She smiled. 'She wanted to come herself, but…'

'The risk of infection's too great. I understand,' Rosie said, and took the drawing. 'Please say thank you to her. Look, Freddie—Penny's done you a special drawing of a doggie.'

'I like doggies,' he said. 'Thank you.'

She had to hold back the tears.

Leo squeezed her shoulder and murmured, 'It's going to be all right, Rosie, I promise you.'

He brought in a selection of savouries from one of the local cafés to tempt her that evening; and again he made her go out for some fresh air when Freddie fell asleep.

'You haven't slept for a day and a half,' he said when she came back all of ten minutes later. 'Take a nap now.'

'But—'

'I'm here. I'm not going anywhere. Freddie's safe with me. Sleep,' he said.

'I…' She shook her head. 'I can't.'

'Then let's try it this way.' He scooped her up in his arms and sat down in the chair next to Freddie's bed, then settled her on his lap and held her close.

'Leo, we can't—'

'Yes, we can,' he said, completely implacable. 'Go to sleep.'

Rosie didn't think it was possible; but whether it was the warmth of Leo's body, the regularity of his breathing or just the fact that she felt safe, curled in his arms like this, she actually fell asleep.

For four hours.

'I'm so sorry,' she said when she woke and realised how late it was.

'Don't apologise. You needed that.'

'But you should've gone home hours ago.'

'To an empty flat.' His eyes were very dark. 'I'm right where I want to be. By your side.'

'But we…' She swallowed hard. 'We're not together.'

'We could be,' he said.

She dragged in a breath. 'It's too complicated.'

'Then let me make it simple for you,' he said. 'I grew up in a world where I didn't know who I was supposed to be—my father changed the goalposts constantly, and nothing I did was ever right. I thought it was me, and that I was unlovable. Emilia made me think that maybe the problem wasn't me after all, and love might actually exist— but it was so easy for my father to push her out of my life. So I decided that a family wasn't for me. I didn't want to bring children into the mean-spirited world I'd grown up in. And I didn't want to make some kind of dynastic marriage with someone I didn't love and then start making the same mistakes my father did.' He stroked her face. 'And then I met you. And the twins. And suddenly everything was possible. Love and a family… Everything I'd told myself I didn't want, but actually I did. And when you came to Tuscany, it was the first time I could remember feeling really happy at the *palazzo*. Having the place full of the twins' laughter, sharing the garden with you.' He looked her straight in the eye. 'Making love with you and falling asleep with you in my arms. It was perfect.'

It had been like that for her, too.

'And, at the charity ball, I was so proud of you. You saved someone's life—you didn't fuss about your dress or anything, you were just cool and calm and sorted everything out, even though you didn't speak the language. I love you, Rosie. You're everything I want—you and the twins. We can give them a fabulous life together—and you're the one who can help me make the world a better place. Marry me, Rosie.'

Words she'd never thought to hear again.

And she knew Leo wouldn't change. He'd be there right by her side. He'd stick to his vows to love, honour and cherish her.

How she wanted to say yes.

But there was her past. Michael. The press had dredged it up once, and they'd do it again and again. She'd end up dragging Leo down. She remembered him saying that he'd fixed the problem with Michael's associates—but supposing it was only temporary? Supposing they came back? Supposing they regrouped and wanted more and more? Supposing they got past Leo's security and hurt the children, his mother or him?

'I can't,' she whispered.

She tried to wriggle off his lap, but he wouldn't let her. 'Why not?'

Did he really need her to spell it out? 'I can't fit into your world. I'd drag you down.'

He kissed her. 'No, you wouldn't. You've changed my world, Rosie. You've shown me what love and family really means. My mother adores you—so does everyone at the *palazzo*.'

Could it possibly be true? She'd really made a difference to his world? He really, really wanted her there?

'Through you, I've realised that I can give our children a life like the one I didn't have when I was growing up— one where their parents love and respect each other. One where we'll be firm when we have to, but fair, and our children will always know we love them and want to have fun with them.' He paused. 'I love you, Rosie.'

He loved her.

She could see the sincerity in his dark eyes. He felt the same way about her that she did about him. Something that went deeper than the fear that numbed her every time she thought about what Michael's associates could do.

Didn't they say that love could conquer all?

Looking at Leo, she saw strength and compassion and deep, deep love.

And that gave her the courage to admit to her feelings. 'I love you, too, Leo,' she whispered. He was everything she wanted—a man who'd be there in the tough times as well as the good times, reliable and kind and having time for the children. A man who really loved her instead of just expecting her to be some kind of trophy wife.

'Then marry me, Rosie. Forget the dukedom. It's not important. At the end of the day, I'm a doctor and you're a nurse. We're a team at work and we'll be a great team at home, too. And I don't care whether we live in London or Italy: as long as I'm with you, I'll be happy. And I can make you and the twins happy, too. Keep you safe. Make you feel loved and respected, the way you deserve to be.'

Even though she was sleep-deprived and had spent the last couple of days worried sick, she was mentally together just enough to realise that he meant it.

They really could have it all.

Be a real family.

But there was still that one last fear. The one thing that stopped her being able to step forward and take what he was offering her. 'Michael's associates… How could you fix it, when the police couldn't? How could you find out who they were?'

He stroked her face. 'I don't like the man my father was, but maybe he's done us a good turn, in the end.'

'How?' She didn't understand.

'His reputation apparently still has a ripple or two,' Leo said dryly. 'His name is definitely remembered in certain circles. And let's just say that my team have, um, avenues open to them that might not be available elsewhere. So I believe them when they tell me that nobody will ever threaten you or the children, ever again. You're safe with me. Always. Marry me, Rosie.'

You're safe with me.

She believed him. 'Yes,' she whispered.

He stroked her face. 'You're sure?'

'I'm sure.' She dragged in a breath. 'I'll be honest—I'm still scared that somehow Michael's associates will find a way round your security team. That they'll hurt you. But if you're prepared to take that risk, then I can be brave, too.'

'The alternative's being without you. Missing you every single second of every single day. And I don't want to do that,' he said simply. 'And they won't find a way round my security team. As I said, my father was, um, good at warning people off. I'm not my father, but people will remember him. And maybe we can turn his legacy into love. Together.'

'Together,' she echoed, and reached up to kiss him.

Leo stayed with Rosie that night, curled together in a chair.

And in the morning, they got the news they'd both been hoping for.

'It isn't meningitis,' Leo said, and lifted her up and whirled her round. 'We're still not sure what the virus is, but provided his temperature stays down and he keeps responding the way he has, you can take him home at lunchtime.'

'The perfect day,' she said. 'Freddie's all right. And we have a wedding to plan.'

He kissed her lingeringly. 'The perfect day.'

EPILOGUE

One year later

'YOU'RE QUITE SURE you don't mind looking after the children tonight?' Rosie asked her mother-in-law.

'Very sure. You know I love spending time with my grandchildren,' Beatrice said.

'And we like being with Nonna,' Freddie and Lexi added.

Since they'd moved to Florence, where Leo had taken over as the head of the clinic that the Marchetti family supported and Rosie worked there as a nurse, the children had really blossomed. They were almost as fluent in Italian as they were in English. And Rosie rather thought that Beatrice had blossomed, too; she seemed much less frail. Confident enough to come and stay in Leo and Rosie's townhouse in Florence for the night, while they attended the clinic's annual charity ball. And, best of all, her past was staying exactly where she wanted it to stay: in the past. True to Leo's promise, Michael's associates had left her alone.

'Now, off to the ball with you,' Beatrice said. 'And hopefully there will be no wasps, tonight.'

'Hopefully,' Leo said with a smile. 'Though Rosie can

ask for adrenaline herself now in Italian, thanks to your teaching, Mamma.'

'Ah, now I leave the medical terminology to you, Leo,' Beatrice said with a smile. 'You look lovely in that dress, Rosie. I'm so proud of my new daughter.'

'And thank you for lending me your diamonds again, Mamma,' Rosie said, hugging her warmly.

'It's good to see them being worn. Just as they should be, by the Duchessa di Calvanera,' Beatrice said.

'Send us some pictures from the ball,' Lexi begged, 'so we can see all the other pretty dresses, too.'

'We'll try. Be good for Nonna,' Leo said.

'*Sì*, Babbo,' the twins chorused.

Rosie was still smiling when Leo drove them across town to the hotel. 'Funny to think it's a year since my first trip to Florence. And what a year it's been. Our wedding, moving here to work in the clinic...'

'It's been a good year,' Leo agreed, parking the car.

'Just before we go in,' she said, 'I have a little news for you.'

'Oh?'

'You might need to brush up on your nappy-changing skills.'

He stared at her. 'Nappy-changing?'

She spread her hands. 'This is the twenty-first century. Duke or not, I'm expecting you to be a fully hands-on dad.'

'Hands-on...?' The penny finally dropped, and he punched his fist in the air. 'We're going to have another baby!'

Which was when Rosie realised that Leo really *did* think of the twins as his own. He'd always been careful to treat them as if they were his own children; and now she knew he loved them as much as she did.

'You,' he said, 'have just made me happier than I ever

thought possible. I know we're not supposed to breathe a word until twelve weeks, but right now I want to climb to the top of the hotel and yell out to the whole of Florence that I'm going to be a dad again. And that I love my wife very, very much. And...'

There was only one way to stop her over-talkative Duke. She smiled, and kissed him.

* * * * *

LET'S TALK
Romance

For exclusive extracts, competitions
and special offers, find us online:

- facebook.com/millsandboon
- @MillsandBoon
- @MillsandBoonUK

Get in touch on 01413 063232

For all the latest titles coming soon, visit
millsandboon.co.uk/nextmonth